a
in

Pleas...   ...e on overdue books

60000 0000 73261

Dear Readers,

I'm pleased to give you *Trace of Fever*, book two of my new series of *über* alpha hunks featuring private mercenaries who are big, capable, a little dangerous and (I hope) oh-so-sexy. If you read the first book, *When You Dare*, then you already know why I call them my men who "walk the edge of honor."

My novella in the anthology *The Guy Next Door* got things started by introducing you to characters related to the heroine of *When You Dare*. Next out is *Savor the Danger*.

To see more about the books, visit my website at www.lorifoster.com. And feel free to chat with me on my Facebook fanpage—www.facebook.com/pages/ Lori-Foster /233405457965.

I'm very excited about this new series, and I hope you will be, too!

Lori Foster

LORI FOSTER

TRACE OF FEVER

MILLS & BOON

First published in Great Britain 2012
by Mills & Boon, an imprint of Harlequin (UK) Limited,
Eton House, 18-24 Paradise Road, Richmond, Surrey TW9 1SR

© Lori Foster 2011

ISBN: 978 0 263 90204 4
ebook ISBN: 978 1 408 97513 8

048-0712

Harlequin (UK) policy is to use papers that are natural, renewable and recyclable products and made from wood grown in sustainable forests. The logging and manufacturing processes conform to the legal environmental regulations of the country of origin.

Printed and bound
by CPI Group (UK) Ltd, Croydon, CR0 4YY

To the Animal Adoption Foundation, a no-kill animal shelter in Hamilton, Ohio.

The AAF does remarkable work for animals. Liger, one of the cats that my son adopted from the shelter, is featured in the book. If it wasn't for the AAF, a truly beautiful, lovable, BIG cat might not be a part of our family now.

The AAF will always be one of my "pet projects" whenever I do fundraising.

To learn more, visit www.AAFPETS.com.

Lori

TRACE OF FEVER

CHAPTER ONE

ARMS CROSSED AND HIS shoulder propped against the wall outside the elaborate, corner high-rise office, Trace Rivers considered his options. Having an inside source would shorten his job. As a pseudobodyguard, he hadn't been given the opportunity to uncover shit yet, and he was getting antsy. But if he could turn someone who was privy to the info he needed, then he'd get somewhere.

Murray Coburn was dirty. Trace knew it. Hell, a lot of people knew it. But they couldn't or wouldn't touch the bastard without rock-solid evidence. The legal system had failed.

Trace would find the evidence eventually, though, and then he'd mete out his own form of justice.

Until then he had to contend with the odd assortment of disreputable punks and bullies working for Murray.

He also had to contend with Helene Schumer, better known as Hell—a name that suited her well. She never missed an opportunity to grope him, to boss him, to make his job more trying than necessary. But as Murray's current paramour, Hell had privileges denied to others.

If Murray uncovered her perfidy, he'd kill her without remorse. That thought didn't bother Trace at all, but Murray would also lose trust in him, and that couldn't happen.

The unsavory idea of using Hell didn't sit well with Trace, but it would be expedient, especially since the lady acted like a nymphomaniac around him.

As she approached now, her intent obvious in the slanting of her eyes and the curve of her painted mouth, Trace did his utmost to ignore her. Luckily he was saved from her assault when the timid receptionist, Alice, approached with a message.

Using the name he'd given for this cover, she said, "Mr. Miller?"

Trace kept his gaze on Hell, but replied, "What is it?"

"There's a woman downstairs asking to see Mr. Coburn. Your presence is requested to see what she wants."

In theatrical fanfare, Hell paused with her feet braced apart, her hands on her rounded hips, her chin at a haughty angle. "A woman? Who the hell is she?"

The receptionist ducked her head. "No idea, ma'am."

"Tell them to keep the woman there until I arrive." Though he could have communicated directly with the staff downstairs, Trace dismissed the young woman to do the chore, to remove her from Hell's wrath. Hell's viciousness was one of the things Murray seemed to enjoy most about her, so he never required her to curb her more cutthroat tendency of mauling the messenger.

"I don't want another woman seeing Murray."

Vicious and territorial. Of course, she had to know that Murray screwed anything in a skirt, with and without consent.

"He's out anyway." The bastard had left two hours ago, and though he'd been favoring Trace as his personal protection, this time he'd taken another man with him.

"Find out who she is and report back to me."

"I don't think so." Everyone in the organization feared Hell, almost as much as they feared Murray. Except for Trace; he felt only contempt—for them both.

And maybe that accounted for Hell's constant pursuit, and Murray's apparent regard.

As he started toward the elevator, Hell stepped in his

way. In her spiked heels, she stood eye-level to his six-foot height. Her long dark hair hung sleek down her back, her lips and nails painted shiny red. A sheer camisole, stretched tight over her enhanced boobs, was cut low enough to display not only her cleavage but damn near her navel and tucked into a pencil-thin skirt. She looked killer-gorgeous, as always.

Gorgeous, and evil. She stared at his crotch. "How convenient for you, that you're being called away."

God, Trace despised her. "Yeah? How's that?"

As daring as always, she reached out a hand and cupped his balls through his slacks. "I anticipated a private moment with you."

Far from enjoying her touch, Trace didn't trust her not to mutilate him. He grabbed her slender wrist and squeezed the delicate bones. Though he knew he caused her pain, her lips parted and her eyelids went heavy.

She licked her lips and searched his gaze. "If you were naked, I would have my nails in you right now."

Which was a damn good reason not to get naked with her. Trace smiled in triumph. "But not this time, Hell." He removed her arm by squeezing until she gasped and her fingers opened. He tossed her aside. "I have work to do."

"Trace?"

On a sigh, he turned back to her. "What?"

"I want you to take me shopping."

"Not in my job description, doll."

"It is—if Murray orders it." She rubbed her reddened wrist over her breasts. "And Murray will order anything I want."

Having nothing to say to that, Trace turned away from her and stepped into the elevator. When the doors closed, he let out a breath of relief.

Since he'd infiltrated the organization three weeks ago,

posing as a bodyguard, Hell had been the toughest part of maintaining his cover. Eventually he'd have to deal with her. As a medicinal chemist, she supplied any and all drug persuasions that Murray might need for his human trafficking venture. Lackeys captured the women and Murray, the bastard, sold them to the highest bidder—after Hell ensured their compliance through risky drugs.

Trace looked forward to the moment when he'd deal with her.

When it came to annihilating the scourge, he didn't discriminate against women. Helene Schumer had to go; the world would be a better place without her.

PRISCILLA PATTERSON SIMPERED and feigned distress as two hulking brutes tried to bully her toward a secluded conference room of the office building. What they intended to do to her there, she couldn't say.

They were not gentle, making her show of defenselessness difficult to maintain. Her arm got twisted; someone pulled at her ponytail, making her gasp.

And then suddenly, a quiet but stern voice spoke up. "Let her go."

Just that easily, she was free. She twisted to find a face to go with that deep voice, and froze.

Wow.

Unlike the Neanderthals who'd taken pleasure in manhandling her so roughly, this man looked smooth and debonair and…sexy.

He strode toward them with a frown that brooked no arguments. Standing easily six feet tall, he was muscular but not overly bulky, clean-cut but not in a too-polished *GQ* way. Very fair hair, straight and a little too long, contrasted sharply with the most piercing golden-brown eyes she'd ever seen. He wore khakis and an obviously expensive black T-shirt. She detected the bulk of a Kevlar vest beneath the shirt.

A black-leather shoulder holster held his gun. The belt around his waist carried two extra magazines, a stun gun, baton and mace. His black lace-up steel-toed boots could be deadly.

The man was ready for anything.

But maybe not ready for her.

That bright caramel gaze drifted over both of the hulks with contempt. "I'll handle her from here."

Grumbling, the men moved away.

He took her arm. "Come with me."

Priss tried to resist, but he was far more physically persuasive—without really hurting her—than the other men had been. "Where are we going?"

"Farther away for privacy."

"Oh. Okay." In her flat shoes, she hustled along beside him, feeling very short and suddenly unsure of herself. "You work here?"

He didn't reply but drew her around the corner, shielding her from prying eyes. He, on the other hand, stayed in view, and Priscilla assumed it was so he could keep an eye on the others.

Cautious and suspicious—qualities she appreciated.

He gave her a very slow perusal, from her dark reddish-brown hair in its high ponytail, to her crisp blue blouse and her over-the-knee, old-fashioned skirt, to her flat-heeled Mary Janes…and then back up again. "What are you doing here?"

"Oh." She pretended to be flustered by his direct stare. And truthfully…she was. But only a little. This was too important for her to fudge it.

She hugged her big satchel purse to her chest and said with just the right quaver, "I came to meet Murray Coburn."

"Why?"

She widened her eyes. "Well, that's actually private."

He stood there, waiting, his gaze unflinching, direct.

Ha. He didn't know her fortitude if he thought a little stare-down would discomfort her. Pasting on what she hoped was a winsome smile, Priscilla blinked her eyes at him. "Oh, I should introduce myself." She held out a hand. "I'm Priscilla Patterson."

He looked at her hand, and his left eye twitched.

He didn't touch her.

"Yes, well…" She tucked her hand back in close to her body. "Will you please tell Mr. Coburn I'm here?"

"No." And then, striking an exasperated stance, he asked again, "Why do you want to see him?"

When she started to look away, he caught her chin and lifted her face. "I don't have time for this, so stop the coy act."

This time her eyes widened for real. He knew she was acting? But how?

Shaking his head, he released her. "Fine. I'll have the men show you out."

"No, wait." She caught his arm—and was stunned at the unyielding strength there. It was like grabbing thick rock. "Okay, I'll tell you. But please don't make me leave."

He crossed his arms, which effectively shook off her touch. "I'm listening."

"Murray is my father."

So still that he looked like a stone statue, the man stared at her. Only an infinitesimal narrowing of his eyes showed any reaction at all. "You're fucking with me."

Okay, so coarse language didn't really shock her, not anymore, not at twenty-four when much of her life had been spent on the sordid side of survival. She still gasped. "Sir, really." Fanning her face as if to alleviate a blush, Priscilla frowned at him. "I assure you that I'm serious."

A noise at the front of the lobby drew his attention, and after a quick look, he cursed low. Catching her arm, he dragged her farther out of view and bent close. "Listen up, lady. Whatever harebrained plan you have to cozy up with Coburn, forget it."

With complete honesty, she said, "Oh, but I can't."

He snarled, and then he shook her. "Trust me on this— you don't belong here. You don't belong in this building, much less anywhere near Coburn. Be smart and take your pert little ass out the door and away from danger."

Pert little ass? Frowning, she looked behind herself. From what she could see, her ass—pert or otherwise— looked nonexistent thanks to the shape of the skirt.

A deliberate choice.

But because he looked genuinely concerned, which was surely at odds with the duty that would be assigned to him, Priscilla shrugged. "Sorry. I didn't come this far just to walk away."

Footsteps sounded behind them. His jaw tightened. "There's a back exit. Go down the hall, hang a left, go through the—"

So stubborn! "Excuse me." Priss stepped around him just as a behemoth rounded the corner, followed by the two men who'd bullied her earlier and another, equally disreputable-looking fellow.

She'd seen plenty of pictures, so she knew right away who stood before her.

Murray Coburn.

Dark, slick, massive in build with an enormous neck and back, he looked exactly as she'd expected, right down to the trim goatee and calculating gaze.

"What's going on here?" Murray sized her up, and

though she knew she wouldn't be to his liking, his gaze turned smarmy. "Who are you?"

Again Priss held out a hand. "Priscilla Patterson. I'm your daughter."

TRACE SWALLOWED DOWN a curse. He wanted to toss the girl, in her ridiculous clothes with her ridiculous ponytail, over his shoulder to carry her out the front door—away from harm.

He wanted, quite simply, to kill Murray in front of her, then kill the rest of them, too. Little Ms. Patterson might be traumatized for life, but damn it, she'd be alive.

Unfortunately he couldn't do a damn thing except stand there looking bored and mildly put out.

Murray's gaze swung to him, blue eyes as cold as the arctic zeroing in. "What the fuck is this, Trace?"

"A nuisance, that's all. I was just getting rid of her." Trace clamped a hard hand onto her arm.

With a flick of his hand, Murray stopped him from taking a single step. He dismissed the other men and after they'd walked away, he looked at her again. His brows were down in that fierce way that made most people quake in fear.

It was an affectation wasted on Trace.

Beneath his well-trimmed goatee, Murray's mouth was flat and hard. "Bring her up to my office."

And with that, he walked away to the private elevators.

Fuck, fuck, *fuck*. Glaring at the girl, Trace asked, "Happy now?"

She looked almost smug when she said, "Getting there." She gave a pointed look at his hand on her arm.

Ignoring that silent command, Trace high-stepped her toward an empty conference room on the lobby floor.

"Hey!" She tried to free herself, but couldn't.

Funny thing, though, Trace noticed that she moved in an expedient, stylized way that, against someone without his level of skill, might have gotten her free. "You're going to hurt yourself."

She worked up a few tears, letting them glisten on her long dark lashes. "*You're* hurting me."

"Not yet," Trace told her, unmoved by the false show of emotion. "But the idea of putting you over my knee gets more tempting by the second."

That left her tight-lipped and silent—with no remnant of tears to be seen.

Trace propelled her into a room and toward a conference table with chairs. "Sit." When she started to defy him, he filled his lungs and made a move toward her.

She dropped into a seat. "Why are you doing this?" Hands gripping the chair arms, she summoned up lost bravado and lifted her chin. "You heard what Mr. Coburn said. He wants you to take me to his office."

"Yeah. But I heard what he didn't say, too."

She shook her head. "What are you talking about?"

"I have to search you."

Aghast, she said, "I beg your pardon?"

"Beg all you want." He was so pissed right now, he might enjoy hearing it. "I'm still going to check you over. *Everywhere.*"

Her eyes widened in alarm.

Too late, honey. Trace nodded at her, grim, but sort of anticipating it, too. "Every nook and hollow, honey, inside every piece of clothing."

She sputtered, and Trace noticed the flush blooming in her cheeks.

With her entire small body pulled tight in rebellion, she gasped, "You're insane!"

Trace propped his shoulders against the wall. "If you

want to see Coburn, I have to ensure you aren't hiding a weapon, or a transmitter, of any kind."

"No."

"Fine." Perfect, in fact. "Then leave. Right now."

She hesitated. "But…"

Again, Trace took his gaze over her. She tried to hide her body under the prim clothes, but he wasn't fooled. He'd bet his favorite knife that this particular babe was in no way innocent. Whether or not she was Murray's spawn, he couldn't say. There did seem to be something of a resemblance in the color of her hair, though hers was a shade or two lighter than Murray's. And when she connived, which she'd been doing from jump, she had a certain look about her that reminded him of Coburn.

Trace glanced at the chunky black watch on his wrist. "Make up your mind, but make it up fast. What's it to be? Do you want to leave, or do you want my hands all over you?"

The new gleam of tears looked authentic, but her chin didn't lower. "I'm not leaving."

Trace pushed away from the wall. "Up with you, then." He caught her elbow, drawing her to her feet. The top of her head barely reached his chin. She had a delicate bone structure, but was clearly filled with underlying steel.

He turned her. "Put your hands flat on the table and spread your legs wide."

For a span of five seconds, she didn't move. Her shoulders were rigid, her neck stiff. That high, dark red ponytail hung almost to the middle of her back. Freed, her hair would just kiss the top of her ass.

He smoothed his hand down that long tail—and his palms burned.

As if in slow motion she plopped her heavy, loaded purse onto the tabletop. First her left hand, then her right, landed on the table, fingers opened for balance.

Trace gently kicked her feet back a little, then said, "Open up, honey."

Her narrow back expanded on a breath of courage. She lifted her right foot and dropped it back down a few inches away.

Trace took great pleasure in saying softly, "Wider."

When she still barely moved, he stepped up behind her. Holding her waist, he nudged her feet far apart, as far as the skirt would allow.

The muscles in her bare calves strained. The skirt pulled taut around that rounded behind. Her shoulders remained as proud and stiff as ever.

They were in a position of lovers, so it was no wonder that he suddenly noticed her delectable scent. Baby soft, and woman sweet.

His nostrils flared—and he forced himself to step away.

"Stay like that." Moving to the side of her, Trace up-ended her purse on the tabletop. Photos, pen, notebook, makeup, brush, comb, mirror, tissues, calculator, candy bar, book... "Jesus, everything but the kitchen sink."

"Bastard," she whispered.

He tsked. "Now, is that any way for a schoolgirl to talk?"

"I'm a grown woman."

"Yeah? How old?"

He could almost hear the sawing of her teeth before she ground out, "Twenty-four."

Trace opened her wallet and checked her driver's license. "Twenty-four," he agreed. "But dressed like a parochial pupil." With no more than a casual glance he memorized her address. Seemed odd that she'd live in the same state as Murray if they'd never met.

Soon as he could, he'd have the address checked out.

But just in case Murray had the same thought... Trace

glanced at her, saw her gaze was averted, and slid the license into his pocket.

He rifled through the rest of her belongings, searched the interior of the purse for any hidden pockets. "Speaking of your clothes…" He glanced at her. "I'm not fooled, so you can save the prim act."

She whipped her head around to burn him with a look. The tight ponytail emphasized her high cheekbones, the straight bridge of her nose. "You're suggesting *what,* exactly?"

Trace examined a photo of her as a younger girl with a woman who looked a lot like her. Maybe her mother.

Even when young, she'd still looked pugnacious, as if preparing to take on the world. The photo left him unsettled. "You're up to something, and I don't like it."

"It's none of your business."

He continued his examination of her belongings, saying casually, "Who gets killed around here is my business."

There was a pause, but no real fear. "You think my own father would kill me?"

Trace scrutinized her. She was more subtle, but in her own way, he had no doubt that she could be every bit as lethal as Hell. The edge of danger was there in her clear green eyes, in her too-cool voice. Under the circumstances, she was one amazingly composed cookie.

He'd have to remember that.

As she watched him look her over, Trace stepped around behind her. "Eyes forward."

"I don't trust you."

"As well you shouldn't." He put his hands on her throat. Silk. Warm, sleek silk. Slowly, he dragged his fingers down to her shoulders, then down each arm. So slim, and so damn young.

In a real pat-down, he'd be thorough, but fast. Not this time. If he could get her out of here, he was willing to cross the line. Priscilla Patterson might be an enigma with a double agenda, but he still didn't want to see her slaughtered. And if she played with Coburn, that's what would happen.

"Easy now." He put his hands over her breasts—and realized she'd bound herself. He quirked a brow. "Hiding something?"

Strained, she rasped, "I'm modest."

"Uh-huh." He went down her ribs to her concave belly, over the lush swell of her hips, the length of her thighs, and back up under her skirt.

She jerked.

Voice low and rough, Trace said, "Be still." Keeping one hand on the small of her back, he reached up between her legs. Very skimpy panties—and nothing else.

Well, heat. Lots of heat.

He brought his palm to the soft flesh of each inner thigh, cupped over her crotch where he felt her springy curls beneath the silky material of underwear, and—

"You can tell I'm not hiding anything!"

"You're hiding something, all right." Reluctantly, Trace brought his hand out but his fingers and palm continued to tingle. For a moment, he clasped her hips and just held her like that, bringing himself under iron control. When she started to straighten, he said, "Not yet."

Her forehead hit the tabletop and she groaned. Her legs were still straight, leaving her bottom high, in the perfect position for sex. This way, a man would go so deep—

As if knowing his thoughts, she locked her hands over her head and gave a low growl, bringing a reluctant and crooked smile to his mouth.

She didn't intimidate easily, and he'd tormented himself enough. "Straighten up so I can unbutton your blouse."

"*Why?*"

"I need to go beneath the binding."

She started to shake. Trace had a feeling it was repressed rage, not nervousness. But she did straighten her
arms, levering her chest up and away from the table.

As he started on the small buttons, she asked, "What
will my father say when I tell him what you did to
me?"

"Why don't you tell him and find out? But know this—
it's what he expected me to do."

She twisted to look at him over her shoulder. "You're
serious?"

"He's a high-level businessman with plenty of enemies.
Protecting him is my job. No one here knew he had a
daughter, so why should we just believe you?" The buttons were all opened now, so Trace turned her to face
him.

Wide elastic circled her upper body. It could have been
a girdle or some such, definitely not meant for a woman's
chest.

It was so tight, he didn't see how she could even hide
her breasts under there, much less anything else. But
then, he'd stopped looking for a real weapon almost from
jump.

This little exercise was all about making her rethink
her plan.

"You can breathe with that restriction?"

"I breathe just fine."

He met her gaze. "Lower it."

Her arms hung loose at her sides, her stance relaxed,
and Trace knew what she planned. He saw it in her
eyes.

Smiling again, this time in anticipation, he whispered,
"Try it."

She looked startled. "What?"

"You want to attack, honey. I see it." He looked at her

mouth. "If your modesty is worth blowing whatever plans you have, then go for it."

Her teeth locked. She seemed to be considering it.

"But know," Trace told her, crowding in a little closer, "you can't best me. Whatever you think you know, whatever capabilities you think you have, it's not enough. Not even close."

Time ticked by slowly while they stared at each other. Her breathing deepened, her eyes narrowed.

"Now or never," Trace taunted, and he knew that for whatever perverse reason, he wanted her to react. Every nuance, every flicker of her thick lashes, fascinated him. Never had he met a woman like her. She had to be as crooked as Murray to be involved in any way, but still she intrigued him.

Slowly, her gaze still locked with his, she lifted her hands, hooked her fingertips in the top of the elastic binding, and began tugging it down.

Trace continued to watch her face; he saw her lips part on a deeper, cleansing breath. She had to be more comfortable now, but why hide her curves in the first place?

Reaching toward his back, he withdrew his knife and clicked it open.

Priscilla's gaze finally left his, but only to look at the blade in curiosity. She tipped her head, then brought her attention back to him. "Automatic switchblade, ergonomic handle, three-and-a-quarter-inch blade."

"You know your knives."

"I know weapons." She still didn't look scared as much as defiant. "What do you plan to do with that?"

"Don't move." Trace tried not to stare at her breasts, now reddened with deep groves showing from the squeeze of the damned elastic. Her nipples were dark pink, soft and luscious.

Catching the top of the binding, he stretched it out

from her body and slipped the tip of his blade inside. Like carving through butter, the elastic separated as he sliced the knife downward. It fell away from her body.

Looking her over, Trace replaced the knife in a back pocket. His gaze zeroed in on her breasts. "You really tortured those poor beauties."

She didn't make a sound.

"Care to tell me why?"

Her chin lifted. "Boobs are distracting."

"That's usually the purpose, right?"

Rather than answer, she held up her palms. "Do you mind?"

His abdomen clenched. Trying not to sound affected, Trace gestured with his chin. "Knock yourself out." *Please, go ahead,* he thought. *Touch yourself.*

With a slight moan, her head tipped back and she put her hands to her breasts in a slow, deep massage. Her eyes closed and she heaved another deep breath.

Definitely affected, Trace noted that her hands were small, and her breasts...were not. It was sinfully enticing, watching her soothe the irritated flesh while making those soft, cooing sounds of pure pleasure.

Such a contrast it made, her feminine, unadorned hands with the short, clean nails—rubbing over those pale, voluptuous breasts, working them as if to alleviate an ache.

Trace clamped his hands over hers, and her eyes shot open.

Through his teeth, he said, "That's enough."

The tip of her tongue came out to moisten her lips. "Getting to you?"

"Trust me on this, you don't want to find out." His hands were twice the size of hers, so his thumbs and each fingertip sank into pliable, soft flesh. Acutely aware of that, of her, he said, "Will you leave now?"

Her small nostrils flared on a quick inhalation. "Not on your life."

Furious, Trace pushed back from her but kept his tone calm and detached. "Button up your blouse and tuck it back in."

She did so in haste, proving she hadn't been as comfortable with her partial nudity and provocative display as she'd wanted him to believe. "It's not going to fit right now."

Stepping to the side, Trace jammed all her belongings back into her purse, glad that he'd kept the license. When shit went south, as it was bound to do, he wanted a way to identify her. Given all his computer expertise and resources in the government and military, tracking her would be a piece of cake.

"Done?"

She smoothed her hair and nodded. "*Now* may I see my father?"

It pissed him off enough that Trace didn't reply. He just handed her purse to her, took her arm and started her out the door.

Gut instincts told him that things had just gotten horribly complicated. And he could put the blame squarely on Ms. Priscilla Patterson's too-proud shoulders.

CHAPTER TWO

PRISS STRODE INTO THE private elevator as if she had every right, as if her heart weren't bumping hard against her ribs, as if her nerves weren't sorely jumbled.

Keeping her cool had taken real effort, but good God, of all the scenarios she'd planned for, expected and discounted, being intimately groped by a man like him, a man so unlike the other men in the organization, had never factored in.

In the elevator, he held silent, but she saw him twice look at her blouse. She could *feel* his gaze, damn it, deep inside herself. And she knew what he was looking at.

Without the binding, her boobs were far too noticeable. The damned buttons gaped and the material strained.

"Enjoying yourself?" she asked with a heavy dose of sarcasm.

If anything, her jibe only made him intensify his study. He stood there, negligence personified, his hands clasped behind his back, his stance casual and relaxed. "I can see the outline of your nipples."

She nearly strangled on her fury. "Go to hell!"

"What are you? C cup? Maybe even a D?"

Oh, God, she did not want to stand here alone with him, closed up in such a small space with his heat and scent invading her lungs. "None of your damn business."

He lifted his hand in front of him, not to touch her, but to imagine it covering her right breast. His face screwed up while he pretended to heft her. "I'd say a full C."

A fine trembling started in her neck and went down her spine. She needed to stay composed to face off with Murray Coburn, but for whatever reason, this man wanted to demolish her control. "I say go kill yourself."

He cracked a smile.

And what that smile did for him.… She couldn't deny that he was devastatingly handsome. Probably a cutthroat villain, but still gorgeous. That disheveled fair hair and those intense, oddly colored eyes…she shivered.

He lifted a brow. "Cold?"

"No." She had to distract him. "So I didn't catch your name."

"No one gave you my name."

"It's a secret, then?" She tried to hunch her shoulders to make her chest less noticeable. "How strange."

"That doesn't help," he said of her posture, "and if you're really interested?" He held out a hand. "Trace Miller."

She disdained touching him again. "Is that your real name or an alias?"

With a grin, he retracted his proffered hand. "What do you think?"

"I think you took my driver's license."

He went still for a heartbeat, giving her a small measure of satisfaction. Lifting her hands in a "woo-woo" way, she intoned, "I know all, see all." Then she curled her lip. "And besides, you suck at stealth."

The elevator stopped and the doors opened with a silent *whoosh*. Trace took her elbow to keep her from stepping out. Bending to her ear, he said on a mere breath of sound, "Actually, I excel at stealth, which tells me that you have to be trained to think otherwise. So now I'm wondering, what is a trained and deceptive woman doing here, claiming to be the daughter of one of the most powerful and fearsome businessmen in the area?"

Shoot. She shouldn't have baited him. He was good, and of course he'd know it, the egomaniac. When she tried to pull free, he easily restrained her.

And then another voice intruded.

"Well, well. What the *fuck* is this?"

Priss looked up at the female, and then had to look up even more. Good God, an Amazon. A really spiteful-looking Amazon all decked out in killer duds as if on the make.

Putting on her sweet and innocent face, Priss said, "Hello. I'm here to see Murray Coburn."

And suddenly Trace was in front of her. She realized why when the Amazon tried to crowd closer, no doubt to intimidate her physically. Wow. Priss braced herself behind him, trying to see what happened. His big shoulders shifted, flexed under her hands, and then he went still again—all without making a sound.

The Amazon had been forced back several feet, heaving and furious.

Oh, he was good, all right. Really good. She hated to be impressed, but she just couldn't help it.

Sounding less than charming, Trace said, "Now, now, Hell, retract your claws. Murray wants to see her."

A venomous snakelike hiss precluded the snarky response. "Did he specify in one piece?"

Priss stiffened. The woman wanted to attack her without provocation?

"No, he didn't, but until he tells me otherwise, that's how she's going to stay."

Outraged, she fairly screeched, "Damn you, Trace."

He didn't budge, and Priss had to admit he made one hell of a blockade.

Was his protectiveness truly motivated just by his hired position? She didn't think so.

Going on tiptoe to see over his shoulder again, Priss

realized he was rock solid, not an ounce of give to his muscles. Huh. She squeezed just a little, fascinated despite herself.

When was the last time any man had caught her interest? Not counting Murray, since her interest in him was all toxic.

The Amazon drew her attention with a slow, contemptible smile.

"One of these days, Trace, definitely sooner than you think, I *will* settle up with you. Count on it." And with that she spun on her very high stiletto heels and sashayed away.

"Friend of yours?" Priss asked.

He turned on her so fast, she jumped back a foot.

"You don't look happy," Priss noted. *What an understatement.* "It was just a question. Don't implode or anything, okay?"

He fumed quietly, and even in his rage, he looked self-possessed. "Under no circumstances will you provoke that woman. Do you understand me?"

Intrigued by the warning, Priss tried to see around him to wherever the woman had gone. He didn't allow it.

His big, hard hand clasped her face, none too gently. "She will slit your throat and smile while doing it. And no one here will stop her. Do you understand me?"

"Uh…" It wasn't easy to speak with the way he smooshed her cheeks, but she felt compelled to point out, "You stopped her."

"This time." He leaned down, close enough to kiss her, but his eyes said he had far from affectionate gestures on his mind. "I won't always be around."

"Duly noted. Now you can stop abusing my face." He released her and she worked her jaw. "Jerk. I bruise easy."

His eye did that interesting twitching thing again before he grabbed her elbow and hustled her forward.

The surroundings were decadent. Authentic art on the walls. Twelve-foot ceilings. Polished-marble floors. And tinted windows everywhere.

When she balked, trying to take it all in, Trace all but dragged her. "This way."

"So dear daddy is rich, huh?"

"You'd be better served to note his power, not his financial status."

"Got some influence, does he?"

That she'd dropped her Little Ms. Innocent facade didn't faze him at all. "More than you could realize, or you wouldn't be here."

They passed a desk where a cowed woman kept her head down and her shoulders hunched. Pathetic.

To her, Trace spoke gently, as if addressing a child. "He's expecting us, hon. Tell him we're here."

"Yes, sir." Using an intercom, she announced, "Mr. Coburn, Mr. Miller is here with a young lady."

"Send her in. Trace, too. I want him in on this."

Priss started forward, but Trace didn't, so she got pulled up short. "Well?" She gave his shoulder a shove. "What's the holdup now?"

He chewed his upper lip, and she could have sworn he looked agonized. After a long hesitation, he yanked her away from the desk and tightened his hold on her arm. "Listen to me, and listen good. Give him no personal information that might make it easier for him to have you tracked. Protect your privacy as much as you can. I'll stall them as much as *I* can. When you leave, don't go anywhere familiar." His thumb rubbed her arm. "Do you have money on you?"

Agog, Priss stared up at him. "You're actually trying

to protect me?" Had she misunderstood his role in all this?

In a precise, angry tempo, he asked again, "Do. You. Have money? On you?"

"Inside my shoe."

He straightened, his expression impressed. "Good girl."

If he didn't stop referring to her as a child, she just might brain him. And then it dawned on Priss. "That's why you swiped my driver's license?" A short laugh—caused by nerves and something else, something sort of like gratitude—escaped her. "You took it so that they couldn't?"

"Let's go." He started her on her way again. "It's never a good idea to keep Murray waiting."

At the enormous double doors, Trace turned the knob, took a quick survey inside and gestured her in.

When she entered, Priss saw why he'd checked before letting her past him.

The Amazon waited.

A little more subdued now, she sat on the corner of Murray Coburn's massive desk. Sunlight poured through the wall of windows behind her, bathing her in a glow, putting blue highlights in her inky-black hair.

Her gaze, narrowed and mean, tracked Priss's every movement.

Despite herself, Priss stepped a little closer to her self-appointed protector.

"Priscilla Patterson," Trace said, as if formal introductions were just the thing for the situation. He gestured toward her father. "Murray Coburn. And the lovely lady with him is Helene Schumer."

Lovely lady? Priss bit back a gag.

Behind his desk, Murray surveyed her. "You made it this far, girl, so don't start cowering now."

Had she been cowering? Well, hell. That was the impression she wanted to give, but this time, it hadn't been feigned.

She felt like she'd entered a viper's nest.

"Where do you want her?" Trace asked, taking personal responsibility for seating her.

Murray's gaze crawled all over her, lingering on her breasts. She wanted to clobber Trace for that.

"The chair there will do," Murray said, indicating a padded seat in front of his desk, far too close to the Amazon's pointy-toed shoes.

Priss eyed the woman. What was it Trace had called her? Hell—short for Helene. Yeah, that suited her.

Sinking back into her veneer of shy reserve, Priss gave a tremulous smile. "Thank you so much for agreeing to see me. I know this is a shock, that *I'm* a shock. And I wouldn't blame you if you'd refused me."

Air unchanging, Murray said, "Sit."

That one blunt word, said as a succinct command, left her nettled. Priss wiped all hostility from her manner and moved forward. Gingerly, she perched at the edge of the chair, ready to bolt if the Amazon took aim at her head.

Trace stood behind her. To Murray, he probably looked positioned to restrain her if necessary. Priss hadn't known him long, but she was a good judge of character, and despite whatever role Trace Miller played in her father's evil enterprise, she knew he wouldn't hurt her.

To get the ball rolling, Priss opened her mouth—and Murray forestalled her.

"I've never fucked a red-haired woman."

"Oh." His bluntness unsettled her. So he'd make no pretense of being a smooth businessman, of being anything other than a crude bully? He had enough money and power that he didn't have to bother hiding his true nature in the sanctity of his office?

Or did he already know she'd never have the chance to share what she learned?

If only she could blush on cue, Priss thought, but that little trick eluded her. Instead, she touched her long ponytail. "My hair color is that of my grandmother. My mother had darker hair." She nodded toward the woman perched on his desk. "Beautiful, much like hers."

Hell leaned toward her, her body vibrating with menace.

With a casual lift of a hand, Murray warned the Amazon to stay back. She retreated, but she wasn't happy about it. Slowly, her father came out of his seat.

Priss eyed him warily. Would he try to kill her outright, as Trace suspected?

When Murray propped a hip against the front of his desk, Priss nearly melted with relief. Until his big feet bumped against hers.

No way in hell was he unaware of the contact. Priss fought the need to shrivel away from his foul touch. Her gut told her that the understated move was in no way fatherly.

A test? Or a warning?

Whatever Murray's real intent, she didn't know. She just knew it made her stomach pitch. Given that she trusted her instincts, she also knew to be on guard.

Murray nodded toward her chest, his gaze heated, his mouth a little too slack. "Braless?"

Now her face flamed. "I—"

Trace shifted. "She had herself bound with some sort of tight sports bra. But since that could have concealed a weapon, I cut it off her."

He hadn't been kidding about telling Murray! Priss waited to see how he'd react. It wasn't what she'd expected.

"I see." Murray's gaze lifted to hers. "Your mother was busty?"

Good God, the cretin hadn't yet asked her mother's name, but he wanted to know her bra size? He was more disgusting than she'd ever imagined.

Inside, Priss churned with fury, but outside, she stammered like a virgin. "She was, yes." Belatedly, parts of her rehearsed spiel shot to the forefront of her mind. "After you left her, she never wanted another man. So she did her best to…conceal her figure."

"As you did with whatever undergarment Trace removed from your person?"

"Yes." She tugged at the material of her blouse, trying to get the gaping front to close. "I'm not at all comfortable like this."

"What you have is an asset. You should be proud."

Oh, this was *soooo* not a father/daughter conversation. "Sir, I want you to know—"

"Give me your mother's name."

Well, 'bout damn time! A deep breath didn't ease the tension in her chest. "Patricia Patterson." Priss waited, but there was no recognition, and predictably, no real interest. She forged on. "I'm twenty-four, so it would have been close to twenty-five years ago that you knew her."

"I'd have been thirty-two." He rubbed at his goatee in fond remembrance of the past, then caught himself. "She's dead?"

Priss ducked her head, as much from grief as to hide the incandescent rage she felt when she thought of the way her mother had suffered before finding the grace of death. "Yes. Three months ago."

"How?" Murray asked.

"She had a stroke. It didn't take her right away.…"

As Priss replied, Murray turned to Hell and requested a drink. He even smiled at Hell's disgruntlement and gave her an intimate kiss that left his mouth shiny with the red gloss of her lips.

His disinterest in her struggle couldn't have been more plain.

As Hell slipped off the desk and went to the other side of the room to pour the drink, Murray pulled out a hanky and wiped his mouth.

All while Priss told the emotionally draining, all too horrific story of her mother's ordeal.

When she'd contrived this plan, she'd expected an unfeeling monster. She'd been prepared for a sleazy villain. But this…this total lack of propriety…the man was a psychopath. He couldn't possibly possess a single ounce of real emotion.

Somewhere along the way to building his empire of corruption, he'd become so comfortable with his power and influence that he didn't bother hiding his innately vicious nature anymore. He had a network of conspirators who would lie for him, cover for him, and enable him.

Involuntarily, her hands curled into fists. While Hell handed Murray his drink, Trace gave a barely perceptible nudge to her shoulder. He didn't look at her, and his stance remained alert, on duty as it were, but she caught his warning all the same.

It could be deadly for her to show her hand this early in the game.

With ice cubes clinking, Murray sipped his drink, and then asked, "So she suffered?"

Jaw tight, Priss nodded. "Immeasurably, yes."

He took another drink. "I don't remember her."

Of course he didn't. Theirs hadn't been a true relationship by any stretch. He'd used her mother for financial gain, and only by the turn of fate had her mother escaped with her life intact.

Deliberately, Priss relaxed her muscles. "I understand. It was a long time ago."

"I won't give you a dime, you know." He swirled the

drink, clinking the ice cubes again while smiling at her. "If you're here for money, you're wasting your time."

As if she'd take anything from him—other than his black heart. "Please, you misunderstand. I don't want or expect anything from you. It's just that, with my mother gone, I'm alone now."

Murray's eyes glinted, and they went over her again. "No other relatives? No husband or at least a boy-friend?"

"No, sir. That's why I wanted to meet you. And…" She tried for shyness. "That is, if you were interested, I thought we could get to know each other." She rushed to add, "No obligation at all, I swear. It's just…you're the only family I have left now."

That request pushed Hell over the edge. "Don't be pathetic." Moving to stand in front of Priss, she put her hands on her hips and thrust her breasts forward. "Why should Murray believe you're family? How could he pos-sibly be related to a homely little bitch like you?"

Trace snorted, and Murray laughed.

"What?" After an evil glare at Trace, Hell whipped around to face Murray. Her arms went stiff at her sides, her hands knotted. "You see a family resemblance?"

"Not at all. But despite the absurd clothing, she's far from homely." He gave Trace a man-to-man look. "What do you say, Trace?"

"Sexy."

Grinning, Murray lifted his drink as if in toast. "There. You see, Hell?"

She snatched up a paperweight from Murray's desk. "She won't be so sexy when I finish with her."

Jesus, Priss thought, stunned by the violent intention. Was now the moment when she should run? But no, once again, Trace stepped in front of her. He even managed to catch the projectile when Hell let out a screech and threw it.

Not at all affronted by her outburst, Murray laughed aloud, then jerked Hell around to face him. "You are such a jealous bitch, Helene, and usually it amuses me." His laughter died and his gaze hardened. "But not now."

Taking that warning to heart, Hell retreated.

In a milder tone now, Murray said, "This is business." He tweaked Hell's chin. "And you should know better than to ever interfere with business."

For whatever reason, that appeased Hell. She even gave a lazy smile. "I see."

"Business?" Priss asked. Could it really be that easy to get in his inner circle?

Holding out a hand toward her, Murray snapped his fingers, but not understanding, Priss waffled.

Trace took her purse from her and handed it to the big man. He dumped the contents onto his thick mahogany desk, picked up her wallet and searched through it.

Frowning, he asked, "No ID?"

Trace had been right about the driver's license. His boldness blew her away. "I, uh, only recently moved here. From North Carolina, I mean. That's where my mother and I lived."

"If you didn't drive, then how'd you get here?"

"Bus?"

"You're asking me?"

Priss realized how she'd said that, and rephrased her answer. "I didn't know if you meant here, as in your office, or here, Ohio. Either way, I took the bus."

Murray's eyes narrowed. "Where are you staying?"

Her brain scrambled, but with Trace's warning in mind she came up with a lie. "I'm in a hotel." She named the location, which was a good five miles from where she'd actually rented an apartment.

Hell picked up a photo. "Your mother?"

"Yes."

She smirked. "I see why Murray left her."

Oh, soon, Priss thought. Very soon she would make Hell pay for that insult. "My mother never blamed him. She said she knew it was a brief affair and hadn't expected anything more." Transferring her attention back to Murray—in time to see him studying her calves—Priss said, "That's why she never contacted you about me. She knew you hadn't been involved enough to want responsibility for a child."

He laughed. "Is that what she told you?"

"Yes. That you were a powerful, accomplished man, and that she couldn't burden you, knowing your preferences."

"She was protective of you."

"Yes."

"And she was right." He crossed his arms over his chest.

Priss saw that they were twice the size of Trace's arms, to match Murray's thick neck and colossal back. But put to the test, Priss would place her bet on Trace every time. He had a quiet but lethal edge to him that instilled confidence in his ability. He might not be savage like Murray, but he would be effective.

Probably why Murray had hired him.

Behind his goatee, Murray's lips curled in a smirk. "I never wanted a child, but you're here now, aren't you?"

Priss took that as a rhetorical question and kept her mouth shut.

Taking her arm, Murray pulled her, not gently but without overt hostility, from the chair. Not giving her much choice, he turned her in a circle, inspecting her from every angle. "I've made up my mind."

"About?" she asked hopefully.

"We'll get acquainted over lunch."

Still recovering from that sudden spin, Priss said, "Oh!

Yes. Lunch would be great." *I could kill you over lunch.*
There'd probably be plenty of time.

"But not just yet."

Confused, Priss said, "What?"

Murray surveyed her with a critical eye—and disdain
of her person. "You're not exactly a fashion plate, now,
are you? If I'm to be seen with you in public, we need to
do some…adjustments."

"Adjustments?"

"Surely you realize that more flattering clothes are
required, along with a makeover of sorts." Before she
could protest, Murray said, "My treat of course." And
then with a smarmy smile, he continued, "It's the least I
can do."

Sounding bored, Trace asked, "Want me to take care
of it?"

Murray nodded. "Yes, that will work. Take her shopping for a new wardrobe, and then make an appointment at the salon. Total do-over, Trace. Hair, makeup,
waxing…" He gave a salacious smile. "Whatever she
needs."

Priss tried not to look as appalled as she felt.

Trace continued to look bored. "No problem."

By way of dismissal, Murray said, "On your way out,
stop by Alice's desk and set the lunch appointment on my
calendar."

"Do you have a specific date in mind?"

Still holding Priss's arm and giving her that very non-
paternal appraisal, Murray shrugged. "Whenever I'm free
after she's had the work done."

"Got it."

Priss gaped at the autocratic management of her life.
No one had even bothered to consult her. "Shopping?"
She tried to sound appreciative. "That's so…generous of
you, but really, I don't need—"

Hell loomed near again. "Do you realize what an important man Murray is? Do you realize his stature in society? He can't be seen with you when you look so—" she searched for a word, and settled on the not-so-insulting "—common."

"Oh, but…" But Priss *really* wanted to deck Helene. Just one good palm shot to the nose, hard enough to leave her a bloody mess, but not hard enough to drive her cartilage into her brain. Priss forced a nervous smile. "It's just that I didn't want to impose."

Hell made a rude sound. She scooped up the contents of Priss's purse and dumped it all in her arms. "You imposed the minute you showed up here claiming a relationship. Accept Murray's generosity. You need it."

"Down, Helene. That's not necessary." Chuckling at the exchange, though it wasn't in the least funny, Murray asked her, "Isn't that right, Priscilla?"

"Well, of course.… I mean…" She struggled to get everything back in her purse. "If you're sure that's what you really want to do—"

He dismissed her ramblings. "Drive her home, Trace. Make sure that she's secure." He gave Trace a telling look. "Wherever she's staying."

"I'll see to it." And again Trace took her arm to lead her from the room.

Behind her, Priss heard Hell muttering something indistinct and she heard Murray laughing some more while playfully shushing her.

After closing the doors behind them, Trace gave her arm a jerk, drawing her from her thoughts. "Come on, then."

Mulish, Priss made him drag her every step. He only went as far as the poor receptionist's desk. "Hey, hon. Can you check Murray's calendar for me? He wants me to set up an extended lunch."

"Sure, Trace." After tucking her short brown hair behind her ear, Alice began typing. Her slender fingers flew over the keyboard. While she did that, Priss again studied Trace. He spoke so kindly to Alice, in a tone he hadn't used on Hell, or on her. He actually sounded... gentle. Kind.

So, did old Trace have something going on with the mousy secretary? Priss considered it—and shook her head. No, not likely.

Alice peered up at Trace with big brown eyes. "He's free tomorrow for a few hours."

No, no, no. She wasn't ready yet.

Trace frowned, and to Priss's relief, he said, "That's not enough time for me to prep her."

Alice glanced at Priss with new sympathy. "Oh. I see."

Oh, what? What did she see? Priss wondered. Put out that Trace so thoroughly ignored her, she started over to a leather chair to sit, but without looking away from Alice, Trace caught her wrist and kept her ensnared beside him.

"Early next week he has three hours free. That'd give you through the weekend to...finish."

"That'll work. Pick a swanky place and set the reservation. Wherever Murray likes best, okay? I'll get the details from you later."

Priss tapped her foot in impatience. She couldn't cross her arms, not with the way Trace kept her trapped in his hold, so foot tapping was the only way to express her annoyance.

But then Trace's big foot came down over hers, not hard, but with a clear message. He didn't even look at her while he gave the silent order for her to be still. The jerk.

"Got it," Alice said.

"Thanks, honey." He straightened again and, after removing his foot, turned his dangerous stare on Priss. "Let's go."

Without a word of complaint, she followed him to the elevator. She was more than ready to breathe in some fresh air untainted by corruption and evil.

This time the elevator took them all the way to the basement and into a private parking garage.

"I parked out—"

Trace jerked her closer, making it almost look as if she'd tripped, when she hadn't. As he helped her straighten, he breathed near her ear, "Monitored."

"Ah." She knew better than to start looking around, but the idea of surveillance made her skin crawl.

Was Murray watching her even now? She fought off a shiver of dread.

When Trace stopped at a spiffy, shiny-clean, black Mercedes with darkened windows, Priss lifted her brows. "Wow."

He opened the passenger door, and she more than willingly got in.

"Buckle up." He shut her door, circled the hood and folded his big body in behind the wheel. With both doors closed, he took several deep breaths, then braced his hands on the steering wheel, squeezing and working until his knuckles turned white and the muscles in his forearms bulged.

Impressive. Knowing no one could see her through the dark windows, Priss lifted her brows. "Is it safe in here?"

By way of answer, he whipped his head around to pin her in place with white-hot rage. "I should save myself a lot of trouble and just kill you now, before Murray has me do it."

Oh, shit. Priss reached for the door handle, but the

locks clicked into place, and she knew she wouldn't be going anywhere, not unless Trace wanted her to.

Possibilities and probable scenarios winged through her mind. Should she fight right now, or wait until they were out on the street? How should she attack? Face first, or the more susceptible crotch?

She peeked over at Trace, and knew no matter what she tried, he'd be ready. Well, hell.

CHAPTER THREE

AWARE OF PRISCILLA seething beside him, Trace put the car in gear and headed for the exit ramp. "What does your car look like and where did you park?"

"Umm…"

He sensed her tensing beside him, probably waiting for sunlight to hit the car before she launched herself at him. Such a foolish, but brave, consideration.

He shook his head. "I never hit a woman." He glanced at Priss. "First."

Confusion softened her hostile edge. "What?"

"I don't suggest you try me, Priscilla. I'm seriously pissed enough right now to give you that paddling you so very much deserve."

Understanding that he'd just been letting off steam, her shoulders slumped. She even scoffed. "Paddling? Don't be an ass." She dropped her purse onto the floor in front of her seat and put her head back. Almost as an afterthought, she said, "I'd never allow that."

She honestly thought she could stop him if he was inclined toward a little discipline? What a joke. But she was correct to relax. He had no intention of abusing her in any way.

Far as he was concerned, she'd been abused enough for one day.

"I parked two blocks away, just in case, ya know? It's a dark blue Honda Civic coupe."

"I'll have someone pick it up."

"Just like that, huh?" She stretched, yawned. "You don't need my keys?"

"No."

When she slipped her feet from her shoes, wiggled her toes and let out a sigh, Trace's temper shot up another notch. "Feel better now?"

"Well, yeah." She turned her head to see him, and even smiled a little. "Knowing that you're not really thinking about murdering me is a huge relief."

"Don't get too comfortable. You're not out of the woods yet."

She shifted toward him. "Yeah, I get that. So what's going on here? What's with the wardrobe and all that nonsense?"

"You require a whole new look to showcase your dubious charms."

"My…" Her jaw went slack as everything finally fell into place. "That son-of-a-bitch! *I told him I was his daughter.*"

"You think Murray cares about a kid he's never known? Get real." Trace couldn't believe her naivete. "No way in hell will he allow anyone a claim on his empire. Being related makes you a bigger possible threat, not more endearing."

"But…people saw me with him. A whole building full of people!"

"People who work for him." And that said it all—or should have.

"And they do what he says, when he says?"

"That's about it." Those who wouldn't be an accomplice to his ruse of legit business, or an alibi when the facade cracked, would be as susceptible to harm as Priscilla.

"So, what's he going to do, sell me to the highest bidder?" When Trace scowled, not about to confirm or deny that, she asked, "Out of the country, or just someplace isolated? I bet he has contacts in California and Arizona, right?"

Trace did a double take. What did Ms. Priscilla Patterson know about any of that? Murray Coburn hadn't gotten his fame by making mistakes or leaking information. "Come again?"

"Oh, give it up, Trace." Rather than look afraid, or even worried, by the reality of Murray's malevolence, she seemed speculative. "We both know how Murray made his fortune, right?"

Dangerous. "Why don't you enlighten me?"

She turned so that her shoulders were in the corner of the seat and she half faced him. "You need me to go first? Is this a test of some kind? Fine. No problem." She leaned toward him. "Human trafficking."

Trace tried not to show any reaction.

"I assumed the sick bastard would stick with immigrants. I mean, I know the employment agencies— profitable as they might be—are just a front for the real moneymaker." She looked out the window at the passing scenery—and didn't ask where he took her. "But if Murray discovered good income with homegrown females, I guess he could be expanding his business enterprises."

No way in hell would Trace corroborate any of her supposition—and it had to be supposition. No way in hell could she have any hard facts, because they were few and far between, and near impossible to uncover.

Trace didn't trust her, not in any way, shape or form. But her theory brought about some interesting questions. "What do you know about human trafficking?"

In a barely audible mutter, she said, "More than I want to."

A chill of alarm ran down Trace's spine. "What was that?"

She gave an aggrieved huff. "Look, I'm not stupid,

okay? Before coming here, I did as much studying on the subject as I could. I know how so many poor immigrants are abused, promised good jobs only to be recruited into prostitution and worse. And I read that white females are in higher demand, because they're not as commonly traded as immigrants."

Trace did a little more white-knuckle squeezing. "If that's what you think, then what the hell are you doing here?"

She shook her head, making that long reddish ponytail swish. "No more questions."

His teeth came together. "Oh, no, you don't, Priscilla. Refusal is an option you don't have. If you want to live through this, which is still doubtful by the way, you will tell me everything."

She sighed. "It's a horrid name, isn't it?"

Lost, he glanced at her. "What? Priscilla?"

"Yes. Mom shortened it to Priss, so that's what people call me—at least, the people who know me well. But that's not much better." She rubbed at tired eyes. "It makes me sound stuck-up, like a straightlaced Goody Two-shoes. I thought finally, for once in my life, my name would be worthwhile."

"Because you wanted Murray to believe you're some Little Ms. Innocent?"

"Yeah." She eyed him. "You don't think he bought it?"

Trace snorted. "He's not a fool. I don't think he's completely onto you, but he's definitely suspicious."

"But you are onto me?"

"I know you're a fraud, Priscilla. I know you have something planned, something that might get us both killed. And I know you're out of your league."

She looked sleepy. "All that, huh?"

While she was being marginally agreeable, Trace pushed his luck. "Is he really your father?"

"What do you think?"

"I think skewed personal vendettas are the most dangerous kind." And somehow, this was personal for her. Because of her mother? Likely. Especially if she had no other family.

"Personal vendettas are always a good reason to get involved." She studied him. "So why are you here?"

Trace kept his gaze on the road ahead. "It's a job."

"Bull." She laughed, and the sound was pleasant despite the strain. "Okay, so you're good at deciphering situations. Me, too. Wanna know what I think?"

Trace tipped his head toward a squat brick structure with a purple awning out front. "There's the boutique where you'll shop."

She didn't pick up on the subject change. "I think you're more than capable of killing, but not innocents. You kill people who deserve it. You're good, so that means you're a professional of some kind. Government operative maybe?"

When he sat there, stony-faced, she shrugged.

"Okay, maybe not. I suppose you could be an independent contractor. Actually, that's a better fit because you seem like the independent sort, more so than a man who takes orders."

Good God. He didn't look at her.

She smiled. "The way I see it, everyone knows Murray is scum, but he has friends in high places. He does bigtime contributions to political campaigns and that buys him enough immunity. For added insurance, he has a few senators neatly tucked into his pocket."

If that was all he had, the authorities could have eventually brought him down—and Trace wouldn't be on the case right now.

He pulled into a parking spot on the street across from the boutique. "We're here."

Priscilla reached for his arm. "Extorting women from other countries is dangerous enough. But when you start tampering with legal citizens, someone is bound to get fired up. Whoever that someone is, he hired you to shut down Murray's operation."

Interesting take. Except that no one had hired him. No one needed to. "That's one hell of an imagination you have there, Priss." Trace pulled free of her unnerving touch. She was good, he'd give her that. But she'd missed the motivation entirely.

Human trafficking had hit him on a very personal level, so he'd made it his mission to demolish anyone and everyone involved, starting with the biggest, most obvious organizations. Thanks to his best friend, Dare Macintosh, they'd made great headway already.

And now he wanted Murray Coburn.

Trace left the car, put change in the meter, and went around to Priss's door. She'd just stepped out when his phone rang. Again, not trusting her to be more than a foot away from him, Trace held her arm while he answered. "Miller."

"It just occurred to me," Murray said. "I should know if she really is my daughter, right?"

Trace saw how the sunlight shone on Priss's hair—and yeah, the name Priss suited her, whether she realized it or not. The bright day amplified the red in her long ponytail, showing a dozen different shades of brown and auburn.

She looked nothing like Murray. A good thing, that. "Up to you."

"I need to test her DNA. Discreetly. Helene said it'd be best to get some of her hair, but it has to have a root attached, so get a couple of good ones, pulled out, not cut. Got it?"

Now that he had the opportunity to slant things however he wanted, Trace pondered the situation. Which would be more advantageous to his plan, if Priss was *not* Murray's daughter, or if she was?

He shrugged. At this point, it was all still up in the air, so he'd just have to play it by ear. "Not a problem."

Murray gave a few more instructions on the type of clothes he wanted to see her in. "Talk her up, see what you can find out, okay? But be discreet. I don't want her to bolt. Not yet."

While Trace listened, Priss put up a hand to shield her eyes and looked around. Her nose scrunched up a little and her mouth pursed.

And damn it, she stirred him.

Without meaning to, he used his thumb to caress the soft skin of her arm right above her elbow.

She gave him a quizzical look, then a more pointed look at his hand, her brows lifted.

Trace released her. "I'll check in later," he told Murray, and then closed the phone and stowed it back in his pocket.

When Priss started toward the designer store, he caught her arm and she went full circle until she faced the opposite way. Trace led her to the equally small phone store a block up.

"What are we doing?"

"Getting phones." He had a hell of a lot of stuff to accomplish tonight. It cramped his brain, trying to ensure that he wouldn't forget anything.

"For me?"

"For myself."

"But you have a phone," she pointed out.

"Be quiet." He went in, towing her along, and bought two prepaid phones with a limited number of minutes on them. Since he changed them out often, it was always a good idea to grab them when he could. Of course he paid in cash. On the way out of the store, he asked, "Where are you really staying?"

"You didn't buy the hotel?"

"No." But luckily, it appeared that Murray had. "I'll figure out how to keep the cover for you, but I'm glad you listened to me when I told you to keep as much private as you could."

"But not from you?"

"Not from me," he agreed. He stopped in front of the clothing store. "Murray more or less owns this place. Say nothing inside, got it?"

"Nothing at all, as in being mute? Or nothing as in nothing important?"

She couldn't seriously find any humor in this situation. "It could be bugged, and Twyla is part of his inner circle. Just because she acts old and flighty, don't let her fool you. She's sharp as a tack and as cutthroat as they come." Catching her chin, Trace tipped up her face. "Where are you staying?"

Priss gave in without hesitation. "I got a place a few blocks away from that hotel. It's a dive, but they didn't ask too many questions when I wanted to rent by the week and pay in cash."

Smart. And devious. Trace put his hand on the doorknob. "Don't bitch about the clothes that you try on. Blush all you want—"

"What makes you think I'll blush?"

"If you don't, we won't take them." Her eyes widened a little over that, and Trace *almost* smiled. "We're not leaving without a variety of outfits. Tomorrow, after Twyla has gotten a fix on your size, I can come back to pick up more."

"Just how much stuff am I expected to take?"

He shrugged. "Four, maybe five outfits. But no matter what, don't forget your role."

"Of a timid little mouse?" She fluttered her eyelashes dramatically.

"It's a stretch, I know. But you started it, so try to keep up." Trace pulled the door open, determined not to smile at her antics. In truth, he enjoyed bantering with her far too much. It was risky, in more ways than one.

As soon as they stepped inside, Twyla was there. She had to be sixty-five, but insisted on dressing like a stage performer with an abundance of garish makeup. She drew on her black eyebrows with such a severe arch, she had a look of shock about her at all times.

"Trace, how lovely to see you!" She floated toward him, her long caftan drifting out behind her while her perfume wafted ahead.

"Twyla." He allowed her to kiss his cheek—and to squish her aging bosom against his chest. While removing Twyla's dark lipstick from his jaw, Trace nudged Priss forward. "We need a wardrobe makeover. I'm hoping you can get us set up with two outfits today, and then after you know her size, maybe pull a few more together so we can come by tomorrow to look at them."

"Hmm." Twyla ran a professional gaze over Priss. "Turn around."

Wary, Priss did a slow, uncertain turn.

"Keep going."

When she faced Twyla again, her cheeks were hot. Interesting. Did she blush at being sized up, or was she really that good at maintaining her cover? Soon enough, he'd find out.

"Shoes? Undergarments? Jewelry?"

"Why not?" Trace gave Priss a warning frown. "Get her started while I step outside to make a call. But I'll want to see her in each outfit."

"Of course." Twyla clamped onto Priss's arm. Her long painted nails looked obscene against Priss's pale skin. Trace watched as Twyla yanked her forward in the same manner one might use with a recalcitrant mule.

Looking back over her shoulder, Priss said, "Trace?"

That small voice, accompanied by the look of fear on her face, almost got to him. She was such a contradiction in so many ways that she kept him off-kilter. "You'll be in good hands, Priss. I'll only be a moment."

Refusing to be drawn in by her, he stepped out into the bright sunshine and, using the prepaid phone, put a call into his friend Dare.

"Macintosh."

With his free hand, Trace rubbed the back of his neck, trying to work out the growing tension there. "It's Trace, and I've got a small conundrum."

"How can I help?"

"I'm going to need a backup tail."

"For you?"

"No, for Priscilla Patterson."

"Huh." Dare made a sound of amusement. "Sounds like an interesting conundrum."

"She's claiming to be Coburn's estranged daughter, and she showed up saying she hoped to get acquainted with him."

"Shit."

"Yeah. But it gets better." Even as he spoke, Trace surveyed the surrounding area—and spotted the dark car parked half a block away. His gaze went right on past so no one would know he'd noticed it. "I'm being watched so I have to make this fast. She left a dark blue Honda Civic two blocks up from Coburn's office. I need it moved someplace safe before he or his henchmen find it. Wouldn't hurt to have the plates switched out, too, just in case."

"No problem. I'll send Jackson up to take care of it, and then he can stick around as the tail, and anything else you need him to do."

Trace nodded. "Yeah, that'll work." Jackson was a newer recruit to the operation, but credible to the extreme. "I'll call you later tonight."

"Consider it done."

Having Dare Macintosh involved really helped lighten the load. "Thanks."

"Trace?" Dare hesitated only a second. "Watch your back."

"You bet." He hung up and reentered the shop. After accompanying Hell here on one of her extravagant shopping expeditions, Trace already knew the routine. He went on through the front of the establishment, past a thick velvet curtain and into the back dressing rooms.

Everything was ornate and fancy, with luxurious fabrics and mirrors everywhere. Taking a cushioned seat and propping his feet up on a small round lacquered table, Trace inspected the various curtained dressing rooms. Beneath the hem of one curtain, he saw small, narrow feet.

Priss.

The feet didn't move for the longest time, so Trace cleared his throat. "Step out so I can see, Priss."

He heard a loud groan, and then in a whispered hush, "It's *indecent*."

He'd known it would be, and still his pulse sped up. Resisting the urge to clear his throat, Trace said, "I'll be the judge of that. Now stop hiding."

The curtain parted, she peeked out, looked around and didn't see Twyla, and with her face twisted in disgust, she took one long step out.

Without even realizing it, Trace dropped his feet back

to the floor and sat forward. Beneath his skin, he burned. Muscles twitched and tightened. "Turn around."

Eyes rolling, Priss did a turn—but far too fast for a thorough exam. And still it was enough.

God almighty, the girl was built with luscious curves and blatant sensuality. There'd be no hiding flaws, not in that sheer bit of nothingness.

But she had none. She was…perfection.

His mouth went dry. "Again, slower this time so I can actually see you."

She gave a low complaint, but did as told.

The zigzag design of the sheer mesh dress left key places exposed, like her thighs, her belly, and an abundance of cleavage. It crossed over her breasts, just barely hiding her nipples with the doubling of fabric. Same for the notch of her thighs, and the cleft of her rounded behind.

Only an idiot would misunderstand Murray's intent in having her dressed so provocatively—and Priss wasn't an idiot. Is that why she went along?

Twyla strode back in with a pair of black stiletto heels. "Nice." She tilted her head back to give a practiced study of Priss in the mind-blowing dressing. Brows down, she gave a few yanks to the material, lowering the neckline, rearranging the hem a little higher. "For this getup, you don't need hose. But try on these shoes."

Priss looked agonized. "I can't walk in those."

"Guess you'll have to learn, won't you?" Twyla handed the impossibly high heels to her.

When Priss bent to slip them on, Trace just knew one of her breasts would break free of the meager constraint of mesh. He held his breath, waiting, but no, she stayed in place.

Barely.

Priss straightened again, and he saw that she had

gorgeous legs. Really gorgeous. Long and firm and sleek.

Damn. Trace rubbed a hand over his mouth. Murray would go nuts seeing her like this, whether she was his daughter or not.

He drew a breath and fulfilled his role. "She needs her hair loose."

Priss shot him a killer look, but she didn't argue as Twyla began working the rubber band free without concern to any hairs that snapped free.

"I'll take it."

Twyla gave him a questioning look, but handed over the rubber band, now entwined with several long hairs. Trace stuck it in his pocket.

That took care of one chore; collecting a sample for the hair follicle test.

Priss's long hair tumbled down in thick, shining hanks that landed over her shoulders, around her breasts and, as he'd suspected, to the top of that stellar ass.

"We'll take it," Trace said, because if he'd said anything else, Twyla would be onto him.

"Shouldn't we know the price?" Priss asked while fingering the material, trying to cover herself more.

She tugged at the hem, and Twyla smacked the back of her hand.

Trace interrupted before any real hostilities could start; he had no idea how much more Priss could take without losing her cool composure. "Make the next one a little more reserved, for everyday wear. Maybe some tight jeans and a few halters."

Trying to appear uncertain rather than furious, Priss said, "And maybe some shoes that are more practical?"

Twyla looked to Trace.

He shrugged. "We don't want her falling on her face. Get her something with a thicker heel."

"Ankle boots will work," Twyla announced. "With those legs, they'll look great." Then Twyla added to Priss, "With this dress, undergarments are out."

Priss squeaked. "I have to be *naked* underneath?"

Twyla ignored her; Trace couldn't. "You want to look your best, Priss. Trust Twyla. She knows what she's doing."

"Indeed." Twyla waved toward a stack of undergarments on an ornate table. "I assume you want to see her in the selection I choose? With her coloring, I think it's best to stick to black and red."

"Yeah." Trace frowned at the rasp in his voice, and firmed his tone. "I'll see them on her." It was expected, he told himself. What would Murray think if he dodged the duty? Twyla would tell him, no doubt about that.

After that lame bit of rationalizing, Trace made himself sit back again. Aware of Priss staring at him with wide eyes, he avoided her gaze and said, "Let's wrap it up though. I have a lot to do yet today."

"She can model the underwear for you while I go grab some jeans and halters."

As soon as Twyla left the room, his gaze jumped to Priss's furious face. She looked scalded, her cheeks were so hot, and ire lit her green eyes.

He had not one iota of sympathy for her. Not yet anyway. Very softly, almost as a goad, he asked, "Regrets?"

Those burning green eyes narrowed. She grabbed a fistful of underwear and, without a single totter on the stilettos, stalked back behind the curtain.

In an agony of suspense, Trace watched the movements of her feet.

She left the heels on, damn her.

He saw her step into a tiny scrap of black lace and his lungs constricted. A few seconds later, she stepped out.

This time he didn't leave his seat. He wasn't sure he

could. His eyes burned and his cock twitched. Gaze glued to her, he said, "You know the program."

Smug at his palpable reaction, Priss turned—oh, so slowly. The panties were no more than a thong, leaving her entire delectable backside beautifully bare. For such a small woman, she had wide shoulders that tapered to a minuscule waist, and then flared again to those incredible hips. She wasn't skinny by any stretch, but her waist dipped in and there was only the slightest curve to her belly. The bra lifted her breasts until they looked ready to tumble over the strip of material meant to restrain them. Again, her nipples were barely concealed.

"Well?" Giving him a coy look, Priss flipped her hair over her shoulder. "What do you think?"

He thought he wanted to fuck her, bad, even knowing she was off-limits.

Propping his forearms on his knees, his hands hanging loosely, Trace looked her over again. Hell, he couldn't stop looking her over. She had no tattoos, no piercings to mar her fair, beautiful skin. And with those tiny panties leaving little to the imagination, he didn't need X-ray glasses to see that she'd never been waxed. Little Ms. Priss liked to keep it natural.

Why the hell that excited him, he couldn't say.

"Cat got your tongue?" she fairly purred.

Trace forced his gaze off her mound and up to her face. "Adequate."

"Hmm. Maybe the others will be better." She hefted her breasts in her hands, rearranged the elastic of the thong, and basically tortured him. "Sit tight, okay? I'll be right back."

Witch. She knew she looked good and she wasn't above mocking him now that Twyla wasn't around to see.

Never in his life had he known such a brazen, sexy

and self-confident woman—who also managed to be somewhat…pure.

Pure sensual appeal. Pure innocence.

Pure trouble.

Calling himself a masochist, Trace settled back in his seat and waited for her next reveal.

IGNORING THE FLUTTERING of her stomach and how her pulse sped with nervousness, Priss pulled on the red ruffled boy-short panties and ridiculous matching bra. This set covered more skin, but was sheer enough that, if Trace looked close, he'd be able to see through it.

And she *knew* he'd look closely. He'd already seared her with the heat of his intensity.

As a modest woman who cared little about attracting male attention, the entire scenario was torturous for her. She figured it may as well be torturous for Trace, too.

Priss drew a breath, shored up her audacity and parted the curtain with fanfare.

GOD ALMIGHTY. Trace gripped the arms of the chair and tightened his abdomen. He searched his brain for a blasé response, and finally said, "Cute." So damn cute that if she didn't get changed fast, he'd be on her and to hell with his cover. "Hustle it up already, will you? We're running out of time."

PLEASED WITH HIS noticeable turmoil, Priss stepped back into the small room and changed into the heart set. The thong had a red heart in front that just barely covered her triangle of pubic hair, and the lace bra had red hearts, almost like pasties, only big enough to hide her nipples. She wasn't unfamiliar with exotic lingerie, but never before had she worn it. When it came to underwear, she was more into comfort.

Her embarrassment lingered, and already her feet ached from the arch of the shoe. But she drew in a breath and asked with saccharine sweetness, "Trace, are you ready?"

No. He wasn't ready. Somehow he had to regain control of this situation. Right now she had the upper hand, and that was untenable.

With the perfect plan in mind, Trace shook his head, but said with what he hoped sounded like indifference, "Quit stalling."

And then he pulled out his cell phone.

This time, she was all but naked. What little material covered her proved mere decoration, like icing on a very sweet cake—a cake he wouldn't mind eating, slowly, top to toes and everywhere in between.

Priss stood with her hands on her generous hips, her feet apart, her shoulders back.

How such a small woman packed so many perfect curves, he didn't know. But she managed it with flair. Boy, did she ever.

"Good enough."

When she smiled at him, he lifted the cell phone and used it to take a picture.

Squawking, Priss leaped behind the curtain and her face went up in flames. *"What do you think you're doing?"*

"Suddenly shy?" Content with her appalled tone and burning-red face, Trace looked down at the phone. Oh, yeah, that'd do. He pushed a few buttons, then put the cell phone away. "Don't worry, honey. I emailed it to myself." His smile felt like a leer. "No one else will see it."

Unappeased by that promise, she glared at him. "You—!"

"Now, Priss. Modesty at this late date is more than suspicious. You wanted my approval." He shrugged—and struggled to keep his attention on her face and off the curves that showed even beneath the curtain she clutched to her chin. "You've got it, with my admiration, too."

Before either of them could say any more, Twyla returned. Quickly, Priss released the curtain, but she looked truly miserable now, and on the verge of attack.

Trace smiled. She deserved to squirm, the little temptress.

Twyla glanced at Priss, studied her in minute detail, and announced, "She needs a Brazilian bikini wax."

Priss strangled on a gasp.

"Want me to have my girl take care of it?" Hands on her hips, Twyla said, "She always does a good job."

Trace fought back a gag. At her age, Twyla was still...*no,* he did not want that mental image stuck in his head.

"I don't know." Pretending to think about it, Trace looked at Priss. She had murder in her eyes, so yeah, she'd likely figured out that Murray had no intention of being a father, but every intention of using her to his advantage. "There's a certain appeal to leaving her au natural."

"You can't be serious."

"I'll give it some thought, maybe discuss it with Murray—"

Priss choked, earning a frown from Twyla.

"—and then get back to you."

Shrugging, Twyla said, "Suit yourself." She handed Priss a stack of clothes. "Jeans and three halters."

Priss held them in front of her body and said a heartfelt, *"Thank God."*

"Priscilla," Trace warned.

He got Twyla's approval for the stern tone. "Try each of the halters with the jeans, and then we'll be done for the day."

Priss closed her eyes a moment, but that didn't help

one iota. Trace had done her in, but good. Flaunting her body while he looked as uncomfortable as she felt had been hard enough. But with him visually caressing her, *and taking a damn photo,* she wanted to shrink into the floor with mortification.

And then he'd had the nerve to discuss things *very* private to her as if they held no meaning, as if she wasn't even a real person. *Would he really mention it to Murray?*

Oh, God, she'd kill him first. And at the moment, with him looking so damned pleased with himself, killing was a real possibility.

Okay, she got it. Murray played by his own rules, and somehow got away with it. He had more reach than she'd realized. She wouldn't turn tail and run—even if Murray allowed her escape now, which she doubted. But no way in hell would she let anyone wax her. Just the thought of it left her shuddering.

She'd always been a very private person; from the age of five she'd been independent in her bathing. Even her mother hadn't intruded on her personal hygiene. Anyone who came at her with the intent of stripping her, positioning her, and leaving her hairless would end up maimed. If it came to that particular showdown, she'd win, period.

As to that photo…Priss seethed, then decided that one way or another she'd get Trace's phone from him and she'd delete *everything.* If he lost important information, well, tough titty. It was no more than he deserved after pulling that nasty stunt.

With that decision, even knowing that Trace had already sent the photo to himself, Priss was able to relax a little again.

Nodding at the box under Twyla's arm, Priss asked hopefully, "Are those the boots?" If she had to wear those mile-high heels a minute longer, she'd cry. In her day-to-day life, she didn't bother dressing up, and she didn't bother trying to impress the opposite sex. She wore her old-faithful jeans with casual tops and, more often than not, sneakers.

Out of the corner of her eye, she looked at Trace. Given his response to seeing her, she wouldn't have to work hard to get attention from him. She now knew that, in the future, if she wanted anything, all she had to do was strip down. Like most men, he became putty at the sight of a naked woman.

Not an ideal situation, but to gain her end goals, yeah, she could deal with that.

Twyla produced the boots, and they were unlike any Priss had ever seen. Studs decorated the vamp of the black leather boots with a peekaboo toe. At least they did have a thicker heel.

"Oh, how cute," Priss gushed, even though she thought they were absurd. "I'll just go try these on." She tipped her head and looked at Trace. "Did you want to see these outfits, too?"

He scrubbed a hand over his face and, without a word, indicated for her to get a move on.

It was all Priss could do not to gloat. Especially since Twyla hung around, forcing Trace to endorse his ruse. The big faker. Even as she tugged on the skin-tight jeans, Priss wondered if Trace was as deadly as she'd assumed.

Not that she doubted he could kill, but had he? Anytime recently?

It took mere seconds to pull on the boots and don a halter. The first one, made like a silk corset, fit her like a glove. Trace approved it with a terse nod.

The second, made of stretchy lace and resembling a camisole, was the most comfortable. He barely looked at her in that one, but Twyla gave it her stamp of approval.

The last, red with white polka dots, was Priss's favorite for the simple reason that it was the most concealing.

Trace appeared to agree. "She'll wear that now. Get her more of the same jeans, in different washes, and a few cocktail dresses. I'll come by tomorrow to pick up everything."

Twyla began collecting the items. "This goes on Murray's tab?"

"Yeah, thanks."

Trace kept his gaze off Priss, annoying her. She wouldn't let him get away with that for long.

In fact, as soon as they were alone again, she intended to call him on a few things. And then she'd make him pay for putting her through that little rendition of exhibitionism.

CHAPTER FOUR

THE SECOND THEY PULLED away from the curb, Trace beat her to the punch. "Not a word, Priss. I mean it."

She opened her mouth, but after giving his frown due attention, she retreated. "What is it? What's wrong?"

He gave her a disbelieving look.

She let out a breath. "Yeah. That question sounded preposterous even to me. For God's sake, I've just been forced into the most revealing outfits for your entertainment, and for Murray's eventual enjoyment, so all kinds of things are wrong."

"It's fucked three ways to Sunday, I agree."

She scowled, and again started to speak, only to have Trace interrupt her.

Glancing in the rearview mirror, he said, "We're being followed."

She didn't look. She obviously knew better, which sharpened his curiosity about her.

Slowly, barely, she leaned toward the window to use the side-view mirror. "Who do you think it is?"

"No idea, so try not to annoy me for a few minutes." He dug out his cell phone and dialed Murray. Most people would have to go through Alice, but Trace had a direct line.

That meant he had the ability to interrupt Murray while working, and while doing…other things. This happened to be one of those times.

"This better be good," Murray complained, grunting a little, sounding winded.

Trace went icy cold with disgust, knowing just what Murray was doing. "Sorry to interrupt."

"Helene will take that up with you later, I'm sure." He chuckled and, in the background, Trace heard Hell's deep moans.

Christ. "I'll get right to the point." Right now, Murray was likely trying to keep Helene calm enough so she wouldn't butcher anyone. She had a mean jealous streak, and Priss had pushed all her buttons. A good fuck would help her expend some energy and tension. "I'm being followed."

Murray said dumbly, "What's that?"

"If you put the tail on me, no problem. I get that you're cautious and I can accept that. I'll let him follow along like a good employee. But if you didn't, I'm going to lose the fuck, or shoot him. Your choice."

There was a moment of silence, and then Murray's loud guffaws nearly split Trace's ear drums.

Aware of Priss watching him, Trace turned another corner, going nowhere in particular. "What's it to be, Murray?"

"Lose him, and if you can't, feel free to kill him with my blessing. He deserves no less for being a shitty tail."

"Got it." More than aware that Murray hadn't confirmed or denied putting the tail on him in the first place, Trace disconnected the call. "Hold tight, Priss. If I don't lose the bastard, I'll have to kill him."

"Squeamish about a little bloodshed, are you?"

"Not at all." And obviously, neither was she.

"So what's the problem?"

"Don't really have one." Right now, there were half a dozen people involved in Murray's operation that he'd take great pleasure in annihilating. "But we have more important things to do right now."

With that said, he took a sharp turn and accelerated. When he hit a hundred, Priss said quietly, "Okay, maybe this isn't—"

"Hold on."

He took another turn, hit the expressway, and got off on an exit two miles down the way. He pulled into an old, dilapidated movie theater another mile off the exit. Steering the Mercedes behind the ramshackle screen, he put it in Park, took out his gun and waited.

Beside him, Priss sat stock-still, her breath held.

Only the rush of muted traffic on the main road could be heard. Gun held balanced on his knee, Trace turned to her. "Breathe."

She inhaled sharply, almost choking. "You lost him?"

"I think so, but we'll wait here a minute to be sure."

Still wide-eyed, she looked around. "Are you familiar with this area?"

"Nope." Trace visually outlined her face; the pert nose, the lush mouth, the long dark eye lashes and keen green gaze. "At least, not as familiar as you are with fetish wear."

Her gaze jerked over to him. Those delicately arched brows pinched down. "What are you talking about?"

"You." Using the gun, he gestured at her body. "In that boner-inspiring fluff called underwear. You're more than comfortable with it. Hell, a real innocent wouldn't even have figured out *how* to wear it, much less used it to taunt me."

Her lips curled. "Oh, poor Trace. Did you feel taunted?"

"Yeah." He stared at her mouth. "I did." It occurred to him that he hadn't seen a single freckle on her. Not on her face, not on her body.

Curious, given the color of her hair.

He tapped the gun against his leg, drawing Priss's attention to it. It'd help if she showed just a modicum of uncertainty. Not that he didn't appreciate her cool cooperation in this now jumbled case, but still… "So tell me, Priscilla Patterson. What did you do before you decided to bedevil me?"

PRISS PONDERED the idea of lying. Again.

"Don't bother."

Damn, he was astute. So what the heck? She put her chin up. "I'm the owner of an adult store."

That annoying gun-tapping stopped. His eyes narrowed, and then he gave a dramatic, negligent shrug. "Somehow, with you, that makes sense."

"I'm not sure I like it that you think so." Was he trying to pigeonhole her? Jerk. "And you know, it's really conceited of you to think I'm here on account of you."

Trace wedged his shoulder against the door, getting comfortable. "Is that right?"

"Yeah." Priss reached over and patted his cheek. "You're just an unexpected perk." She rested her hands on her thighs, aware of Trace looking at her chest in the stupid halter. "I'm here for Murray."

"Because he's your father?"

"Yeah." She slanted him a look. "And because I'm going to kill him."

For long seconds, Trace said nothing. He reholstered the gun, shifted back in his seat and put the car in gear. "You're not killing anyone, Priss, but I'd like to hear more about this dirty little store of yours."

"I am so killing him, as soon as I can." And in the same even, nonchalant tone, she said, "The shop is great, not at all dirty. It's well run—by me—and it stays busy. It supported me and my mother before she passed away."

Thinking of her mother hurt, so she shook that off.

"How big is it?"

"Not even as big as Murray's office. Most of our business is DVDs and books, along with the occasional battery-operated item." She bobbed her eyebrows at him. "The underwear…well, we have a few crazy things, like crotchless panties and pasties and bondage bras, but mostly just for display. When people want stuff, they order out of a catalog, and we get a percentage of the sales."

Trace drove out, and there wasn't a single sign of their tail. "Go on."

"What else do you want to know?"

His gaze kept moving around the area, alert, cautious. His question sounded almost as an afterthought. "You ever wore any of the merchandise before?"

"Nope. I'm a comfy cotton kind of gal."

He nodded, then tossed out, "How did your mother die?"

Lacking a smooth transition, Priss wondered if Trace hoped to take her off guard, or was it just his way? Even as he questioned her—and listened to her answers—he kept constant surveillance of the area.

When they were on the main road again, he stuck with back streets rather than return to the highway.

"Mom had a stroke."

"So what you told Murray was the truth?"

She nodded.

Trace drove with one hand and, with the other, he reached over for her knee. "I'm sorry."

Priss badly wanted to cover his hand with her own, but before she could really think about it, he withdrew again. "You haven't exactly been nice to me, Trace, so why should I believe you care?"

He shrugged. "We're each stuck in our role, and you know it." He glanced at her, then away again. "I lost my parents, both of them, long ago. Regardless of everything else we have going on, I know how it is to go through that."

Priss accepted his explanation. "Thanks."

"It was rough?"

"Yeah." Such an understatement. "Mom suffered for a long time before she died. She was...incapacitated. Unable to care for herself. Little by little, she wasted away, and in the end, her death was a mercy."

Putting his hand back on her knee, Trace squeezed in a show of comfort. "You cared for her yourself?"

"The best I could." Her chest hurt, remembering how inadequate she'd been. "There wasn't anyone else. But I still had to work, and we'd laid low for so long—"

"Staying out of Murray's radar?"

"Why else? Not that mom thought Murray would have any real interest in me, not as a father anyway. She didn't trust him, with good reason. And yes, that's why we had a sex shop. Mom said Murray never would have thought to look for us there."

"He'd have assumed she went back to her middle-class upbringing?"

Priss nodded. "So she hid where she knew he wouldn't look for her. But because of our lifestyle, we never had much insurance, or much cash put away."

They rode in silence for a while, and Priss—thinking Trace's nosiness had been appeased—closed her eyes. It had been a long, very tumultuous day. And it wasn't over yet.

After ten minutes or so, Trace asked, "You asleep?"

"No." It had been so long since she'd had any real sleep, she'd forgotten what it was like.

"Who's running the shop for you while you're here?"

"My partner, Gary Deaton." Priss hated to think about

that, because no way would Gary keep up things the way she wanted.

"Partner, as is business, or personal?"

"Personal? *Eewwww*. Hardly." Such a repugnant thought made her shudder. "Business only, thank you very much. And actually, he's not really a partner. More like an employee. I just call him a partner because he works as many hours as me, sometimes more. Right now, while I'm here, definitely more."

"Anyone else in the picture?"

"No, and what do you care anyway?"

"Just wondering if anyone else is involved in this harebrained plan of yours." He turned another corner, and they ended up on a road familiar to her. "Or if you have someone back home who'll start looking for you soon if you don't check in."

Priss wasn't really worried, but she wouldn't take Trace lightly, either. "Thinking about killing me again?"

He gave a short laugh. "Killing you, no."

So what was he thinking of doing with her? She didn't dare ask. Keeping Trace Miller, or whatever his real name might be, at arm's length was a dire necessity. "Life on the lam doesn't lend itself to romantic entanglements."

His thumb rubbed over her knee, and Priss wondered if he was aware of doing it, if he did it on purpose to turn her on, or if it was an extension of the thoughts she saw flickering across his face.

"Trace…"

"It occurs to me that I didn't see a single freckle on you. Not on your face." He gave her a quick, level look. "And not on your body."

"Yeah, so?"

"That's kind of curious, don't you think, given the color of your hair?"

Priss lifted his hand and dropped it over next to him. "Okay, first off, hands to yourself. Got it?"

He said nothing, but she saw the corner of his mouth tilt up in the slightest of smiles.

"Secondly, did you happen to notice that my brows and lashes are a darker brown without a hint of red?"

"Meaning?"

"Meaning I'm not like some redheads who are..." Her face heated. "Red all over."

"Yeah?" He glanced at her lap meaningfully. "Do tell."

Priss punched him in the shoulder. "I don't like what you're thinking."

"You don't know what I'm thinking." And with another provoking grin, "Do you?"

Like she'd say it out loud? No way. Priss crossed her arms. "If you were hinting that you think I dye my hair, I don't. Everything on me is natural."

"We'll see."

"No, *we* will not see a damn thing!"

Under his breath, Trace said, "I damn near saw today. If I'd moved a foot closer for a better look—"

"Stop it!" Priss felt heat throbbing in her face, and she hated it. "And that reminds me. I want you to delete that damned picture."

"Not a chance. Seeing you in that getup was a trophy moment for me." He pulled into a lot, put the car in Park and looked around. Forestalling her anger, he said, "You weren't kidding. This place really is a dive."

Well, hell. She hadn't even noticed that she was back at her run-down apartment. It unnerved her that he'd distracted her enough to make her unaware of her surroundings. That could be deadly.

Sooner or later, she'd take him off guard, and then she'd get his phone and smash it. If he had emailed the picture to himself, well, at least she'd have some payback. Until then... "What now?"

"Now we go in, get some of your stuff and make it look like you're staying at the hotel. If anyone checks on you there, and you aren't around, you can always claim you were out late hitting bars or something."

"Barhopping doesn't work with my cover."

His jaw tightened. "I'll think of something. But from here on out, you're in survival mode. Got it?"

"No." Nothing and no one would keep her from doing what needed to be done. Priss tried to open her door, but it still didn't budge. "Unlock it."

Instead he pulled her around to face him. He started to blast her, but something funny happened. Instead of reading her the riot act, he stared into her eyes, then down at her mouth. His entire demeanor changed. He looked just as tense, but now for different, hotter reasons.

He still stared intently at her mouth when Priss heard the lock click open. She glanced down and saw that Trace had reached back for the door, all without breaking that disturbing, electrifying visual contact with her.

She met his gaze again, and softened. Damn, but resisting Trace wouldn't be easy, not if he kept looking at her like that. "You're coming in, too?"

"Yes." Suddenly, almost violently, he turned away from her and left the car. Still a gentleman, he strode around to her side and opened her door. "Let's get this night over with."

Well. That sounded insulting. Priss would have let herself out, except that she had to extract the room key from a hidden pocket in the design of her purse.

"Fine." She moved out of the car to stand beside him. "But when we go in, watch where you step."

"Why?" Taking her arm, he started for the entrance,

again surveying the area all around them. "You have land mines hidden around?"

Priss ignored him. "It's this way." She took the lead, steering him toward the side entrance. Nearby police sirens screamed, competing with music from the bar next door. "I'm on the second floor."

They passed a hooker fondling a man against the brick facing of the building. Priss stepped over and around a broken bottle. Tires squealed and someone shouted profanities.

Distaste left a sour expression on Trace's face. "This dive needs to be condemned."

"Maybe, but it's shady enough that no one asked me any questions when I checked in."

"It's also shady enough that you could get mugged, raped or murdered in the damned lot and no one would notice."

Priss shook her head. "I'm not worried about that." They went up the metal stairs, precariously attached to the structure.

After muttering a rude sound, Trace said, "There's a lot you should be worried about, but aren't."

No reason to debate it with him. Her options on what to worry about, and what to ignore, were pretty damned limited. "This way."

The ancient run-down house had been reworked in better years to accommodate four separate tenants. She was on the back corner, facing the bar.

Trace nodded toward the rowdy establishment. "It fired up early."

"My understanding is that it opens with lunch and is going pretty strong by early dinner. It won't bother me. I'm used to that type of noise."

Trace gave her a long look, but Priss refused to meet his probing gaze.

Using the key, she unlocked the dead bolt and then the door lock. "Careful now."

"Careful of what?" Trace asked.

They stepped in and before she could turn on a light, a low growl sounded. Behind her, Trace froze.

But not for long.

Somehow, before she even knew it, Priss found herself behind Trace, pressed to the wall. When she realized he'd pulled his gun, she smacked his shoulder. "Don't you dare shoot my cat!"

His confusion was palpable. "Cat?"

"Yes, as in a pet." Priss stepped away from him and found a lamp. Though she'd checked in days before contacting Murray, she wasn't yet entirely accustomed to the space. She fumbled for a moment before getting the light on.

Liger, her enormous kitty, came over to her and rubbed his head against her shin. Priss knelt down to hug him, to stroke along his broad back. She got a throaty purr in response.

Gun now hanging limp at his side, Trace stared at her. "You have to be kidding me."

"Put away your gun, Trace." She dropped to her butt on the floor and let Liger crawl into her lap. Because he was twenty-three pounds of solid love, he overflowed in every direction. Priss laughed as he ran the edge of his teeth along her knee, then rolled to his back.

"Good God. That's a domestic cat? Really? I've never seen one so big."

"He's a Maine coon. They're naturally large."

"You're telling me that's a normal size?"

"For the males, yeah. I found him at a shelter a few years ago. Isn't he beautiful?"

"Actually…" Trace holstered the gun and hunkered down beside her. "Yeah. He is."

For whatever reason, that surprised Priss. "You like animals?"

"Sure." He held out a hand to Liger. "Is he friendly?"

Priss rubbed her nose against the cat's neck. "Very. He's also really smart. He's a big lover boy, aren't you, Liger?"

The cat watched Trace, then put a giant paw on his thigh. He let out another snarl, making Trace go still.

"That's just his way of checking you out. He won't bite," Priss assured him. "I mean, he will, but not unless you were doing something you shouldn't."

"He has his claws?"

Priss glared. "Of course he does. Declawing is cruel!"

Trace paid no attention to her affront. He stroked the cat and Liger closed his eyes in bliss. "He has a tail like a raccoon."

"I know."

"What did you call him?"

"Liger." She hugged the cat again. "Because of his lionlike ruff, and his stripes."

"He's the wrong color."

True. Being mostly black with gray and white stripes, Liger didn't resemble a lion or a tiger. "I was going by size and that great roar of his."

The cat abandoned her to crawl up on Trace's lap, then stretched up to sniff his face. Trace grinned, petting Liger and rubbing under his chin. "He really is a nice guy, isn't he?"

"He's wonderful. Maine coons are like big affectionate dogs. They enjoy attention and have, for the most part, very gentle natures."

"For the most part?"

"He detests bugs and can get pretty vicious with them."

Trace laughed at that mental image, but then sobered. "I hate to tell you this, but he's going to be a big problem."

Priss froze. "What are you talking about?"

"Sorry, honey, but he has to go."

CHAPTER FIVE

SNATCHING THE GIANT cat away from him, Priss held him protectively.

With his chin tucked into the longer hair on his chest, Liger continued to purr.

Priss looked equal parts alarmed, furious and defensive. "Listen to me," Trace said.

"No, you listen." It was the darkest, coldest tone he'd heard from her. "If you touch one finger to my cat, I'll…"

She didn't finish the threat, unable to think of anything dire enough.

Rolling his eyes, Trace rose back to his feet and surveyed her apartment. It was clean but ragtag, spare beyond measure, and in no way secure. "I'm trying to make sure the cat stays safe. Anything or anyone that can be used against you is in danger. That's why I asked you if you were involved with anyone else in any way."

"Oh."

He cut his gaze to her. "What did you think? That I was hitting on you?"

Her right shoulder lifted. "You had just seen me all but naked."

God, he didn't need her to remind him; the image would be forever burned into his brain. "You flaunted your near nakedness, but here's a news flash for you, Priss. You're not the first naked woman I've seen."

"And probably not the best-looking, I know." Hefting

the big cat in her arms, Priss stood and went to a well-worn couch. She collapsed onto it in a sprawl. She looked at Trace through slumberous eyes and an edge of curiosity. "But you looked like you enjoyed the show."

What the hell did she want? A confession that she'd deeply affected him? Well, she wouldn't get it.

"I have a pulse, so of course I enjoyed it." The apartment was really no more than two spaces, the living, eating and sleeping area all rolled into one, and a tiny bathroom with stained sink and toilet bowl, and cracked tiles in the shower. There were no barricades, no alternate escape routes other than a window in the bathroom and one behind the couch. It wouldn't do. Almost absently, he added, "You're stacked, Priscilla Patterson. And that's a problem, too."

"Too?"

"The cat?" Fists on his hips, Trace turned to face her, and saw desolation in her big green eyes. As susceptible to real tears as any other guy, he gentled his tone. "Priss. You need to move Liger someplace safe."

She shook her head, and hugged the cat tighter. "There isn't any place. I'm all he has."

And he was all she had? Looked like it. Trace frowned as he considered things, then he withdrew the prepaid phone again and dialed Dare.

His friend answered on the second ring. "What's up?"

"I need a favor."

With a shrug in his tone, Dare said, "Name it."

"The conundrum I told you about? Well, she has a cat."

"Is that a euphemism, or are you talking about a pet?"

Trace grinned. "Pet. A *big* pet." He lowered the phone to ask Priss, "How much does that monster weigh?"

"He's not a monster, but he's twenty-three pounds." She stared at him with grave distrust. "And what exactly are you doing now?"

Back to the phone, Trace said, "He's a twenty-three-pound cat, if you can believe that. Thing is, he's a sweetheart, so fair game. And I just know he'd make a powerful weapon against her."

"Yeah." Dare went thoughtful, but only for a moment. "You want me to keep him out of harm's way? Hell, my girls would love it. They enjoy all things furry. Since I'm not on assignment right now, I'll be around to make sure they get along."

Relieved that Dare had offered, Trace let out a breath. "If you're sure, I could drive Priss and her cat down there tomorrow. She needs a damned makeover anyway. Coburn ordered it."

"Damn. That's not sounding good."

"No." But Trace didn't want to go into Murray's motives yet. If he did, he'd want to go kill the bastard now instead of sticking with the plan. "Maybe you could arrange for a beautician or whatever to be there, to help cover the trip. If Priss returns with her hair changed, and her nails done up, no one would think anything of it. And Jackson could make sure we got out of town without being followed."

"Yeah, I think we can manage that. I'm pretty sure Chris has a friend who's a hairdresser."

Amused, Trace shook his head. Dare's wife, Molly, though very pretty, wasn't into long hours spent at a salon. But Dare's good friend and employee, Chris, had a variety of acquaintances ranging from football players to beauty queens—all of them guys. "Unless something comes up, I could have her down there late morning."

"Plan to eat lunch here."

"Thanks." The mention of food made Trace wonder—

when was the last time Priss had eaten? Now that she'd slouched comfortably on the couch, her exhaustion showed. He frowned. "I'll call when we're on our way."

After hanging up with Dare, Trace went to the blinds and peered out. The parking lot adjoined the bar on one side, a back street on the other. He didn't like the layout, or the noise level, or the lack of security. Even the shittiest joint should have some safeguards in place.

This place had none.

"You made arrangements for Liger?"

He nodded. "It'll just be until you're in the clear, Priss. That's all."

"But we don't know how long that might be."

"No." Trace rubbed his face. "Have you eaten?"

"Not since breakfast."

And it was now well past dinnertime. "All right. Let's get your things together."

"How much should I gather?"

"Everything you might actually need. If I can help it, you won't be spending any nights here."

"Such a shame." She looked around wistfully. "I was already settled."

He wouldn't debate it with her. She was moving, period. "We'll get you checked into a hotel, but not the one you mentioned. I don't want you any place where Murray knows to look for you." He'd take her to the same hotel where he was staying, as close as he could keep her.

"Won't that make him suspicious?"

"I'll think of something." He watched her rise from the couch. "After that we'll grab some food."

She hesitated. "And Liger?"

"He'll stay with you for tonight. Then tomorrow we'll take him to stay with my friend." Trace watched her, and saw her gearing up for an argument, based on concern and fear. "Don't look like that. Dare will be really good to him, I promise. He has two dogs who love other animals. Between them, they'll make him feel right at home."

Trace knew she didn't want to. She had that look of stubborn machination coming over her; he could practically see the variety of alternate plans flitting through her thoughts.

He used stark reality to convince her. "Would you rather one of Murray's henchmen find him? Trust me on this, Priss, they're more than capable of using the cat to hurt you. It would be…ugly."

Given the look on her face, she knew exactly what he meant.

Her shuddering breath and trembling lips left fear in his soul. *Do not cry. Please.* Priss had a body like sin, and the disposition of a hedgehog, but seeing her love for that big fat cat…well, it struck something tender deep inside him.

Very softly, Trace said, "You okay?"

Regaining her self-confidence, she firmed her lips and nodded. "Thank you for thinking of it." And then in a less intense voice, "I'd die if anything happened to him."

Which meant Trace would do every damn thing in his power to see that it never came to that. "This way he'll be safe." Now if only it was that easy to ensure Priss's safety. "Let's get going. We'll have a long day tomorrow."

"All right." She left the cat on the couch and went into the bathroom. In one overnight case, she had everything already packed. From behind the fold-out couch, she produced a large duffel bag stuffed full. "Other than this, I need to get Liger's litter box and food." She lifted the cat's leash and harness off the door knob.

Amazed, Trace looked at her paltry belongings. "You hadn't unpacked yet?"

"I hadn't planned on sticking around too long. And I

didn't want to have to leave anything behind if I got boned on this deal."

"The deal to...kill Murray?"

"That's right." Priss's smile felt like an alarm. "You might think I'm a silly girl acting on impulse, but I had a plan, Trace. A sound plan. And if you hadn't shown up, I'd be that much closer to ridding the world of a very rotten soul. Now that I know seeing my cat again depends on my success...well, let's just say I'm doubly motivated to get this over with."

Trace saw the gleam of success in her eyes, and the cocky tilt of anticipation on her sexy mouth. For a slight, shapely female with an innocent face, she was so damn bloodthirsty.

Contradictions. Nothing but constant contradictions.

So why the hell was he starting to find that so exciting?

PRISS STRETCHED AWAKE IN the much-cleaner and better-smelling hotel room. The sheets were smooth, the pillows soft. She had enough space to actually move around without bumping into anything.

Sunlight crept in around the haphazardly closed curtains. It would be another gorgeous June day. Time to get up—except that she couldn't move her legs, not with Liger stretched out in full splendor across her. He had her blankets pinned down so that they only covered her waist.

The air-conditioning—something unavailable at the apartment—kept the room cool. With a yawn, Priss crawled out from under Liger and sat up on the side of the bed. Her long hair hung in her face and the now-rumpled T-shirt she wore covered only to the top of her thighs. But for now at least, for this particular morning, she was safe.

So many changes in such a short time.

Her mother's death had been both a devastating loss and a blessing. Not a day went by that she didn't miss her, but at least now she didn't suffer. That had been the worst for Priss, seeing her mother in misery, fading away in small, painful increments.

Leaving her home should have been an upheaval, but with her motivation driving her, Priss had gone through the packing, the driving, and the new town by rote. Comfort took a distant second to reaching her goals.

She'd settled in, found Murray's location, and even found Murray. She'd been right on track.

And then she'd met Trace…whatever his last name might be. She wasn't buying the name he'd given her. Trace had as many, maybe more secrets than she did.

She enjoyed sparring with him verbally, found him physically appealing and was intrigued by his cocky attitude of capability. By far, he was the most tempting man she'd ever met.

Because she really didn't know enough about him to be so captivated, her reaction to him was kind of…well, sick.

Sure, her instincts were good, and her gut told her that Trace was hero material. Despite a lack of facts, she'd already decided he was one of the good guys, an alpha male who would step into danger to protect others, just as he had—so far—protected her.

And her cat.

He was the complete and total opposite of Murray Coburn. So why was he working for that bastard? Or was he?

Liger stretched leisurely, yawning widely enough to show his abundant razor-sharp teeth. He opened his big yellow eyes to blink at Priss, then gave the cutest little

meow that sounded small and girlish in comparison to
his opulent body.

Priss grinned. "I know. That was a long night. We're
not used to it, are we? And now you want breakfast." She
scratched his head, his favorite spot under his chin and
then along his back. "Me, too, buddy. But first things
first."

On her way to the bathroom, which was now twice the
size of the one she'd used the day before, Priss glanced
at the connecting door.

In the very next room, Trace slept.

Her heart pounded, and that was the biggest change
of all. For all intents and purposes, she saw men purely
as customers, easily coerced into buying the latest and
most expensive porn. She joked with men, argued with
and rejected them. Unlike her mother, Priss felt at ease
in male company.

But a pounding heart? Nope. Not once had she ever
met a man who affected her *that* way.

Before leaving the bathroom Priss splashed her face
and cleaned her teeth. A glance in the mirror showed her
looking a little worse for wear.

Not that she gave a flying flip.

Using both hands, she shoved back her hair from her
face and gave herself a critical inspection. Before meeting
Trace, she'd always accepted herself as a sexless woman,
apathetic in most situations, detached from the customary
interests of young females, methodical in her approach
to life.

Yes, she'd loved her mother. So damn much. But
beyond that one single person, no genuine affection had
ever touched her. She'd been a woman set on correcting
wrongs, with no other available emotions.

But around Trace she felt so much that her head swam
with the conflagration of sensations. She'd gone to sleep

thinking about him and, she just realized, she'd awakened with him on her mind.

Utterly pathetic.

She had just given Liger his food when a tap sounded on the connecting door. Priss's heart leaped into her throat.

With excitement.

Not dread, or annoyance, or even indifference.

Pure, sizzling stimulation. Suddenly she was wide-awake.

Tamping down her automatic smile, Priss leaned on the door. "Yeah?"

"Open up."

Still fighting that twitching grin, Priss tried to sound disgruntled as she asked, "Why?"

Something hit the door—maybe his head—and Trace said, "I heard you up moving around, Priss. I have coffee ready, but if you don't want any—"

Being a true caffeine junkie, she jerked open the door. "Oh, bless you, man." She took the cup straight out of Trace's hand, drank deeply and sighed as the warmth penetrated the thick fog of novel sentiment. "Ahhhh. Nirvana. Thank you."

Only after the caffeine ingestion did she notice that Trace wore unsnapped jeans and nothing else. Her eyes flared wide and her jaw felt loose. Holy moly.

"That was my cup," Trace told her, bemused.

But Priss could only stare at him. Despite the delicious coffee she'd just poured in it, her mouth went dry.

When she continued to stare at him, at his chest and abdomen, her gaze tracking a silky line of brown hair that disappeared into his jeans, Trace crossed his arms.

Her gaze jumped to his face and she found him watching her with equal fascination.

A little lost as to the reason for that look, Priss asked with some belligerence, "What?"

With a cryptic smile, Trace shook his head. "Never mind. Help yourself, and I'll get another."

Oh, crap, she'd snatched away his cup! "Sorry."

He lifted a hand in dismissal and went to the coffee machine sitting atop the dresser. His jeans rode low on his hips. The sun had darkened his skin, creating a sharp contrast to his fair hair.

Another drink was in order, and another sigh of bliss. Hoping to regain her wits, Priss said, "God, nothing in the world tastes better than that first drink of coffee."

Trace looked over his shoulder, his attention zeroing in on her mouth, then her chest and finally down to her bare legs. "Oh, I don't know about that."

Sensually stroked by that hot glance and the low timbre of his suggestive words, Priss followed him in. So did Liger. Now fed, the big cat strode past her and leaped up to Trace's bed, disturbing the covers that Trace had already smoothed back into place. Liger chose to stretch across the pillows near the headboard. He pawed the soft cotton a moment, showed his claws, yawned and relaxed.

Trace gestured toward the small round table and two chairs. "Take a seat, Priss."

Last night, after relocating to the hotel, she and Trace had eaten dinner at that table. It had been…nice.

A revelation even.

They'd shared quiet conversation, talking about every-thing under the sun without either of them giving away anything too personal or important. Pure chitchat. A way to pass the time.

For Trace, it had seemed mundane, a casual occurrence that he'd indulged many times.

For Priss, it was a profound thing to sit across from a man and really, truly enjoy him—his appearance, his sense of humor and wit, his intelligence and his attention. Even while eating a loaded cheeseburger, he'd stayed alert to every sound in the hallway and parking lot, and every movement she made, no matter how big or small. Having his undivided interest, protected by his irrefutable competence, had been really nice.

"I don't mind sitting." But first…Priss finished off her coffee and looked at the full pot. "Is it all right if I get a refill?"

"Help yourself."

When Priss moved toward the coffee machine, rather than give her room, Trace leaned back on the edge of the dresser and watched her. She could detect his early-morning scent of warm skin, musky male and palpable sex appeal. *Delicious.*

Would he smell that sinful up close, if she put her nose in his neck, or near that solid chest? Or…maybe lower?

She eyed his gorgeous body, and raised a brow. "Doing a little flaunting of your own this morning, huh?"

"In deference to your delicate sensibilities, I pulled on jeans. Isn't that enough?"

Enough for what, her peace of mind? Ha. Being around Trace, especially with him like this, half-naked, sent her heart racing like a marathon runner's. "Maybe it would be," Priss admitted, "if you didn't look so good."

The compliment sent his right eyebrow arching high.

"Oh, *come on,* Trace. You know what you look like." She visually devoured him again, more blatantly this time, and noticed a rise behind the fly of his jeans. *For her?*

Well-well-well. Flattering.

"I'm sure you've had more than your fair share of adoration."

He recovered with a level look of mockery. "I'm

thirty years old, brat, so you can assume I've seen some adoration—and suffered bouts of total rejection."

"Rejection? Really?" She found that hard to fathom. "Either you've known some stupid women, or there's a side of you I haven't yet witnessed."

"It's safe to say that you've seen only the side I chose to show you."

"Hmm." It was difficult to absorb Trace's provoking words, given that his body hair fascinated her. It scattered over his chest and trailed down his abdomen. Even the hair on his forearms, covering muscles and large bone, somehow seemed supersexy. It was shades darker than the pale hair on his head, but then, his lashes and brows were dark, too. And that interesting beard stubble…

Unable to stop herself, Priss reached out and stroked her fingers along his jaw. "I like this early-morning side of you. You look…I don't know. Raw and very manly."

Other than the narrowing of his eyes, Trace held perfectly still.

Catching herself, Priss dropped her hand and went to the table. "I don't suppose we could order up breakfast?"

For long moments he continued to study her. "I'd rather we get ready and go out. Anything that can be checked, like room service for two, should be avoided."

"To maintain both our covers?" Not that Priss expected him to admit to a cover. It was enough that he'd put her in a room close to his, near the ground floor, with access to stairs and back exits that disappeared into busy roads.

"To keep you safe." Trace joined her at the table. "If Murray suspects you of being anything other than what you say you are—"

"I know, I know. I'm fish food." She made a face. "We need to talk about something else, at least until I'm awake enough to show my true contempt for good old Murray."

"How about you tell me why you want to kill him?"

She had wondered when he'd come back around to that. "On an empty stomach? Bleh."

"You'll tell me later?"

"Sure," she lied, "if you'll change the subject to something more palatable for now."

"All right." Trace sipped his coffee with more restraint than she'd been able to show. "How'd you sleep?"

"Like the dead, thank you."

He gave a theatrical wince. "Bad analogy, all things considered."

Because Murray might well want her dead. She winced, too. "Sorry." A glance toward the window provided inspiration for conversation, as sunlight seeped in even with the drapes drawn. "It looks like it's going to be a beautiful day."

"You and I will both keep the windows covered and, whenever we're out of the rooms, the connecting door has to be locked."

"Prying eyes?"

"Anything is possible. My guess is that Murray still has me under surveillance, which is why we were followed. It stands to reason that with you now in the mix, the scrutiny will be amplified."

True, all of it, but given the impact of Trace shirtless, being mellow and kind, even threats to her person didn't help her to concentrate. "I thought of a more interesting topic than weather and menace."

He saluted her with his cup. "Go for it."

In anticipation of his reply, Priss licked her lips. "How many women have you slept with?"

Trace missed a single beat, but only one, before saying,

"A very odd question over morning coffee, and none of your business."

Priss made a habit of being brutally honest with herself, so she had to admit that she wanted it to be her business. And how would it hurt, as long as Murray didn't find them out? If her plans went as expected, she wouldn't be around long enough to get entangled in Trace's life. Why not find a little enjoyment while the prospect existed?

Who knew when she might ever meet another man who made her feel warm and soft, excited and safe? In twenty-four years, Trace was the first. He could be the last.

And if her plans for Murray went awry? Well, she could end up dead.

Somehow, dying a virgin seemed the ultimate insult. But then, maybe that was just her morbid sense of humor trying to help her keep her fear at bay.

Resting a forearm on the table, Priss leaned a little closer to Trace. "Too many to count, huh? So...were any of them virgins?"

With his coffee cup almost to his mouth, Trace paused. His gaze sharpened, and his shoulders suddenly tensed. "Why are you asking?"

A tinge of heat went up Priss's neck. Her private life was hers and hers alone—at least until Trace agreed to a little side activity. If he did agree...well, then he'd already have the answer he wanted. "That's cheating to answer a question with a question."

Trace sat back, his expression frosted. "No." He shook his head, disbelieving, even a little pissed. "No way in hell are you trying to claim—"

The buzzing of his cell phone cut him off. He was practically incandescent with smoldering frustration.

Oh, yeah, the cell phone. She needed to grab that when the opportunity presented itself. Odds were she could access his email and delete the photo from his messages, and the phone's memory. Unmoved by his attitude, Priss sipped at her coffee. "Think that's Murray?"

The phone buzzed twice more before Trace gathered himself. "More than likely, so don't say a word."

After she more or less agreed with a shrug, Trace went to the phone and opened it.

KNOWING IT'D BE MURRAY, Trace said in the cold, aloof way that impressed his current boss, "Miller."

"Good morning." Murray's jovial voice blasted into his ear. "I trust you're up and on the clock?"

Well, hell. Something had Murray in a good mood, and Trace had already come to realize that boded ill for those around him. Murray was happiest when tormenting the hell out of others. "Absolutely." Trace sent a warning glare at Priss. She silently mouthed back at him, mocking him, pricking him further.

"I stewed all night on my darling daughter." At that Murray snickered. "I don't trust her."

"Me, either." Trace knew damn good and well that Priss was up to her pretty neck in revenge. Somehow, he had to keep the game going, and still keep her from doing anything too stupid.

Like attempting to kill Murray.

If she did try it, she'd end up not only dead, but sorely used and abused first. Just thinking about it made Trace icy cold inside.

No way in hell could she be a virgin.

"You get her clothed?" Murray wanted to know.

"For the most part, yeah. Twyla did a great job. You'll like her choices."

"So she's a looker?"

"Decked out right, yeah, she is." Trace checked the clock on the nightstand. "I have to stop by there again to pick up a few more things that Twyla was putting together for her. She'll have enough for a week, including a night out."

"Good. Take Priscilla with you when you go. From here on out, I want you to stick close to her, see what she's up to, keep an eye on her."

"I can do that." In fact, that worked fine for Trace. If he kept Priss close, he could ensure her safety. Anytime she was out of his sight, he'd have Jackson tail her. If need be, they'd all blow their covers to keep an innocent alive—but it'd piss him off royally if Priss ruined his large-scheme plans by putting herself in such a dangerous position.

He wanted Murray, but he wanted Murray's contacts, too. He wanted the whole damn rodeo, every fucking one of the corrupt bastards, from the lowest minion to the top dog himself. Anyone who had sold, traded, advertised, transported or handled captive women was on Trace's radar.

He'd have them, too—one way or another.

A silky tone to his voice, Murray said, "I'm glad you find her attractive, Trace, because it occurs to me that the best way to gauge the truth of her fresh-faced innocence is to take her for a ride."

Trace froze. He had the simultaneous reaction of rage and…carnal interest. He zeroed in on Priss. She glanced up, caught his expression, and judging by the way her eyes widened, picked up on his conflict.

"A ride?" Trace repeated.

"That's the easiest way to see how experienced, or inexperienced, she really is. And since Helene isn't keen on me doing the riding…"

Drily, his stomach churning at the level of Murray's sickness, Trace said, "Because she's your daughter." He prayed that was the reason, but he had his doubts.

His doubts were confirmed.

"No, no." Murray gave a deep chuckle. "Helene doesn't buy the relationship, and even if she did, I doubt that familial connections would factor into her prejudice. One of Helene's more appealing qualities is her complete lack of respect for societal taboos."

Yeah, he'd noticed. Trace concentrated on not squeezing the cell phone hard enough to shatter it. "I see."

"Do you? Then let's just say it'll be simpler if you do the honors." Murray paused before saying with a hint of menace, "You don't object to that plan, do you?"

Shooting for world-weariness, Trace asked, "Are we talking seduction, coercion or rape?" Priss perked up even more at that. Her green eyes steeled with indignation—directed at him.

But Trace also saw a hint of fear that washed some of the color from her face. Not much had shaken her so far, so what had done it this time?

The idea of being forced?

With his guts burning, he wondered if Priss had first-hand knowledge of such a thing.

He wanted to hold her, to reassure her…but hell if he would. A little fear was just what Priss needed to drive home the jeopardy and wake her up to the foolishness of her plan.

Murray laughed at Trace's question. "Since I'm making it your job, do you have a preference?"

Closing his eyes against Priss's expression, Trace shrugged. "I'm not a natural-born rapist, but it's your show, your call."

His deference delighted Murray. "I like your attitude, Trace, I really do. You have great conviction to the duty of your post. I'm glad I hired you." His laughter faded. "Let's go with seduction first. After all, Helene assures me that for you, seduction should be a piece of cake."

Trace snorted. "Is she trying to get me killed, then?"

*What the fuck was Hell doing discussing him like that
with Murray?*

Murray laughed again. "Now Trace, you know I'm not
the jealous sort. I have no reason to be, right?"

"No reason at all."

"I like to indulge Helene whenever possible."

Which meant…what? That Helene could have him?

With the game wearing on him, Trace rubbed the
bridge of his nose. "You're generous with her."

"I don't mind her admiring eye. It's often valuable to
me. Just remember that my generosity has a limit."

"Always."

"So…I may assume that this new assignment won't
cause you any trouble, whether little Priscilla is truly an
innocent or not."

"No trouble at all."

"Excellent." Murray's words reeked of arrogance.
"Keep me informed."

"Of course." Even as Trace closed the phone, he heard
Murray's humorless laughter, and it left him on edge.

The sick bastard was up to something—but what? And
how much damage would it do to Priss?

CHAPTER SIX

IT DIDN'T SURPRISE Trace when Priss jumped up to confront him. "What was that about?" Dread left her pale and angry. "Why were you talking about rape? What are you planning? What is *he* planning?"

Trace studied her face. Without makeup, her long hair rumpled and hanging in tangles, she was still so damn sexy that he had to fight to keep his body from reacting.

Again.

He wanted to protect her, to soothe her, and he wanted to be inside her. Right now.

Through the oversize T-shirt she'd worn as a nightgown, he could see the generous swell of her breasts, and even the outline of her soft nipples. From the jut of that stupendous rack, the shirt dropped over a flat belly down to rounded, shapely thighs. She was so small boned, Trace thought, her wrists and ankles fragile, feminine.

"Trace," she warned, as if she had any leverage against him. "Tell me what's going on."

"All right." He closed the small space between them. "Seems you and Daddy Dearest have a few things in common."

She breathed too hard, too fast. "What are you talking about? I have nothing in common with that pig."

Trace lifted a hand and smoothed the backs of his fingers over her velvety cheek. And even that, such a simple touch, roused him, sent his temperature up and his voice down. "Murray thinks I should fuck you."

Falling back a step, Priss blinked at him. *"What?"*

Never had a woman looked so shocked—or so sexy. "That's where our morning conversation was headed, right? You were eating me up with your eyes, talking about sex and virgins, deliberately prodding my curiosity." He opened his hand to cup her jaw. "Well, you know what, Priss? I'm beginning to think you're both onto something. Maybe that's the natural course we're due to take."

Her tongue slipped over her upper lip. "Sex?"

Damn, did she have to sound both fearful and hopeful? "What do you think?"

Her expression changed, her breathing deepened even more. She shook her head, but Trace ignored the insubstantial denial.

"Come here, Priss." And with that, he pulled her softness against his harder body. She was pliant, but unsure. So warm and rounded in all the right places.

He tipped up her stubborn chin, bent down and put his mouth to hers.

In an instant, he was lost.

MURRAY SAT BACK IN HIS CHAIR with his feet on the window ledge so he could stare out at the vista. This time of day, the morning sun looked brilliant. Only a few spun clouds crawled across the azure sky.

His thoughts rioted, heated. Would Trace do as told? How long would it be before he had her naked, under him?

What would Priscilla think of that? Would she try to run? Was she terrorized?

Was she his daughter?

"I don't fucking believe you!"

Helene's strident, angry tone shattered his musings. Turning his head to find her in the doorway, Murray scowled just enough to show his displeasure. "You should have knocked."

"Since when?"

"Since you felt you had the right to curse me." He turned his chair, tipped his head to study her. Then he patted his lap. "Come."

Like a good lapdog, she obeyed, but grudgingly. Once she'd seated herself on his thighs, Murray cupped her generous and firm breast. The best money could buy, he thought.

But Priscilla's tits had looked real.

He squeezed. "Now, what did you have to say?"

Lifting her chin in defiance, she stared at him. Helene wasn't a woman to quail; that was something he found so enticing about her. No matter the roughness of his mood, his sexuality didn't scare her.

Nothing scared Helene. Yet.

She shook back her long hair so that her breasts were better displayed. "You *ordered* Trace to fuck that little tart?"

"This is your business, why?" Through the thin material of her blouse, Murray felt her nipple stiffen. He smiled.

"You've never done that before. When interested, you use the women yourself, and then you sell them off."

"True." And because she accepted the acts as a part of his business, she choked down her jealousy. But with Priscilla, she knew it would be different. He stated the number one reason why. "No other woman, however, has claimed to be my daughter."

Fury brought color to her face.

Anticipating her reaction, Murray said, "You didn't expect me to give her a trial run, did you?"

Helene had the good sense not to push him. "I doubt she's your spawn, but until you know, why not just save her?"

"Envious of the attention she's getting?"

Helene's eyes sparked.

Leaving her breast, Murray reached beneath her skirt. He watched her eyes as he cupped his hand, none too gently, over her heated sex. "You have an uncommon interest in Trace Miller, no?"

Some of her confidence waned. She licked her lips, and Murray saw the moment she decided to challenge him with the truth.

"Yes, I do."

That admission was accompanied by a rush of moisture against his palm. Damn, but her bold sexuality never failed to stir him. "You want him for yourself?"

Again she measured her response, and chose to be audacious. "I have a new drug that I'd like to try on him."

A new drug? Fascinating. Since she'd joined him, Helene had come up with many variants of aphrodisiacs and hallucinogens that alternately made the women compliant, blindly aroused and occasionally comatose. Only on the rarest occasion had her concoctions ever caused death. "It works on men?"

"I believe so, yes." She quickly added, "I would only experiment with Trace, and only with your authorization."

Murray worked his thick fingers beneath the minuscule crotch of her lace panties. "You know your place, Helene," he said approvingly.

"By your side. Or under you. Or over you." She stifled a sharp moan. "Wherever you want me, Murray. You know that."

"Yes, wherever." Her capitulation to his every twisted

desire gave her priority over others; there was nothing Helene wouldn't do for him. That type of loyalty covered a lot of ground, sexually…and otherwise.

"Murray," she whispered, her heavy eyes closing, her smooth face flushing with desire.

Murray considered things. He hadn't gotten to where he was by making hasty decisions. "You know, Helene, I might let you have your playtime with Trace. *Might*," he emphasized when Helene's lips parted on an anxious moan. Right now, Trace had shown himself to be an unparalleled employee; sharp, intelligent, exceedingly capable in all ways.

And still new.

He was so good that it sometimes stymied Murray, wondering why a man with Trace's assets would bother working for anyone else. He had the skills to be independent, yet he lived in hotels and made himself accessible day or night. In so many ways, Murray felt that Trace should be an adversary, not a lackey.

If Trace ever proved untrustworthy, if he failed in any way, Murray might enjoy watching Helene have her way with him.

"Her way" was seldom comfortable for others.

"But right now, love, I want you on your knees. You've stirred me with your impudence, but my time is limited. Get me off, and you can take care of yourself after I've gone."

On a broken breath, Helene slid off his thighs and to her knees on the thick carpet. Excitement lit her icy-blue gaze as she opened his belt buckle and slid down his zipper.

At the feel of her hot little mouth on his cock, Murray closed his eyes and put his head back. Yes, he enjoyed Helene. For now.

Every good whore had her uses.

And as far as he was concerned, they were all whores.

PRISS TASTED LIKE WARM, wanton woman.

But she kissed like a schoolgirl.

Drawn inexplicably by the snare of inexperience, Trace teased her lips with his tongue. She had the most amazing mouth, so full and soft, so damn sexy.

On a shaky breath, she parted her lips, and he dipped his tongue inside.

Priss went very still, poised on tiptoes, breathing fast and hard through her nose. Unable to help himself, Trace held her head in both hands and fit himself to her more securely, deepening the kiss, gently ravaging her sweet mouth.

She moaned, excited and accepting, but not really... participating. He had the awful suspicion she didn't know how.

Could it be possible? Trace eased back to look at her. Her eyes were closed, her nostrils flared, her body leaning into his, flushed and ripe.

Over a *kiss*.

Slowly, her thick lashes lifted to reveal her dilated eyes. "Trace?"

Son-of-a-bitch. He knew women, and while he suspected Priss was devious enough to outact an Emmy winner when it suited her purpose, he didn't think she was faking it now. The woman reeked of sexual purity, of carnal curiosity and a craving of the unknown.

Why him? Why the hell did he have to be the one to gain her attention? Not that he much liked the idea of anyone else initiating her—*Jesus, what an old-fashioned idea*—especially not that freak, Murray.

Priss looked at his mouth with naked yearning. Each

deep breath caused her breasts to strain against the soft cotton tee, repeatedly drawing his attention to them.

Her tongue touched her upper lip, then retreated. "What's wrong?"

Trace wanted to implode. Seconds ago, she'd edged near panic at the mention of rape; now she sounded as eager as he felt.

But he didn't dare follow through with all he wanted. Not yet. Not with so much on the line.

"Go get dressed." Taking a deliberate step away from her, and then another, Trace tried to distance himself from her. He could see the fine trembling in her small but lush body. Her nipples pebbled against the T-shirt, begging for the touch of his fingers.

Or his mouth.

A delicate flush warmed her skin.

He steeled himself against it all. "I'll see you back here in ten minutes."

Confusion, and then shame, shadowed Priss's hungry expression before that stubborn chin of hers went into the air. "In a hurry to leave, are we?"

"We have a lot to get done." Unable to bear the hurt still visible in her gaze, Trace turned his back on her. His pulse pounded and his guts clenched. "Wear your regular clothes, something comfortable for a long ride." *God, I'd like to take her on a long ride, with both of us naked, her straining under me—*

"Where are we going?"

Pushed to the limit, Trace ignored her question; conversing with her further would do nothing to cool his desire. He needed away from her. He needed her fully dressed.

Besides, the fewer details she knew, the better. For her, and for him.

As he gathered up his own change of clothes and shaving kit, he said, "Ten minutes, Priss."

Priss sauntered up behind him, so close that he *felt* her nearness like the static of a violent storm. It sizzled along his nerve endings, sent a thrumming through his blood.

"You are so damn secretive," she complained, and then to Liger, "Let's go, baby. We didn't want to shower with him anyway."

The second the connecting door closed, Trace dropped back against a wall, squeezed his eyes shut and groaned softly. Shower with her? Hell, yeah, he'd love that. The idea of running soap-slick hands over all of her rich curves and sexy hollows was enough to take out his knees.

He remembered how she looked in that itty-bitty thong and barely there bra, not just her body, but her defiance, her pride. Few women could have handled that situation with such cool emotional control.

He knew a cold shower was in order. It would help with his boner, but not with the rest of his turbulence, because with her, it was more than the physical attributes that got to him. So much more.

Shit.

For reasons beyond the obvious, he needed to avoid added involvement with Priscilla Patterson. It wasn't just the job he had to protect, but his heart, as well.

And just when in hell had he gotten a heart?

Other than the people he'd die for, his sister and his best friends, everyone was a means to an end, a way for him to carry out an assignment. They made up the puzzle pieces necessary to put together a clear picture. Period.

He kept bystanders as safe as he could, but he did not *care* for them. Not that way.

Not *this* way.

Trace pushed off of the wall and stalked into the bathroom. He turned on the cold water full blast and shucked off his jeans.

It would be a change of pace for him, but he needed to repel Priss, to make her *not* want him. Fighting himself was difficult enough—fighting her, too, would be impossible.

Whatever it took, he needed Priss to see him as one of the bad guys. Given his self-appointed role in this undercover sting, and the heinous things Murray required of him, it shouldn't be too hard to do. He'd just act out his part, and in the end, she'd despise him almost as much as she did Murray.

And with that decision made, Trace stepped into the icy water and prayed for a clearer head, and a surcease of the sensual torment.

PRISS STEWED IN HER ANGER, stoking the embers even as she showered, as she brushed out her long hair and dressed. Even as she brushed Liger, talking to him in a crooning voice she hoped hid her real emotions.

Why had Trace kissed her, only to reject her? A game? A test?

She had to put aside her desire for him to get his phone and delete that hideous photo from his email before he stored it anywhere else. And she had to ingratiate herself with him somehow to get him to reveal his real purpose with Murray.

When Trace tapped at her door, she jumped.

"You ready?"

Her jaw tightened. Pushing up and away from the bed where she sat with Liger, Priss cleared her throat. "Yeah, I'm ready."

He opened the door. His gaze moved over her, from her hair tied in a high ponytail to her sloppy T-shirt and jeans, down to her flip-flops. "You are such a chameleon."

"You said comfortable clothes."

One hand braced overhead on the door frame, the other braced to his right, Trace nodded. "It's fine." Suddenly he looked resigned. He stepped in and his eyes narrowed. He held out a hand.

There was something in his eyes, something dark and dangerous that she didn't trust, she just didn't know. But he kept his hand out, so she accepted it.

He pulled her forward.

Would he kiss her again? Her heart thumped in a frantic rhythm. Would he apologize and explain? Would he—

Trace turned her to face the dresser, her back to his chest. His hands slid from her shoulders down her arms to her wrists.

He put her hands flat on the dresser. "You know the drill."

The drill? Her eyes widened at her reflection in the dresser mirror. *He wouldn't dare.*

With one foot, Trace nudged her into a wider stance. "Just relax. I'll be quick about it and then we can get out of here."

"Like hell, I will!" But when she started to turn, he held her, his arms like steel, his determination inflexible. "Damn you, Trace, you already know—"

"What?" His mouth was very close to her ear, his breath warm and soft. "That you're some sweet little girl just looking for her daddy?"

Priss kept her mouth shut; she had never been a "sweet little" anything.

Stepping up so close that his hard body touched all along her back, Trace said, "That you don't have a secret agenda, an agenda that could jeopardize a hell of a lot?"

"Like *your* agenda?"

He didn't take the bait. His fingertips, rough textured, hot and firm, stroked the insides of her wrists. "Am I to accept that you're exactly who you claim to be, Priss, a woman without secrets?"

His sarcasm, though spoken calmly, almost seductively, left her lungs aching with anger. "You bastard."

"You have that right." His hands flattened over hers; his gaze met hers in the mirror. "Now stand here like a good girl and let me do my job."

No way in hell would she give him permission. And she couldn't really fight him without giving herself away. Since she wasn't sure a fight would accomplish anything substantial, she simply stared at him, daring him to get it over with.

His mouth quirked. "You've got backbone, honey, I'll give you that."

It might have been a compliment, except that his hands then went exploring, up her arms, into her armpits, down her rib cage and hips. His fingers prodded, stroked, caressed.

"I am not your honey." Her breath labored; she would *not* let him hear her pant, not with anxiety or excitement.

As his palms coasted up the inside of her thighs, higher and higher, right to the sweet spot, Trace roughly whispered into her ear, "I bet you taste like honey, though, don't you?"

Oh, God. This wasn't a frisking. It was a damn seduction. She couldn't bear to look at her reflection, to see how he affected her even when mocking her.

Turning her face away from the mirror, Priss rasped, "Stop it."

And he did, at least to a point. More methodical now, less inciting, Trace checked her waist, under her breasts, and then pulled the neckline of her T-shirt out to peek into her cleavage.

Priss jerked away and, hands fisted, turned to face him. "Satisfied?"

That strange quirky smile came again. "You have got to be kidding."

Right there in front of her, as if it weren't a personal thing to do, he adjusted his jeans.

Her mouth went slack. Good grief, he had an erection! And she'd just then noticed that he was all decked out in his defensive gear again, bolstered by the Kevlar vest under his dark polo, his utility belt once again loaded with a knife, nylon cuffs, stun baton, Glock, extra rounds...

He picked up her purse and rifled through it. Since seeing her remove the room key from a hidden seam the night before, he checked every crease and pocket. When he found nothing untoward, he handed it back to her.

Trying to be cavalier about all that had just happened, as well as his fully armed appearance, Priss folded her arms under her breasts. "Expecting a war this morning?"

"Every morning, afternoon and night, actually." He nodded toward Liger. "Gather him up and let's get on our way."

So now he'd act as if he hadn't just felt her up? She scooped up the big cat, who sprawled back in her arms like a baby with a little meow of pleasure. "You're a real dick, Trace, you know that?"

He opened the door, looked out, then hefted the cat's bag of supplies. Already in alert mode, he said absently, "Yeah, I know."

And then there was no more conversation as they took Liger and all his paraphernalia to Trace's car.

IT WORKED IN HIS FAVOR, and was even a little amusing, that Priss gave him the silent treatment. He hadn't antici-pated her being that female about things. So far, nothing with her had been ordinary or expected. But the fewer questions she asked, the fewer lies he had to tell.

When he went through a fast-food drive-through for breakfast sandwiches, he didn't ask for her preference, and she didn't offer up any suggestions. Because he had very specific drinks in mind, he didn't order any juice or coffee to go with the food. Although her nose twitched at the delicious smell, she didn't say a word when he set the bag of warm biscuit sandwiches on the floor near her feet.

Which was perfect.

Unfortunately, it couldn't last. Some things she needed to know, so minutes later as Trace pulled into the nearly hidden, private garage, he said, "Enough already, Priss. I need your attention so stop pouting."

The muscles in her jaw flexed, but she sounded bland enough when she replied. "Go to hell."

He ignored that. She had to be curious about where they were, and why. At the bottom of a sloping drive that took them underground, Trace reached out the window and pushed a private code into a gate keypad that protected the garage.

A large fence lifted, allowing them in. "I made sure we weren't followed, and if you ever need to come here, you should do the same."

Her green eyes looked mysterious and oh, so alert in the dim lighting of the garage. "Why would I come here?"

Trace pretended surprise. "A question? Seriously? Common sense prevails over stubbornness, huh? Terrific."

Her right hand balled into a small but credible fist. "I repeat, Trace *Miller,* go to hell."

Trace couldn't help chuckling. For some reason, it almost made him proud that she'd recognized the last name as fictitious, even though no one else had thought a thing of it.

He gave her a telling look. "I'm guessing that you might need the garage because you're definitely up to something—something shady and absurd—and it doesn't take a rocket scientist to know you're in over your head. Sooner or later you'll realize it, and I only hope it's in time for you to make a strategic—and safe—retreat. In case I'm not around to save your luscious ass, I wanted you to know about the garage."

She tipped her head, then said with a straight face devoid of humor, "You think my ass is luscious?"

He fought off another grin and shrugged. "Even for a man with hands my size, it's big enough for a handful. But it's not out of proportion with your equally notable rack."

That must not have been the sweet talk Priss wanted, given her darkening expression.

Both hands fisted. "Pig."

"You asked." Trace pulled up next to a '72 Chevy 4x4. The rough body of the truck was mostly green but with a driver's side beige truck-bed panel. "This is a protected, private garage. If you're ever in danger, on the run, and you know your car has been made, you can pull in here and switch out your ride for another."

That stunned her. More observant now, she sat up higher and looked around. "Hey. That's *my* car." She pointed to the blue Honda.

"Yeah. I had it moved here." He watched her. "Had the plates changed out, too."

That left her eyes rounded. "How many of these cars are yours?"

"Five." They ranged from disreputable to nondescript to ultimately expensive and classy. Whatever was called for, the vehicle would match.

When no longer in this area, they'd be traded in for different cars, stored in a different garage rented in the appropriate place.

Trace patted her thigh in a dispassionate way that didn't even come close to representing how he felt. "Get Liger and I'll get his stuff and our food."

"So there *is* food for me?" she quipped. "Because, you know, you did promise me breakfast."

"Did I?" He hauled out the big cat's belongings, two water bottles and the bag of breakfast.

"Yeah, and I'm famished." Arms overflowing with the giant kitty, Priss followed him to the passenger door of the truck. She eyed the rusty, mismatched exterior, the loose residue of dirt in the truck bed, the redneck bumper stickers in various stages of wear. "Slumming it?"

"Being cautious." He opened the door and stored Liger's stuff behind the bench seat. "Hop in and buckle up."

"The seat belts work?"

She sounded dubious. "Yeah, smart-ass. Safety first, you know." He took the cat from her, which sent Liger into a deep, rumbling purr. That the cat liked him was almost a compliment.

After Priss had secured herself, Trace gave Liger a few strokes along his furry back, then handed him into Priss. "He'll ride in your lap?"

"I'm not about to stuff him into a carrier, if that's what you're asking. He'd complain the entire way."

The carrier would have been more convenient for his plans, but he could improvise.

Trace went around to his own side of the truck. "Let's get the food together before we get on the road."

He made sure to give her the biscuit first. He really did want to ensure that she ate, since it was going to be a long day for her and she wouldn't get another chance until they got to their destination.

"So do I need a code to get into the garage?"

He shared a password with her. "Punch it in, then press Enter and the gate will lift. On your way out, it opens automatically at your approach."

What Priss didn't know was that the gate had a two-step function. A secondary, numerical password cleared the login. If anyone accessed the garage without the numbers, an alert was sent out, notifying him of the breech.

Whether she wanted him to or not, Trace would be aware of Priss's use of the hidden garage.

And he would know if she shared the password with anyone else.

"You won't forget?"

"No." Priss appeared unconcerned with the simple configuration of letters. "Should be easy enough to remember. So, care to tell me why all these precautions are necessary?"

"That you don't already know the answer to that just shows how naive you are."

"If you say so."

"I do." Only after Priss had taken two big bites of her biscuit sandwich did Trace pick up her water bottle, open it and hand it to her. "Here you go."

Distaste curled her lip as she accepted the water. "This is all we've got?"

"Yup. Drink up. You need to stay hydrated." And he needed to get her to Dare's secure home without risking his friend's identity or location.

As if water were somehow objectionable, she wrinkled her nose as she dutifully drank.

Though Trace watched her with regret and attentiveness, she didn't appear to notice. In no time she'd finished off half the bottle—more than enough.

Small as she was, it shouldn't take long now.

Priss glanced his way. "Aren't you going to eat?"

"In a minute." Settling his shoulders back against the door, Trace kept his gaze on her, unwilling to break that last small connection. "You go ahead."

She gave him a funny look, but then, even to his own ears he sounded especially gentle, and remorseful.

"Suit yourself." Priss finished off her sandwich, and then she finished off the water. After gathering up her wrapper and the empty bottle, she let the cat down onto the floor of the truck, onto a blanket she'd placed there. As she straightened again, she yawned and stretched.

"Comfortable?" Waiting for what would happen left Trace's every nerve ending sizzling in anticipation.

"I'm fine." Priss frowned at him. "You know, since we're just sitting here shooting the bull..."

When she trailed off to yawn again, Trace encouraged her, asking, "What is it?"

For a moment, she fiddled with her seat belt, but then she met his gaze. "I don't know what to think."

Hell, she'd put him in such a tailspin, he didn't know what to think, either. "About what, exactly?"

Priss licked her upper lip, a habit he'd already recognized as a sign of uncertainty. She wanted to ask him about the kiss, about why he'd stopped. He'd bet his life on it.

But instead she asked, "Where are we going?"

"You'll find out when we get there."

She let out a long, exaggerated sigh. "So I'm just supposed to go along blindly and see where I end up?"

After drinking that water, she didn't really have any choice. His stomach knotted with the awful reality. "Trust has to start somewhere, honey, and it's going to have to start with you trusting me."

That didn't sit well with her at all. "Because you don't trust me, I gather?"

Trace saw her eyes going vague and said softly, "Not even a little."

She fought the sleepiness sinking in. "Then why did you kiss me?"

Could one small admission hurt at this point? He didn't know, and he didn't really care. He looked into her slumberous eyes and said, "I had to taste you."

Her arms loosened; her hands relaxed on the seat at either side of her hips. She let her head slump back against the seat. "I don't understand."

Which part, Trace wondered, the kiss, or this? Watching her fade, he almost hated himself.

It was done, Trace told himself. Necessary but unfortunate. There was no point in second-guessing things, indulging in self-recrimination.

He picked up her wrist, puzzling her. "It's okay, honey."

"What is?" She half laughed, then frowned and lifted one limp hand to her head. "What are you talking about?"

While looking at her, wanting her, Trace said, "Don't fight it." If she fought it, it'd kill him.

Alarm swept some of the vagueness from her beautiful green eyes—but she couldn't muster up enough concern to react as she'd probably like to. "It?" Then she looked at the water bottle. "Oh, no."

"The drug won't hurt you so don't get worried about it. You're just going to sleep, that's all."

"I don't want to sleep!" She struggled to stay awake, her expression filled with deep hurt and awful fear.

Damn, damn, *damn*. He couldn't take it. "Come here, Priss." He pulled her closer as he leaned toward her, and he put his mouth to hers. Gently. Softly. A careful eating kiss, thorough and yet reserved.

When he let up, her eyes were closed, but still she whispered, "Why...why did you kiss me again?" In the next instant, she slumped against him, boneless and limp, held back only by the seat belt.

Even though Trace knew she wouldn't hear him, he put his face in her neck and said in a raw whisper, "Because with you, Priss, once just wasn't enough."

CHAPTER SEVEN

HE'D DONE A LOT OF atrocious things in his lifetime. He'd maimed many men, killed more than that, all without this awful, gnawing remorse. The things he did were part of the job, his self-assigned duty to society. He removed the scum, or took them out of commission, without blinking an eye.

Along the way, he'd occasionally had to manipulate an innocent, always without real harm.

But this time, with Priss…an unbearable churning of guilt, regret and anger left him keyed up and furious.

What was it about Priscilla Patterson that turned him inside out like this? More than most, he understood the need for a clear head, for uncompromised dedication to seeing the job through.

Murray and his ilk, his associates and admirers, were a waste of humanity at best, a threat to unprotected people at worst. After what had happened to his sister, no way in hell could Trace let any of them slide. He'd see them all in hell before he quit.

But with Priss in his arms, her damned oversize cat staring at him with unblinking eyes, Trace wanted to rage against the fates. Why had she come into his life at this particular moment?

Drugging Priss was necessary; he couldn't put his friend Dare, or Dare's new wife, at risk.

Would Priss understand?

Would she forgive him?

"Shit." After scrubbing a hand over his face, he then drifted it more gently over Priss's silky hair. She wore that damned ponytail again, which was a shame. He liked her hair long and loose. It was so damned sexy.

Out of self-preservation, he levered her away from him and into her own seat. Drugged, she looked deceptively sweet and demure.

Right.

The woman didn't have a demure bone in her small, lust-inspiring body, and she epitomized deception. So why the hell should he care if she forgave him or not? They had jack squat in common. It wasn't like they'd ever be in a relationship—beyond their joint but denied efforts to destroy Murray Coburn.

Yeah, he believed that to be her motive. Why she wanted to destroy Murray—that's what he needed to figure out. Once he had all the facts, he could decide how far she was willing to go, and how much she'd sacrifice, *who* she would sacrifice, to reach her goal.

Using just one knuckle, Trace smoothed over her temple, her cheek, and down her pale throat, pausing where her pulse beat steadily.

Shaking his head, he accepted that he was more pathetic than a high school geek on his first date.

The buzzing of his cell phone brought him out of his absurd mind-set of regret. Liger continued to stare with what looked like recrimination.

"You don't know anything about it," Trace told the cat as he dug out the phone and flipped it open to answer with a succinct, "Miller."

"Where are you?"

Murray. It needed only this. Bland, his constant throbbing of anger tamped into submission, Trace replied, "At this precise moment, or overall?"

"Never mind that. I don't really give a shit. I just need to know that you can be back here by seven tonight."

Trace's mind whirled with possibilities, but he still sounded robotic and detached when he said, "To the office?"

"Yeah. Is that a problem?"

"You want me there, I'll be there." Trace glanced at his watch. Yeah, he had enough time to make the trip, put Priss through the routine and get back. His gaze went to Priss; he'd hate it if he'd drugged her for no reason. "What's up?"

"I want you to accompany me on some business tonight."

An exchange? The sick bastard wanted him to take part in selling women?

Both with fury and anticipation, Trace's heart clenched and every muscle in his body tightened. This was the first time he'd been invited to witness a business deal; it could be the in he'd been looking for.

Seeing Priss passed out beside him, knowing she might be next in Murray's deadly game, Trace almost snarled into the phone, "I see."

There was a pause, and then Murray asked silkily, "Am I sensing some animus here?"

"No." He kept his reply short to minimize the chance of Murray hearing real animus—like the "I'm going to take great fucking pleasure in tearing you apart" kind of animus. "Seven at the office. Got it."

"Good. So tell me, is everything going well with Priscilla?"

Given the perfect segue, Trace rubbed the back of his neck and said, "She's a bumpkin, Murray."

"Are you referring to something specific?"

Cursing silently, Trace looked away from Priss; even with her passed out cold, he couldn't bear to see her while betraying her privacy in such a way. His hope was that he could preserve her modesty by gaining Murray's interest in her...down-to-earth uniqueness.

She was certainly different from the elite socialites surrounding Murray. As regular patrons of the finest beauty spas, those pampered ladies considered a Brazilian wax a fashion necessity.

In contrast to their polish, Priss's wholesome and uncontrived beauty could be considered a novelty.

"No tattoos, no piercings." Trace pinched the bridge of his nose and said, "And she's never been...trimmed."

"Come again?"

Plain speaking didn't feel right when Priss was the woman under discussion. Trace sought less crude, insulting words. "She's au natural."

Heightened, almost electric delight came through the phone as Murray asked in a hushed, gleeful tone, "You mean...?"

So he had to spell it out? "Between her legs." Trace flexed his free hand, trying to release the building tension. Basic, territorial instinct made it nearly impossible for him to discuss Priss so intimately with Murray. "Otherwise, she's as groomed as any other woman."

"But our little Priscilla is too private to bare herself for the full works, eh?" He chuckled. "How novel."

In this instance, Trace could speak truthfully. "For her lifestyle, a neat trim might not be de rigueur."

"Being lower-middle class, you mean?" He said it with a sneer, as if lack of wealth reflected on her character.

Trace stared at the far wall of the dimly lit garage. "I got the impression she lives on a tight budget."

Murray's voice went chilly. "It occurs to me that this report means you must have seen her naked."

"No." *Not yet.* But if Murray had his way...

"No?" He sounded surprised, and terse with annoyance. "Then how would you know?"

The image of Priss in the revealing clothes again came to the forefront of Trace's mind. Not that it was ever tucked too far away. Since first seeing her mostly bare, he'd been far too aware of her and her body. "It was hard to miss with the skimpy panties that Twyla chose for her."

"Ah. You don't say."

Definitely terse. Trace continued to talk as if he had no interest in the situation other than the tasks assigned him. "She wasn't at all comfortable modeling the clothes."

"Shy?"

"Mostly just modest, I think." And a real fury when the mood struck her. "I'd say she's the real deal. Innocent, I mean. Like I said, a country bumpkin."

He could hear Murray breathing, the sick bastard, but he said nothing. He just waited.

Finally Murray said, "There's a certain charm to her lack of sophistication, isn't there?"

Yeah. A whole lot of charm. Trace forced himself to focus. "That's what I told Twyla."

"What, exactly?"

"That it was your decision to make, not mine." Deference to Murray didn't come easy for Trace, but he managed. "I know you said to get her done head to toes, but if you liked the idea of her being natural, then I didn't want to change things. She can always be waxed, but the reverse isn't true."

Tension built, sending Trace's thoughts toward exit plans that'd keep Priss safe—and then Murray laughed.

"Ah, you are always thinking ahead, aren't you, Trace? Always putting my interests first."

Always considering ways to kill you. Trace pushed out

an angry breath. "You don't pay me to make decisions for you, Murray."

"No, but I have a feeling that if I did, you'd excel at that, too. You have an uncanny knack for knowing my mind. There's definitely room in my organization for a man of your unique skills to advance up the ladder."

Back teeth locked together, Trace said, "Thank you."

Done with the frivolous conversation, Murray returned to business. "I look forward to my lunch with Priscilla. Naturally I'll want you to be there."

Thank God. As long as he was close, he could ensure her safety. "All right." Again, Trace said nothing else. Verbosity was not a trait Murray admired in others.

"Tonight, I may have some added duties for you."

"Anything I need to know about ahead of time?" If it involved participating in the abuse necessary to corral women like cattle, Trace knew that he'd have to advance his plans against Murray.

He'd kill him and damn the consequences before he'd further damage an already traumatized woman.

"Our buyer might need a little…education on the proper way to handle a deal." Amused by the possibilities, Murray chortled. "The ignorant fuck is trying to dicker with me over the price of the merchandise, after we'd already negotiated the details."

Trace remained silent. It turned his stomach that Murray truly thought of human beings as no more than a product to progress his wealth. But at the same time, relief that the task could be handled guilt-free eased the tension in his muscles. Hell, he'd take pleasure in demolishing anyone involved in Murray's business.

"You can handle that, can't you, Trace?"

"Yeah, I can handle it." But he'd need a safe place to stash Priss, just in case this was a diversion.

Murray continued with smooth intent. "And if I need him shot to impress the other buyers?"

Trace shrugged. "I'll shoot him." Then he added, "But I can impress the others without wasting a bullet, if you'd prefer that."

"Good man." As always, with the confirmation of imminent violence, Murray returned to his good humor. "I'll see you at seven, then." And with that, he disconnected the call.

In the silence that followed, Trace heard Priss's deep breathing. He didn't want to look at her, to acknowledge what he'd done to her, but he couldn't stop himself.

While he'd spoken to Murray, she'd shifted a little and now she slumped toward him with her head in an awkward position.

Ignoring Liger's eerie stare of accusation, Trace reached past Priss and released her seat belt.

As she tumbled toward him, he eased her head down to rest against his thigh. Her long ponytail bunched in his lap, and Trace smoothed it out. In the darkness of the garage, he couldn't see the red highlights in her amazing hair, only the deep browns.

Visually examining every inch of her, Trace noted that her smooth, soft skin looked very pale, her long lashes left shadows on her cheeks, and her lips were slightly parted.

So were her knees.

For the longest time, Trace just looked at her. For once, instead of being on guard, her expression appeared serene and at peace.

When sleeping.

When drugged.

He couldn't keep his hands off her, off the warm flesh of her arms, the silk of her hair. To him, the ponytail looked torturous, pulling at her scalp.

Feeling like a bastard, Trace withdrew his knife, lifted her hair and, using just the tip of the blade, cut through the rubber band.

Priss didn't stir.

After massaging her scalp to ease any conceived discomfort, he spread out the long locks, trailing them across his lap, feeling the coolness, the weight of her hair.

Jesus, she was dead to the world, so why was he was tormenting himself like this? He wasn't going to take advantage of her right now, so he'd be smart to buckle her back in and get this cursed trip over with.

The cat jumped up into the seat to watch him more closely. Cautiously, given that soul-deep stare, Trace reached out to rub Liger's ear, and got a small meow in return.

"I won't hurt her." But he knew he already had.

Maybe in acceptance of his statement, maybe out of feline laziness, Liger curled up against Priss's side and started purring. He overflowed the seat, but didn't seem to mind.

He only wanted to be next to Priss.

At least the cat trusted him, Trace decided. It was a start.

Taking the time to rearrange both woman and animal, Trace buckled Priss back into her seat and let Liger get comfortable next to her. He started the truck, put it in gear, and drove from the garage.

With Priss so soft, warm and sexy beside him, it was going to be a very long drive.

AT THE FUZZY EDGES OF HER mind, Priss realized that the radio music had suddenly stopped—and she was no longer in motion.

The stillness closed in around her.

Confusion gnawed on her contentment, and she peeked

open one eye to see Trace behind the wheel of what looked like the dashboard to an old truck.

Window open, he spoke outside the vehicle, into what looked like an intercom. Priss stayed very still and listened.

"No one followed us. But I might need a minute or two to bring her around."

Another voice, deep and mellow, came through an intercom, but Priss couldn't catch what was said.

"Yeah," Trace replied. "She's been out pretty damn hard."

Out? She tried to think, but that hurt her head. The truck moved forward, slowly now, and stopped beneath some shade.

Little by little, as the fog cleared, memories tumbled back in.

Being at the garage. Eating breakfast. Talking to Trace, being kissed by him...

Drinking the water.

Oh, God.

Everything slammed back into her sluggish brain. Trace had drugged her!

How long had she been out? What had he done to her? She attempted to take inventory of her body, but other than remaining lethargy, nothing seemed amiss.

The sudden pounding of her heart did more to revive her than anything else could have. She had to concentrate hard to hide her awareness, to keep from jerking upright and lambasting Trace with her fury.

Where were they, and what did he have planned?

She felt Trace draw nearer. She breathed in his scent, and heard him say, "It's okay, boy. I bet you're ready for a break, aren't you? Even though you slept most of the way."

He spoke to Liger. She felt a furry tail drift past her, and panic settled in.

She would not let Trace or anyone else hurt her cat.

That didn't really make sense, given that Trace had wanted to protect Liger. But how could she trust him on anything after he'd tricked her into drinking water with drugs in it?

"Good God," came yet another voice, this one right outside the truck. "Are you sure that's a domestic cat?"

"A friendly one, yeah." The truck moved as the driver's door opened. "Don't be a sissy, Chris. He's as gentle as a lamb."

A man laughed. "Hand him out. I'll see what Dare's girls think of him."

The bench seat shifted beneath her. "Just be careful. I don't know what he'll think of the girls and I don't want him spooked."

"Damn, you are a big boy, aren't you?"

Liger gave his sweet little meowing reply, which made the man laugh again. "Don't worry, Trace. I'll take good care of him."

She recognized the name Dare from Trace's phone call. But Chris? His girls? Just where had Trace taken her, and *why?* At least she knew they meant no harm to her cat. Even now, she could hear Chris talking to Liger, soothing him, coddling him with soft words. And he'd sounded sincere enough when he told Trace that he'd take good care of Liger.

So her cat was safe—but was she?

As subtly as possible considering that her limbs still felt leaden and her head stuffed with cotton, Priss slid her hand back and opened her seat belt. It made a quiet but distinct "clink" and the belt loosened.

Aware of Trace's gaze now on her, of him looming closer, she kept her eyes closed, relaxed, her body boneless.

His hand touched her cheek, moved over her jaw, then under her chin. "Priss?" His fingertips felt *so* warm, and oddly gentle. "Come on, honey. You've been out long enough."

Honey? How dare he?

Remembering all the training she'd put herself through, Priss reacted without warning. Her fist came up hard and fast. She aimed for Trace's nose, which would have done the most damage. But at the last second he turned and she connected with his left eye instead. Even in the close confines of the truck cab, she got some momentum on the punch.

Trace jerked back with a curse.

Swinging her feet up and pulling her knees to her chest, Priss kicked him in the sternum.

He wheezed as he went sprawling backward through the open driver's door of the truck.

In a flash she had the passenger door open, but her legs were so weak, she fell out in a rather inelegant sprawl.

She didn't stay down. No way.

Though her head pounded, she surged to her feet and after one fast glance back at Trace, she bolted forward— and right into something rock-solid.

More staggered now than ever, she reeled back.

Arms of steel went around her, locking tight and incit- ing pure, red-hot terror. Like a wild woman whose life depended on getting away, Priss fought. She utilized every escape method she'd ever learned, but sadly, she didn't gain even the slightest edge toward release.

And then Trace was there. "Let her go, Dare."

Without a word, the immobilizing arms opened and she ended up crushed close to Trace's chest instead. "It's all right, honey." His voice was low, melodic. Apologetic. "Take it easy now. No one's going to hurt you."

The frantic pumping of her heart subsided. For reasons that had to allude to insanity, she felt...safe. It was Trace she'd been escaping, Trace who had slipped something into her water. And yet it was there, in his tone, in the way he rocked her side to side.

Remorse.

Caring.

Fighting off nervous tears, Priss shoved back from him. Not out of his arms, because she still needed the support, but back enough that she could glare into his face.

Already his left eye was swelling, turning purple. That gave her grim satisfaction.

"You drugged me."

"I know." He stroked a big hand over her hair. "I'm sorry about that. No choice, really."

It occurred to her that her hair hung loose and tangled around her shoulders. Where had her rubber band gone?

"No choice?" She sneered at him and, finally feeling grounded, slapped his hands away from her. "Of course you had a choice."

From behind her, a man said, "No, he didn't."

Priss whirled around, and almost toppled herself again. A man—a big man—stood less than two feet from her. His size didn't alarm her, not when she was already used to Trace's size. This one stood a few inches taller than Trace, but looked no more imposing for it.

It was the way he completely towered over her smaller stature that put her on alert. Early thirties, short brown hair and electric-blue eyes.

Dangerous. Just like Trace.

Her throat tightened, and she stepped back against Trace. Casually, as if he'd expected no less from her,

Trace looped his arms around her and clasped his hands over her stomach.

"Priss, this is my good friend, Dare."

Dare nodded. "Trace would no more give away my location than I would his. You're an unknown, lady, and around here, we don't take chances."

Around here, meaning...what? The location, or the business?

Dare wasn't exactly hostile, but close enough to rile Priss. And with Trace's arms around her, well, she wasn't afraid. Nervous, yes, but her fear was on temporary hold. "I'm known enough that he's seen me nearly naked."

Dare's gaze lifted above her, no doubt to meet up with Trace's.

She heard Trace sigh, and felt his shrug. "Murray's orders."

Dare nodded in understanding.

Understanding! How in the world could he understand *that?* The big jerk.

"I'm known enough for him to take a picture of me almost naked, too." Priss scowled fiercely. "With his stupid cell phone. And he still has it!"

That sent Dare's right eyebrow up, but he said nothing.

Trace stiffened behind her. "Damn it, Priss...."

Feeling braver by the second, she again left Trace's secure hold to confront Dare. "And I'm known enough that your good buddy has felt me up, *twice*."

The left eyebrow lifted to join the right. Dare shrugged. "If that's true—"

"It is!"

"Then I'm sure Trace had his reasons." He looked to Trace for confirmation.

Clearly growing irritated with her, not that she cared, Trace growled, "For the most part."

And damned if Dare's stony face didn't show her a quirk of a smile—there and gone. Her hands balled into fists and her neck stiffened. "Why, you—"

A female voice suddenly intruded. "What in the world is going on out here?"

Trace muttered, "Shit," under his breath.

At the same time, Dare said, "Molly," in dark warning.

Priss looked up to see a top-heavy, average-looking woman of average height, with average brown hair and an exceptional look of outrage aimed at the men. She wore a pink T-shirt and jeans with flip-flops.

Her kind of woman.

Sensing an ally, Priss took two steps toward her, but Trace pulled her up short by grabbing her arm.

"No, you don't," he told her, and no matter how Priss yanked and pulled, she couldn't free herself.

"Settle down, will you?" Trace said near her ear. "You're not helping things."

The woman's expression pinched even more.

Dare started toward her in a ground-eating stride. "Back inside, Molly," he said, sounding more cajoling than commanding. "I'll explain in private."

Like hell! Priss didn't want to lose whatever opportunity this might be, so she shouted, "Molly, help me. Trace drugged me to bring me here, and Dare manhandled me when I tried to escape." And before Trace could muzzle her, if indeed that was his intent, she added, "Some other guy stole my cat!"

The woman's mouth dropped open, then firmed shut again. With one raised hand, she halted Dare's progress. Dare dropped his head and groaned.

Molly looked around, and then pointed off to her right. "Over there. Chris has your cat, and he's a good guy, so you don't need to worry about that."

Priss looked, and sure enough, some guy sat on the

grass beneath a large shade tree, not far from Trace's truck, with Liger in his lap. Two beautiful Labradors were on their bellies, their ears perked, their tails thumping.

Like a king, Liger held court, accepting the attention from the guy and the dogs.

Dare said, "Those are my girls, Tai and Sargie. They're gentle, so don't worry about the cat—if you can call that monster a cat."

"He is not a monster," she said in defense of him, almost forgetting her situation. "Liger is very sweet."

"Declawed?"

"Of course not." She would never do that to Liger. "But he only scratches when necessary."

Trace maintained his hold on Priss's arms.

Looking much like a beach bum who had just awakened, Chris wore a ratty T-shirt. But unlike Molly, his hairy legs were bare beneath rumpled tan cargo shorts and he was barefoot.

Priss didn't want to, but she knew she had to get control of herself. "I suppose Chris is the person who'll be caring for Liger?"

Dare said, "Chris pretty much cares for everything around here."

"He's good with animals, Priss." Trace's thumbs rubbed up and down the backs of her arms, almost wringing a shiver from her. "You don't have any reason for all these hysterics."

Oh, that got her anger right back up there at the boiling point. She gave him a look that could kill. "Hysterics?"

Before she could say more, and before Trace could reply, Molly was there. "Hello. I'm Molly. And I believe I heard Trace call you Priss?"

Priss eyed her. "Yeah."

Molly just smiled. "Why don't you come inside with me? I'll get you something to drink."

"You're Trace's friend?"

"Yes."

And she was expected to accept a drink? "What, do I have stupid stamped on my forehead?"

Confused, Molly shook her head. "I don't—"

"I told you. He *drugged* me."

Molly looked at Trace.

Dare said again, "Molly...."

She waved him off. "I know. It's all hush-hush and top secret and Trace is honorable, so whatever has happened, there's a reason for it. I get it."

Priss glared at all of them. "Well, I don't."

"We'll indulge girl-talk, that's all," Molly promised Dare. "I won't pry and I won't divulge anything."

"Anything like what?" Priss asked.

Molly continued to smile, and that smile made her look very pretty. "Anything that they—" she indicated Dare and Trace with a nod of her head "—think is a security risk."

Sensing Molly would be easier to crack than Trace or Dare, Priss asked, "Like?"

"Full names, which are always off-limits."

"So his name isn't Trace Miller?"

Molly did a verbal stumble, then said, "Of course it is."

Of course it wasn't, or else Trace and Dare wouldn't have let out a collective breath at Molly's answer, and her straight face. "Anything else?"

"Location of course, which has to be kept private, at least until they know they can trust you, which from what I can tell means only after you've married one of them."

For some reason, that made Priss's face redden. "That's what you did?"

Molly grinned hugely. "Yes. Dare is my husband."

Dare said again, *"Molly,"* this time in exasperation.

"Oh, really, Dare." Molly flapped a hand at him. "Just what do you think she could do with that information?"

"That depends on how connected she might be, who she knows, and what she's up to."

While husband and wife groused at each other, Priss looked around and saw land and more land, all of it secured with towering fences, gates, and high-end security. "Wow. This place is a fortress."

"Of course." Molly returned her attention to Priss. "The guys also don't want me to discuss whatever it is they're up to, not that I even know, so however connected you might be, don't waste your time on me. Usually I'm as in the dark as you are right now."

"I'm not that in the dark," Priss insisted. And truly, every minute it seemed some new aspect of Trace was revealed to her. "I know Trace is undercover with Murray."

Dare went still, but Trace just rubbed his face.

"By the way, Murray is a real scumbag human trafficker, just so you know."

And suddenly Dare was beside Molly, his arm around her protectively. For her part, Molly tried to hide it—and she almost succeeded. But Priss saw the flash of…something dark and grim in her eyes. A bad memory?

Interesting.

So Molly was somehow involved. Was that motivation enough for Trace to go after Murray? Maybe, but Priss didn't think that covered it. Not all of it.

"I also know that Trace is working with Dare."

No one confirmed or denied her claim.

"And I know, given the cost that goes into a place like this, that they have to have a successful enterprise to afford this much security. Stands to reason that to be successful, they have to be good at what they do. And that, of course, would coincide with all the absurd secrecy. I mean, drugging me? Is that not bizarre?"

"Maybe it was a little overkill." Molly frowned at Trace's hands on Priss's arms until he spread his fingers wide and stepped back, releasing her. "Thank you," she told Trace. She patted Dare's hand, letting him know without words that she was fine.

He gave a small nod and stepped away from her.

With her composure restored, Molly put a slim arm around Priss's shoulders and turned her toward a...well, an *incredible* home.

Priss stalled.

How the heck had she missed a house that damn big? The place was beyond anything she'd ever seen. It was the type of home she had always supposed Murray had, big, lavish, impressive and protected.

Priss whispered, "Toto, I've a feeling we're not in Kansas anymore."

Molly laughed. "In the big scheme of things, where you're at isn't all that important. Come on. We'll just make you comfortable and let the guys work out the rest of it, okay?"

Suddenly Priss wasn't at all sure she wanted to go off with this woman. Molly was far too accepting of things.

But when she looked back, both Trace and Dare stood there, arms crossed over their chests, dominating stares watching her.

Had she unsettled them with her deductive reasoning?

She put up her chin. "That sounds very nice, Molly. Thank you." And even though she felt a little sick in her stomach, very confused, angry at being manipulated and…well, sort of fretful at being away from Trace, she allowed Molly to lead her inside.

But along the way she made note of everything, including security cameras, and multiple avenues of possible escape.

CHAPTER EIGHT

THE MINUTE MOLLY AND Priss disappeared inside, Trace cursed. He actually wanted to hit something, but a tree would break his knuckles, he didn't want to put another dent in the truck, and Dare would hit back.

Chris Chapey, Dare's longtime best friend and personal assistant, approached with the enormous cat draped over one shoulder so that he could keep an eye on the trailing dogs. The bottom half of Liger filled his arms, and the long tail hung down to the hem of Chris's shorts.

Without even thinking about it, Trace started petting the cat. After a few hours in the truck together, he and Liger had an understanding of sorts.

Dare watched him, but said only, "That cat is a beast."

"He's an armful, that's for sure." Chris hefted him a little higher, and got a sweet meow in return.

Both dogs barked in excitement, but quieted when Liger gave them a level stare.

Chris laughed at that. "You want me to head in to keep an eye on things?"

"That's why I pay you the big bucks, right?" Dare stared toward the house. "You can tell Trace's lady—"

"She's not mine."

Both Chris and Dare gave him a certain male-inspired look, a look that said they understood his bullshit and would let it slide—for now.

Okay, so she was his responsibility, at least for the time

being. Feeling that a warning might be in order, Trace said, "Try to lose your normal sarcasm, Chris, okay?"

"Are you kidding?" Chris snorted. "I heard every word exchanged over here, and I have a feeling that one would make mincemeat of me if she thought I was getting out of line. She sure as hell put you two in your place."

That only worried Trace more because for the most part it was true. Hell, it had been true from the second he met Priss. "Just be on guard. I know Priss, and you can believe that it's going to get worse before it gets better."

"Maybe the makeover will help her chill."

Obviously Chris hadn't read Priss very well. "Fat chance. It's going to be a cluster-fuck, so prepare yourself."

"She's not keen to the idea, I take it?"

Trace shook his head. "Especially since she knows why Murray wants it done." And that just fired his blood all over again. "Speaking of Murray, I have to be back earlier than I thought. He wants me in his office by seven."

Though Chris was well trusted by both of them, he rarely involved himself in business. "Matt will be here soon. Send him in when he arrives, and I'll go—" he bobbed his eyebrows "—prepare your girlfriend."

"She is *not* my—" Damn it, Chris was already walking away, rendering his protests useless. After a deep breath, Trace redirected his thoughts. "I don't like her being in there alone with Molly."

Dare clapped him on the shoulder. "Don't worry about it. Molly is reasonable."

Forgetting about Chris's keen hearing, Trace said, "Then she's the only woman I know who is."

Chris, now several yards away, waved a hand back at them. "I don't believe I'll tell either woman that Trace said that. Some women like to kill the messenger!" Carrying the cat and followed by the dogs, Chris went up the walk and in the front door.

"You trust this friend of his?"

"Yeah. Chris and Matt have been friends forever, and Matt's been over before. He's okay." Dare leaned back against a thick tree trunk. "I take it Priss has you tied up in knots?"

There wasn't much point in denying it. And maybe admitting things to Dare would help him get them under control. "I want her."

"No shit. Tell me something I don't know."

Trace had trusted Dare forever, as a good friend, a partner in the business and as an honorable man. He knew Dare had uncanny instincts and deadly skills.

But he thought he had covered his reaction to Priss.

"Damn." Trace ran a hand through his hair. "Do you think Molly and Chris picked up on it, too?"

After a short sound that might have been a stifled laugh, Dare said, "They're neither blind, deaf or stupid. So...yeah. I'm betting they noticed."

Trace frowned.

With a shake of his head, Dare dismissed his concern. "It's not a big deal, Trace. Don't sweat it."

The mild, even amused reaction to his predicament surprised Trace. "She's off-limits."

"You think so?" Dare looked down at the dappling of sunshine through tree limbs, then back at Trace. "Why's that?"

"What do you mean, why's that? Hell, Dare, I barely know the woman."

"You knew her well enough to take her picture."

If Dare smiled, he was going to flatten him. Period. "She's somehow involved with Murray, claiming to be his damned daughter while plotting...something. From what I can tell, she's hiding more than she's sharing."

"Hmm." Dare turned his head, studying Trace. "You know, she sounds a lot like you, except you claim to be Murray's bodyguard. Maybe Priss has her reasons, just like you do."

God, Trace hoped so. He wanted her to be…righteous. "Until I know what those reasons are, I have to leave her be."

There was no disguising Dare's laugh this time. "Good luck with that."

Trace bunched up as he faced his longtime friend. "You don't get it, damn it. Murray *wants* me to fuck her. The prick told me so. He even made it a damned order."

Dare's expression went taut. "What reason did he give?"

"You know Murray's type. It's probably twofold. He says he wants to know if Priss is as innocent as she tries to portray."

"Innocent? Are we talking about the same girl?"

"Woman," Trace corrected, because even though Priss was young, only twenty-four, he couldn't bear to categorize her as a kid, not when his thoughts were usually mired in lust. "But yeah, one and the same."

Disbelief had Dare shaking his head. "I'd say ballsy, proud, even conniving. Definitely contrary. But innocent?" He looked more than dubious. "Of *what?*"

Trace made a lame gesture. He believed Priss to be sexually innocent, or at the very least, inexperienced. In Priss's defense, Trace said, "You should see how she is with Murray. The charade is convincing."

"Didn't convince you."

"No." If it had, he wouldn't have "felt her up," as Priss put it. And he sure as hell wouldn't have taken her picture. But what she lacked in sexual experience, she made up for with shrewd cunning.

Dare drew him back into the conversation. "Then

there's the possibility that it didn't convince Murray, either."

"I'm better than he is."

"No doubt. But it's risky." Considering things, Dare pushed away from the tree. "Want me to check out her background?"

He did, but...

"Anything I find will go straight to you, no one else."

Trace nodded. "I know. But I have her driver's license, so if it's valid, researching her should be easy." And then Trace would know if anything she'd told him was true.

"We can get started right now. We'll use the computer in Chris's house."

"You can access the departments we'll need from there?"

"Are you kidding? Chris's computer is better equipped than mine." Pointing a finger at him, Dare said, "In the meantime, don't make a misstep until we know everything."

In other words, don't get in too deep until he'd dug through Priss's past and knew more about her than she knew of herself. "You use that rule when going after Molly?"

Dare grinned. "No."

"I didn't think so."

The grin faded and Dare looked away. "The minute I found Molly in that goddamned shack, drugged and mistreated, I knew she was different from the other women who would be sold, and I was lost."

Since "lost" was exactly how Trace felt about Priss, he commiserated.

Neither of them could remember that awful time without going cold in rage. It was for Trace's sister, Alani, that Dare had gone into Mexico. The bastards had known

Trace—his face, his style—and it was because of him that Alani had been taken. Since they could identify Trace, it made more sense for Dare to go.

But that hadn't made it easy.

That sense of helplessness was something that would always eat at Trace; he'd desperately wanted to go after his sister himself.

Dare had brought Alani out, just as Trace had known he would. But he'd brought Molly out, too. And somewhere along the way, he'd fallen in love with her.

Now he and Dare shared a vested, very personal interest in destroying every human trafficker they could locate. Odd as it seemed, Ohio had become a hotbed for human traffickers, both in sex slavery, and debt bondage where loans were paid off with slave labor and sexual submission. Without a state law to make the offense a felony, and with few officers trained to recognize the crime, too many creeps were setting up shop in the state.

Molly had been taken right in front of her apartment building, located in a small, quiet town. Sadly, hers wasn't an isolated case.

Dare said, "Most times, she acts like she's forgotten." He sounded almost tortured. "I think she does that for me."

Seemed possible to Trace. Molly was a strong woman, and despite Dare's capability, she often appeared as protective of him as he was of her. "Molly's okay, Dare. Whatever she suffered, she's fine now—happy even—so relax."

Deliberately, Dare drew in a deep breath and let it out. "What's Murray's other reason for trying to force you on Priss?"

Glad for the change of subject, Trace explained, "Sick jollies, maybe. But I also think he's trying to trip me up, to see how far he can push me."

"And?"

Trace met Dare's level gaze. "And what?"

As the sound of a car approached, Dare shielded his eyes from the sun and looked toward the road. "How far will you go, Trace? That's something you need to decide, and soon." He gave Trace one more quick glance. "Before that girl decides it for you."

And with that, Dare stepped away to the control box. No one entered or left Dare's property without him knowing.

Presumably the car at the gate was Matt, the man who would work over Priss, head to toes. Even from a distance, Matt looked flamboyant with bleached-blond hair, dark shades and a purple convertible.

It was unreasonable and it made little sense, but because he'd be working on Priss, Trace disliked him on sight.

PRISS FELT SICK AND confused over what had been done to her. Just when she'd started to trust Trace, to think that they were somehow connecting...

She closed her eyes as a great well of hurt pulled at her, making it difficult to interact, even though she really liked everyone.

Chris was genuine, and hilariously witty. Matt was all serious business over the task of improving upon her very humdrum appearance.

And Molly, well, Molly sensed her upset and tried to put her at ease, to make her more comfortable. But the truth was, Trace had touched her, kissed her and then he'd drugged her. His remorse meant nothing, not when on the heels of apologizing, he'd dropped her off among strangers and then left her.

Where the hell was he?

Even in her agitation, Priss concentrated on not crossing her arms or shifting her feet too much. She didn't want to bump her hands into anything and maybe ruin her pretty French manicure, or mar the sexy red polish on her toes.

It felt very new to be spiffed up like this, and if it wasn't for her need to get closer to Murray, she'd never have allowed it. But Murray had ordered it, and if she refused, she'd give herself away and possibly miss the opportunity to destroy him.

That she wouldn't do.

Since the makeover took place in Dare's family room in front of a small audience, it was doubly awkward. The family room connected from the kitchen, and that meant Trace or Dare could come upon them at any minute, too.

But they didn't.

Dare's house was enormous, and beautiful, and masculine. Molly told her that she hadn't changed a thing after moving in, except to put away her belongings and turn one of the rooms into an office for her personal use.

Chris Chapey, Dare's personal assistant and, she gathered, a very close friend, did a good job at keeping everything well organized. Chris was a funny guy with sinful good looks, a great body, a wicked sense of humor and edgy sarcasm. He kept Dare's home running smoothly.

But personally, his tastes tended toward grunge chic. He was sloppy, disheveled and half dressed, but somehow on Chris, it worked.

Though it wasn't overly obvious, Priss figured he was also gay. That helped ease her discomfort with him. Matt, too.

And Molly, well, Molly was so cheerful, so accepting of the bizarre circumstances of Trace showing up with a drugged woman, that Priss couldn't help but wonder about her.

What had she been through to make everything else seem so ordinary?

Molly came from the kitchen carrying a tray filled with cans of Coke and two glasses with ice. "Priss, would you like a cola? Or something to eat?"

So that someone else could drug her again? Did they all think she was an idiot? She gave Molly a look of disbelief. "We've already been through this."

Molly blushed. "But the Cokes aren't even opened yet."

Forgoing the glasses, which Priss assumed were for the ladies, Chris snagged a can for himself.

"Neither was the water before I drank it."

Matt said, "Priss needs to sit still until I'm finished and until her polish has dried."

When he'd first arrived, Matt had set up a makeshift salon, unloading everything he'd need, including a vinyl cover on the floor, a special chair with a tray in the front, and a big mirror, in record time. He moved at a frenetic pace and expected her to keep up. "But I'll take a drink over ice. Thank you."

Glaring at him through the mirror, Priss said, "If I wanted a drink, I'd have a drink. But I think I'll be safer sticking with stuff that I've bought or prepared myself."

Molly winced. "I could be your official taster, if you want."

Chris rolled his eyes over that dramatic offer, and Matt pretended not to hear.

So far she'd noticed that Matt was good at playing deaf, dumb and blind when necessary.

"No, thanks." Truthfully, she was still too furious to be hungry or thirsty. Where was Trace? What was he up to? How dare he do this to her?

Sure, he'd introduced her to everyone, including Matt,

but then, on his way out, he'd told her to "behave," in the same tone he might have used with an unruly kid.

It almost made her blush to recall her sharp reply of "Bite me."

Trace hadn't said anything more; he'd just left her.

That was some time ago. At first she hadn't thought about it so much, not with Matt giving her orders left and right and playing with her feet and hands. After all, she knew Murray had ordered this, and that Trace had brought her as a means of protecting her.

But now that she had to sit still, her thoughts rioted over Trace, over the things he'd done and the possible reasons why.

Being honest with herself, Priss knew she was as upset with how he'd touched her, and then stopped, as she was with the fact that he'd abused the fragile beginning of her trust by tampering with her drink.

She wanted to believe that, whatever his role with Murray, he had a good reason for doping her. He hadn't hurt her, and now even the residual effects of the drug were gone. She was wide-awake, alert, and she wanted to see him. If she had to go through this, the least he could do was stay accessible.

With drink orders handled, Molly returned to a plush, padded easy chair to watch in fascination as Priss got the works. Though Chris stayed close, Molly figured he was the plant, there to ensure no one said anything they shouldn't. He mostly played with the animals, which were all in attendance.

The big, open family room had a deck out back that faced a beautiful lake. Thinking she heard something—a voice maybe—Priss tried to turn that way to look, but Matt maintained a hold on her hair.

"Sit still."

"Go to hell." She strained her eyes, and saw nothing but the outdoors.

Where had Trace gone to and what was he doing that was so important he had to ignore her?

Chris laughed, drawing her attention.

That one had mockery down to a fine art, and it made Priss scowl. "What are you snickering about now?"

"You're damned funny, Priss, that's all."

Molly said, "Chris," in admonishment.

He took a long drink from his Coke, and then grinned at Priss. "You're blustering enough, but it's not fooling anyone."

Her eyes narrowed. "Meaning?"

Chris saluted her with his soda can. "You've got it bad, hon, and it couldn't be more obvious."

Afraid he might be right on the money, Priss looked away from him. "I have no idea what you're talking about." She wiggled her bare feet, annoyed by the cotton stuffed between her toes. She pretended to admire the red polish.

Matt tortured another length of hair, pulling it taught, painting it in white goo, and then wrapping it in aluminum foil.

She now resembled an alien from space. Matt claimed the procedure would give her hair depth, whatever that meant.

"Chris is right, you know." He physically repositioned her head so that she faced forward. He wasn't all that gentle, either. "You're so lovesick, it's almost embarrassing to witness."

Molly frowned at them both. "Leave her alone, you guys. Hasn't she been through enough?"

What did any of them know about what she'd been through? Even Trace didn't know, so he couldn't have shared—except for the "knockout" drink he'd given her, which he'd done on purpose, and which all of them seemed to take in stride.

Besides, the last thing she wanted was pity from anyone. She could deal with anything else but that. "Actually I was thinking that Matt reminds me of Meat Cleaver."

Chris tucked in his chin. "Who?"

She waved a hand—carefully so that she didn't mar her manicure. "He's a popular guy in porn videos. One of our big sellers, actually."

Chris promptly choked on his Coke.

Matt's hands, busy only seconds before, now held suspended over her head. Highly affronted, he glared down at her. "I beg your pardon."

That particular tone tickled her. "Yeah, seriously, you do. He wears his hair just like yours. I think he's done… Oh, I don't know, maybe a dozen pornos now. He's a real star." She winked at him. "Popular with the men and the ladies."

Matt looked horrified. "I assure you, I would never—"

"I said he looks like you, not that he is you. Shoot, none of the male porn stars are built as good as you are. Definitely not the straight guys."

"Uh…thank you?"

Priss snickered. "It's sexism at its best. The women all have enormous boobs, and the guys *are* boobs."

Chris sat forward, more interested in this than he was in nail polish. "What do you know about pornography?"

"I know it's lucrative, because I own an adult store."

All eyes went round.

Molly sat forward, too. "You do?"

"Yeah. Movies are our biggest seller. And through our catalogue sales, the toys do pretty good, too."

"Toys?"

"Molly," Chris interjected, "shouldn't you be working on a book or something?"

Molly refused the suggestion. "I'm taking mental notes." She bobbed her eyebrows. "Believe me."

"You're a writer?" Priss asked her. Why had no one told her that?

"Yes, and I'm thinking a thread with a porn producer would make a great story. He could be a supervillain. The wheels are already turning."

Chris groaned.

For a few minutes, they discussed books. Priss was amazed by Molly's success as a bestselling novelist. Not that she should have been. After all, Trace and Dare were exceptional men. Why wouldn't they associate with exceptional women?

And thinking that, especially with any comparisons in mind, nearly depressed her. She shouldn't care what Trace ultimately thought of her...but she did.

To shake off that thought, Priss asked, "So your latest book will be a movie?"

"Yes, it's very exciting." Molly moved to the edge of her seat. "But I'd rather hear more about your business."

"No," Matt said, and he resumed his work on Priss's hair with a little more pain than necessary. "This is not a topic for a mixed audience."

"Prude," Priss accused. And then to Molly, "I inherited the place when my mom passed away."

"Oh." Molly blanched. "I'm so sorry."

"I'm adjusting, but thanks." No way did she want to get into a depressing talk on her mother's demise.

"So..." Molly cleared her throat. "You run it by yourself now?"

"I have an employee-slash-partner." Priss shrugged. "He's watching it for me while I'm away."

"Huh." Molly tilted her head. "Does Trace know about your shop and your partner?"

"I told him." Priss felt peeved all over again. "Honestly, he didn't seem all that interested."

Chris whistled low and reclined back on the floor, braced on his elbows.

"What's with the whistle?"

Matt answered for Chris. "It's clear that you've got the hots for Trace."

"I've only known him a couple of days!"

Undeterred, Matt continued, saying, "But if you don't adjust your attitude you're setting yourself up for disappointment."

"My attitude?" It felt like they'd somehow come full circle. "My attitude is just fine."

They all gave her a pitying look.

Priss rolled her eyes. "Okay, not that I'm buying into any of this, but...what do you suggest?" She said it with enough sarcasm to impress Chris, but actually, she could use a male perspective on things.

The guys were gay—but still guys.

Chris set Liger aside. The big cat went to a windowsill to recline in the sun. "Stop playing the tough guy. It's ridiculous and not very believable."

Ridiculous? Heat flooded to her face. "I'm not *playing* anything!"

"Yeah, right." He finished off his Coke and crushed the can. "I was there when you leaped from the truck with blood in your eyes, remember?"

Good God, she had been attempting an escape, not putting on a show. She gripped the arms of the chair and tried to moderate her tone. "Then you should remember that I had good reason for..." She glanced at Matt, wondering how much he knew about Dare and Trace and whatever enterprise they owned. She brought her gaze back to Chris. "Well, you know why I reacted that way earlier."

"Maybe. In part." Chris shook his head.

"In part? Are you nuts!" Did none of them get the insult in what Trace had done to her?

"Look, Priss, if you were afraid of Trace, or even mad at him, you wouldn't be obsessing over him now."

Her neck stiffened with indignation. "I'm not obsessing." Was she? Well, maybe a little. *Where was he?*

Molly leaned forward, attentive and interested. "Are you and Trace...you know. Involved?"

"No." Firm, Priss shook her head. "We're not." Not that she hadn't tried to involve him, but so far, for the most part, he'd been resistant. "Not beyond a couple of kisses."

Molly brightened. "He kissed you?"

"A couple of times." Should she tell Molly about the picture Trace took? Or how Trace has touched her under the guise of frisking her? Maybe not, not with Matt listening in. It'd only cause a need for more explanations than she could give.

"I'm not surprised," Matt told her. "You're already attractive. You have good, basic bones to work with."

"Bones?"

"But when I finish fine-tuning you, you're going to be stunning. Physically *irresistible*. So you should use your feminine appeal instead of the balls-to-the-walls attitude if you want Trace's attention."

Stunning? Irresistible? Somehow Priss doubted it. She glanced in the mirror and...yeah. Not great, especially not with foil in her hair.

She ignored Matt's insult to her attitude in favor of concentrating on the possibilities. "Use it how?"

"Anger is just another form of caring. If you didn't care, why get mad?"

Uh, because he had *drugged* her. Hello! But for her own sake, Priss knew she should keep that to herself. She sighed.

"Don't be so available, emotionally or physically."

"Way too much excess of both," Chris agreed.

Matt put his hands on her shoulders and gave her a squeeze. "Instead of you working so hard, let Trace work a little."

Hmm… Could she make him work a little? Did she want him to? Yeah, she did.

"Baloney." Molly glared at both men. "That's bad advice, so don't listen to them, Priss."

"No?"

Molly shook her head. "I never played those games with Dare. I always tried to tell him what I was thinking and feeling. Well, once I trusted him, I did. And I pretty much had no choice but to trust him from the get-go."

Fascinated, Priss opened her mouth to ask about Molly's personal situation, but Molly cut her off.

"And now we're married."

Interesting. But what if she never trusted Trace? What if he never trusted her?

Chris snorted. "Apples and oranges, Molly. Trace and Dare are two *very* different men."

Priss wanted to expound on that. They were different, but they also shared similarities that spoke volumes. They were each capable, cautious, dangerous, rock hard and edgy. They stayed highly attuned to their surroundings, and to everyone around them.

If she shared what she'd noticed, Priss thought she might be able to get some dialogue going, and maybe trick Molly or Chris into giving away some deets—like where the guys worked, or who hired them.

What Trace wanted with Murray.

But even if Molly and Chris didn't understand the

necessity for secrecy, she did, and there was the chance that Matt was an outsider.

Meeting his gaze in the mirror, Priss asked him, "How much do you really know?"

He said quickly, "I know *nothing*." Using the end of a comb pick, he separated another section of her hair, keeping all his concentration on his chore. "Not a single thing. And I want to keep it that way. God forbid one of those two decides I'm a security liability."

His reaction intrigued Priss. "Because they would do… *what* exactly?"

Chris snorted. "Nothing." And then to Matt, "Don't talk stupid."

"Yeah," Molly complained. "You're going to give Priss the wrong impression."

"Worse than my initial impression with my *very sleepy* ride here? Not likely." Given what Matt said, Priss knew he was aware of something. Maybe not the whole scope of what Dare and Trace did, not the particulars, but he knew enough that he didn't want to be involved.

Smart guy.

Before she could really question him, Matt announced, "All done with your hair. Now, it only makes sense to get the waxing out of the way before we start on your makeup—"

Her flesh crawled and her stomach knotted. "No."

"—because I don't want to do your makeup until after your hair is styled, so—"

"No. No waxing." Priss shook her foil-filled head. On this, she could not relent. "Forget it."

"And," Matt said, emphasizing the word dramatically, "it's my understanding that Trace has less time than anticipated, so we shouldn't dawdle."

"I said no!"

Matt waved off her protests. "Molly, is there a more private room we can use?"

Straightening in her cozy, padded chair, Molly looked from Matt to Priss and back again. "Um...I suppose the—"

"Hairdresser—" Priss spoke through her teeth, deliberately insulting, her temper frayed and her volume elevated "—you're not listening to me. *There will be no waxing.*"

The sleeping dogs lifted their heads, alert to the new tension in the room. Liger gave her a wide-eyed stare.

Molly cleared her throat, but didn't move.

Eyes downcast and brows raised, Chris slipped across the room and out the door to the back. He closed the door quietly behind him.

Priss just knew he was slinking off to tell Trace about her refusal, but so what? Yes, she understood that this was part of Murray's game to test her, and she knew Murray wouldn't be pleased, that he might even be done toying with her, if she disobeyed a single command.

But in this, she didn't care.

Staring at that closed door, she muttered, "So Chris knows where Trace is, but he wasn't going to tell me? What a complete butthead."

Matt stood his ground. "At the very least we have to do your eyebrows, legs and underarms."

Incredulous that he hadn't yet let it go, Priss swiveled around to face Matt. *"I can damn well groom myself."*

Rolling his eyes, Matt put his hands on his hips. "You do not want to be an unrefined girl. And I do not want to do half the job. It makes no sense to be so beautifully polished in parts, but to remain so...bohemian in other ways."

Mortification tightened her chest. "Come at me with hot wax." Priss stared right into his eyes, her voice soft, deadly. "I dare you. Really, I do. Try it, and let's see what happens."

His expression looked comical. "You're *threatening* me?"

"I'm telling you that you'll be wearing hot wax if you don't let it go."

He threw up his arms. "Fine. Be that way. Go about like a troglodyte, like a…an ape. See if I care."

"Thank you." Troglodyte? Sheesh. With that settled, Priss's tension eased enough that she could breathe freely again. She stood, checked her fingernails and her toenails and declared herself dry. "Looks nice," she said while admiring her hands.

"At least I got something accomplished," Matt grumbled.

Priss stretched. "Molly, you got any music? It feels dead in here right about now." And she didn't want Trace to find her all out of sorts. The guys said to be less obvious, so that's what she'd try to do.

Molly rushed to a small panel on the wall, relieved no doubt to have something to do. "I can play my favorite tracks on surround sound. It's in every room. Decadent, huh?"

With a glare at Priss, Matt said, "Nothing but the best for Dare." He blew Molly a kiss. "And that includes *you*, doll."

Priss laughed at the veiled insult. "You might as well have said I'm in the category of the worst. But all things considered, I forgive you for the slight."

Matt made a face. "Oh, wow, I'm so grateful for your benevolence."

The music started, and it was a song Priss loved. "How long will I have this stuff on my hair?"

"Depends. I'll check it in twenty."

Twenty minutes to liven up her disposition. "Do you dance, hairdresser?"

At five feet eleven inches, and with his bleached-blond hair adding an inch more, Matt stared down at her. "Challenging me?"

"Why not? I've never had much opportunity to dance, so I'm sure you're better. But I feel like cutting loose a little, and we've got twenty minutes to waste. What do you say?"

For her part, Molly had already set aside her drink. "I'm in!"

So were the dogs. They anxiously awaited direction, ready to leap on anyone who showed interest in the game.

Priss caught Matt's chin and gave it a squeeze. "Come on, hairdresser. Lose the sour expression. It doesn't suit you."

"No." He still appeared peeved. "It doesn't."

"Look at it this way—" she held out a hand "—you can further polish me with a few lessons."

"You've truly never danced?"

There was a lot she'd never done, but once she took care of Murray, that would change. "Only in the privacy of my own room, and even I was appalled at how bad I am."

His mouth twitched before spreading into a grin. "Oh, okay. But when I'm all done with you, I better see some sincere appreciation for the transformation."

"Guaranteed." Especially if he made her stunning, as he'd promised. She couldn't wait to see Trace's reaction to that.

Matt took one of Priss's hands, one of Molly's, and the next thing she knew, they were all three dancing as the dogs bounded around them, barking in excitement. Liger watched with little interest.

And Priss had a blast.

CHAPTER NINE

TRACE FOLLOWED BEHIND Chris as he led the way from his smaller house down closer to the lake, up to Dare's much larger home. They'd accomplished only a little, but he now knew that Priss's ID was authentic, and that she lived in Ohio.

"She was seriously ready to blow, Trace. I know pissed when I see it, and that girl was pissed. Big-time."

Dare flattened his mouth, but couldn't keep quiet. "You say Matt wanted to wax her?"

"Yeah." Chris looked back at them. "I think *he* thought he was supposed to…you know…style her *everywhere*."

Trace locked his teeth together. He did not want to have this discussion again. Not with his friends.

"I don't blame her for complaining." Dare frowned at Trace. "Hell of a thing to ask a girl to do, especially in a private home instead of a salon."

Trace stopped dead in his tracks, fed up, pushed over the edge. "She's not a girl. She's a grown woman who put herself in this predicament by plotting against Murray."

Dare and Chris stopped, too, then turned to face him. They both crossed their arms and waited.

"Mutt and Jeff," Trace muttered over their belligerent, accusing expressions. "How you two can act so much alike, I don't understand."

Chris was the first to drop his arms. "We don't." And then, "What the hell are you talking about?"

"He's deflecting," Dare told Chris, not changing his

stance one iota. "Guilt is a son-of-a-bitch, and he's got it in spades."

Chris cocked a brow. "Because he wanted her waxed?"

"Hell, no, I don't want that."

Chris half smiled. "I see."

"He's feeling guilty because it was no doubt Murray's idea to put Priss through this, and Trace agreed to it, even knowing how Priss was going to feel about it."

"No, I did not," Trace told him, so tense that his neck ached. "I'd already told Murray…" Shit, he didn't want to tell them what he'd said to Murray in order to convince him.

Dare looked at him with disgust. "This ought to be good."

"Well, it's not." In fact, it sucked. "Let's just say I handled it."

Dare continued to stare at him. "No waxing?"

"No."

Chris asked, "Does Priss know how you handled it?"

"No."

"Then maybe you ought to tell her before she murders Matt."

Trace started on his way again, this time taking the lead. "She's five-four and weighs less than one-twenty. Matt can handle himself."

"Says the man with the black eye."

Rather than throttle Chris, Trace lengthened his stride. Though he'd needed some space from Priss to put things in perspective, he probably shouldn't have left her alone with the others. Had she grilled them? Had she exposed his undercover stint to Matt?

No, she wouldn't do that.

And Trace realized that he did trust Priss, at least a little.

She wouldn't give him away, but that didn't mean she wouldn't dig for information. Hell, she'd had over an hour to work on them. In the meantime, he'd used the excuse of doing a rudimentary check on her background, and touching base with Jackson, to regain his bearings.

As he neared the back door of the house, Trace's pulse quickened. Was Priss still fired up? Would he need to console her? Reason with her?

Even after she decked him, he still looked forward to her every reaction—and then he heard the loud music.

And the laughter.

Chris cleared his throat. "Huh. I guess Matt talked her off the ledge."

Dare said quietly, "Shut up, Chris."

Trace tuned them out as he stormed up to the glass door and opened it.

While Molly stood off to the side laughing, both dogs bounding around her, Priss snuggled up against Matt and got twirled right off her feet.

She put her head back and laughed aloud. Her hands clung to Matt's shoulders.

Her pelvis flattened against his.

Long ropes of hair wrapped in silver foil stuck out around her head. She wore a cape and she had cotton wrapped in and around her toes.

For a woman set on murdering her father, she looked mighty happy.

Liger was the only one to notice Trace's entrance. The big cat jumped down from the windowsill and started his way. Chris and Dare crowded in behind Trace.

And still Trace stood there in the open doorway, frozen with some anomalous, churning emotion.

Yeah, Matt was more than able to handle Priss. The son-of-a-bitch had just picked her up off her feet. Again.

And again, Priss held on to him.

Near his ear, Chris said, "Yeah, uh, this might be a good time to remind you that Matt is gay."

"Somehow," Trace told him, "that's not mattering to me much right now."

Dare said, "You never know when to quit, do you, Chris?"

As Matt twirled her around, Priss laughed without reserve, and Trace wanted her so damn bad that he couldn't see straight.

Only when Liger hunkered down in front of him did Trace draw his gaze away from Priss. The cat's ponderous backside twitched and shifted left and right as he prepared to leap up into Trace's arms, whether Trace wanted to hold him or not.

But he did. He needed an ally right about now.

Trace opened his arms.

Chris and Dare backed up.

In one agile leap, the cat came up to Trace's chest, and that finally grabbed Priss's attention.

Huffing from her exertion, her face flushed and her expression happy, she looked toward the door—and went still.

Dare pushed past Trace and went to the wall unit to turn down the music.

Into the silence, Chris asked, "Everyone having fun?"

"God, Chris," Dare said. "Trace is going to kill you if you don't shut up."

"Really?" Priss struck a pose of annoyance, one hip cocked out, her arms crossed, her chin elevated. "And here Molly and Chris assured Matt that you weren't the type to cause bodily harm."

"They must have been jesting." Trace was well used to Chris's warped sense of humor, so Chris wasn't in any danger. But Matt… Trace zeroed in on him. In a tone more lethal for the quietness of it, he asked, "What are you doing?"

"Harmless dancing?" Matt replied in a nervous question, unsure of the right answer.

Priss suddenly stepped in front of Matt, which left Matt bemused. "Don't act snarky with him, Trace. I asked him to dance with me. We had some time to kill before this crud comes out of my hair. And *you* were nowhere to be found."

Matt pulled her aside, earning a glare from Trace. He quickly held up his hands, palms out, to prove he wasn't touching her. "Speaking of time, we can go wash your hair right now, if everyone will just excuse us."

"I need a minute with Priss first." Trace eyed her militant stance, and had to fight a smile. She had a backbone of steel. He liked that. "Alone."

"Only a minute," Matt admonished. "Any longer, and her hair could be ruined."

Trace looked around the room at their audience.

"Yeah, right." Chris opened the back door with a flourish. "Privacy beckons from beyond. Knock yourself out."

Patience personified, Trace watched Priss as she tried to think of some reason to refuse. In the end, she stormed past him, the dogs hot on her heels. With a salute to the others, he carried out the cat and closed the door behind them.

The dogs continued on down the hill, all the way to the lake. Tai waded in and lapped at the water. Sargie sprawled out on the sun-warmed grass and watched her.

Arms folded, foil glinting in the sunshine, Priss stared after them. Silence reigned for half a minute, then she said, "Heck of a shiner you've got there."

Again his mouth quirked with a grin. "It'll probably look worse in a few more hours." One thing about Priss, she would always amuse him. "You took me by surprise so it was a direct shot."

Subdued, she hung her head. "Pure reaction to realizing I'd been drugged. Sorry."

Pure reaction? Meaning she was trained enough to react by instinct? Every hour he learned something new about her. If she was trained, that would be a good thing. Not that she could possibly have enough instruction to deflect the likes of Murray. "I'm fine, Priss. Don't worry about it."

"I won't." She took a few steps away and peered off at the lake. "It's beautiful here."

"You should see it early in the morning." Trace set Liger on a settee and moved up behind Priss. He wanted to touch her. Hell, he wanted to consume her. "The fog rises off the lake, the leaves rustle, fish jump and birds sing. You see the blinding sunrise across the surface of the lake. It's really something."

"Does anyone swim in there?"

"Everyone does." Without thinking, he added, "I can bring you back sometime when we're not so pressed for—" Trace caught himself before finishing that awesome thought. Pressed for time or not, the odds of him ever returning here with Priss were slim to none.

Gaze cynical, Priss looked at him over her shoulder. "Yeah, right. Maybe we'll do that." She turned to face him. "Sometime when we're not at odds, when we're not dealing with a madman who enjoys selling women, when you haven't just drugged me earlier in the day?"

Trace rubbed the back of his neck. "All of the above."

"You know, something just occurred to me." She stared at his swelling eye before shaking her head. "We'll be leaving here soon."

"Yes." The sooner the better. He didn't dare risk getting to Murray late. And before that, he had to ensure Priss's safety. Jackson could keep an eye on things, but damn it, he hated relegating responsibility. Not that anyone, least of all Priss, expected him to take on that task. But he wanted to.

He insisted on it.

"Do you plan to drug me for the return trip, too? Because I have to tell you, no way in hell will I willingly ingest anything from you or your friends."

He'd been wondering about that himself. "I hope I won't have to."

His answer made her both belligerent and wary. "So tell me, what are my alternatives?"

He reached out a hand, and after a brief hesitation, Priss took it. Her fingers felt small and soft, cool to the touch despite the warmth of the day.

They were not the hands of a killer. They were, however, the hands of a woman feeling desperate rage above all else.

Trace led her to the narrow seat where Liger rested in regal splendor. Squeezing in between cat and woman, Trace seated himself beside her, keeping his hold on her hand.

Matt opened the door. "We seriously need to finish the process with her hair."

"Two more minutes," Trace said.

Matt balked over the delay, but finally said, "Fine. Two minutes and no more." He ducked back inside.

"Oh, wow," Priss teased. "He really is terrified of you, isn't he?"

Trace smiled. "It was noble of you to try to shield him earlier."

"Yeah, well." She huffed out a breath and looked down at their clasped hands. "You were mean-mugging him, and I wasn't sure what you might do."

"And you figured whatever I did, you could stop me even if another man couldn't?"

Her gaze snapped up to his. "Actually, I figured I was to blame, so why should Matt catch the brunt of your temper?"

Noble. Kind. More and more, Priss appealed to him, not just physically, though God knew that was enough to weaken his knees. But she was protective and bold. And sweet. Sometimes.

"Matt knows I wouldn't hurt him." Trace watched her expression. "Not without good reason."

"I'm dying to hear what you consider a good reason, but first..." She tugged her hand free, settled back and crossed her legs. "What's the plan? And it better be good, because I won't be easy to fool again. If you want me out when we leave here, plan on clubbing me over the head, and don't plan on me making it easy for you."

Trace kept getting distracted with the glinting foil. He gestured at her head. "It's difficult to think when you look like this."

"Try wearing it. Now talk."

Forever amusing. Her droll humor was nearly as sharp as Chris's, and that was saying something. "I did a background check on you using your driver's license."

Her jaw loosened and her face went blank in surprise. Then she sat forward. "Oh, my God." She smacked her own forehead. "How did I forget that you still had that?"

"Other things on your mind?" Trace shrugged, unrepentant. "Now I know that at least part of what you told me is true."

Cautious, Priss watched him. "Which part?"

"You're from Ohio."

Her eyes darkened. "What else?"

"I verified your age."

"And?"

He wasn't ready to tell her everything he'd learned, not yet. "You do own an adult store. It earns enough to sustain you, but you're never going to be financially comfortable."

"My idea of comfort probably differs from yours."

"Your employee, Gary Deaton, is in his early forties. He has a minor criminal record, and a big-time case for you."

Her eyes went wider.

"You officially took over running the place about six months ago. Three months ago, it became yours." *Because her mother had died.* Trace shook his head. He didn't want to get into a big discussion on her mother, yet. "That's all."

Relief washed over her. "That's all? Good grief, isn't that enough?"

Not by a long shot. He softened his tone. "What did you think I'd find?"

"Too many things for us to go into now. Matt's returning. And I really don't want my hair ruined just because you chose a warped time for deep discussions." More anxious than not, Priss stood. "One more thing, though."

Trace stood, too. "Yes?"

Matt opened the door and tapped his foot.

"I don't give a fig what Murray thinks about it. No one is seeing me naked, not for any reason."

Trace touched her jaw, smoothed his thumb over her chin. "Not even me?"

On a sigh of pure exasperation, Matt shut the door again.

"Not if you have hot wax with you, no." Priss met

his gaze without flinching. "Otherwise…I might be willing."

He tried to hide his surprise—and his pleasure. "Is that right?"

She shrugged. "Let's just say I understand what motivates you, so I can maybe get beyond it."

Not kissing her proved impossible. It was tricky, but Trace managed to bend close without losing his good eye on the edges of silver foil. He brushed his mouth over hers, felt her warm breath, the softness of her lips, and had to force himself to draw away.

"Don't worry about any of that. I…" Damn. He shook his head. "I convinced Murray that you weren't the type to allow it."

"Not the type?"

"I believe I used the term *country bumpkin*. I said you'd revolt, and he agreed to leave you au natural. You can thank me now."

Priss snorted. "It's humiliating, knowing you discussed that with him, with Matt and probably with your buddies Chris and Dare, too."

He cupped his hands around her neck. "I know, and I am sorry. But surely it's better than the alternative of—"

She smashed a hand over his mouth. "I'd have hurried along my plans to kill Murray before letting anyone invade my privacy that way."

"You are *not* killing anyone." Regardless of solid motivations.

"That's not for you to decide."

It was, but she hadn't accepted it yet. Trace caught her wrist, kissed her palm and lowered her hand. "Dare and I agree that you can leave here fully conscious. Just know that until everything is resolved—"

"Everything, meaning what?"

He ignored her interruption. "—you'll be watched. Forget privacy, Priss, because you won't have any. Until I'm satisfied that you won't throw a wrench into my plans, you're going to have a tail 24/7."

For reasons Trace couldn't understand, she smiled at him. "Fine by me." She patted his chest. "Just don't plan on being satisfied anytime soon."

She stepped around him to pick up her cat, opened the door, and said into the room, "Hairdresser, I'm ready. Let's get this over with."

Two hours felt like ten as Trace paced the kitchen, waiting for Priss's unveiling. Chris and Dare were with him, but Molly had gone along with Priss and Matt.

He glanced at his watch again. "Can't you hurry Matt along?"

Busy at the computer, Chris made a face. "For the umpteenth time, no. He's creating art, or so he says. Leave him to it."

"I'm going to be late."

"You've got plenty of time," Dare told Trace as he finished making sandwiches. "Even if you hit traffic, which you shouldn't, you'll get back with a couple of hours to spare."

"I'll have to get Priss settled before I take off."

"Jackson's on hold. He'll be ready when you are."

From the doorway, Priss asked, "Who's Jackson?"

All three men looked up.

As if in slow motion, Dare set aside the knife he'd been using to cut chicken salad sandwiches into quarters.

Chris pushed back from the computer and let loose with a low whistle.

Trace stared. Damn, he'd known she was a looker, no disguise could hide that. But he hadn't realized...

Matt beamed. "Stunning, am I right?"

"Well, say something, guys." Molly slid in around the two of them and came forward, grinning. She carried a bag of products that Priss would use to re-create her current look. "Doesn't she look fantastic?"

"Yeah, she does." Dare pulled Molly in close, kissed her and whispered something in her ear. She looked at Trace and laughed.

Chris saluted his friend. "Great work." And then to Priss, "You can copy it?"

"I'm not an idiot. It's a little makeup and some hair product. Easy-peesy."

Trace barely followed the conversation. Priss's long hair had been trimmed and shaped so that now it somehow fluffed around her face, looking like she'd just come from a little bedroom activity. The subtle red coloring showed more, and looked sexier.

Green eyes that had always been direct now looked sultry and suggestive, even while she awaited his verdict on the results. Her lashes looked longer, her lips more lush—and none of it was obvious.

She looked good enough to tempt a saint, and it dawned on Trace that Murray, who was nowhere near sainthood, would think so, too.

Furious at the situation, at the overriding conflict of what he had to do versus what he wanted to do, Trace drew a tight breath. "Yeah. Fantastic."

Propping her hands on her hips, her attitude unaltered by her beauty, Priss glared. "So why do you sound so disgusted, then?"

Dare pulled Molly closer to his side. "You look very nice, Priss. It's just that Trace isn't a man who likes to share, but he's currently not in a position to deny others."

Trace continued to stare at her, and he saw her dawning understanding. She gave a peek back at Matt, aware of him as a trusted friend but not a part of the inner circle. Hell, Priss didn't know what that inner circle protected, and still she went along.

"Got it. Well, it's not Trace's problem. Maybe he should recall that." She turned to look at the wall clock. "Shouldn't we be hitting the road?"

The woman looked like living, breathing sex, but she talked like a businesswoman. Trace hated it. All of it.

Dare indicated the array of food. "I fixed lunch. You have to be getting hungry."

Matt went straight for the grub, but Priss declined. "No, thanks."

Trace scowled. "Enough already. You need to eat." Hell, she hadn't had anything, not even a drink of water, since her breakfast sandwich early that morning.

The makeup and tousled hair lent a whole new air to her expression of sarcasm. "I'm nothing if not a fast learner."

Bemused, Dare picked up a sandwich, took a bite and then offered her the rest. "Safe enough?"

"You guys are tricky, so I'll pass."

"For the love of…" Trace let that sentiment trail off. Seeing her so hot, so sexy, had done enough to destroy his calm. "Don't push me, Priss."

"Or you'll do what? Dope me?"

Matt glanced up, then deliberately away, whistling softly to himself.

Trace took one hard step toward her—and his cell phone rang. Scowling, he retrieved it from his pocket, looked at the number and then at Matt. "Out."

Matt grabbed two more sandwiches and his drink and headed to the family room. Chris caught Molly's arm and urged her from her seat. "We'll go with him."

Rolling her eyes, Molly went along, but said to Dare, "I'll expect an update."

He just nodded. The dynamics of their relationship amazed Trace. Apparently Dare confided everything in his wife.

Must be nice to be that secure with a woman.

He eyed Priss, who stood still in front of him, in no way considering his possible need for privacy.

Trace answered the phone. "Miller."

"How's it going, Trace? Is Priss cooperating with the stylist?"

"It's fine. And yeah, she is." Truthfully, she'd done her best to bully Matt, but luckily he wasn't a pushover.

"Got a report on the results? I have to admit, I feel like a kid on Christmas, waiting to unwrap a gift."

Yeah, Trace knew just how Murray's mind worked. "She looks good. You'll be pleased."

Jovial, Murray asked, "Is she there?"

Maybe he'd overestimated Murray's level of trust. Not that Murray ever fully trusted anyone. He was forever trying to catch Trace in a lie, but Trace remained careful of what he said, and when, to avoid that particular scenario.

Lacking inflection, Trace said, "She is."

"Great. Put her on. I want to talk to her." No doubt to verify Priss's whereabouts for himself.

Ice shot through Trace's veins. Murray could have only one agenda in mind, to intimidate Priss, embarrass her or try to trip her up. An inner battle raged, but in the end, he said, "Here she is."

He handed the phone to Priss without saying another word.

Her eyes widened. With the mascara and liner, the effect was exaggerated. "Who is it?" she mouthed.

"Murray wants to speak with you."

Just that quick, Dare went to warn the others to silence.

Trace put a finger to his mouth, alerting Priss before hitting the speaker button on the phone.

She chewed the gloss off her bottom lip, drew in a deep breath and took the phone. "Murray! Hello. How are you?"

Trace stood as close to her as he could.

Murray said, "Having fun, honey?"

"It's amazing. I had no idea that a professional could make such a difference with my hair. I mean, I take good care of myself, but this is…well, it's decadent. I don't even look like me anymore."

She gushed just as any neglected young lady might when introduced to the benefit of unlimited pampering.

Trace smiled at her, feeling unaccountably proud of how quickly she adapted to appease Murray.

"I look forward to seeing the results myself."

"Of course, whenever is convenient for you. And Murray, thank you so much. It wasn't necessary, I told you that and I meant it. But this is just…well, it's the most fun I've ever had."

"I'm glad you're enjoying yourself." A beat of silence, and then, "I understand you switched hotels?"

Shock rippled through Trace. How the hell had Murray known that already? Had the son-of-a-bitch planned to do her harm so soon?

Trace would have told Murray a story about her move as soon as he saw him, but he hadn't thought to prepare Priss—

Unfazed, she put a hand on his chest to reassure him. "It was the oddest thing," she said to Murray, sounding exactly like the naive young woman she claimed to be. "Trace felt certain that someone was watching us, and he didn't think it was safe to stay where I was. He insisted that you would want me moved to a more secure place."

Murray wasn't expecting that quick reply. He paused, cleared his throat. "Trace is right, of course." And then with suspicion: "You say he caught someone watching you?"

"I don't know if he caught anyone exactly. He just said he felt someone was. He looked around, and then he said I should move. I was going to call you to tell you, but he promised me that he'd take care of that when he saw you again. I'm—I'm not sure, but I think maybe he didn't want to give me your phone number."

"Really? How silly of him." But Murray didn't offer up the number. He wanted no direct links to Priss, and everyone knew why.

If—maybe *when*—she turned up hurt or even dead, there could be no trails leading back to him.

"I'm glad he relocated you, Priscilla." Tone silky, he asked, "Where are you staying now?"

Priss looked at Trace, and he prayed she'd remember to give her old address, the one she'd first lied about to Murray. He'd left enough of her belongings there to fool Murray if anyone went by and checked to see if she was in residence.

Without missing a beat, Priss related her old location to Murray, but she went one better by not dwelling on it. Overtalking a lie never gave credence; just the opposite. Priss handled it like a veteran. She gave the location, and then went on to chat about her clothes, her makeup, her painted nails.

In no time, Murray cut off her rambling enthusiasm to ask for Trace again.

God love her, Priss had done an excellent job of both boring Murray and convincing him of her ruse.

Even Dare seemed surprised by her expertise. He and Dare shared a look; Priss was a natural-born liar.

Not exactly a sterling quality for a young lady.

Trace took the phone. "Was there something else, Murray?"

"Yeah." He bit off the word. "You *knew* she was being watched?"

"Of course. But again, I didn't know if it was you or someone else. You told me to ensure her safety, so that's what I did."

With a lethal edge to his tone, Murray asked, "Who else did you think it might be?"

"An old boyfriend, a friend—no idea, really. I know she claimed not to have any relatives, but how do we know for sure? You didn't say anything about tailing her, but I knew she had eyes on her."

"You didn't tell her it was likely to be me?"

"No. When she asked me why anyone would be watching us, I told her that you were a powerful man and a lot of people were jealous of you."

"Good cover." His voice lowered. "It's uncanny, Trace, this sixth sense you have."

Trace said nothing to that. Truth was, he should have known Murray would immediately check on her story, but he hadn't even thought of it, and it pissed him off.

He had to stop being so distracted by Priss.

"So tell me." Slick anticipation sounded in Murray's tone. "Have you had her yet?"

Trace closed his eyes, wishing like hell that he'd taken the phone off of the speaker function. Priss didn't need to hear this, but it was too late to do anything about that now. He could feel her staring at him, not so much with accusation as with uncertainty and curiosity.

Dare said nothing, did nothing. Trace knew he didn't want to embarrass Priss further.

Opening his eyes again, Trace locked his gaze with Priss's. "No time to work on that yet."

"You slacker, you." Murray chuckled. "Helene told me

that you'd be right on it. I think she expected you to rape the girl as soon as I gave the order. She's been fuming around here all day."

"Fuming?" God, Hell would be the death of him.

"That's right," Murray said with interest. "If I didn't know better, I'd swear she was jealous."

Priss gave him a look of pitying disgust and turned her head away.

"But you do know better." Trace caught her elbow before she could move too far from him. "Because you know I'm not an idiot."

"Yes. But lately, I'm not so sure with Hell."

Christ, did that mean Murray would turn on his lover? Or worse, let her turn on someone else? Anything seemed possible.

"Anyway, I have other things to do now. Finish up with Priss as soon as you can. I don't want you to be late tonight."

"I'll be there."

"I'll see you then."

After Murray disconnected the call, rage made the impulse to throw the phone nearly impossible to ignore. Instead he shoved it back in his pocket and looked at Dare.

His friend, not being an idiot, either, joined the others in the family room. Trace stepped up to Priss. "You okay?"

She flipped her hair back. "Why wouldn't I be?"

The way her hair tumbled drew his hands. He lifted one long lock, expecting it to be stiff with hair spray. But Matt was even better than he'd thought. Her hair was soft, silky, and it turned him on. "Murray put you on the spot. That could've rattled anyone."

"I'm not as delicate as you seem to think I am."

"Maybe not." He cupped her face in both hands. "But you are soft and small and, at select times, very sweet."

She made a rude sound. "Sweet, huh? You're as deranged as Helene."

"I want nothing to do with that bitch on wheels."

With a humorless laugh, Priss said, "I don't think you have a choice on that one. Just as Murray's willing to sacrifice me to test you, he's willing to sacrifice you to test her. Everything is about tests with him. And I get the feeling few people ever pass muster."

She was right, of course. And astute. "When you live your life as Murray does, trust is a hard commodity to find."

"What about the life you live?"

Unwilling to go into that with her, Trace shook his head. He could count on his fingers the number of people he trusted, and so far, she wasn't one of them. "You think fast on your feet. That was a smooth story you told."

She shrugged, but some sad truth sent her eyes downcast.

Had her life involved a lot of lies? From what he knew after her background check, she hadn't attended public schools or held a job outside of the porn shop.

He had his suspicions of course, and most of them centered on the relationship her mother must have had with Murray. Eventually, Priss would tell him everything. And in the meantime, he'd left it up to Dare to do more digging.

"Will you be able to remember that twisted tale, to keep your story straight?"

Long lashes lifted and she stared up at him. "What do you think?"

He thought her ability for slick manipulation made her beyond suspect, and yet, at that moment, it didn't matter.

Trace stepped closer, close enough that he felt the warmth of her small body and sensed her trembling anticipation. "I'm going to kiss you, Priss."

Slowly, Priss nodded. "And you know what?" Her attention dropped to his mouth. "I'm going to let you."

CHAPTER TEN

THE KISS LINGERED UNTIL Trace knew he had to end it or else find a room. If he did that, he'd be late getting back to Murray, because a quickie with Priss would never satisfy him. Sure, it'd take the edge off, but what he really wanted was to linger with her, to spend his time sating them both. Soon, he told himself.

When the timing was right.

Responsibility had never felt so heavy.

"You, Priscilla Patterson, are a mighty distraction."

"I never was before." She put her forehead to his sternum. "But I'm glad I am now. Truth is, I need the distraction as much as you apparently do."

"Worried?" He smoothed her hair again. He couldn't wait to feel it on his bare skin. They were moving at the speed of light, and the circumstances weren't exactly conducive to seduction, but that didn't seem to matter. The chemistry was there, taking over, driving them both, and he felt defenseless against it. Against her.

"Just wondering about something." She levered back. "Murray doesn't trace the calls?"

Leading her toward a bar stool, Trace shook his head. "I have a router on the phone. He can't."

"Ah. Clever." She studied him. "So you and Dare run a high-tech operation, as I suspected. I can't see you guys running to the local security warehouse and picking up run-of-the-mill routers. So is it the same type of device a government official might use?"

Avoiding the questions, Trace picked up the platter of sandwiches. "You need to eat."

She couldn't hide her disappointment. "I need to stop trusting you so much, at least until you start to reciprocate a little."

"You've been trusting me?" He gave her a long look. "Could've fooled me." Hell, it felt like she fought him at every opportunity.

Propping her chin on a fist, Priss sighed. "Like I said, it needs to be reciprocated. And until then, I'm not accepting any food or drinks from you or your cohorts."

"They're friends, not cohorts."

"Even Dare? And what about this Jackson person?"

Trace was about to chide her for constantly trying to pry, but everyone filed back into the kitchen.

Matt said, "I need to go. I have other appointments today." Without a single ounce of hesitation, he cupped Priss's shoulders, drew her forward, and gave her a smacking kiss right on her slightly parted lips.

It was a toss-up who was more surprised, Priss or Trace. Priss blinked rapidly, Trace snarled and Chris laughed at them both.

"I enjoyed working with you, Priss. You were more than entertaining, and a font of information on all things kinky."

Trace narrowed his eyes. Was Matt trying to rile him? *All things kinky?* Just what the hell had they discussed? "What does that mean, Matt?"

"She schooled us on the porn marketplace. Very informative." After a meaningful glance at Trace, he turned back to Priss. "I hope to see you again."

She went still, unsure what to say. Trace filled in the silence. "Did you want to bill me, or get paid now?"

"I almost hate to charge, it was all so fascinating."

Trace growled. "But you will."

Grinning, Matt said, "Yes." As he turned away, he added, "I'll get something in the mail to Dare. He can pass it along to you. *I* certainly trust you."

Matt's emphasis meant that Priss *didn't* trust him—not that Trace needed a reminder of that.

Chris walked out with Matt, and Molly again tried to get Priss to eat.

"Why is everyone playing my nursemaid? It's not like I'm emaciated or fainting from hunger." She refused the food. "Thanks anyway, Molly, but I'm not going to starve."

Annoyed, Trace stalked off.

Priss turned on her seat. "Where are you going?" And then with a touch of alarm, "Are you leaving without me?"

He stopped, flexed his hands a few times, and pivoted to pace right back to her. "I would not leave you here."

"No?" She cleared her throat and asked hopefully, "Would you drug me again?"

His teeth ground together in frustration, but he didn't lie. "If necessary."

All reserve vanished and Priss threw up her hands. "Jerk!"

Trace touched her jaw, but she leaned away. "I'm going out to get Liger's belongings. Soon as that's done, we'll leave." He hesitated, left eye flinching, then bent to her mouth again. He kissed her before she even realized what he would do, but no way in hell did he want Matt's kiss to remain fresh. *"Together."*

For only a moment, Priss looked dazed, then she gave an embarrassed glance at Dare and Molly. After regaining her aplomb, she leaned her elbows back on the bar and shrugged. "I'll be right here, waiting for you. Not like I have much else to do."

"Be good, Priss."

She went hoity. "Meaning you don't want me grilling anyone?"

"Exactly." And before he wasted more time bantering with her, he exited the room. He'd be busy much of the night with Murray, but the next day...maybe the next day he'd have to advance things a bit. Until he got Priss out of his system, he knew he wouldn't be one hundred percent. Yet to deal with Murray, he'd need all his wits, and then some.

PRISS WAVED AFTER TRACE'S fast-retreating back, then swiveled around to Molly. "Good riddance. Can you believe his nerve? The man slips a Mickey into my drink and then expects me to just act like it didn't happen."

"That would be my cue." With a nod at the ladies, Dare went off after Trace.

Molly surprised Priss by chuckling. She lifted her cola in a toast. "You have Trace befuddled, I'll say that. When I first met him, he was so cool and detached, it kind of freaked me out."

Despite Trace's succinct warning, Priss wasn't one to miss an opportunity for info. "Yeah, when was that exactly?"

Molly didn't take the bait. She sipped her cola before setting aside the can. "He's warmed up some, but he takes his self-assigned responsibilities very seriously, which means he's usually a real somber guy. It's kind of nice to see him chasing his own tail for once."

Trying for subtlety, Priss asked, "Self-assigned responsibilities?"

Molly laughed. "Did I tell you what actor was chosen to play my lead male protagonist in the movie?"

The change of topic threw Priss enough that she asked the appropriate questions and got engaged in Molly's explanations, and before she knew it, Trace, Dare and Chris all returned.

As they strode into the kitchen, each of them tall, well built and strong, oozing capability in various degrees, Priss couldn't help but admire them. "Studs galore."

Molly choked on another laugh. "Yup."

With the guys close enough to hear, she asked Molly, "Do they run in packs? Like wolves, I mean."

Easily amused, Molly played along. "They must. Wait until you see Jackson. He fits right in." She blew a kiss to her husband when he gave her a dark look. "A regular Romeo, that one."

Chris snorted. "Not according to Alani."

Hearing a new name, Priss asked, "Who's Alani?"

And everyone clammed up. An almost depressed air settled over the previous camaraderie. She frowned, wondering about the mysterious Alani and the esteemed Jackson.

"Sorry," Chris said softly, speaking to the room at large. And without missing a beat, he added, "I'm going to take very good care of your cat, Priss, don't worry. For the time being, he'll stay at my place at night to keep Dare's girls from sticking their noses into his cat box. But when I come up here, I'll bring him with me."

"You don't stay here?" She'd been going on the assumption that they all lived in the house together.

He shook his head. "Did you see the smaller house that's closer to the lake?"

"Yes." She'd noticed it when she was outside with Trace, but hadn't paid much attention, not with her and Trace's conversation.

"That's my house. I like my privacy."

Priss rolled her eyes. "I can't imagine any place getting more private than this setup."

"True enough. But with those two—" he nodded at

Dare and Molly, already cuddled close on the opposite side of the bar "—it's nice to move out of hearing range each night."

Dare reached over to smack Chris on the back of the head, but he ducked away.

Trace said, "The honeymoon will never wear off for those two."

That sounded really nice to Priss. With her mother's mental instability and then lingering illness, and the uncomplimentary atmosphere of her workplace, she'd never really been around traditional families, much less happily married couples. Molly and Dare looked *very* happy together.

Priss let out a wistful breath.

Chris mistook that for something altogether different. "While we move this stuff down to my place, did you want to say goodbye to Liger?"

And just that easily, her mood darkened. "I love that big cat, Chris."

All joking aside, he said, "That much was obvious."

"You damn well better pamper him."

"Guaranteed."

Molly reached across the bar to touch her arm. "We'll all give him plenty of attention and love, I promise. Please don't worry about that."

They did seem like animal lovers; Dare's girls were certainly pampered. They were members of the family, which made it all the more special.

Priss took her time talking quietly with Liger, hoping he'd understand her absence and not feel abandoned. He touched his nose to hers, gave her one of his sweet little meows, then went to lie by Tai and Sargie.

It was almost as if he wanted her to know that he'd be fine. She swallowed a lump of emotion and blinked back hot tears.

By the time she and Trace were back in the old truck, ready to pull away, Priss did feel better about leaving Liger behind.

"At least he'll be safe," she said as much to herself as to anyone else.

Trace put a hand on her knee. "That's more than I can say for you."

Dare leaned in her window. "Be smart, Priss, and listen to Trace."

Priss scowled at him. "Why doesn't he have to listen to me?"

After a long stare-off, Dare peered past Priss to Trace and said, totally deadpan, "Listen to Priss."

Trace grinned. "I'll try if she will."

Priss put up her chin. "I make no promises—but whenever possible, I'll try."

Dare reached in and ruffled her perfectly styled hair, much like she'd seen him do with his dogs. Trace didn't like that, which amused Priss. His territorial tendencies were new to her. Sure, her employee Gary tried to act possessive, but that idea was so laughable that it annoyed more than it complimented.

As Trace backed out, Priss waved to the assembly in the driveway. It included Chris, Dare and Molly, with both dogs and Liger lounging in the sunshine.

It was the strangest thing, but it felt like she was leaving…family. Not the dysfunctional family she and her mother had formed, but a *real* family.

Pressing a fist to her chest to try to contain the hurt in her heart, Priss accepted the sad truth: after she retrieved Liger, the chances of her ever seeing these people again would be slim to none, and slim was out of town.

They were nothing to her—just as she was nothing to them. For the first time, she really felt the loss.

"You okay, Priss?"

God, it amazed her how easily Trace picked up on her moods. He'd done that from the very beginning, which either made him lethally perceptive, or…a truly wonderful guy.

Resting her head back against the seat, she looked at him. He had a gorgeous profile. She'd teased Molly about the guys always being handsome, but to her, Trace was by far the most incredible. Even this Jackson person Molly had mentioned couldn't hold a candle to Trace, she was sure of it. "I'm fine."

He shook his head to let her know he didn't buy it, but he didn't press her, either.

For the longest time, they drove in companionable silence along gravel roads that turned to paved and eventually gave way to busier streets that melded into highway ramps.

While Trace repeatedly stole looks at her, Priss took note of all the beautiful scenery. There were rolling green hills, natural lakes and ponds, and many horse farms.

"Kentucky?" she finally guessed.

"Yeah." Trace turned on the radio, not loud but on a music station. "Not far from home, though. We'll cross the bridge over into Ohio in just a couple of hours."

It was such a nice concession, having Trace give her even a small but obvious fact, that she felt she owed him a truth. "You know, if it makes you feel better, my sense of direction sucks. I doubt I'd be able to find my way back here even if I had a GPS."

Trace grinned. "Dare wasn't worried." He ruined what could have been a nice compliment by adding, "There was nothing in your background to suggest you'd be a threat in any way."

"Mmm." Priss looked out the window at a field of cows. "Let's hope Murray sees it that way, too."

The mention of Murray soured Trace's mood. "I can't get over how you look."

And he didn't sound happy about it. Curious, Priss watched him. "So how do I look?"

"Hot." His mouth tightened, but he said, "Fuckable."

Startled, she felt heat tinge her cheeks. "You smooth talker, you."

"Forget smooth." He squeezed the steering wheel. "I'm worried about how Murray's going to react when he sees you."

His worry started to chew on her, too. "I'm his daughter, remember?"

Trace cursed low. "Murray's not going to care that you're supposedly related."

Supposedly? So he still didn't believe her about that? Well, truthfully, she couldn't be one hundred percent about it herself. Her mother's best guess put Murray as the paterfamilias, and that was all that mattered to Priss.

"What do you think he'll do?"

Trace gave her a lingering glance, then returned his attention to the road. "Given how you look—"

"Fuckable?"

"Yes. And like a prime piece of salable property."

"Oh." That wasn't much of an improvement, but she got his point. Murray was in the business of selling human property. If he thought he could make money off her…

"I wouldn't be surprised if he tried to use you to cement a deal, sort of as the icing on the cake, and at the same time he could remove you as a threat to his empire."

Her skin started to crawl. "You think he sees me as a threat?"

"To get where he's at now, Murray had to be shrewd in the beginning. But these days, his lust for power warps everything else, and now he's just a deranged, sick paranoid who sees everyone as a threat."

Yeah, she'd gotten that impression.

"No way in hell is he going to let anyone get close, most definitely not a daughter. A dissipated son, maybe. Murray could relate to that. But a fresh-faced, moral daughter? Not in this lifetime."

So her con had been wrong from the very beginning. And if she'd really done her homework, she'd have known that. But no, she'd gotten high on her need for revenge, and she'd gone off half-cocked on righteousness. "Damn."

"Yeah." Trace rolled one shoulder. "Look at it this way, what you're presenting and the way you're presenting it is the antithesis to what Murray wants in his life."

Now that her perspective was different, Priss knew he was probably right. "I see your point." It sickened Priss to even consider it, but she said it anyway. "Maybe I should have tried to…you know, come on to him?" She fought off a gag.

"Hell, no!" Trace sent her a furious glare. "He'd have used you, then shared you, then sold you."

Her temper unraveled without warning. "Then what should I have done?" Hurt squeezed in on Priss, prodded by memories of her mother's fear and the irreversible damage done to her. Her mother had lived in hell, never able to escape the past or the constant terror of being caught again. She saw things that weren't there, ran from men who only wanted conversation, and for all intents and purposes, she'd kept Priss hidden.

She'd kept her a prisoner.

For her own good. Or so her mother had always said.

Her life had consisted of undue caution, warnings, crying jags and wretched, clinging panic.

Priss said again, more quietly this time, "What should I have done?" If she didn't make Murray pay, then it was all for nothing—her mother's suffering, her abysmal up-bringing, all of it.

Her life had little enough meaning already. Without this one driving purpose, she'd have…nothing at all.

WHEN PRISS GOT QUIET, it bothered Trace. He knew right where her thoughts had gone. He didn't want to push her, but the sooner they got it all out in the open, the sooner they could deal with it.

She sat slumped beside him, her head resting against the back of the seat, one hand beside her, the other braced against the door where it met the window.

The casual pose didn't fool him; he could feel her throbbing tension, and the pain she tried to hide.

Trace reached for her hand and gave her fingers a squeeze. Quietly, he asked, "Do you want to talk about your mother?"

Without looking at him, without even an ounce of real interest, Priss said, "No, why? You want to talk about what it is you and Dare do?"

Exasperated, Trace released her. "What does one have to do with the other?"

"I was raised not to trust any man." Leisurely, she rolled her head to face him. "That includes you. *Especially* you."

They needed a break, and she needed to eat. Thinking food might improve her disposition, he pulled into a gas station with a small store attached.

"Come on. Pick out some food and then I'll tell you what I can."

She immediately perked up. "Really? You mean it?"

"That hungry?" He smiled at her newly animated expression.

Priss shook her head. "That curious."

The second he parked the truck, she opened her door and got out. Trace had to hustle to keep up with her. He grabbed her arm before she could step into the store.

"You need to show a little more caution, at all times."

At a more sedate pace, they entered, and Priss grabbed a burrito, chips, a soda and prepackaged doughnuts. Trace bought his own drink, but he was careful not to touch Priss's food. He was afraid if he did, she'd find a reason to refuse it.

When they returned to the truck, he scanned the area and found it clear. While Priss prepared her food, he put in a call to Jackson.

Priss pretended preoccupation, but he knew she listened to, and memorized, every word.

Jackson answered on the first ring but said nothing.

"I need you on duty tonight."

Recognizing Trace's voice, he said, "Yeah? Doing what?"

There was something about Jackson that often rubbed Trace the wrong way. Maybe it was how Jackson and his sister, Alani, always squabbled. Or maybe it was that women ogled him nonstop.

Feeling a little tetchy about the idea of Jackson keeping an eye on Priss, Trace growled, "Does it matter?"

"Nope."

"Then what's the problem?"

Like a parent schooling a kid, Jackson said, "I kind of need some instruction here, Trace. I'm not psychic. Or did you want me to guess?"

Shit. Trace rubbed the bridge of his nose. "I thought Dare had told you."

"Nope. Nothing specific anyway."

He let out a breath that didn't really do much to hedge his possessiveness. "Murray wants me to accompany him tonight."

Jackson's whistle of surprise was nearly drowned out as Priss choked on her drink. Trace reached over and rubbed between her shoulder blades while she bent forward, coughing.

"So he's finally biting." Jackson sounded duly impressed with the progress. "'Bout damn time."

A little early, actually, which was why Trace had to assume this might be a trap. "While I'm gone, I want eyes on Priss. Every minute."

"Got it."

"I need you ready to intervene if it comes to that." And once again, Trace despised that he might have to rely on someone else. That it had happened with his sister still burned him. He didn't want to entrust Priss's care to anyone else. He trusted Jackson's ability to handle things or he wouldn't be working with him, but...that wasn't the point.

"She's going to be at your hotel?"

"No." Trace gave him the address of the original place Priss had booked. "Murray already questioned her, so I'm guessing he'll have someone check up on her."

"So she needs to be there. Are you expecting the visit to be friendly or hostile?"

"I have to assume friendly, but in case I'm wrong, that's why you're watching. You can notify me if shit goes south once you have her safe. And if I should hear of anything to make me think it might not be friendly, I'll send you the text code."

Within the organization, Trace, Dare and Jackson shared codes that identified every probability, and that could be simply and quickly sent without anyone else knowing what they meant.

Now, after what she'd been through, Alani also knew the codes. It made Trace feel marginally better about her being out and about again, picking back up on her life.

"When I finish with Murray, I'll take over watching Priss."

"You going to stay with her?"

He shook his head, even knowing that Jackson couldn't see him. "If I thought I could slip her out of there unnoticed, I would, but if anyone's watching…"

"Yeah, probably too chancy." Trace didn't need to finish that thought; Jackson understood. "I'll go by there now to get the lay of the land, find the best retreat if necessary. Tell her she won't see me, but I'll be nearby all the same."

Nearby watching Priss's every move. Trace's jaw tightened. "Thanks."

"So…" Jackson cleared his throat. "Your sister is on her own right now?"

Hackles rising even more, Trace asked softly, "Why are you asking?"

"You're usually right up her… That is, you're usually looming over her. When you can't do it, you have Dare watching over her."

"What makes you think that's not the case now?" Alani swore she was fine, that she could carry on without all the supervision. True, she was extra cautious now, and Trace doubted she would ever again take chances with her safety. But it wasn't just for her that Trace continued to keep a close eye. It gave him a measure of peace, too.

"We met up to discuss remodeling my place. If either of you had been watching, I'd have known."

"She met with you at your request, I suppose?" Absently, Trace watched Priss all but inhale her food. She must have been famished, and he was the one responsible for that. He reached over and lifted from her jeans a tiny piece of onion that had fallen from the burrito wrapper.

She mouthed a silent, "Thanks."

Again Jackson cleared his throat. "Yeah, my suggestion." Then in disgust, he said, "But I doubt it'll happen. You know your sister and me—oil and water. How the hell she gets any business with her surly disposition, I'll never understand."

"Yet you broached the idea to her?"

Jackson sounded defensive. "I wouldn't mind a professional touch at my new place. Being that she's your sis and part of the biz and all, I felt obligated to go to her first."

"Uh-huh." Trace watched as, with another big bite, Priss finished off the food. "Leave my sister alone, Jackson, you understand me?"

Slowly, Priss turned her head to stare at him. "So you *do* have a sister?"

Shit. He'd said more than he should. "I have to go."

"Yeah, you should go." Jackson sounded every bit as acerbic as Trace felt. "And don't worry about Priss or Alani. I've got it covered."

Trace opened his mouth, but Jackson disconnected the call. He snapped his teeth together. "Son-of-a—"

"A sister, huh? The mysterious Alani, I take it?" Priss gathered up her garbage and put it all back in the bag. "You know, Trace, you might as well tell me everything, otherwise I'll just go by supposition."

Hell, she already knew far too much. He put the truck in Drive. "Such as?"

Leaning closer, one hand on his thigh in a gesture of sympathy, Priss said softly, "Your sister was the victim of human traffickers."

Trace gripped the steering wheel and said nothing.

"That would account for why you're involved with Murray now, and why everyone went all hush-hush when Chris accidentally said her name. Don't worry, I understand." She rubbed his thigh. "Your secret is safe with me."

CHAPTER ELEVEN

TRACE CONCENTRATED on the traffic, on the surrounding area and on not responding to Priss's astute guess.

After a minute of silence from him, she retreated back to her own seat. The second she stopped touching him, he felt her withdrawal, both physical and emotional, and he hated it.

Tension built inside him. "Priss…"

With little interest, she said, "Hmm?"

Damn it. Why he felt so drawn to her, so…entwined with her, Trace couldn't say. But he didn't want a barrier between them, not now. "I do have a sister."

"I know." She sounded even more remote. "I heard you say so."

Loyalties divided, Trace sought a response that would pacify her. "Alani's life…her issues…they're private. Hers to share, not mine."

At least he had her attention again. Priss watched him, still guarded but also sympathetic.

Finally she sighed. "I can understand that." She turned her head to look out the window at the passing scenery. "That's exactly how I feel about my life and my issues."

Trace was quick to say, "It's not the same."

"With neither of us sharing any real details, we'll never know if it's the same or not, will we? But I mean it, Trace, I understand why you don't want to discuss your sister's personal and private business."

She sounded genuine enough, but Trace wasn't

satisfied. "You're here with me, Priss. In the thick of things. I require details from you." That is, beyond the details he'd already gleaned in his cursory background check on her.

"Yup. In the thick of it." She laced her fingers together over her stomach and relaxed in the seat. "Now that I've eaten, I feel better."

"You were feeling bad?"

She rolled one shoulder. "Melancholy maybe. Anyway, describe Jackson for me so I'll know the enemy from the babysitter."

"I doubt Jackson would like being called a babysitter." Not that he gave a damn what Jackson liked.

"No?" Priss lifted her brows. "How about deadly enforcer? Bodyguard? What exactly should I call him?"

Her continued detachment wore on Trace. "Odds are you won't need to refer to him at all. But so that you can recognize him if it does become necessary, he has dark blond hair, green eyes. Around my height, but bulkier."

"As in more muscular?"

He scowled. "I suppose."

"Huh." She lifted a brow. "Hard to imagine, really."

"What?"

"Anyone being more muscular than you. I mean, you're pretty ripped."

Trace shifted. He was flattered, but also uneasy. Priss was in a strange mood and it didn't bode well. "Like I said, he's bulkier with it."

"Mmm." Tipping her head, Priss studied his shoulders, his chest. She shook her head as if to clear it. "So he's good-looking?"

What damned difference did it make? Trace frowned at the line of questioning. "Hell, I don't know. My sister says he looks like a lake bum."

That got her grinning. "Really? That's intriguing. Most of the lake bums I've seen are tan, fit and athletic."

Yeah, that sounded like Jackson—if you added in razor-sharp reflexes and uncompromising competence. "You'll be safe with him."

"From what I overheard, I wonder if your sister and Jackson have something going on."

"No." Trace shook his head, sure that they didn't. Did they? He ground his teeth, and then moved on to more pertinent information.

For the remainder of the long drive, he instructed Priss on probable escape routes from the old apartment. Being an expert, he remembered every egress and where it led. "Jackson will look it over himself, and I'm guessing that if it becomes necessary, he'll come in through the window in the bathroom."

She did a double take. "You think he'd fit?"

"It's the window least likely to be noticed, and yeah, you'd both fit." Jackson knew how to squeeze in and out of tight places. And Priss, if it came to that, would learn.

Going over details on security, Trace told her not to open the door to anyone and not to leave the apartment for any reason. It'd be best to keep her windows locked but leave the drapes in the front room parted enough for any of Murray's henchmen to see her. If they knew she was inside, they might not feel obligated to have her presence verified.

"When you go to bed, it wouldn't hurt to bar the door." Murray was so unpredictable that she couldn't take too many precautions.

Priss toyed with a lock of hair hanging over her shoulder. "So...if you finish with Murray in time, do you think you might come in to see me?"

She obviously hadn't understood when Jackson asked

him the same thing. "No. I might be keeping watch, but from a safe distance."

"Oh."

Trace saw her disappointment. He wished he could return to her, but that'd really be pushing their luck.

The next two hours passed pleasantly enough. They talked, but not about anything controversial. After returning the truck to the garage and retrieving the Mercedes, they stopped to pick up the rest of Priss's clothes from Twyla. It was right at closing time for the shop. Trace kept checking his watch, but he was still on track to meet Murray.

Twyla wanted to gush about how improved Priss looked even as she admonished her for not wearing the new, more provocative clothes.

"I'm saving them for Murray," Priss told her with the appropriate giddiness of a schoolgirl. "After all, he bought them for me."

Twyla approved. "And don't you forget it."

They exited the shop with Twyla dogging their heels, trying to continue the conversation. But the day had been too long already for unnecessary politeness. Trace helped Priss into the car and shut the door. While Priss gave a happy wave to Twyla, Trace ignored her and went around to the driver's side.

"You were rude."

"She's under Murray's umbrella, so trust me, she's used to worse." Glad to be out of there, Trace added, "She's aware of every scheme, so don't start feeling sorry for her."

"I wasn't."

"You waved like she was a close friend."

"Fulfilling my role as a giddy girl, that's all." Priss settled in her seat. "Besides, I've known a lot of women like Twyla, prickly and bossy. But that doesn't mean she's in cahoots with a maniac."

"She is."

"You sound so sure." Priss chewed her lip. "But how do you know that?"

"Murray broke me in by having me accompany Hell on a few shopping trips." He gave her a pointed look. "Believe me, I overheard plenty."

Until Priss relaxed, he hadn't realized how keyed up she was. "So you never…"

"What?"

Priss rolled in her lips, but didn't hold back. "You haven't taken other women there to be outfitted? You haven't…been a part of their abuse?"

"No." His shoulders tightened. Fuck, no. Even before his sister's ordeal, he'd never stood by and watched anyone mistreat a woman, and he never would. It was the one big conflict in his cover. Put to the right test—a test against his morality and conscience—how would he handle things? He wanted Murray and all who associated with him, but he knew where to draw the line. "Never that, Priss."

With the smallest of relieved smiles, she nodded. "Good to know."

A few miles from the apartment, they went into a small grocery to buy Priss more supplies. While she loaded a cart with junk food and a few basics, Trace grabbed other necessaries she might need like toiletries and a few magazines that'd help give credence to her being in residence.

Back in the car, Priss looked over a magazine, and then put it back in the bag. "It's going to feel emptier now, without Liger there."

"I'm sorry." Trace knew how any living, breathing creature could offer comfort when the shadows started to close in. He suspected that Priss had a lot of shadows in her life. "Maybe you can watch TV or something to help pass the time."

"Maybe."

Minutes later, he pulled into the lot and, without being obvious, scanned the area. Nothing seemed out of place, but to be sure, he told Priss, "We're back in our roles, okay?"

"Yeah, I get it." She opened her door and stepped out, hefting several of the packages into her arms.

The second the slick, black sedan pulled into the lot, they both noticed. Priss straightened, tracking the car as it pulled past and parked toward the back of the lot, away from the street.

Suspicion narrowed Trace's gaze as he watched the vehicle; absently, he handed the additional bags to Priss. "Get in your apartment and lock the door."

She stiffened with alarm. "What are you going to do?"

He gave her a small push even as he started toward the car. "Do as I say, Priss."

Three big bruisers stepped out of the car. The driver sent a smarmy smile toward Trace.

Jackson should already be in place. Trace hoped he had the good sense to stay put because he wouldn't need his help, but later, Priss just might.

PRISS GOT TO THE TOP of the rickety steps and rushed to the front door of the apartment. Though she scanned the area, every nook and cranny that led to the apartment access, there was no one else on the landing, and no one near the stairs.

For the moment, she felt safe enough.

She wasn't a dummy; she wouldn't take unnecessary

chances that would divide Trace's concentration. Not with one man against three.

Impressive as Trace might be, those odds *sucked*.

After she unlocked the front door and tossed the heavy bags onto the couch, she darted to the railing to observe the confrontation taking place.

The three hulks facing off with Trace looked like professional assholes. Black T-shirts, black slacks, dark sunglasses.

Could they be more clichéd?

Oh, God, oh, God. Trying to read Trace's body language, Priss gripped the railing and held her breath. The men awaited his approach as if they'd come there specifically for him.

Murray's men? Another test—or something else?

Trace looked…well, he looked relaxed. Maybe even amused.

Stride casual, he continued to advance on the men without a single obvious concern.

Other people were in the lot, out in front of the bar next door, driving by on the street—but no one paid any attention to them.

With less than four feet separating them, Trace stopped. His voice was firm, clear, reaching Priss where she waited safely out of reach of harm.

"Who are you?"

The man who'd taken the lead spit near Trace's shoe. "None of your fucking business."

"I'm not asking again."

The guy laughed and reached for…a gun!

Priss gasped at the same time the guy said, "Screw yo—"

His reply ended when Trace put his boot to the idiot's jaw. Shattered sunglasses went flying and the man's head snapped around. He lurched back to slam into the side of the car. The gun slipped from his hand.

Trace kicked again, and the fellow slid down into a heap on the ground.

It happened so fast that Priss was left with her mouth hanging open and her eyes flared wide. For a very brief time, the other two men had the same reaction.

Seconds later they shook off their surprise.

One of them pulled another gun while the third attacked Trace. Though she wasn't a girlie-girl by any stretch, and she was never given to drama, Priss barely swallowed back a scream.

She started to race down the steps, determined to find a way to help, but in seconds she saw that Trace had the upper hand. *Again.*

Dumbfounded, she watched the battle unfold, and she watched Trace dominate.

Oh, he got hit. Several times, in fact.

But nothing seemed to damage him, or slow him down.

After taking a blow to the chin that he barely registered, he retaliated with a hard knee to his combatant's groin, bending the other man double. A punch finished him off and his sunglasses hit the pavement, too.

Two guns and two pairs of sunglasses now littered the ground around them.

The third man launched himself onto Trace's back, attempting to choke him from behind. He found himself flipped onto his back, and his head made solid contact with the parking lot.

To Priss's amazement, Trace wasn't done. He went to one knee, caught the man by the shirt front and, after flipping those sunglasses away, pounded his face with heavy fists. When Trace finished, the hapless fool was bloody, battered and out for the count.

The brutality of it didn't faze her. Given their initial hostility—both in tone and manner—she understood what those men had intended, just as she understood why Trace reacted as he did.

It was the effortless way Trace handled them all that blew her away. The brutes got their asses handed to them, and then some.

Only fallen, groaning bodies remained of what could have been a serious threat.

Systematically, Trace went from man to man, disabling and further disarming each of them. When he finished, he stood back to survey his handiwork.

As if he'd only just then remembered Priss, he glanced back and found her standing at the rail.

She swallowed down her guilt for disobeying an order and gave him a thumbs-up signal for his success.

Now he looked furious. He pointed a finger at her. *"Inside."*

Lord have mercy.

On a gulp, Priss nodded and, backing up, pretended to do as ordered. When Trace returned his attention to the men, she moved back to her vantage point at the railing and watched as he opened the back door of the sedan. Showing no signs of strain, he hefted up the first heavy thug and shoved him into the backseat without worry for any additional injury he might cause. The second brute got piled in on top.

Trace closed the door on them.

Going back to the first man that he'd knocked out, Trace kicked him a few times, not hard enough to cause more damage, but enough to bring him around and get his attention.

Jolted, the guy tried to jerk upright but crumpled on what must've been a bad leg.

Trace smiled as he hauled him to his feet. Leaning

close, he said something low, something that Priss couldn't hear, but it sent the man into panicked struggles.

That's when Priss caught the glint of Trace's knife.

Oh, wow. She squeezed the railing tighter, refusing to blink.

As the man tried to fend off Trace, a brief struggle occurred, ending with a loud howl of pain. Trace withdrew his knife, sheathed it, and shoved the cursing man behind the wheel of the car.

He slammed the door and waited. Finally, after some fumbles, the man started the car and, a little haphazardly, drove out of the lot. He hit the main road with a screech of his tires.

After the car was completely out of sight, Trace gathered up the thugs' discarded weapons, went to his car and locked them in the trunk.

His attitude floored Priss. He behaved as if nothing out of the norm had happened.

She rushed back down the stairs and toward him. "Wow." When he glanced at her with a frown, she said again, "Just…wow. That was amazing."

His left eye flinched. "I told you to go inside."

Priss drew up short at his deadly calm and eerily quiet tone. "Yeah, you did." She tried to sound reasonable. "But if you hadn't handled things so *handily,* I needed to be where I could call out to others, or make a run for it, or—"

Trace took her arm. "You and I need to talk."

She did not like this overly controlled mood of his. "So…you have time to talk? I mean, don't you need to get going?"

"Stop dragging your feet."

She wasn't…was she? Straightening her spine, Priss took the lead. Or she tried to. But Trace kept her right at his side, without a word, without even paying much attention to her. Only half under her breath, she said, "You're being a bully."

At the top of the stairs, he stopped to stare at her open door. "Un-fucking-believable."

"There's no one around." Now she sounded defensive. Yeah, she knew better than to run off and leave the door standing wide open. "You have to admit it, Trace, I had reason to be distracted."

He started marching her forward again. "Left to your own devices, you'll end up dead."

"That's not true." Hadn't she already survived twenty-four years with an unpredictable madman as a father? "I'm good at survival."

He pulled her into the apartment, closed the door and locked it.

Priss gulped. Yeah, okay, so now nervousness took over. Not really fear, because she felt certain that Trace wouldn't hurt her. But he was just so…dangerous. In every sense of the word. His mood, his ability, his speed and strength, had all combined to annihilate three overgrown, trained thugs.

Thugs who were sent to attack him—or maybe her. Instead they'd limped away, their tails tucked between their legs, their weapons confiscated. If Trace weren't being so unpredictable, she could almost laugh about it.

Instead, with him standing there staring at her in a fulminating rage, she squirmed uneasily.

"You showed them, huh?"

His eyes narrowed.

She clamped her lips together. God, she'd sounded like a sap. Trying for a cavalier attitude, Priss leaned back against the door. "Now what?"

"This." Slowly, he stepped up to her. His right hand flattened on the door beside her head.

Eyeing his planted hand, she saw bruised knuckles

and unshakable resolve. She inhaled a shaky breath. "This?"

He traced the fingertips of his left hand along her jaw, up to her temple and then flattened that hand on the door at the other side of her head.

His pelvis pressed into hers, and she couldn't miss the tension surging through him.

Oh. *This*. Sharpened awareness left her eyes heavy, her heartbeat rapid. She tried to focus on his bruised jaw or his black eye. But all her attention zeroed in on his mouth. "You're going to kiss me?" *'Bout damn time*.

"And other things."

Oh, boy, *other* things. "Like?"

His mouth brushed the side of her throat, opened and sucked her skin in against his teeth.

Her toes curled and her stomach bottomed out. "Trace…"

Without haste, he worked his way up to her lips with hot, open-mouth, wet kisses. Every inch of his progress tantalized. All the while he kept her body pinned in place with his.

The fact that he didn't use his hands only amplified his touch.

When his mouth finally met hers, she was so primed, so hungry for him, that she groaned aloud. That seemed to break him. The next thing Priss knew, he'd lifted her, helped her to wrap her legs around his waist, and he had one hand down the back of her jeans, the other under her T-shirt over her right breast.

CHAPTER TWELVE

"I WANT TO TALK TO her myself."

Murray tangled his hand in Helene's hair—and pulled. "Who are we talking about, sweet?"

She winced, but didn't fight him. Her lip curled. "Priscilla."

"Ah." Murray loved how Helene always simmered near the boiling point, no matter the circumstances, no matter his mood or how rough or gentle he might me. "Jealous, much?"

Heat flared in her light blue eyes. "Jealous, not at all!"

"You're a liar. I can see it." He cuddled her big, firm breast. "You're vibrating with hatred."

Her lips parted as he found her nipple. "Hatred, yes. She's trying to use you. I know it. I don't trust her."

Very softly, he asked, "You don't trust me?" He applied more pressure to her nipple, tugged.

"Ah—God, I *do*, Murray. Of course I do." She panted. "Always."

"Then trust me to know what to do with little Priscilla Patterson." Releasing her, Murray pushed her back and fumbled with his slacks. Submission always fired his blood. He loved it. He wallowed in his power. "It doesn't concern you."

Looking dismayed for only a moment, Helene stared at his crotch, then began working up the hem of her tight skirt.

She would willingly forgo her own pleasure in favor of blowing him. That attitude earned her a reward of sorts.

Murray stopped her before she dropped to her knees. "Raise your skirt more. Expose yourself."

Confusion sharpened her features before she licked her lips and did as told.

A scrap of black lace covered her sex. With one hand Murray rubbed himself, and with the other he spread her blouse, exposing those magnificent tits.

Yeah, that look suited her. It needed only one more alteration.… "Drop your panties."

Helene shook back her long, glossy black hair. "All right." Slipping her thumbs beneath the waistband, she eased the material over her notable hips and down her thighs.

She would have stepped free of them, but Murray shook his head. "Leave them there, around your ankles."

Getting into the game, she asked, "You like that?"

Yeah, he liked it. He stroked himself faster, harder. "Bend over my desk."

Her extraordinary rack expanded as she sucked in a deep breath. Exhilaration scalded her cheeks.

"Well? Don't just stand there. Get on with it." He kept his gaze on her sex, already damp with wanting him. "I have shit to do before Trace gets here." And no way in hell would he do any of it with a boner.

Not when Helene was kept around for this very purpose.

She let out a moaning, shuddering breath and hurried to obey. Making a show of it, she flattened her hands on the desk and slowly slid forward until her chin nearly rested on the surface. Arching her back, she spread her legs as wide as she could with the restrictive material hobbling her ankles.

Breathless, she asked, "Like this?"

"That'll do." Now that she'd positioned herself, Murray stood back to look at her. He could see her getting wetter, and it incited his lust. "So you want to talk to Priscilla?"

She went still, then began panting. "Yes." Her flesh shimmered with excitement. "I could make her tell me things."

"With your drugs?" Helene loved to test the effects of various narcotic blends on unruly women who dared to fight their fate. And he had to admit, it was usually more effective than beating or starving them.

"Yes," she moaned. Her hands curled against the desktop; her thighs tightened. Now writhing, she whispered, "I have the perfect formula for her. She would be pliable, pathetically agreeable…"

Murray chuckled. Helene enjoyed anything and everything he did to her, and if she could be cruel to someone else in the bargain, that was enough to send her into an orgasm.

"I sometimes wonder, Helene."

Eyes closed, she concentrated on breathing. "About what?"

"What type of warped, abusive upbringing you must have had."

"What?" Surprised, she twisted to see him, her lust temporarily abated. "Me?"

"Don't move."

She went still again, her body radiating heat. "No, it wasn't like that, Murray. My parents adored me. *Everyone* adored me."

And then her parents had died, leaving her alone, spoiled rotten, left to her own devices to find a way to remain pampered. Maybe that explained some of it. Not that he really gave a shit. Her sickness was her own, and it complemented his.

"You're a fucking princess, is that it?" He stroked himself against her ass, teasing them both.

"Yes," she whispered on a breath of sound. "A princess."

All but begging for it, she wiggled her ass, and Murray gave in. He clasped her hips and with one hard stab, surged into her.

They both groaned harshly, and after only a half dozen strokes, he felt himself boiling toward release.

Helene didn't realize it, but much of his lust stemmed from knowing things she didn't know.

Things about Trace, about Priscilla.

He had a certain way of doing things, a way guaranteed to give him the perspectives he needed to judge loyalty. Helene would discover his true methods soon enough, but for now, she served her purpose.

He didn't care about her pleasure, never had and never would. But when she cried out, her inner muscles clamping around him, it pushed him right off the precipice of control. He pounded into her one last time. Objects toppled, and Helene gasped at the pain in her hip bones as they connected with the edge of the desk. They both went quiet in that suspended moment of orgasm.

He collapsed over her, sweaty, limp, sated.

Done with her.

Already his mind moved on to other things. With his pants drooping and his cock now limp, he stumbled back and fell into his chair. Kicking it around so he could look out the window, he let out a long lazy breath.

Helene understood the dismissal.

As silently as she could, she straightened her clothes and, wobbly on her high heels, slipped from the room.

He didn't notice her satisfied, gloating smile—and he

wouldn't have cared anyway. To his mind, Helene posed no real threat. Not to him.

And no one else mattered.

ADRENALINE CONTINUED TO RUSH through his blood, obliterating common sense and sound reasoning.

Playing havoc with his conscience.

Filling his hand with her soft breast, Trace found her nipple with his thumb and knew he had to taste her.

Right now.

Pushing her shirt up and pulling her bra down, he bent and covered her taut nipple with his mouth.

On a soft moan, Priss sank her hands into his hair, trying to get him closer.

It wasn't enough.

But what would be?

The second he'd seen the men in the slick car, he'd known who they were and what they wanted. The dressing didn't matter—he always identified trouble. Years of trailing the most vicious society elements had honed his instincts to the point that he recognized a threat even before it got in range.

Still, he'd given the men a chance, offering the opportunity for them to state their names and their business without bloodshed.

Pulling a gun meant they passed on the pleasantries, and that gave him plenty of reason to pound out some frustration.

He assumed Murray sent them, either as another test for Trace, or because he'd short-circuited his plans for Priss.

But even pounding on the henchmen hadn't expended enough energy to ease his ever-growing tension. Priss was the source of that tension, and only she could release him.

He wanted her. *Insanely.* More than he could remember ever wanting a woman.

It defied logic.

"Trace…" she whispered.

Needy. Ready. Willing, and oh, so ripe.

"I don't know enough about you." He growled the statement as much to himself as to her when he switched to her other breast. He plumped her up with his hand, circled her nipple with his tongue, and drew her deep.

"You…" She gasped and her body arched. "You know more than I know about you."

True. All of it. Out of necessity, he had to deceive her. He had to use her.

So what the hell was he doing getting intimately involved with her?

Cursing, Trace shoved himself away and let her feet drop back to the floor. He turned to pace and, running both hands through his hair, put needed distance between them before facing her again.

That was a mistake.

The sight of her, limp against the door, shirt up and legs braced apart, nearly felled him. Her bra cups were beneath her breasts, lifting them almost like an offering. Her nipples were tight and wet from his mouth, her eyes glazed, and her lips parted.

He shook, when normally he was rock steady.

Getting involved with her would be a mistake, but given the level of his lust, how she affected him, he couldn't see any way around it.

Making the decision helped to steady him. "As soon as possible, Priss."

She drew in a shuddering breath. "What?"

"I need to be inside you." He flexed his fingers, loosening his fists, reaching for control. "As soon as possible."

"Oh, okay." She licked her lips—and nodded. "When?"

Incredible. It would be funny, except that he felt like he suffered a thousand torments. "I don't know. I have to see how things go tonight with Murray."

Some of the daze cleared from her eyes. She swallowed twice. "Murray." She said his name with derision. "What will happen tonight? You'll be okay?"

"Not sure." That's why he had to wait. What if he took Priss now—against a damned door, with his knuckles bruised and adrenaline pumping—and then Murray caught onto him and killed him? Hell, maybe Murray was already onto him and that's why he'd sent the goons. With Murray, nothing was ever certain or clear-cut—except Trace's hatred of the man.

Organizing his thoughts, he took a cautious step closer to Priss. It'd help a lot if she'd cover her chest and maybe stop looking so sexually ravenous, so innocently open to him.

It'd help if she wasn't the most appealing woman he'd ever met. "In case shit goes sideways tonight—"

"No! Don't say that." Taking him off guard, Priss launched away from the door and threw herself against him. Her arms locked around his neck, her body squeezing into his.

At least her shirt dropped down to cover her breasts.

Against his shoulder, she said, "I…I don't want to scare you, Trace."

He tried to pry her away, but she held on. "Scare me?"

"I mean, I don't want to scare you off." She huddled closer. "I figure nothing much actually scares you. Not with how you fight, but—"

"Priss." Holding her shoulders—safer ground there— he levered her back. "What is it?"

Uncertainty held her silent for a heartbeat of time before she blurted, "I like you. A lot."

He was a coldhearted bastard, a killer when necessary. And still he softened.

"Don't you dare smile!" Knotting her hands in the front of his shirt, she tried to rattle him. "I like you more than I ever thought I'd like anyone. I'm not asking for anything. Well, not for much. Sex. And I guess protection. And if you wanted to help me kill Murray that'd be—"

Ice shot through his veins, obliterating his smile. "You're not doing anything with Murray, damn it!"

She hesitated, and Trace saw the moment she decided to placate him. "Sex and protection, then?"

A thousand curses rushed through his beleaguered brain. No one could be that transparent. She had to have an endgame, but damn it, he didn't know what it might be. "No way in hell are you serious."

"You bet I am." Showing her own annoyance, Priss went on tiptoes. "Until today, I'd never danced with anyone."

What did dancing have to do with anything? He shook his head. "I don't understand you." And that was an aberration, too, because he *always* figured out motives and personalities. More often than not, he understood others better than they understood themselves.

"It's easy enough. You see, things like dances are out when you don't attend public school, when for all intents and purposes you don't even exist."

He felt a little sick. "Priss..."

She poked a finger into his chest. "Interaction with other kids, especially boys, was a huge no-no." Taking a step back, she looked beyond him. Her voice lowered, turned pensive. "Can't draw attention from anyone, can't be noticed in anyway. Hide. All the time hiding."

The way she folded her arms around herself made her look very small and alone.

"Everything was about caution and fear, about avoiding other people because no one could be trusted, and everything was a risk. Even when my mom felt forced to take a chance, strictly for survival reasons, she didn't let me."

"She kept you locked away?"

Priss closed her eyes for a moment. "The silliest things were so noticeable."

"Like what?" Trace wanted to hear it all. Every awful detail. Gently he encouraged her. "Tell me."

"Like…fresh breezes." Bleak, so sad, she looked at him. "Wherever we lived, the doors and windows stayed locked. I played inside. By myself."

That was no way to raise a child, and Trace hurt for her. "You got out sometimes?"

She shrugged. "We shopped, but always in silence. We even drove in silence because Mom was always on the lookout, always waiting for the boogeyman to appear. Normal jobs, like…I don't know, a cashier or a waitress, left her too exposed. It's what Murray would have expected, she said. And so she had the porn shop, a place Murray would never look for her, and—and—"

His throat closed as she choked up. He reached for her, but she slapped his hands away.

"No, don't you offer me comfort like it's going to matter. It *won't*. Nothing will matter as long as Murray is free to do as he pleases, free to ruin more lives." Her fist thumped against her chest. "He ruined *my* life, damn you."

"No." Trace had to deny that, because believing it hurt too much. "A woman ruined wouldn't be so foolishly brave, so funny, or so smart."

"Brave?" That made Priss laugh, but the sound held no humor. She turned somber, too serious. "You can help me to stop him."

So many emotions ran rampant, taking off in a surge, that Trace barely recognized himself. Thunder roared in his ears, his heart raced.

Grabbing her shoulders, he shook her. "Goddamn it, you will *not* do anything with Murray! Do you understand me? You will avoid him when you can, and when you can't, you will allow me to handle things!"

Priss shoved him back. "Fine. It's plain how you feel about this." Looking mulish, she took a stand. "So forget the...protection."

He reached for a calm that didn't exist. Not around her. Not *with* her. "Priscilla—"

"You make my name sound like a growl." She inhaled. "I still want the sex."

That blurted statement almost knocked his heart through his chest.

"Oh, come on, Trace." Grudgingly, she admitted, "You know if I haven't danced, I definitely haven't done...that. But I want to. With you."

The unspoken words *before it's too late* hung in the air between them.

For one of the few times in his life, Trace suffered a complete and total loss. Priss made him frenzied, when that went against every fiber of his basic being. She robbed him of his natural demeanor, one of calm control and precise direction.

She turned him inside out—and God help him, he was starting to like it.

Making sure not to touch her again, Trace stepped around her and headed for the door. "Lock up behind me. I'll check in when I can."

"Running away?"

"Retreating strategically." He paused at the door. Facts remained, danger persisted. He couldn't go like this, not without letting her know that his protection extended beyond his own physical presence or influence. He opened the door and stepped outside. After scanning the area and finding nothing amiss, he looked back in at her. "No matter what happens with me, you won't be alone, Priss. Remember that."

Trace closed the door on her expression of devastation. Because he'd admitted he might not live through this? Maybe.

But could she really care that much, that quickly?

Why not? He knew he did.

He could go back in and reassure her that he had no intention of allowing any outcome other than the demise of Murray and his operation and operatives. But that'd lead to her talking to him, and maybe touching him, and his resistance waned already.

In order to see that outcome, he had to stick to plans.

Trace waited on the rickety walkway, listening for the click of the lock. When he finally heard it, he forced himself to leave. The metal stairs rattled with his rushing footfalls. Though he knew Jackson lurked about, hidden from view but accessible, he continued his surveillance of the area.

Murray wouldn't be happy that he'd disabled three of his men, but he would respect the ability that made it possible. Now if he could just control Helene while corralling Murray and his many cohorts into a corner... well, he just might be able to get this tangle with Priss all worked out.

And then he could have her.

That was incentive enough to keep him on his toes.

PRISS WENT TO THE WINDOW to look out. She watched as Trace drove away, and with every second that passed, she felt angrier, sicker and lonelier.

She dropped the curtain and moved away from the window.

What if Trace didn't come back to her? She pressed her palms against her eye sockets, but still she saw her mother's haunted face, the unrelenting fear that ate away at her peace of mind and her sanity.

Sure, Trace had mad skills. No one could deny that. But he couldn't dodge a sniper's bullets, or fend off a sneak attack, and Murray was capable of anything. Every supervillain she'd ever seen in a movie crowded back into her brain. Though she tried to block the thoughts and the images, they flickered with the vividness of a colorized movie reel—ways of torturing, of disposing of bodies, of murder and mayhem and sickness.

The fear wasn't for herself, but for Trace.

Instead of Jackson babysitting her, he should be used as backup. If she knew where Jackson hid himself, she'd go to him and demand he do just that.

But she didn't know the guy, and being blond described about a third of the drunks tripping in and out of the bar next door.

With nothing else to do, Priss went to the couch and flopped down on her back. She covered her eyes with a forearm and concentrated on how Trace had kissed her, where he'd touched her.

It had all been so incredibly…intense. And intimate. More intimate than anything she'd ever known.

She wanted him. Bad. She hadn't known such want existed, but now she'd met Trace and he'd done something to her, tainted her brain or stirred up her dormant sexuality or…something.

She wanted more. A lot more. With Trace.

He had to come back. He just had to.

But if he didn't, she'd still get to Murray—one way or another.

"How'd you get the shiner?"

Trace shut the office door behind him and stalked over to stand by the enormous window. Heavy storm clouds had rolled in, bringing the dark of night earlier than usual. The weather matched his mood.

He stared down at Murray in his seat. Hatred wormed through his heart, but he kept his expression temperate. "Three guys showed up at Priscilla's apartment."

One of Murray's brows climbed high. He covered his surprise quickly. "Three men you say? And all you got was a single punch in the eye?"

Trace shook his head. "No. Priscilla did that earlier."

Murray lost his relaxed pose. "The hell you say."

"Just a disagreement." He wanted to settle the issue of the thugs, not talk about Priss and her tendency—and talent—for violence. "Not a big deal."

Raising a hand, Murray stalled Trace's effort to talk about his henchmen. "Did you strike her back?"

Bastard. He couldn't keep the frown off his face. "No."

"Why not?"

"She's your daughter."

Murray's eyes narrowed as he studied Trace. "There is that, I suppose."

"And a hit from me would do her real damage. Maybe even kill her."

"You're a man of control." Murray shook his head. "You can discipline without damaging. And the truth is, an unruly woman can benefit from a slap every now and then. If nothing else, it damages her pride enough to keep her in line."

Maintaining his relaxed pose was impossible. Trace paced to the front of the desk and redirected Murray's malice. "Your three buffoons barely touched me, but they're not going to be much good to you anytime in the near future."

Irritation put a twitch in Murray's jaw. "You didn't kill them?"

"Not without a direct order from you, no." He waited for Murray to deny sending them, but he didn't. "Did you want them dead? That's why you sent them after me?"

Instead of answering that, Murray asked, "How bad are they hurt?"

"Some broken bones, probably a few concussions. I stuck them back in the car and last I saw, they were limping off to the hospital."

Murray sat back in his chair and crossed his legs. For several seconds, he looked stunned before outrage took over. Slamming his hands down on the desk, he cursed. "You won't kill them, but you didn't think to call me before rendering them useless?"

Now that Murray had lost his cool, Trace regained his. Hell, he enjoyed seeing Murray riled. "I'm telling you now. Without knowing for sure if you sent them, or why, I was left to my own discretion. If you want me to bother you with every little detail that comes up, just say so." He shrugged. "But I was under the impression that you wanted me to handle shit."

Murray's face reddened with bluster. "I do, damn it."

"They were shit," Trace explained. "They've been handled."

For a full minute Murray fumed in silence while Trace stood there, waiting, almost hoping the bastard would attack so that he could end this damned farce.

Instead, Murray rocked back in his chair and guffawed. "I'll be damned."

The mercurial mood swings were not a good thing. They made Murray all the more unpredictable and dangerous because you couldn't gauge his reaction. "So I should assume this was no more than another of your tests?"

Grinning, again dodging a direct answer, Murray pointed at Trace's face. "You say Priscilla blackened your eye, huh?"

Trace touched his fingertips to the bruise. He couldn't tell Murray what had really happened, or how adept Priss had been at *almost* escaping. "She took offense."

"Looks like."

"She threw a damned book at me." A book, if it hit him the right way, could have done the damage, and it was more believable than the truth.

Grinning hugely, Murray teased, "Came on a little strong, did you?"

"Something like that."

Murray roared. "God, I love it." He hit the intercom. "Alice, get Helene in here. I have something to share with her."

Damn and double damn. The day had been a cluster-fuck from the get go. All he needed now was Hell's psychotic participation.

A minute later, Helene strode in looking like a woman on a mission. Her eyes were always cold, but now…something was different. She looked glacial with loathing.

Had Helene begun dipping into her own pharmaceutical concoctions? Hazardous. But that would explain a few things.

A tight skirt hugged her long thighs, emphasized by the deadly height of her heels. Beneath her blouse, Trace could easily see her long, stiff nipples.

Excited? About what?

"Come in, sweetheart." Murray motioned to her. "I have something to share with you."

Shaking back her long hair and propping a lush hip on the corner of Murray's desk, Helene eyed Trace. "What happened to you?"

"You're going to love this," Murray told her. With grand fanfare, he announced, "Priscilla attacked him."

"Not an attack," Trace corrected, aware of Hell's heightened attention. "More a loss of control."

His meaty paw high on her thigh, Murray leaned closer to Hell as if to share a confidence. "She threw a book at him."

Like a snake preparing to strike, Hell coiled, zeroing in her anticipation of cruelty. Even her tongue flickered out, serpentlike, to dampen her lips. Breathless with malicious desire, she whispered, "I could discipline her."

The offer repulsed Trace.

It had the opposite reaction with Murray. He studied her with fresh interest. "I'll think on it."

Like a kid given a special gift on Christmas, Helene rejoiced. "You mean it?" Off the desk, she rushed around to Murray and bent to kiss him. "Just give me the word and I'll handle it. I know just what to do with her—"

"Hush." He put a finger to her lips. Looking past her to Trace, Murray laughed. "She gets into her work, doesn't she?"

Trace worked his jaw, words beyond him.

"Oh-ho." Murray pushed Helene back and stood with a rush of glee. "What's this, Trace? You don't want Helene near your little protégé?"

Helene whipped around to glare at Trace. "What does it matter to you? She's nothing. Less than nothing!"

"She's my daughter," Murray reminded Helene. "And that's why Trace cares. Isn't that right, Trace?"

He gave a halfhearted shrug.

Body rigid, Helene conceded the possibility of that, but still hissed to Trace, "Nothing to *you* personally."

"I'm charged with protecting her."

Helene leaned closer to him, her dilated eyes glittering, her breath sweet. "It's none of your damn business."

Aware of Murray taking it all in, Trace clasped her arm and moved her out of his line of vision. "You misunderstand, Murray. Whatever you want to do with Priscilla is your business. It's Helene's twisted little heart that sort of sours my stomach." And then to Helene, "It's kind of pathetic, the way you get your jollies, don't you think?"

She lashed out. "Bastard!"

Trace caught her wrist before her palm connected with his face. In front of Murray, uncaring, he wrested her into a chair none too gently. His hands squeezed her wrists, keeping her still. She'd be bruised later, and he didn't give a damn.

"Don't ever," he warned through his teeth, "try to slap me. You won't like the consequences."

Helene gasped in air, equal parts furious and aroused. Psychotic bitch.

Trace stepped away from her and turned to Murray, ready to explain if necessary, only to find him smiling his Cheshire cat grin.

To Helene, Murray said, "Trace's right, of course." He took his suit coat from an ornate hook on the wall. "I'll reprimand you later for that little display of rebellion."

Shit. Trace didn't want to feel guilty about Helene. He glanced at her, but the threat of punishment had only stirred her more. A flush stained her skin and her eyes were heavy, smoky with lust.

"You ready?" Trace asked Murray. He needed some fresh air in a bad way.

"I am." On his way to the door, Murray paused to stand over Helene. "And you…"

Tremulous with excitement and fear, she flattened her back in the chair. "Yes?"

Murray cupped her face. "I think you *should* go see Priscilla. Take some of your drugs, the ones that help expose the truth. Ferret out her feelings—on me, on Trace, and on sexual deviance. Don't hurt her, but otherwise…have fun. I'll touch base with you when I finish my business for the night."

His legs suddenly leaden, his heart missing a beat, Trace stood there, immobilized, sick. Murray didn't trust him—didn't trust anyone—and so his unending suspicions would never be satisfied. Trace's instincts screamed for him to kill them both, right now, before they could touch Priss.

What to do?

Helene squealed like an excited schoolgirl. Leaping from her seat, she threw herself against Murray for a long, intimate, tongue-twining kiss.

Hearing his own heartbeat in his ears, Trace slipped his hand into his pocket. If he could use his phone without Murray noticing, he could alert Jackson to the problem.

But Murray released Hell and, anxious to be on his way, slapped Trace on the back. "Let's go. You can drive. I don't feel like taking an entourage tonight."

Think, Trace. Get it together. Forcing concentrated thought, he said, "You don't want backup?"

"You are my backup." He glanced at Trace. "Think you can handle that?"

"As long as we aren't ambushed by an army, yeah, I can handle it."

"That's what I'm counting on. I don't want to alert anyone with a damn parade of cars or people. And I want to show this little fuck that I don't need a contingent of men to demolish him."

"All right." It was risky. Trace knew it, so Murray had to know it, too. He was counting on the buyer coming alone, or with only a few men. But then, Murray had gotten to his position in the game by leading the front lines. He wasn't a coward; no, he was more like a bully, always up for cruelty, especially when he could administer it himself. Maybe this was how he fed his sickness, by taking part every so often.

They left the office with Helene rushing past them. On her way to her own office, no doubt to gather the tools of her trade, she blew a kiss to Murray, and sent a look of fierce satisfaction at Trace.

She would demolish Priss. Murray's order not to hurt her just meant no broken bones or scars. Anything else was fair game.

Helene would abuse her, sexually assault her, and leave her more destroyed than Priss could ever imagine. Priss had her strengths, but she wasn't on a par with Helene.

He couldn't let that happen. Jackson was on the scene, and he could handle things, Trace knew it. But he wouldn't leave this to chance.

If necessary, he'd kill Murray. Tonight.

While Murray mused over what would take place between the women, Trace calculated how much time he had. Jackson was in the area, and he had dossiers on all the key players, including Helene. He'd recognize her if he saw her.

They were still in the garage when Helene rushed down and got into her own sporty little BMW convertible. From the passenger seat, Murray watched her, smiling in indulgence, rubbing his thigh, calculating.

Trace started the car. "You might not have a daughter left when Helene finishes with her."

"She knows better," Murray murmured. "Helene is something. Pity she's so unstable."

What the hell did that mean? Helene pulled out ahead of them at top speed, her tires squealing, her long hair blowing back with the top down.

It wasn't until they'd nearly reached their destination that Murray got a phone call, distracting him enough for Trace to send Jackson the code. He prayed he was in time, and when he got a single hum of the phone in reply, he knew Jackson was on it.

Murray was so involved in a heated debate with someone that he paid no attention at all, either to Trace's use of the phone in his pocket, or the single, barely detectable sound of reply.

But Trace was a world-class multitasker. He not only got the message to Jackson, he caught every word of Murray's conversation.

A supply of women would be coming in very soon. Twelve of them, all young, and all American. The specifics were vague, but Trace knew they could be anywhere from sixteen years old up to thirty. They would be attractive, and right now, they'd be frightened beyond measure.

Priss would be safe, but with this new information, the restriction in Trace's chest didn't ease much. He had to find out when the exchange would take place. *He had to.* Once the women were dispersed, finding them again would be nearly impossible.

But for now, he had to put on the show Murray expected. If he blew it, he failed everyone, Dare and Jackson, Priss and the females who would be sold.

In a nearly deserted part of town, where only vagrants and addicts would roam, Murray directed him into the front lot of a building that claimed to be an employment agency. The crumbling brick building, enclosed by high chain-link fencing, had been reduced to rubble in sections with only the central part of the structure still holding. Opaque windows, bars on the front door, and security cameras everywhere left no doubt that it was monitored… by someone.

A second, more substantial fence was topped with razor wire, facing in, not out. Anyone with a good eye would wonder why an employment agency wanted to keep applicants in, rather than keep out criminal elements.

Trace already knew the reason. The agency was a criminal operation preying on immigrants and minors of both sexes. Sometimes the victims were runaways and neglected teenagers, sadly labeled throwaways, though he could never think of them that way. Kids with their fair share of bad luck already heaped on them made easy prey.

Trace's muscles clenched. He'd seen too much to ever be immune to the plight of those enslaved by others.

He'd seen hotels where repressed workers wouldn't look him in the eye, where others spoke no English at all, making one wonder how they applied for the job, and what hopes they might have had when they'd first come to the country. He'd seen restaurants with kitchens hiding labor exploitation.

And he'd had his own sister snatched away as punishment against him because he cared about the victims caught up in human trafficking. Hell, he cared about all victims.

He especially cared about Priss.

The new batch of females were likely down on their luck with no family or close friends to notice their disappearance. They had no one—but they had him.

And he would not let them down.

Little by little, law enforcement was catching up with the growing issue of human trafficking. Many cities now had programs to train social workers, religious outreach groups, educators and Hispanic community advocates. They learned how to spot, and where to report, signs of trafficking.

But it wasn't enough.

Only by ridding the world of the key players would they ever make a dent.

"Fucking asshole." Murray closed his phone and slapped it down on the dash.

"Problem?" Trace asked.

"I lost part of my cargo."

A vise closed around Trace's heart. "Come again?"

Murray stewed for a moment before taking his phone back up and stowing it in his pocket. "The idiot forgot to ventilate the trailer." He glanced at Trace. "One of the bitches died."

So he'd failed after all, before he'd even had a chance to make a difference.

"I'll have to raise my price for the rest." Murray opened the passenger door. "The buyer isn't going to like it, so on top of teaching him not to negotiate an already negotiated deal, you might have to stress the importance of being a game player."

"No problem." Trace could stress things all right. Gladly. And when it came time to kill Murray, he just might take his time and enjoy it.

CHAPTER THIRTEEN

ALTHOUGH HE STAYED alert and ready for anything that might happen, Jackson seemed relaxed as he sat back against a rock wall. He wore his cowboy hat low, had his boots crossed at the ankles, a knapsack rested beside him and he'd been nursing the same beer—mostly a prop—for over an hour.

Some men got bored when on surveillance. Not Jackson. He lived for this shit. He loved it. Fine-tuning his instincts hadn't taken as long as it might for some. By being forced into the right spot, at the right time, he'd learned that he was born to kick ass, to protect.

To operate outside the law.

Yeah, that was the best part. Dare and Trace had connections that would make the president of the U.S. of A. jealous. Senators, wealthy businessmen, foreign dignitaries, hell, they probably knew the prez himself.

Those types of connections provided clearance to do what had to be done when legal venues stifled progress. They were good men, walking the edge of honor, never teetering too far to the dark side, but accomplishing what others couldn't.

And they'd made him a part of it. Jackson grinned and pretended to slug back another big drink. Life was awesome.

As he ruminated, a hot little number sidled up and tried to get his attention. Jackson winked at her, giving her the illusion of drunken interest, but truthfully, she wasn't his type and even if she was, he was on call. "Some other time, sweetheart."

She pouted, but he looked away to again scan the area. Suddenly, out of nowhere, something felt...wrong. Static. Charged.

Out of balance.

Instincts could be a bitch, but he never dismissed them.

"'Scuse me," he told the little honey as he picked up his bag and pushed away from the wall to stagger over a few feet, taking in the apartment from a different angle.

Everything looked as it should, not that appearances mattered. Not ever.

He found a railing to droop against, finished off the beer and pitched it toward a trash can.

He missed. On purpose.

Narrowing his eyes, he stared at the lighted window of the dive where they'd tucked Priscilla Patterson. Jackson had thoroughly studied her dossier. Cute girl. Big tits. Lousy background.

It didn't take a genius to know that Trace had a thing for her.

Thinking of Trace ramped up Jackson's acuity, mostly because thoughts of the brother dredged up thoughts of the sister. And the sister...Alani burned his ass more often than not. Yeah, she'd been through hell and then some. Luckily Alani was a fighter, not nearly the wilting flower her brother assumed her to be.

If she didn't dislike him so much, Jackson had a feeling they could really set the sheets on fire. He could make her forget anything and anyone from her past.

Strolling again, he moved to the side to see the other window in the apartment. No one paid him any mind, but that didn't keep him from playing up the drunken bit. Deliberately, he tripped over his own feet and almost pitched face-first into the gravel lot.

Two women giggled at him; one was a cutie, the other an older gal desperately hanging on to her youth. He grinned at them both.

Alani wouldn't be caught dead in that type of cheap bar. Everything about the girl screamed privilege and refinement. Her long, fair hair and big golden-brown eyes were a combination guaranteed to make most men notice. Add to that a kickin' body and a smile that could perk up the most flaccid dicks…well, she certainly had his attention. More often than not, he had only to think of her and he'd get half wood.

She'd recently turned twenty-three. So damn young. And fresh.

And ripe.

Thanks to Trace's endless wealth and influence, youth hadn't factored in when Alani decided she wanted her own business. To give the girl the props due her, Jackson admitted that she'd managed the business well.

The fine hairs on the back of his neck suddenly prickled, sending alarm down his spine. Without turning to look behind him, he opened his senses.

Yeah, something was going down.

He heard the screech of tires at the same time that his phone buzzed in his pocket. He withdrew it, saw the code from Trace, and threw off the facade of a drunk with ease.

On his way to the side of the building housing Priscilla, he kept watch to ensure no one noticed him. Then, from deep shadows and out of view of curious gazes, Jackson removed the cowboy hat to slip on a blackout mask. If anyone did see him, they wouldn't be able to identify him later.

He adjusted his hat over the mask and glanced back at the parking lot.

None other than Helene Schumer parked a classy BMW. All long legs, long hair and kick-ass attitude, she stepped out and started toward the apartment only to draw up short. She looked back at her car, realized that with the top down, she couldn't deter would-be car thieves, and moved back to it to close it up.

That was all the opportunity Jackson needed.

He took off in a ground-eating stride, pushed by urgency and honed by skill. He'd get to Priscilla first, and God-willing, the girl wouldn't prove any trouble.

PRISS TIPPED HER FACE back, letting the water run over her naked body but being careful to keep her hair, now piled on top of her head, dry. She didn't want to ruin her new hairdo. The warm shower helped to soothe her, but not enough. Thanks to Trace, she was still primed and restless.

Giving up, she turned off the shower—and heard something, a faint, intrusive noise that didn't belong in the quiet apartment.

Her heart jammed up into her throat, almost choking her. *Oh, my God.* Someone was in the bathroom with her, and her senses told her that it wasn't Trace.

She couldn't see through the opaque shower curtain, so she strained her ears. When she heard nothing else, her anxiety amplified. Whoever had just intruded, he was good. Very good.

Slowly, so as not to give herself away, she reached for the full squeeze bottle of shampoo and got a good grip. Too afraid to breathe, she prepared herself.

She whipped back the shower curtain in a rush, and before her stood a tall, muscular *masked* person. Startling green eyes shone through the mask—and dipped to look over her body with what appeared to be appreciation.

Swallowing back the terror, Priss squeezed the bottle hard and sprayed shampoo into those prying eyes. As he reacted with a disturbingly quiet flinch, she used the bottle like a club, whacking him in the temple, back up across his chin and lifting it for another blow, intent on breaking his nose.

He didn't make a sound, but he did bend and toss her over his hard shoulder.

His hands landed on her wet, naked butt.

When she started to scream, he whipped her around fast enough to steal all the oxygen from her lungs. He slammed her up against the wall, further knocking the breath from her. His eyes irritated by the shampoo, red now took dominance in the color of them. Even so, his gaze fried her as a hard hand clamped over her mouth.

Nose to nose with her, he started to say something, but on an adrenaline rush, Priss brought her knee up hard into his groin.

His gaze went blank before he whispered faintly, "I'm Jackson…" and then he slumped against her with a muffled groan.

Oh, God. Oh, God. Oh, God. In an equally soft whisper, Priss said, "Why?"

Through his teeth, he gritted out, "Company."

"Oh, God!" Her rescuer was big, solid and thanks to her, weak-kneed with pain. Trying to push around him, Priss reached for the doorknob so she could retrieve clothes, but Jackson had recovered enough to grab her back.

He shoved a towel at her. Still in a barely audible voice, he said, "No time."

"But…" She was *naked*.

Taut, pissed off and vibrating urgency, he gave a

cursory glance over her body and then at the ceiling. "Out the window. Fast."

The window? *In a towel?*

A knock sounded on her front door.

Priss froze, but Jackson, after swiping his eyes with her washcloth to remove most of the shampoo, bent to offer his cupped hands as a boost. "Sorry, sweet. No time for modesty. We gotta go *now* unless you want me to kill someone in front of you, and that might put Trace in a bad way with Murray—"

"Oh… Shut up!" No way would the towel stay in place for her climb out such a small window. And she really didn't have any other choice.

Rushing, Priss tossed the towel over the bottom of the windowsill. She wrapped her fingers over the ledge and stepped into Jackson's hands.

Her belly—and more feminine parts—were on a level with his face.

She could feel her skin burning, especially as she propelled forward with her backside in the air a few seconds before she got her hip braced on the window ledge. She pulled her legs through and, after seeing that no one was around outside to witness her disgrace, got ready to drop out.

The front door squeaked as it opened.

Wasting no more time, Priss hopped down as silently as she could to the metal landing. As she moved aside, she wrapped the towel around herself and tucked in the end—not that it did much for her modesty at this point.

Far quicker than she had managed, and with a great deal more grace despite his size, Jackson dropped down next to her. He said right into her ear, "I'm going to lift you down to the ground. You'll have to drop a few feet."

Priss nodded—and he immediately caught her under

the arms. As if she weighed nothing at all, he lowered her over the railing.

She lost the damn towel.

Like a bird with a broken wing, it took a spinning dive to land in a heap below her, which left her dangling naked.

Outside.

With a big guy looking down at her.

Jackson never changed expressions. "Ready?"

This is too unbearable. "Do it, damn you."

He let her drop and she landed hard, first on her feet, then her knees, then her naked butt. "Ouch."

She was still crouched down, trying to assess whether she was hurt or not, when Jackson landed beside her. He whipped off his T-shirt and stuffed her into it, all the while looking up at the bathroom window.

Priss looked up, too, and saw that he'd had the foresight to close it.

She tugged the shirt down as far as it'd go. It smelled of him, nice, hot, manly. But he wasn't Trace and she didn't care how manly he might be. She was so mortified she didn't know if she'd ever recover.

"This way." Catching her elbow, he forced her to her feet again and headed toward the back of the building, but he balked when he saw the littered debris on the ground. Beer bottles, rusted cans, sticks and other unidentifiable items would lacerate her bare feet.

He looked down at her. Priss shook her head and started to back step, but he said, "Sorry," then tossed her over his hard shoulder again.

He jogged to his car, jostling her all the way so that her big boobs repeatedly bounced against his shoulder. One big, hot hand held on to the backs of her thighs, the other just above her behind.

When he dumped her into the front seat of a vehicle

parked in the shadows, she was so grateful that she felt like crying. She didn't though. Instead, she scrambled over to the passenger seat and readjusted the damn T-shirt.

He was behind the wheel in a heartbeat and, without turning on his headlights, rolled the car forward slowly, his gaze going back and forth from the rearview mirror—no doubt watching for the intruder—and the narrow alley in front of him.

"Put on your seat belt."

Priss couldn't draw a deep breath. She couldn't think beyond knowing that this man had just seen her naked in ways she'd never even imagined, in a variety of poses, all because someone had broken into the apartment with the intent of hurting her or...or *something*.

She put on the belt.

After removing a ludicrous cowboy hat, he peeled off the blackout mask and dropped it on the seat between them.

"Who was it?" Priss felt him glance her way, but she couldn't bear to look at him yet. Arms wrapped around herself, knees pressed tightly together, she kept her gaze straight ahead to stare out the windshield.

"Helene."

"But...the door was locked. How did she get in?"

"You kidding? That barracuda has a bag of tricks that'd put Houdini to shame. She wants in, she's getting in, with or without an invite."

Overwhelmed at the idea of what Helene had likely planned, Priss covered her face.

Sounding more curious than concerned, Jackson asked, "You gonna cry?"

"No." She shook her head, resolute. "No, I'm not."

"Then what's wrong?"

He couldn't be that obtuse. "You're kidding, right?"

"Ah, yeah, gotcha. Modesty issue, huh?" He drove in

a deceptively relaxed way. "Look, yours isn't the first tail I've ever seen, okay?"

Fury stole Priss's breath. She reacted without thinking, slugging him hard in the shoulder.

"Ow!" He grabbed her wrist and tossed her hand back at her. "I was trying to *comfort* you, woman."

"Comfort!" He couldn't be serious. No man could be that dense. "You're a...a Neanderthal!"

"Am not."

Flattened by his careless attitude, Priss stared at him in disbelief. He was a gorgeous guy, but still a jerk. Shaggy blond hair, darker and more unkempt than Trace's, piercing green eyes, a strong jaw and...she peeked at his naked chest... Built.

Her chin lifted. "Where in the world did they even find you?" It had to be under a rock. Or deep in a cave.

He glared at her. "*They* who?"

"Trace and Dare."

Giving her a cautious frown, Jackson rubbed at one bloodshot, swollen eye. "That's top secret."

That's top secret, she mouthed, making fun of him, lashing out in her embarrassment.

He went rigid with affront. "Goddamn it, woman, you blinded me, nutted me, and damn near clubbed me to death. Now you have to ridicule me, too?"

He dared to complain to her? "You snuck into my bathroom. You saw me *naked!*"

"Yeah." His mouth twitched. He nodded just a little. "Yeah, I did." As he turned on his headlights and pulled onto the street, he said in an aside, "Sorry 'bout that."

He did *not* sound sorry, not in the least.

"Didn't mean to stare."

He'd been staring? She should kill him. She really should. But...she might need him for protection. And

Trace probably wouldn't like it if she offed one of his operatives.

"Naked woman and all." Jackson gestured lamely. "It's instinct, ya know? Guy's gotta look."

Priss tried to gather herself, but it wasn't easy. Molly hadn't exaggerated: Jackson was drop-dead gorgeous, now shirtless, and outrageously cocky and outspoken.

Hoping to bury the topic of her nakedness, she asked, "Where are we going?"

"My place, I reckon." He pressed a palm to his fly and winced. "I need some ice."

Still feeling very exposed—she wore only a man's dark T-shirt—Priss looked around the interior of the car. "I don't suppose you have a jacket?"

"In this heat?" He shook his head, but offered his hat with gallant fanfare. "That help?"

She took it and dropped it into her lap. "Please tell me you're staying somewhere private."

"Nope." He glanced at her, his gaze dipping to her chest before darting away again. "Above a bar, actually."

Groaning, Priss dropped back in her seat. Worse and worse.

"Where'd you learn to fight?" Before she could answer, he asked, "Does Trace know about your violent tendencies?"

Scenery passed in a blur. Car lights lit the interior, then faded away. It started to rain.

Priss swallowed back her embarrassment and shrugged. "I blackened his eye."

"That son-of-a-bitch." Jackson chuckled. "He could have warned me."

"How am I going to get into your place dressed like this?"

"Want me to carry you again?"

Priss drew back, ready to slug him, but he subdued

her with a charming grin. "Hold up, little girl. I was just teasing."

"Little girl?" Killing him seemed more appealing by the second. At the very least, it'd give her something to do besides feel exposed and vulnerable.

"Now don't go all feminist on me." He slowed to turn a corner. "You're what? Five-two?"

"Five-four."

"'Bout a hundred pounds?"

Her teeth clicked together. "More than that."

"Didn't feel like it."

Again she drew back to punch him, but he only laughed at her, robbing her of any real anger. She ended up swatting his shoulder, and he didn't even seem to feel it.

"Don't bludgeon me, sweetheart. Whatever the exact measurements, you gotta admit you're small."

Petite would be a more polite term, not that she'd debate it with him. "I'm not a girl."

"Grown woman, huh?" His sensual gaze flashed over her, leaving her fidgeting. "Fine, I'll take your word for it."

"Like you even have to." The man had seen every inch of her, from every angle. She covered her face again.

"Yeah," he commiserated, "I did get the vantage point on that, didn't I?"

"Shut up."

He turned onto a different street. "I can take you up the back way. Later tonight, Trace'll probably come by for you."

"You think?" Trace had told her that he wasn't likely to see her again tonight.

"Sure. Whatever his plans, he hadn't counted on this." Jackson cocked a brow and his grin went crooked. "Can't say as he'll be thrilled to know I took you from the shower, but damned if I'm not looking forward to telling him."

So Trace felt like he had a claim? Worked for her. "You enjoy annoying him?"

"Yeah. It's fair." He pulled his car into the parking lot for a busy bar, but drove around the back.

"This reminds me of the place I was staying."

"Yeah, except that I'm a guy and you're...not, and neither place is appropriate for you." He parked the car, got out and came around to her door to play at being a gentleman. "Let's go."

Priss noticed several couples loitering around in plain view. "In front of them?"

"Drunks and hoochies. Don't worry about it."

Eyes narrowing, she tucked in her chin. "Hoochies?"

With a roll of his eyes he caught her arm and hauled her out. "Don't go getting offended on behalf of the female populace. Most of the women that hang out here have hit on me—aggressively—without knowing shit about me, and at least half of them were married. So yeah, they're not exactly paragons of society."

Still affronted, Priss held back. "What do you call the men who behave that way?"

"Names that'd scorch your pretty little ears." He urged her forward. "Now come on."

He marched her right past the people, and Priss did her best not to make eye contact with anyone. One woman stopped molesting the man with her and instead glared at Jackson.

Filled with scorn, she propped her hands on her hips and said loud enough for the whole parking lot to hear, "I thought you said sex was against your religion?"

He tipped a make-believe hat at her. "Yeah, but see, she converted me."

Priss wanted to kill him. She held his big cowboy hat in front of her thighs until they'd passed the people, and then she held it over her behind.

"Not sure the hat is big enough for that."

Steam came out her ears. "You—"

"Just saying you have curves, honey." Jackson laughed as he moved her around ahead of him. "How 'bout I'll be your cloak?"

He'd already seen every inch of her, so Priss agreed with that solution. But damned if she'd thank him.

He paused at a door to unlock it, stepped in to turn on lights and survey the room, then drew her in. "Have a seat." He locked everything back up again. "I'll grab you a blanket or something."

For that, she *did* thank him. Watching him walk away, she noted his long-legged stride, the breadth of his shoulders, the narrowness of his hips. His blond hair was a little too long, sun-streaked and wind-blown, and... appealing.

Was Trace's sister sweet on him? Given all she'd heard, Priss had to think so.

He returned with a flannel shirt, a blanket and a pair of cotton boxers. "Not exactly haute couture, but it'll get you more covered than you are now. Those shorts have an open fly, though, so button 'em up."

Priss took the clothes, and when he just stood there, she shoved him in the chest. "Go away."

Amused once again, he touched a bruise on his forehead. "Yes, ma'am." On his way to the kitchenette, he asked, "Something to eat or drink?"

The way he acted, this could have been a routine social gathering. He was even more cavalier than Trace, and definitely as cocky.

She sighed. "Both." Eating would give them both something to do.

"Coming right up."

Priss pulled on the shorts first. They were loose in the waist, but snug in the butt. "So tell me, what's with the cowboy gear? I heard you were like a beach bum or something."

He stiffened, then looked over his shoulder at her. "The clothes are cover." When she squawked, he lifted a hand in apology. "Sorry. It's, uh, hard not looking."

"You're a pig!"

"Nah. It's just that I admire the female form."

"That's the cheesiest line I've ever heard!" It could have come straight from one of the cheap pornos.

"I'll have you know I'm sincere, and I have plenty of artwork around my place that proves it."

"Bunch of nudie posters?" Priss guessed.

"No, smart-ass. Real art." He kept his back to her, but his ears lifted with his grin. "But, yeah, nudes."

"Figures." She pulled on the flannel and wrapped it around herself. She wasn't really cold, but her skin prickled. Probably nerves. She *had* just escaped... something.

"Gotta tell you, sweet, a photo of you fresh from the shower would go real nice."

Priss snorted. "If it's a photo you want, you should ask Trace." She was still rankled over that. "He's holding on to one."

"No shit?" Jackson half turned.

Now that she'd donned the clothes he gave her, she didn't mind his attention. "Undercover, you said? As a cowboy in Ohio?"

"Whatever. It was workin' just fine." He went back to the fridge. "Who told you I look like a beach bum?"

He sounded irritated, but so what? His endless good humor was beginning to rub her the wrong way. "Molly."

"Ahh. Nice gal."

She looked at his bronzed shoulders and the deep grove

of his spine down his back. "You gotta admit, you have the tan for it."

"Most of it is natural coloring. Everyone in my family is dark." He ran a hand over his head. "Despite the blond hair."

"So you're not a sunbather?"

"Never said that." He cleared his throat. "You know Alani?"

"I know you two are sweet on each other."

"What?" Again he whipped around to see her, and almost dropped a package of lunch meat. "Where'd you hear that?"

She sat on his couch and tucked the blanket around her. Outside, the rain started in earnest. If it had come a few minutes earlier, she might have been spared the audience during her arrival. Of course, she'd now be wet and miserable, so...

"Stop daydreaming."

"Oh." She looked away from the window. "I was in the car with Trace and heard his side of the conversation with you. Sounded clear enough to me."

"Apparently not, cuz I'm *not* sweet on her. What kind of dumb-ass thing is that to say? I like her, sure, even though she's not the easiest lady to be around."

"No?"

Jackson didn't seem to hear her. He continued on as he pulled food from the tiny fridge and piled it on the counter. "She has her reasons for being prickly, and I know it."

"Those reasons are?"

"And there isn't a man alive who wouldn't want her. She's about the sexiest thing I've ever seen." He shook his head. "But I'm not *sweet* about anything." He scoffed. "That sounds like some adolescent bullshit or something."

"You have a very limited vocabulary."

"My balls still hurt. It's affecting my brain."

"Your brain is located a little low, isn't it?"

He paused, then laughed. Shaking a loaf of bread at her, he said, "Good one. I'll have to try to remember this sharp wit of yours."

"If you want sharp wit, you need to meet Chris."

"Met him. Like him." He stuck his head back in the fridge and came out with cheese. "And yeah, he's funny, too."

"So what exactly do you plan to do with all that food?" He now had two or three types of lunch meat and two cheeses set out, along with a variety of condiments, pickles, lettuce and half of a tomato.

"I'm a man of many talents, baby." He gave a bow. "So I'm fixing us some dinner. Don't know about you, but skin-of-my-teeth escapes always make me hungry."

Priss thought about it, then pushed up from the couch. "I'm hungry, too. And that was rather skin-of-our-teeth, wasn't it?"

"Yeah." He gave her a once-over. "You're handling it pretty well."

Inside, she shook horribly. But she'd lived her life hiding from others, so she wasn't about to bare her emotions for someone she barely knew. "Should I be crying?"

"I'd rather you didn't." He popped a slice of cheese into his mouth. "Crying women make me horny."

Priss rolled her eyes and leaned against the counter in the kitchen. "Why, for God's sake?"

"Guess because I like playing the macho role." Jackson turned back to the counter. "And speaking of that—back at your place, it was close but I wouldn't have let anyone hurt you."

She believed him. "I suppose you'd have handled things, however necessary."

"That's about it."

"And that, I assume, is why you're working with Dare and Trace." She took the bread from him. "The more I learn of this elite organization—" an organization that could rescue, or kill, as the need demanded "—the more I like it."

"That's good." Jackson took out a knife to slice the tomato. "Because I have a feeling you'll fit right in."

CHAPTER FOURTEEN

As THEY WENT AROUND to the side to enter a dank, dark section of the building, foul odors assaulted Trace's nose. It was the smell of age, mold and...fear. "I take it this isn't where people apply for a job."

Murray snickered. "We're sure as hell not going to march in the front door." He pressed up too close to Trace's back. "Most think this section is condemned. No one comes in here."

"I can see why." Like an old factory, the brick interior walls led through hallway after hallway, all narrow, all dirty and crumbling and dark. After some maneuvering they reached a room where large, idle machinery, now in disrepair, sat in a twisted heap of metal.

More than half the bulbs were missing from overhead light fixtures, and drafts through broken windows sent shadows moving and dancing, stretching out over the concrete floor.

Trace stopped to listen.

"I don't like this," Murray complained. "Maybe I needed more guards after all."

"You don't need anyone besides me."

"Damn you, you are so cocksure of yourself." His gaze darted around the room. "I like that."

Keeping watch for anything that moved, breathed or seemed out of place, Trace stepped ahead of Murray. "Stay put a minute."

Few ever dared give Murray orders, but all he said was, "Sensing a trap?"

"Just uneasy with the setup. It's too dark and there are too many points of egress."

"Got your gun?"

"I'm not an idiot." Trace continued on with his easy stride along the perimeter of the room.

Sounding irritated, Murray said, "Think you ought to get it out and ready?"

"It's ready. I'm ready." And talking was a distraction. "Wait here." He heard a click and looked back to see that Murray had not only armed himself, but had his gun at the ready.

Would he shoot Trace in the back? Doubtful. The threat Trace felt didn't come from Murray. Not right now.

At the far end of the room, behind rusted metal shelving, Trace's keen gaze detected a shadow that didn't belong. One shadow, one man.

Very manageable.

"Enough of this bullshit. I see you, and I have no patience for games."

A hulk of a man, head clean-shaven, fully armed, emerged from the shadows. "Not a game." Like Trace, he left his gun in the holster. "Just ensuring the safety of this meeting."

Trace gave the behemoth a quick glance, noting the tense way he held himself, the steroid muscles and nervous eye movements. He dismissed him. "You're not the guy we're here to talk to. Where is he?"

"Mr. Belford had the suspicion that he could be in danger for negotiating the price."

"The price is set, and there are no negotiations. A smart businessman should know that."

"Can you guarantee me he'll be safe?"

Trace let his grin come slowly. "No."

Startled, the big man finally reached for his gun, but Trace didn't give him a chance to get it. In one fluid move, his bowie knife left the sheath, flew from his hand and embedded in the shoulder of Belford's bodyguard. The thug yelled and dropped his gun, and seconds later Trace had him in a stranglehold, one arm tight around his thick throat, his fist on the hilt of the knife. He twisted just enough to wring another howl from his target.

"Where's your boss?" When the man hesitated, Trace applied pressure to the knife.

"Gawd, enough! Okay, okay. He's tucked away safe in another room."

Chickenshit move—but with rightful concern. "Which way?"

"South corridor. Four rooms down."

In the darkness, with so many separate cubbyhole rooms to choose from, Belford might have slipped out one of the many broken windows before they found him. The yard was as disjointed as the interior, with plenty of avenues of escape.

"How were you to alert him?" No way in hell would a cell phone work in the bowels of the towering brick factory.

"Walkie-talkie, on my belt."

Trace looked to Murray. He'd put away his piece and now stood with arms crossed, expression studious. "Call him."

Nodding, Trace squeezed his arm closer around the man's throat. "Tell him it's all good. Get him here." When the big guy started to move, Trace warned, "Slowly."

With appropriate caution, the man withdrew the walkie-talkie and pressed a button. "All secure, Boss."

Through the scratchy receiver, Belford said, "Deal is set?"

"Yeah, yeah." Showing too much anxiety, the man said, "It's fine."

"You're saying they agreed to my price?"

Near the man's ear, Trace whispered, "Tell him we're willing to talk about it." Claiming the terms were agreed upon without further negotiation would be absurd—and a clear tip-off that things weren't right.

After more discussion, arrangements were made. With Belford on his way, Trace said to the guy, "Time to sleep."

Alarm racked the big man before Trace tightened his arm brutally, squeezing until he went limp. He was a heavy load, and once he passed out, Trace let him drop without much concern for how he landed on the concrete floor. As he went down, Trace grabbed the hilt of his knife. It came free as if slipping from butter.

He wiped it off on the front of the man's dress shirt.

Blood oozed from the wound to form a puddle on the floor. Trace wasted no time securing his victim's feet together and his arms behind his back with nylon restraints. He shoved the body back, ensuring Belford wouldn't see it as he entered the room.

Murray joined Trace. "Nice work."

Trace came back to his feet and looked toward the south corridor.

"He could bleed to death," Murray mused.

"Do you care? Because I don't."

"No skin off my nose. Good riddance to them both." Murray spat on the downed fellow, then looked around the room and made a sound of disgust. "Hard to believe the bastard keeps the women in this hellhole."

Trace couldn't stop himself from an expression of disbelief. Murray had just given away valuable info. But more startling than that was the idea that he cared how the women were treated.

Imagining them, frightened, mistreated, being kept in the cold, raw room filled Trace with disgust and brought up even more disturbing, dangerous images of his sister in a similar situation. His fists tightened enough to crack his knuckles.

A chill emanated from the concrete floors and the rough brick walls hung with cracked cement, cobwebs and worse. The windows were either blackened with smoke, or jagged death traps of broken glass.

Going for a tone of impartiality, Trace said, "I suppose it's as good as any other prison."

"Maybe. But what's the point of me giving him quality merchandise if he's only going to foul it up in this place? A smart businessman would secure cleaner, and more secure, accommodations."

That Murray referred to women as articles of trade always rankled Trace. But he agreed with the security issue. He nodded toward the windows. "It'd take twenty-four-hour surveillance to keep anyone from making a run for it."

"He's not that dumb. He stores them in the windowless basement. This room is like day care in comparison."

Another piece of information. Trace hid his rage beneath curiosity. "You've seen the basement?"

Murray lifted one massive shoulder. "In years past, I used it a few times myself. But not since I've...*refined* my business."

A tendril of something dark and sinister slithered down Trace's spine. Had Priss's mother been kept here? Had she been one of Murray's first victims? When possible, he'd check to see how long the factory had been shut down.

"Here he comes." Trace nodded toward the empty corridor.

"I don't see anyone."

"Just wait."

Seconds later, a shadow elongated and morphed into the shape of a man.

Trace took the lead, stepping in front of Murray and asking, "Mr. Belford?"

"Yes." Beady eyes darted around the room. "Where's Dugo?"

Assuming it was Dugo now passed out on the floor, out of sight, Trace took a few more steps forward. "Don't worry about that right now." He caught Belford's arm. "I'm sure you understand if we utilize some security precautions."

Belford tried to take a hasty step back. "What do you mean?"

"Simple pat down, that's all." Trace kept his hold tight. "Gotta make sure you're not carrying."

"Oh." His gaze moved past Trace to Murray. "I understand. Of course."

Trace went through the motions, but Belford had no more than a wallet, cell phone and the required walkie-talkie on his person.

To further alarm the prick, Trace relieved him of all three, moving them well out of his reach.

Murray smiled. "Come, Belford. Join us."

More skittish by the moment, Belford stepped forward—and saw Dugo bleeding on the floor. "Dear God, you've murdered him!"

"He's alive," Trace told him. And then, because he had to know, he asked, "Anyone else in the building?"

"No." Belford shook his head in dismay. "No one."

"Be damn sure you tell me the truth. Because if I find out otherwise—"

"I believe," Murray said, "that my man wants to know if you currently have any women occupying the basement."

Belford shook his head again. "No. It's…well, it's set

up for the cargo I'll get from you. That is, if—if we still have a deal?"

"We do," Murray told him. "At the original price we agreed upon."

"Oh, but I thought…" Gulping, he glanced at Dugo. "Yes, that's fine."

When Dugo stirred, Trace shut down Belford's hopes, saying, "He's not going to save you, so forget it."

"Right." Running a hand over his head, then over his gut, Belford cleared his throat. "Well, if everything is settled, then…"

Trace saw the gleam in Murray's eyes. Belford might not understand it, but Trace knew exactly what that look meant: bloodshed, abuse, devastation.

For once, he didn't mind. If anyone needed a little devastation it was Belford.

Casually, Trace moved into position behind him. A worm like Belford didn't deserve a direct face-off.

When Murray nodded, Belford tried to bolt. Trace halted him with a shattering punch to his kidneys and Belford, after bowing forward, collapsed in on himself to join his man on the floor.

Without looking away from Belford, Trace asked Murray, "How bad do you want it?"

"I'll tell you when to stop."

With Belford's face still twisted in pain, Trace lifted him up by his shirtfront, popping several buttons in the process, and went to work. He used his fists, his elbows, his knees and his feet. With every blow, he thought of what this man had conspired to do against women. What he *would* do if Trace didn't stop him.

Murray's time would come, but for now, he could dish out partial retribution to one of the players. Not a perfect solution, but it'd do for now.

As he worked over Belford, Murray talked to him,

taunting him every so often, conveying little details of their arrangement.

Trace made a mental note of every word said while again pretending to be a robot on autopilot to fulfill Murray's vicious request.

Five minutes later, with Trace not even breathing hard and a few of Belford's teeth on the floor mixing with blood and at least one bone broken, Murray lifted a hand to call a halt.

Trace stepped back and Belford, barely conscious, slumped to his ass on the cold floor, hanging his bruised and bleeding head.

Murray moved to stand over him. "Understand, please, this was a lesson in honor. We made a deal and, for me, once a deal is set, there is no further negotiation."

Belford managed a weak nod of assent.

"I figured you'd get the point. *Now.*" Murray chuckled and slapped Trace on the back. "Good work."

Flexing his knuckles, bile burning his throat, Trace thought of Priss. He thought of her jibes and her scent and her headstrong manner, and was rewarded with a cleansing breath of fresh air.

He needed her now more than ever; though he was beginning to think he'd needed her, her specifically, for a very long time.

"We're through here?"

"Nah." Murray nodded toward Dugo. "Kill him."

That wasn't part of the plan, but Trace wouldn't balk over taking out a participant in the human-trafficking racket. In the end, he hoped to kill them all.

He withdrew his gun and took aim.

Murray touched his wrist. "On second thought, Belford might need him to get home. You're so thorough that he's in worse shape than Dugo."

Trace dropped the hand holding the gun. His temper prickled. "Another fucking test?"

Murray laughed. "And as always, you passed with gusto." He nudged Belford with the toe of his custom-made shoe. "You'll take the women, all of them, at the agreed-upon price and, in the end, when you make your profit, you'll realize how valuable this exchange has been."

Belford made a sound of agreement.

Squatting down by him, Murray said, "Unfortunately, I'm one girl short of our agreement. Consider it a toll for making me come here and explain myself. Got it?"

Again Belford struggled to give reply.

"Great. Show up with the money, don't ever try my patience again, and we can put this unpleasantness behind us." And with that, Murray regained his feet and started out.

Trace backed out behind him; the men were fallen, but they weren't entirely incapacitated, and he didn't take chances.

Outside, Murray stretched. "That was entertaining. Two fights in one night, against how many men now?"

"Four." He opened Murray's door for him. "I'm not counting Belford."

That made Murray laugh, and on the drive back to the office, he engaged in small talk, almost as if the extreme violence of the past hour hadn't taken place. It was another indication of his sickness.

Another reason to put him down.

Rain pounded from the sky, leaving the streets steaming from the earlier heat of the day, as Trace escorted Murray into the office. They went past an army of night guards and most of them not only nodded to Murray, they deferred to Trace as they would a drill sargeant.

Idiots, all of them. Most knew what they did, who they

protected, but some of them went by the creed of "seeing nothing, hearing nothing, repeating nothing."

Almost to himself, Murray said, "You're better than all of them put together."

He was, but Murray's mood was strange, too introspective, and he didn't want to find all the guards dead in the morning. "They have their uses."

"True enough." Murray strode into his office and went straight to the bar. "Drink?"

"No, thanks." He wasn't about to muddle his senses with alcohol, and besides, he didn't trust Murray or Hell not to slip something into his drink.

Of course that thought led him to Priss and unrelenting guilt.

Murray sprawled into his chair. "I have a slew of employees on different levels performing many different duties. But for the business I'm in and the security I require, you're far more valuable to me than the rest."

Trace eyed him. He didn't know if Murray wanted to promote him, confide in him or fuck him. "Was there something else you needed from me tonight?"

For the longest time Murray studied him, then he laughed and shook his head. "No. You're free to go."

"You're sure?" If Murray wanted to spill his guts, Trace damn straight wanted to listen.

"Get some sleep," Murray suggested. "You've surely tired yourself after the brutality of the day."

"No."

Amused, Murray tilted his head. "No, you won't sleep, or no, you aren't tired?"

Trace shrugged. "Both, I guess." He looked at his watch. "You think Helene is done with Priscilla yet?"

"Doubtful." Rocking back in his big office chair, Murray cradled the glass of whiskey and propped his feet on the desk. "For tonight, don't worry about Priscilla."

"Great." Thank God Jackson would keep Helene from getting anywhere near Priss. "Then I think I'll get some dinner, maybe hit up a club."

"Missing your social time lately?"

Trace thought about how to answer, and settled on saying, "Following up a fight with a relaxing lay suits me."

"If you can call what you do a fight," Murray snorted. "You're so damn fast and effective, there's no real fight to it."

"Did you want it otherwise?"

Shaking his head, Murray said, "No, that wasn't a complaint, just an observation. But I understand the adrenaline rush, so go and get some relief, but stay on call in case something comes up."

"Always."

"Oh, and, Trace?"

One hand on the door, Trace glanced back.

"I've decided to move up my lunch with Priscilla. I'm anxious to see her now that she's been made over."

One blow after another. Cautiously, Trace turned to face him. "All right." He wanted to ask why the change, but didn't dare push things.

"I have to admit I'm curious about Helene's effect on her, too." Murray watched him. "Think she'll be hysterical, or accepting?"

Staring him in the eyes, Trace said only, "Hard to say."

"Women are all so different," Murray mused in agreement. "And yet, they're all weak."

Trace kept quiet.

"We'll keep the meeting private, but I want you there watching on as security—just in case things get out of hand."

Meaning if Priss didn't go along with Murray's twisted plans? "I can take care of it."

"No, I'll make the arrangements with Alice myself." Murray smiled. "I'll let you know the details."

As far as dismissals went, that wasn't too subtle. Trace nodded and let himself out. Despite what he'd told Murray, he had no interest in clubs or other women.

The sex…yeah, that sounded right. But only with Priss. *God, he needed her.*

Anxious to make a private call to Jackson to check on Priss's welfare, Trace headed straight for his apartment. There was enough traffic to make it difficult to spot anyone following him, but he did notice one set of headlights that stayed too close.

When he pulled into the lot next to the apartment, the car went on past. Trace waited, but didn't see it return. Besides, with Priss elsewhere, the threat was minimal.

Just in case, he waited a minute more, and then pulled into the apartment parking lot. If the coast was clear and no one had followed Jackson, he would shower off the blood and then go to her.

He could hardly wait to get her close, to touch her, taste her…to get her under him.

If fate dealt him a winning hand, tonight would be the night.

BLOOD PUMPING HOT AND FAST, Helene waited just inside the entry doors of Trace's hotel. After finding Priss's apartment empty, she decided she would not waste the night. They thought they were so clever, but they had underestimated her.

Even through the rain, she had a clear view of the parking lot. Trace, always so cautious, furtively checked everything and everyone—but he didn't see her, she made sure of that.

As she waited, he left the car, turned up his jacket collar and, ignoring the rain, pulled out his cell phone to put in a call.

When he started in, she ducked to the side of the foyer, partially behind a tall plastic plant, not really hiding, but not exactly making herself noticeable, either.

She had hoped that Trace would have Priscilla with him, and to that end, she'd brought plenty of her special formula with her, enough to make them both pay, enough that they would finally understand what she could and would do.

Unfortunately, Trace entered alone, speaking intently into the phone.

To Murray? She couldn't hear what he said, but she didn't think so. The usual curt deference reserved for Murray wasn't in evidence. In fact, he almost—but not quite—smiled. No, he spoke to someone else, someone friendlier than Murray.

From his fair hair to his broad shoulders and down that strong back to his powerful thighs, Helene's gaze went over him.

She shivered.

Having Trace defenseless against her, even dependent upon her, would be better, much better, than playing with Priss.

Almost as if he felt her heated interest, Trace suddenly stopped—and oh, so slowly turned to face her.

Their gazes clashed, held.

Something dangerous, something ultimately deadly shone in his mesmerizing hazel eyes. She breathed harder, her stomach tightening, her sex growing damp.

She'd wanted him from day one, but he'd always treated her with contempt. Tonight, he would do as she wanted. He'd have no choice.

"Hello, Trace."

He dropped the hand holding the phone, keeping it lax at his side. "Helene. What are you doing here? Where's Priscilla?"

Gliding up to him, feeling the taut pull of her nipples and the burning rush of lust, she smiled. "You tell me."

"You were supposed to be with her." His brows, so much darker than his light blond hair, pinched down, but his voice remained neutral. "You damned lunatic. I know you didn't finish with her so quickly, so what did you do? Kill her?"

Strange, but he didn't seem overly alarmed by the possibility. But then, maybe he had known Priss wouldn't be there when she arrived. "I never even got to see her. Her apartment was empty."

"Where is she?"

Shrugging, Helene trailed a fingernail down his damp chest. "I assumed you swept her away."

Catching her wrist in a bruising hold, Trace tossed her off him. "Keep your stories straight. I was with Murray."

"So where is she then, hmm?"

"No idea, but I know where *I'm* going." He dropped the cell into his jacket pocket and turned his back on her, striding away.

Rushing to keep up with him, Hell asked, "To bed? That's perfect for me."

"Go fuck yourself." He kept walking. "That's the only way you'll get laid, because I'm sure as hell not touching you."

No one should ever underestimate this man. He was cagey, slicker, and maybe more cruel than even Murray. His reflexes impressed her, and his body combined with his confidence left her desperate to experience him.

She kept a safe distance.

Without looking at her, he said, "Go away, Helene."

"When I came specifically to see you? Not a chance."

Over his shoulder, he pinned her with his sharp gaze. "How'd you know where I was staying?"

"Murray doesn't keep secrets from me."

That made him laugh. "If you say so."

As Trace retrieved his card key from his wallet and unlocked his door, she slowly withdrew two hypodermics from her pocket. She'd meant one for Priss, one for Trace, but having Trace all to herself would be very sweet.

And two needles would work to her advantage, given his caution.

She removed the caps on the needles. With care, she tucked one into the back waistband on her skirt, but left the other visible.

He didn't appear to be paying any attention to her at all.

"You won't be able to ignore me for long." As quickly as she could while still trying to be furtive, Helene reached out to him with the needle, intending to stick him in the shoulder.

Trace turned too fast for her to dodge him. One hand on her throat, the other clamped onto her arm, he slammed her up against the wall.

Her pulse raced.

Staring into her eyes, so commanding, so much fury, he squeezed her arm until she winced—and dropped the needle.

"You conniving bitch." He crushed it beneath his boot heel, leaving a damp spot in the carpet. "You were going to drug me?"

"Yes." Staring at his mouth, Hell licked her lips and leaned toward him. "I have a special elixir just for you, Trace."

Revulsion hardened his expression even more and he put space between them. "What special elixir?"

After flexing her hand to bring circulation back to her arm, Hell braced both hands behind her. The pose was innocent, unthreatening. "Murray wanted a concoction, an aphrodisiac, that'd make the women more pliable, more… agreeable to the sexual side of things."

"Because a comatose woman can't argue?"

"She can't. But Murray wanted the women awake and anxious to meet their fates. Titillating, don't you think?"

"I think you're overselling." His narrowed gaze sharpened. "Something like that doesn't exist."

"It most definitely does—now." It wasn't often that she got to brag on her skills. "My serum makes the blood sing and sets the body on fire. And almost by accident, I've found that it works particularly well on men." She moved up against him. "One dose and you'll be so hard, so throbbing, you'll be begging me for relief. So how about we go inside and get started?"

"Not happening." He pushed away from her as if she were a vile thing. "Go home. Go to Murray."

"I can't." Truthfully, she preferred his resistance. If he conceded to her wishes, if he gave in, he wouldn't be nearly as desirable. She'd been chased, and she'd been dominated. Sometimes, though, she preferred the chasing—or dominating. "I want *you,* Trace."

"I'd say I'm sorry, but I'm not. Stay the fuck away from me." Clearly repulsed, he turned to his door.

Quick as she could, Hell freed the needle and in one motion swung her arm up and around, stabbing it hard into his muscled backside.

As much from reflex, as outrage, Trace backhanded her. The blow sent her sprawling to the floor, her legs in inelegant display and her face stinging. She tasted blood on her lip, and that, too, inflamed her.

Trace didn't realize it yet, but it was too late for him.

Appalled, outraged, he stared at her in incomprehension. "What did you do?"

She licked her bloody lip. "I sealed your fate."

He jerked the needle free, staring at it until it slipped out of his hand. Voice already slurring, he asked, "What the hell did you do?"

Helene forced herself back up to her feet. She straightened her skirt, smoothed her blouse.

She'd been struck before, of course, but never quite like that; Murray had never wanted to bruise her face.

Trace was the most powerful man she'd ever encountered. She worked her jaw and winced. It wasn't broken, but she'd have one hell of a bruise come morning, and probably a fat lip, too. It'd be tough explaining to Murray, but she'd figure out something.

And as soon as possible, she'd make Trace pay for the inconvenience.

She smiled. "Come on, big boy. Inside, before you drop here in the hallway and someone calls the police. None of us wants that to happen."

Because his thoughts were already muddling, he didn't fight her as she led him into the room, but he ground out, "I'll kill you for this."

Cooing to him, Helene said, "I know you'll try." She closed and locked the door. "But not before I've had my way with every inch of your delicious body."

He slumped back to the wall and slowly slid down to the carpeted floor.

"Don't worry, baby." Watching him, Helene peeled off her jacket and dropped it over a chair. "You're going to be wide-awake and very aware of everything I do to you, every kiss and touch, every lick and suck, *everything*. It's only for a half hour or so that you're going to be helpless and I need that time to get you all secured and situated." She stepped over him.

Trace made one last feeble attempt to retrieve his cell phone from his pocket.

She laughed. "Now who do you think to call?"

More succinctly than she'd expected, he said, "No one."

And he closed the phone.

Smiling, feeling indulgent with his continued refusal to accept his fate—the fate she'd give him—Helene took the phone and put it out of his reach. "Oh, Trace." She touched his jaw. "This is going to be so much fun. For me."

CHAPTER FIFTEEN

THE HORROR OF WHAT they'd just overheard left Jackson and Priss staring at each other. It was Priss who reacted first.

"Why are you standing there?" She shoved Jackson hard. "You heard everything. That bitch is going to molest him!"

Looking a little sick, Jackson whispered, "Yeah." He looked away. "Or worse."

Her stomach cramped and her eyes burned. She covered her mouth. "God only knows what she's capable of."

"I shouldn't have said that." Jackson closed the now-dead phone and knotted his fingers in his hair. "And I shouldn't have put him on speaker phone."

"I wouldn't have given the phone back to you otherwise!" Trace had called with instructions for Jackson to do a check on an old factory. He wanted a blueprint to the building, and he wanted to know how long it had been out of operation and who owned it now. From what she'd heard, Jackson would leave much of that research to Dare, who would likely leave it to Chris. Little by little, she was learning the chain of command, and how they worked together as a minimal unit to accomplish so much.

After the business discussion, Trace had also asked about her, and when he found out she was fine and dandy—Jackson didn't mention his cavalier treatment of the shower incident—he'd wanted to speak with her.

Priss was hoping that he'd come to her, that they could continue what he'd started. But before much was said, someone joined him. The conversation was muffled, but when Priss realized he was talking to Helene she'd known something was wrong. She'd asked Jackson how to put the cell phone on speaker so he could hear, too.

Jackson looked almost comically lost, so Priss shoved him again. "You have to go help him."

Shaking his head in the negative, Jackson said, "If he'd wanted help, he'd have said so."

"He couldn't!"

"Baloney. Trace is cagey. He'd have gotten a message through, but instead he ended the call. You heard him, Priss. She asked him who he was calling, and he said no one. And that was the message."

"You don't know that!"

"I know that he wants me to stay right on top of you."

"Idiot!" She wasn't the one currently in trouble.

He frowned at her. "You know what I mean. In the figurative sense. If Trace had wanted me there, he could have said something…but he didn't."

He wasn't going to go help Trace? *"Are you out of your mind?"*

"He *didn't,* Priss." Jackson paced away, looking almost as tortured as she felt. "Jesus. I know Trace. He's slick. If he thought he couldn't handle it—"

Handle Helene raping him? Oh, sure, he could maybe handle that.

But *she* couldn't. And besides, who knew where Helene would draw the line? She could disfigure Trace with her warped idea of lust. And thinking that almost made her scream.

Unwilling to wait for Jackson to come to his senses,

Priss spun around on her heel and headed for the door. "I'm going to him."

"What? No, wait." He caught her before she'd taken two full steps. "You don't have a car."

"I can grab a cab."

Harassed, he shook her. "You don't have any money."

"So give me some money!"

He squeezed his eyes shut. "Helene." Shuddering in real reaction, he whispered, "I wouldn't wish that fate on any guy. Well, you know, some guys are into that perverse shit, but Trace…no way. He'll puke. He'll wash his skin in bleach. He'll—"

Priss slapped him.

Jackson's head snapped around with the strength of the blow, but came back slowly, his eyes narrowed and mean. "Damn it, woman—"

She grabbed a fistful of chest hair and yanked his face down close to hers.

"Oeowww!"

Priss had no sympathy for him. "Let's. Go."

Through clenched teeth, with the first real anger she'd seen from Jackson, he ordered, "Turn me loose. Right *now!*"

Nerves twitching, Priss opened her fingers and Jackson stepped back, rubbing his chest. He glared at her.

"Be reasonable," she said, trying for a more cajoling tone. "He needs us."

"All right. I suppose I should— Wait…what did you say? You want to go *with* me?"

He made it sound like it was the most absurd thing ever. Priss tried to be very clear. "I will not stay here. If you don't go, I will. If you try to go without me, I'll find a way to get there on my own."

As he strode into his bedroom, he said, "You're asking the impossible."

"Not asking. Stating as fact." He returned, pulling a T-shirt on over his head. "I am going. With you or without you. Now what's it to be?"

He glared at her. "Okay."

"Really?" She was surprised at his quick turnaround.

"But only if you promise me that you'll lay low and do exactly as I say, no questions asked and no arguments."

She wouldn't promise him anything. "We're wasting time."

"Promise me, or I swear I'll hold you here and neither of us will go."

Her mouth fell open. "What do you mean, you'll hold me here?"

"You're not dumb, Priss. You know what I mean." Leaning close, nose to nose, he enunciated, "By force. Hell, woman, I'll sit on you if I have to." Only half under his breath, he murmured, "I've kinda wanted to do that anyway."

She drew back, but he caught her fist. "Promise right now that you'll behave."

She'd behave, all right. She'd behave any damn way she pleased. "Sure. I promise."

Disgust showed on his handsome face. "That's about the most insincere promise I've ever heard." He rearranged his hold on her to take her hand in his. "Come on. Let's go."

She was still barefoot and hardly dressed appropriately, but this time, Priss didn't give a single thought to their audience. She cared only about reaching Trace.

For his part, Jackson was as cautious as ever, and even knowing it was necessary, it drove her nuts because it slowed them down. In her mind she kept imagining what Hell might be doing to Trace, and how Trace might react.

Jackson was right; he wouldn't like it. That much she knew.

But if Helene truly had a drug that'd make him more agreeable… No, she wouldn't think about that right now. She couldn't.

Not that long ago she'd left her home, entrusting her business to nasty old Gary Deaton so she could pursue her need for revenge. She'd expected to come up against danger, rejection, abuse.

But never, not once, had she considered anything that had transpired so far.

She definitely hadn't considered falling in love at light speed with a man opposed to all her plans.

Yet…she had.

She'd fallen hook, line and sinker, irrevocably, head over heels, madly, impossibly in love.

"Drive faster," she ordered Jackson, and then ignored his grumbling reply.

The question was, now that she'd accepted the truth, what should she do about it?

Or would she get a chance to do anything at all?

TIED UP WITH HIS ARMS behind his back, his pants below his knees, his legs parted, Trace finally regained use of his limbs. Unfortunately, Hell had secured him tightly to keep him in that exact position.

Propped upright against a heating unit on the wall, Hell used an exposed pipe to secure his wrists. It kept him in an awkward sitting position. He tried moving his arms, but realized she'd fastened them together with handcuffs.

Using the same nylon restraints he favored, maybe taken from his own stash, she'd bound each of his ankles to heavy bedroom furniture, one to the bed, one to a nightstand that was screwed to the wall. When he tried to twist, he realized he had a raging hard-on.

Trace looked down at himself, then dropped his head back in loathing. God, he hurt. A deep, sexual hurt.

As if he'd indulged in hours of foreplay, his entire body throbbed with the need to ejaculate.

Helene stepped over him, one stiletto-clad foot at the outside of each of his knees. She'd unbuttoned her blouse to expose her breasts, and had hiked up her skirt to the top of her thighs.

The bawdy stance showed her lack of panties and her long bare legs. "Finally regained your wits, I see. I figured a guy in your superb shape would recover quicker, and you did."

Trace stared at her, his hatred palpable. "What the *hell* do you think you're doing?" He gasped as she leaned down and teased one finger along his rigid shaft. His back bowed, his breath hissing in.

"Nice. Very, very nice." Positioning herself on her knees between his thighs, Helene licked her lips and bent to brush her cheek along his dick.

"Stop it!" Trace tried to rebel, to reject her, but he couldn't move more than a few inches either way. "You sicken me, Helene."

"And yet—" she held him in her soft, hot hand "—you're so hard for me."

"Hard from whatever you had in that needle. Not for you. Never for you."

She smiled and, still holding him in one hand, stroked her nails over his bare chest. "I have a thing for hairy chests. How did you know?"

"Stop this." He hoped he sounded calmer than he felt. Even though she only held him, her hand still, her fingers not too tight, he felt on the verge of exploding. "Helene, listen to me…"

"I can't wait to taste you, Trace. All of you. I want you to come in my mouth. What do you think about that?"

Succinct, to the point, Trace said, "I'll kill you."

Smiling, Hell stroked her fingernails along the inside of his knee. "Murray won't like that."

"He won't like you sucking my cock, either."

"So maybe we won't tell him about that." She leaned down and licked the inside of his thigh.

At the touch of her hot, moist tongue, Trace almost lost it. He squeezed his eyes shut, clenched his teeth and thought about Priss.

Helene ended the lick just short of his testicles. "You know, if Murray found out about any of this, he would take it out on both of us." Using her thumb, she teased the head of his cock.

It was maddening, and Trace knew if she didn't stop, he'd come. And then he heard a sound, faint but distinct.

Someone had just entered the connecting room.

Damn, damn, damn.

Had Jackson left Priss alone? Was that exactly what Helene had wanted? Maybe she'd had someone follow Jackson after all and knew that Priss would be vulnerable—

Helene lifted her head. "Did you hear something?"

Trace was relieved to see her looking genuinely surprised by the possible intrusion. "Yeah, I did. It was me complaining." He spoke loud enough to cover up any more telltale noise from the other room. "Stop and think, Helene. If you do this, Murray will find out—"

"Shhh." Putting a finger to his lips, she cocked her head to listen. "Be quiet." She stood and went to the table for his gun.

No. "First you think to rape me, and now you plan to shoot someone?" Attention divided by his bodily needs and his compulsion to keep others safe, Trace's voice sounded more raw than usual. "You said it yourself that we don't want the police involved. But if you fire that gun, no way in hell will you keep them away."

"True." She turned thoughtful, and then lifted his stun baton instead, hefting it in her hand, testing the weight of it.

Trace cursed low. It wasn't easy to focus with blood burning through his veins, his skin on fire and his cock twitchy, but he tried.

"That's not much better, Helene. You could still kill with that, and if you leave behind a victim—"

"You mean other than you?"

Hard-jawed, Trace nodded. "Yes, other than me. Murray won't easily accept a mess of yours that he has to clean up.

"Perhaps." She came back to crouch over him.

Though the nearness of that baton left his nerves jumping, he didn't look at it. He wouldn't give her the satisfaction of knowing his unease. "I'll tell him about this myself."

"I doubt that." Her thumb on the button as a tacit threat, she stroked the baton over his body. "The connecting room did seem strange to me. Who's over there, Trace?"

"How the fuck should I know?"

"Oh, I think you know." She moved the baton between his legs. "You're too cautious to be in a connecting room next to someone without doing a full background check."

True, but he wouldn't tell her shit.

She cuddled his balls a second, then sighed and stood. "Make a sound, and I'll switch to the gun and to hell with the consequences."

Picking up more restraints, she moved to the connecting door and stood to the side.

Seconds ticked by, and then a full minute.

At least Jackson was being smart, Trace thought. He was taking his time, not rushing things or charging in like a white knight. Of course, he expected no less of him. If Jackson had been the reckless type, he and Dare never would have brought him on board.

Unfortunately, Helene showed incredible patience. She kept her gaze off his body so she wouldn't be distracted, giving Trace an opportunity to seek ways of escape.

He didn't find many. The handcuffs were so tight that his arms were going numb.

But she had left his watch on his wrist, and he wiggled around until he was able to get hold of it. It wasn't easy from this angle, bound as he was, but he managed to remove the tiny pin hidden in the band. He went to work picking the lock on the handcuffs. If he could get his hands free…

He saw his knife on the table with his gun. The knife was all he needed. But could he reach it with his legs still hobbled?

His gaze jerked back to the door when the knob, ever so slowly, started to turn. It had barely opened two inches when Helene jammed the baton through and pressed the trigger button.

The sound of arching electricity mixed with Jackson's groans. When Helene finally let up, his body fell into the room. Lightning fast, Helene was on him, straddling the small of his back to secure his wrists behind him.

When Jackson stirred enough to react, she zapped him again.

"Helene, stop it!"

"All right." She smiled, and stroked a hand over Jackson's ass.

Jesus, why was Jackson even here? Trace hadn't asked him to come. He'd even closed the damn phone.

Hadn't he?

At this point, after the drugs, things were kind of hazy.

Jackson groaned again.

Dredging up a more commanding tone, Trace said, "Leave him alone."

"Not until he's incapacitated." Helene tossed the stun baton off to the side and wrapped the nylon around Jackson's ankles, too. But she did so over his jeans, which would at least give him a little wiggle room.

With that complete, she backed away from him. "Well, well. It's like Christmas morning." Breathing hard, she looked at Jackson top to toes—and smiled.

Jackson grunted out something that sounded vaguely like "Fuck you." He rolled to his back.

Helene kicked his ankle. "Anyone else in that room?"

Trace stared into the other room, but saw nothing and no one.

Still grimacing in pain, Jackson repositioned his legs, bending his knees and bracing his heels on the floor. To the casual observer, it appeared he only wanted to ease his discomfort. Trace knew better. Though Jackson's arms were tight behind him, he could be deadly with his legs. "See for yourself."

To do so, she'd have to get close to Jackson again. She'd have to get in range.

"Ah, no." Helene crossed her arms and laughed. "If you're even half as good as Trace—"

"Who's Trace?" He glanced over, tucked in his chin at seeing Trace's naked boner, and said with sympathy, "Damn, man, she really has you sprung, doesn't she?"

Helene put her hands on her hips. "I'm not buying it, so save your breath."

"Buying what?"

"You two know each other, and that means if I get too close you'll find a way to…do something to me."

"Nah, sugar. I don't know what that dude did to piss you off, but I'm harmless. I promise."

"Somehow I doubt that." She chewed her swollen lip. "Push yourself away from the door."

With a shrug, Jackson did as she asked. "Now what?"

She circled him, cautiously. "Now you tell me who you are."

"Innocent bystander?"

Though her smile didn't waver, her eyes narrowed the tiniest bit. "You think you're really clever, don't you?"

"Obviously not clever enough." He wiggled some more until he was able to sit up against the wall. "Damn, woman. Care to tell me what this is all about?"

Still playing innocent, Trace realized. Not that Helene would buy it. But at least it kept her occupied, and he *almost* had the lock free.…

As if in deep thought, Helene ran the fingers of her free hand along her cleavage, slowly, back and forth. "You're quite the morsel, aren't you?" Her attention went to Jackson's lap, his abs, and then back to his face. "Hmm. Now what should I do with you?"

Grinning at her, he said, "Did I overhear some discussion about blow jobs?"

She leaned in long enough to slug him in the face, then quickly backed away again.

Trace had never in his life felt so helpless. Who was with Priss? How the hell would this twisted scenario end now that Jackson had flubbed his way into it?

And worse, what would Murray's reaction be to all this?

Jackson flexed his jaw, and continued with his easy

humor. "Maybe I misunderstood. I could've sworn I heard you mention—"

"Shut up!" She stomped back over to her purse and, with her back to the men, fiddled with something. Jackson was about to push to his feet when she returned, one hand behind her back.

He eyed her cautiously. "Change your mind, then, sugar?"

"Possibly." Crouching down near him, but not too near, Helene said, "But not until I have you properly sedated." She parted her knees, giving Jackson an eyeful—and the idiot looked. "When I get done with you, you won't be so damned handsome."

"Well, it's bound to be an improvement. Being this good-looking is a curse. The women won't leave me alone." He smiled at her. "Case in point."

She presented the needle.

Jackson scowled. "You don't need that."

Tapping the syringe, she let one drop leak from the end. "It'll make you all nice and easy to get along with. Better still, it'll shut you up for a bit." Grinning, Helene nodded toward Trace. "How do you think I got him tied up?"

"I thought maybe he was willing."

"No." She smiled. "But don't worry. It's not going to hurt you. Not too bad, anyway. And there are no serious side effects."

"I'm not sure I believe that."

"Oh, stop being a baby. Do you really think I want dead bodies left behind? Well, I don't."

Jackson positioned his feet again. "Lady, you are not sticking me with that."

"Oh, I believe I am." She held it like a dagger in her fist, raised high, ready to stab him wherever she could.

And Priss appeared out of nowhere. Without making

a sound, she slipped into the room, swooped up the discarded stun baton and jolted Helene with a steady stream of electricity.

Trace felt the lock give away. Quick as he could, he started freeing his hands.

Priss held the baton steady, her face twisted with rage, her body rigid. The needle fell out of Helene's hand, and Jackson was quick to use his heel to bring it closer to him.

The handcuffs caught in the pipe, frustrating Trace.

Jackson surged to his feet, then propped himself against the wall, hobbled by his ankle restraints. "Good timing, darlin'."

Dear God. With every second that passed, they ran the risk of Priss's duplicity being discovered. Trace would kick Jackson's ass for this stunt later, but for right now, he wanted to ensure Priss's safety.

Given the circumstances, any other woman would be hysterical. But not Priss. She was clearheaded enough to time her entrance to go unnoticed, to retrieve and use the stun baton with devastating effect—possibly deadly effect if she didn't let up.

Her jaw tightened as she clenched her teeth and kept on firing.

Trace had no choice but to take control. Calmly, his voice low and even, he said, "She's done for, honey. I need you to ease up now."

Priss didn't seem to hear him. She looked determined to inflict more damage.

Helene fell to her back, her body jerking and flinching. Her eyes rolled back and spittle formed at the sides of her mouth.

"Enough." Though she probably felt justified, Trace knew that the last thing Priss needed was a death on her conscience. "I said that's enough!"

Almost as if in a struggle, Priss managed to release the trigger. She panted, her arms still stiff, ready to go at Helene again if she moved.

"That's it." Trace tried to sound soothing. "Good job."

"Damn it." Priss issued the complaint while looking at her hand. "She made me break a nail."

Jackson huffed out a quick laugh. When Hell twitched and moaned, he turned and dropped down atop her, his knees straddling her hips, her arms pinned down, and his body blocking her view of the rest of the room. "I've got this."

"Better late than never." Finally, Trace managed to untangle the metal cuffs from the pipe. He half stood, half leaned on the bed. Until he freed his legs, his range of movement and leverage would be limited. "Give me my knife."

Pulling her gaze away from Helene, Priss turned to him—and went stock-still. "Oh." She stared at Trace's naked body and said again, "Oh."

"The knife."

Face pinching with outrage, Priss looked at Helene again. "She was going to—"

"I know what she was going to do."

Anyone could see that Priss considered inflicting more damage on Helene. Trace said firmly, "Don't do it."

Jackson glanced over his shoulder, then choked down a snicker. "You see what I've been dealing with? It ain't natural."

Too furious and too primed to talk, Trace pulled his pants back up but didn't bother fastening them over his aching erection. If Jackson dared make a single comment about his condition, he'd flatten him.

He said again, "The *knife*." His commanding tone finally got through to Priss and she moved with belated alacrity.

"Sorry." She snatched up the knife and came to him.

Trace held out his hand, but instead of giving it to him, Priss went to work on the restraints, wielding the knife with clumsy inefficiency, sawing needlessly before finally cutting through the resistant nylon. "She made these so tight...."

"Quiet." Taking the knife from her, Trace surged over to Jackson and released his hands. He gave him the handcuffs and, with the most pressing issues resolved, turned back to Priss. "I want you out of here."

In that instant, Helene started to come around. Jackson flipped her to her stomach and secured the handcuffs to her wrists. She moaned, and Jackson said, "Sorry, sweetheart," before giving her a sharp tap to the jaw.

She went out like a light again. He sat back against the wall, his legs over Helene, using her like a footstool, and frowned at Trace. "I can explain."

Trace gave him one hard, direct look. "Shut up."

"Right." Going silent, Jackson concentrated on freeing his ankles.

"Don't be mad at him," Priss interjected. "I insisted—"

Bodily turning Priss, Trace headed her toward the connecting room. "Not another word out of you, and don't you dare move until I come for you."

"Trace..."

"Now."

She jumped at his hard, furious tone, but damn it, he couldn't moderate his temper. When she started to speak again, he gave her his deadliest stare. He'd been through a day of hell, and finding her anywhere near the carnage was enough to send him through the roof. Control? Shot to hell.

With any luck, Helene didn't know who had stunned her, and Trace wanted to keep it that way. She couldn't know that Priss had been hiding in the connecting room, or that she'd been with Jackson.

He could only hope.

But either way, he didn't want Priss still around when Helene came to.

She gave him a look of hurt and left for the adjoining room.

"What do we do with this one?" Jackson asked. He nudged Helene with his feet.

Trace turned his back on Jackson without answering.

He went to Helene's purse and dumped it. Inside he found two more vials of the serum. Apparently she'd planned on one crazy little party for herself.

Jackson was already on his feet, so Trace tossed the vial to him. "Shoot her up with that shit. Use the needle she dropped, but give her a double dose."

"It won't kill her?"

"I have no idea." And at the moment, he didn't really care. One dose had his memory hazy, so hopefully two would leave her completely at a loss as to what had transpired. "When you finish, dump her somewhere. One shot would give you about a half hour of her being pliable before she turns into a hellcat again. Two might buy you more time."

"Got it." After picking up the needle she'd dropped, Jackson eyed Helene's fallen body. "Shame she's such a nut. If she had even an ounce of sanity or compassion, she'd be pretty damned sexy."

Trace didn't see it. To him, raging psychosis negated any physical appeal Helene might have. "It'll be better if she doesn't see you again."

"That's what I figured, too." Jackson tapped the needle, releasing an air bubble, then went back and pulled up

Helene's tight skirt. He made a sound of regret, and stuck her right cheek.

Helene never stirred.

Trace started to go…but he had to know. He grabbed Jackson's arm and pulled him to the other side of the room, away from Helene, and away from where Priss could listen in.

CHAPTER SIXTEEN

WITH A CLEAR VIEW OF Helene still out cold, Trace asked Jackson, "Why the hell are you even here?"

Jackson looked far too uneasy for Trace's peace of mind. "I know you didn't want me here. I got the message loud and clear when you cut the call. Thing is, your little lady was damned insistent that I do something."

"Like get stunned and tied up?"

"You try planning with a hellcat breathing fire in your ear, making demands, prodding you—"

"Priss?"

"She's a terror. That name doesn't suit her at all."

Fine, so Priscilla had been worried. There was no reason, and he'd explain that to her later, but that didn't get Jackson off the hook. "Why aren't you at least alone?"

"There was no reasoning with her. She was hell-bent on heading out the door, with or without me." He met Trace's anger front on. "My only option was to go along with her, or knock her out the same way I did with Helene."

The idea of anyone putting hands on Priss left Trace bunched with rage. "Don't even think—"

Jackson smirked. "Right. I figured you wouldn't like that idea much." He glanced back at Hell, saw she was totally limp, and said to Trace, "I was hoping for better timing to tell you this, but since we'll both be busy tonight… Priss was already riled before she heard you on the phone."

"Riled?"

He shrugged, uneasiness showing. "Over how the whole rescue went down."

"What are you talking about?" A thousand scenarios went through Trace's head. "Did you hurt her?"

"Ah...no. It was the other way around." Jackson crossed his arms. "You know, you could have warned me about her violent tendencies."

Yeah, he probably should have. But since he'd told Priss that Jackson might come by... "I don't understand."

"Her modesty was bruised, that's all." More subdued, Jackson added, "I managed to stuff her out the window and to my car with nary a bruise."

"So why the hell are you grinning?"

Jackson chewed his lips a minute, then coughed. "She was...well, she was in the shower when I got there. Naked. You know..." He nodded. "All wet and stuff."

Trace's heart stopped. "What?" And then with cold menace, he asked, "You saw her naked?"

"Buck-ass. Yup."

Fighting the urge to flatten a trusted friend and colleague, Trace spoke through his teeth. "You looked?"

"Hello! A little hard not to, Trace, okay? She was *naked.*" He ran a hand over his jaw. "Helene was literally at the door, so I, uh...had to hoist Priss up and out the window."

Imagining that, Trace went blank, numb.

"No time to waste, you know? I did give her a towel, but...yeah. She dropped it." In a rush, Jackson added, "Once I had her outside, I gave her my shirt to wear."

Once he had her outside. Meaning...he hadn't just seen a flash of her naked. No. It was way more than that.

Trace had nothing to say. Nothing. The idea of Jackson seeing what he hadn't, for whatever reason, left him sick with fury and possessive rage.

Jackson cleared his throat. "Well...I should take

care of Hell, right? Figure I'll pull my car around to the
hallway exit and just wrap her in a blanket. Since she's
out and can't start fussing, odds are no one will notice."
He squinted one eye, peeked down at Trace's lap and
winced. "You okay, buddy? I mean, that looks mighty
uncomfortable."

Trace stared at Jackson, then turned and walked out.
Okay? Hell, no, he wasn't okay. He'd been drugged with
some strange but powerful chemical substance that made
him ultra sensitive, painfully hard and kept even his skin
singing.

And then to find out what Priss had been through, the
situation she'd been in with Jackson...

Seeing Priss sitting primly on the edge of the bed
dressed in Jackson's clothes did little to assist a return to
coherency.

Especially when Priss's gaze immediately dropped to
his open fly.

Damn. She practically devoured him with her eyes—
and he liked it. He loved it.

He *needed* it.

But now wasn't the time, damn it all. Using care, Trace
fastened his pants the best he could. "Let's go."

"Where?"

Did she sound worried, merely curious or a little annoyed? He let out a breath. "I need you someplace safe
before anything else happens."

Priss nodded, but still she sat there, her gaze bright,
her cheeks flushed with residual anger. "You're really
okay?"

"I will be." If she wanted an apology for him yelling
at her, she'd be doomed to disappointment. She shouldn't
have been there in the first place, and she shouldn't have
been bullying Jackson.

He held out a hand. "Come on."

She inhaled sharply, then propelled off the bed and into his arms, squeezing him tight. Her body was flush against his, touching him, moving, and he lost his fragile grip on propriety.

Tangling a hand in her hair, Trace drew her face back and took her mouth in a consuming, starving kiss.

It wasn't enough.

He wanted to brand her, to claim her, to make her his own in every way imaginable. And she wasn't fighting him. No, not even close. Instead Priss was all over him, accepting and anxious.

Trace let his hands drop to her bottom, lifting her up and against him. He ground against her, oblivious to everything except her taste, the heat of her body and his straining erection.

When he left her mouth to taste her throat, she whispered, "Trace?" with confusion and need.

"I'm sorry." There was her damned apology after all, but not for yelling earlier. "Helene drugged me." He lifted her higher so that he could open his mouth over the tender swells of her breasts.

"I know." Her hands braced against his shoulders, trying to find balance. "I was so afraid...."

Backing her to the wall, he caught her thighs and lifted them to either side of his hips. Oh, God, perfect. The feel of her, her scent swirling around him... He ravaged the soft, fragrant skin of her throat while moving against the junction of her thighs. A few seconds more, and he'd be coming.

He groaned with rampant need that boiled closer and closer to the surface.

A light tap sounded on the door and Jackson cleared his throat. "Well...this is awkward."

God Almighty, he'd kill him yet.

Priss's hand smoothed over Trace's hair, and he heard

her say, "Not now, Jackson. Close the door. Trace will see you in a few minutes."

"A few minutes, huh?" Jackson scoffed. "Yeah, sure. But uh…you're okay, honey?"

Before Trace could decide whether or not to flatten Jackson, Priss hugged him closer.

"I'm fine, I promise." Her hand continued to move over Trace, easy soothing strokes that still incited his every nerve ending. "Now go away."

Trace heard the door close and he felt like a bastard, like a molester, like a weak idiot with no morals and no backbone.

Drugs were a real son-of-a-bitch.

Priss had been through her own kind of hell. She deserved his attention, his comfort. But he had no control at all. Hell, even now, knowing his lack of control to be true, he couldn't seem to pull back from her.

Her hand slid over his shoulder, down to his side. "Trace?" She kissed his ear. "This might be easier on the bed."

He groaned again, his body straining, racked with need.

Feeling her smile on his temple, he heard her whisper, "Or not." And then she moved, gliding against his cock, and even through layers of material, it was enough to devastate him.

"Wait." The single word sounded like sandpaper. Trace fought for a breath, then another. But he would not come in his pants like a green kid. "I can't…I *won't* do this."

"No?"

He wanted her to understand, but he was short on words and long on need. "Not to you."

She went still, and Trace geared himself up for a variety of reactions. Then she wiggled, and he let her free even though it almost killed him. When her feet touched the floor again, she didn't move away from him. Instead she lowered her hands to his erection.

He hissed out a breath. "Priscilla... Honey, this is wrong." *Even though it felt so good.* "Everything you've been through..."

"I'm fine, Trace, really." Her hand circled him, and she looked at him with a softened gaze and a little awe. "But you're not."

He would never understand her. "Everything that's happened today... You're not rattled?"

"Not anymore, now that I know you're safe from Helene." Priss shrugged, tipped her head. "You seem pretty rock steady, too, considering."

"I'm on fire." His hands shook when he cupped her face. "Jesus, I don't know what she gave me, but..."

"But you still handled things when you needed to."

Pride demanded that he explain things to her. "I was just about free when you two showed up. I would have gotten away from her."

Her hands continued to move on him. "I believe you."

"I would have handled things. You shouldn't have gotten involved."

All her attention remained on his cock. "Right now, I'm sort of glad I did."

She sounded awed, and excited. "That's not helping, Priss." Whatever the drug concoction, it had a potent kick that just kept amplifying.

"And you need to get off?"

He stared at her. "You're not acting very virginal."

"Get real." She snorted. "I work in a porn shop."

A fact he'd never forget. "Yeah, I need to get off." Even saying it put him perilously close to the edge of no return. "Afterward, maybe I can clear my head."

"I'd like to help with that."

The things she said, the things she did… "Your first time shouldn't be like this."

"You're right." While staring down at him, Priss licked her bottom lip. "The thing is…I want to…taste you."

His lungs compressed. Hearing her say that nearly took out his knees. He slid his fingers into her hair, holding her head and envisioning the whole thing with devastating effect. He knew he should turn her down, but he couldn't get the words out.

"Can I take your silence for agreement?"

Trace squeezed his eyes shut tight, told himself to refuse before it was too late… "Yes."

"Oh, good. But first I have a question."

He'd never survive this. "What?"

"That bitch didn't have her mouth on you?"

"No." He kissed her hard, and wanted to keep on kissing her. Her lips were soft and open, warm and sweet. One day soon he'd take his time with her. Tonight wasn't it. "No, she didn't. That was her plan, but then you and Jackson got there—"

"I'm so glad." Priss started slipping down to her knees, and Trace knew he wouldn't last. Not beyond a minute. Maybe not beyond the first touch of her sweet mouth.

He tried to go easy, to keep from clenching his fingers in her hair, but the second he felt her breath he was a goner. Her tongue touched him tentatively, exploring, and he suffered a hot surge. "Don't tease, Priss. I can't take it."

She said, "Mmm," and her mouth opened on the head, sliding over him, enclosing him in moist heat. He stiffened all the way down to his toes.

Holding him in her fist, Priss took more of him, almost to the base of his shaft, and he lost it. She might be a novice, but her innocence was more of a turn-on than experience could ever be. He knew he would be her first in so many ways, but this—this had been reserved for fantasies.

With his hands in her hair, Trace held her close, guiding her, showing her how he needed her to move. A ringing sounded in his ears, his limbs trembled, pleasure exploded and he came with a groan of bone-deep satisfaction.

Only vaguely aware of her taking everything from him, swallowing, moaning in her own excitement, Trace eased her away.

As Priss reluctantly released him, he dropped down to sit beside her, his back against the wall, his thoughts blessedly cleared and his body no longer on fire. He labored for breath, and tried to think.

Almost purring, Priss snuggled against him like a content little cat. "That was pretty neat."

Pretty neat. God, it wasn't to be borne. Putting an arm around her, Trace mustered up common sense. "We have to get out of here." He squeezed her to his chest in a brief hug. "I swear I'll not only thank you properly, I'll reciprocate—"

"Reciprocate?" She perked up at that idea, then blushed. "You mean…?"

He could hardly wait. "Yes, but that'll have to be later. Right now, I need you to change into your regular clothes. You have something here in the room, don't you?"

Frowning, confused and maybe a little hurt, she nodded. "Yes."

"Good. After you're dressed, get together everything. Don't even leave behind a hairpin."

"I don't own hairpins."

Her disgruntlement made him smile. She was so incredibly sweet and unique, sensual and independent. And far too daring. He touched the corner of her mouth, then had to kiss her. "I'll be back in minutes, and then we'll get out of here."

She caught his hand as he stood to leave. "Trace?"

Damn, she was beautiful. He pulled her to her feet, kissed her again, quick and hard. "I need you, Priss. *You,* not just quickie relief—though I swear, what just happened is something I'll never forget."

"Really?"

How in the world could she look complimented by that? "Really. But the drugs haven't worn off, and I'm far from done, and you're the only woman I want."

Her expression brightened more. "The only one?"

Trace laughed. After the night he'd had, it was the most absurd of reactions, but still, he laughed again. "We need privacy, honey. And a bed. And I need you naked." He cupped his hand to her cheek. "Let me help Jackson, and then we can get out of here."

She turned away to the closet. "I'll be ready when you are."

Never in his life had Trace expected to find such an… accommodating woman. In so many ways, she matched him, when he hadn't thought that was possible. Until meeting Priss, he'd marveled at how easily Dare had settled into marriage, because it had seemed such an unachievable dream to him. But now…he wasn't sure a lifetime with Priss would be enough.

She made him laugh, when genuine laughter had been missing for so long from his life. Drugged or not, she turned him inside out wanting her. And though he'd kept many innocents from becoming collateral damage, he'd never once felt for any of them the same powerful mix of emotions that Priss wrought.

Even as he helped Jackson stow Helene in the trunk of his car, Trace continued to marvel over Priss and her reactions.

She accepted the violence and danger inherent in what he did, handled herself well in times of stress and uncertainty, and she'd not only gone to her knees for him, she'd seemed pleased by the whole thing.

Jackson closed the trunk of his car with Helene inside. Through the pounding rain, he searched the surrounding area. "I think we're all clear."

"Yeah." But he wouldn't completely relax until he found out how this played out with Murray. Moving back into the shadows under an overhang, Trace said, "Call me when you've dealt with her."

"Sure." After a couple of seconds with only the sounds of the rain and wind Jackson asked, "You two going to be okay?"

"Yeah."

He rubbed his chin, either fighting off another grin, or not accepting Trace's reply. "The thing is…Priss is sort of…well, she's not like other ladies."

Slowly, Trace turned to stare at him.

"Why are you mean-mugging me? I'm not saying that with any personal interest or any shit like that." Jackson sluiced the rain off his forehead. "Look, I just meant…"

"What?" Trace tried to tamp down the absurd anger, but couldn't. Even the chilly rain didn't affect the heat of his possessiveness. "What did you mean?"

"Fucked if I know." Jackson made a sound of disgust. "Forget I said anything."

Realizing he was being an ass, Trace stopped him from taking off. "Wait a minute."

His impatience obvious, his brows raised, Jackson waited.

It rankled, but still Trace said, "Thanks for taking good care of her." He motioned lamely. "With everything, I mean."

"Yeah. No problem." Jackson gave a silly salute. "It's what we do, right?"

No, taking naked women from the shower was definitely not in the job description. Trace shook his head. "I appreciate your concern for her. I do." This was ridiculous. "It's just that—"

"I get it." Jackson clapped him on the shoulder. "I'm a guy, remember? Just stay on your toes because I have a feeling that one will keep you guessing."

No kidding. "I don't suppose you could—"

"Strike the memory of her naked from my brain?" He winked—and stepped out of reach. "I'd lie and say sure, but you wouldn't believe me anyway."

It was more than any man should have to bear. "That's not what I was going to say."

"Then I don't have to disappoint you."

Jaw tight, Trace nodded to the car. "Know what you're going to do with her?" He hoped Jackson had a plan other than dumping her in the river, because Trace was fresh out of ideas.

"Yeah, I figured when she started to come to, I'd take her to an off-the-grid bar and leave her there. She'll look inebriated going in, and once the drug wears off, well, the drunks will be at her mercy."

"That works for me."

"Then I'll get to it before she comes around." Jackson clapped him on the shoulder again. "Tell Priss I said goodbye." Grinning, he got in the car and circled the lot before driving away.

From the shadows at the back of the hotel, Trace kept watch until Jackson was out of sight. Without it being said, he knew Jackson would go into the bar disguised so no one would ever be able to trace Helene back to him. She could tell any story she wanted to, but she'd have no proof. And anything she said would only incriminate her more once Murray found out what she'd done.

For a few minutes more, Trace waited outside. There

were no out-of-place shadows or noises, no suspicious people or vehicles.

Now he could see about getting Priss moved elsewhere, and he could be alone with her.

Finally, he could have her.

He didn't need a drug in his bloodstream to get him excited over that prospect.

TWO HOURS LATER, WITH ONLY a few phone calls, Trace had everything arranged. He'd heard from Jackson that Helene was no longer a problem, and he had them settled safely into a different hotel on the outskirts of the town. This hotel was upscale, and they'd checked in as a married couple.

Trace seemed right at home, and although Priss felt very out of place, she was still content.

Sure, the circumstances were horribly skewed, and before long there would be grave consequence for the events of the night. But Trace had been so attentive that she didn't have any regrets.

Well, maybe except for Jackson seeing her naked. That would leave her red-faced for a good long time.

But other than that, she'd come through it all unscathed, and so had Trace. If anything, she'd forged a special closeness with him now.

Rain battered the bedroom windows of the suite, and storm clouds left the night black as pitch. "I know he said things were resolved, but what did Jackson do with Helene?"

Trace glanced up as he unloaded his variety of weapons on the nightstand. "Other than the jolting you gave her, she'll be all right. Don't worry about it."

Still not trusting her. She sighed, but accepted the evasion. The more she learned of Trace, the more she understood his need for confidentiality. "I'm sort of glad that…you know…you guys didn't kill her."

He went still for a moment before continuing. "There was no reason. Killing her would have only complicated things with Murray." He pulled off his wet shirt and tossed it over a chair, then sat on the bed to remove his shoes.

That jittery, hungry rush hit her again. Trace was the most appealing man she'd ever seen. That he was also strong and heroic was enough to melt her bones.

"No reason to complicate things more." Priss noticed that his hands were shaking again. No doubt the effects of the drug, which seemed to come in waves.

He looked up at her. "If killing her becomes necessary, it'll happen, Priss. You do understand that?"

"Yes." And she wouldn't lose any sleep over it, either. But for now, tonight, given what she hoped and assumed would happen, it was a relief that *no one* had died.

Trace stripped off his socks. "Your shirt is wet, Priss." He watched her with cool control. "Take it off."

Her breath catching, Priss stared at him. He looked enigmatic as he stood to turn back the bed. Wearing only open slacks again, he looked incredible.

And she wanted him.

Without the necessary urgency of earlier, nervousness took over. Not nervousness from fear or even uncertainty. She trusted Trace and she wanted him. But this was all so new. To even feel like this was an aberration for her.

Leaving her shirt on for the moment, she sat in a chair and removed her sandals. "Did Helene say what she gave you?"

"Just that it's something she developed for the victims." He kept his back to her, but his hands tightened. "To make them easier to deal with."

Foul bitch. Maybe they should have killed her after all. "She's as evil as Murray, isn't she?"

"Yes she is. Sick and evil." He twisted to face her. "Thank God Jackson got to you before she did."

"You should have let me keep jolting her." Rather than think about how Jackson had found her, Priss stood and, determined not to balk, pulled off her top. "She deserved it."

"True." Trace walked over to her and caught her hands when she started to open her jeans. "But you didn't deserve to be a part of that."

Priss decided she'd argue that point with him later. Helene had openly insulted her mother, so she deserved a lot.

When Trace simply held her hands out to her sides and looked at her, Priss asked, "Are we going to have sex now?"

His mouth twitched, and his gaze warmed, but he sounded dead serious when he said, "Yeah, I think we are." He lifted his attention from her stomach to her face. "Is that okay with you?"

"Yes." More than okay. She licked her lips. "Will you kiss me?"

"Absolutely."

Before he could do that, which would surely distract her, Priss asked in a rush, "Do you want me mostly because of the drugs?"

With far too much concentration, he moved long ropes of wet hair off her shoulders. "Is that what you think? That drugs are what make you appealing?"

"I don't know." Her brain had been in a tailspin ever since hearing Helene's voice on the phone, knowing she was with Trace, and hearing what she intended to do. Then finding him like that, ready, hurting, needing relief... "It seemed to me that you were sort of trying to resist the whole sexual chemistry until…well, until the drugs made it impossible."

"Silly Priss." Trace held her face and kissed her. It was a long, deep, tongue-twining kiss that left them both breathing deeply. "If all I wanted was relief, I could handle that alone."

Her eyes flared. Was he saying…admitting… "I suppose." Why was *she* blushing? He was the one who'd said it.

And he didn't look the least embarrassed. Very matter-of-fact, actually.

"That, uh, that wouldn't be as much…fun. Right?"

A slight smile went crooked. His thumbs brushed her cheeks, the corners of her mouth. "I could also find a willing woman easily enough."

"I'm willing."

His grin widened before he got it under control. "I meant a woman other than you."

Her temper sparked. "I'm not sure I like where this is going."

"Fact is, Priscilla, the drugs are still with me. I can't deny that. And yes, I was trying to avoid getting too involved with you. You have so damn many secrets that it makes my head swim."

Of all the nerve. "*I* have secrets?" She pushed his chest. "What about you!"

Almost laughing, he contained her hands and pulled her closer. "Truthfully, I want you. With or without drugs." He brushed another, softer kiss to her lips. "But if you're having second thoughts, if you're not sure about this, I can go into the shower, take care of business and then we can get a good night's sleep."

Take care of business? Even though she blushed again, Priss said, "I wouldn't mind watching that."

"No."

Hmm. "Maybe another time, then." She tipped her head back and smiled up at him. "No second thoughts, Trace. I swear. I want you. Right now."

Relief showed in his hazel eyes. "Good." He slipped his fingers under the shoulder straps of her bra and peeled it down. His gaze was so intense, so hot that she felt it. For the longest time he just looked at her.

"Trace?"

"Damn, you're beautiful." And then he bent and drew her left nipple into his mouth.

It was wonderful. Amazing. She felt the stroke of his tongue, the pull of his mouth, all through her body.

He seemed in no hurry now to get on with it. In fact, he took his time, switching to her other nipple and drawing on her, teasing with his teeth until her knees went shaky.

Even when it felt too powerful, too concentrated to bear, his arms locked around her and kept her from pulling away. She could feel his erection again, as big and hard as before. Hoping to encourage him to haste, Priss moved against him, pressing and stroking.

He released her with a low groan. In the next second he had her lifted up and carried to the bed. He laid her flat and went to work on her jeans.

"You have protection?" Priss asked as her jeans got shoved to her knees, then down off her ankles, leaving her in a displaced bra and her panties.

"Yeah." He kissed her belly, her navel, lower.

Wow.

"I figured we'd get together sooner or later, and I don't take chances."

"Responsible men are so sexy."

He laughed, and given that his mouth was against her, it tickled.

Priss twisted to unfasten her bra and fling it away. "Take off your pants."

"Not yet," he said in a rush, staring at her breasts. He breathed harder. "If I do that, I'll lose control, and this is your turn."

"My turn?" She wasn't idiot, so she had an idea of what he meant, how she felt about that. Her stomach flip-flopped and her nipples ached.

Trace slipped his big hand into the front of her panties, touching, seeking. His eyes closed as his fingers parted her. "I want your climax to be a foregone conclusion, because once I get inside you, Priss, I'm not going to last."

"You aren't?" That sounded intriguing—not that she could dredge up a lot of rational thought while he played with her.

"Just relax and I'll explain everything."

CHAPTER SEVENTEEN

TRACE FORCED HIMSELF to pull back. Priss watched him with wide, curious eyes, her body shimmering in excitement. Reminding himself that this was her first time, that she'd been through hell tonight, and that she had a lot of emotional baggage, he gathered himself as much as he could.

He slid his fingers under the waistband of her tiny panties, then said, "Let's get rid of these, okay?" He pulled them down and off her long legs. After dropping them off the side of the bed, he slowly drew a hand from her ankle to her knee, then up the inside of her thigh until he covered her pubic curls with his palm.

She bit her lip, but said nothing.

Trace sat on the side of the bed, looking at her, breathing in her scent, thinking of all he wanted to do to her and with her.

"I feel exposed."

His gaze lifted to hers. "You are exposed." Frowning, he asked, "You aren't worried?"

"No." She drew a couple of quick breaths. "It's just that you're looking at me like...like you're examining me or something."

"I don't want to miss anything." He bent and kissed her navel. "You're beautiful, Priss."

"Matt did a good job."

He smiled. "Agreed, but Matt has nothing to do with this." He kissed her belly again. "Or this." Stretching out beside her, he kissed her breasts. "Or this." He moved his fingers between her legs, parted her and, watching her face, pressed one finger in.

Her hips lifted. "No." She sounded a little shrill. "Matt has nothing to do with any of *that*."

"I'm glad." Gently, Trace fingered her. When she gasped, he bent to her mouth and kissed her, slow, eating kisses that only made him want her more.

Having Priscilla Patterson naked on a bed in a private room, her green eyes heated, her long reddish hair in disarray around the pillows, her long legs open and her breath coming fast…that was as close to heaven as he'd ever get. And for that moment, he thought the rest of the world could damn well wait. He needed this. He needed her.

She gripped his shoulders and her nails, only recently manicured, sank into his skin.

He loved that, too. Damn, there wasn't much Priss did that he didn't love. Even her stubbornness turned him on.

"Oh, God," she suddenly whispered as she put her head back, her body stiffening, trembling.

Trace realized she was close and it not only amazed him, it triggered his own lust. He crowded over her, teasing her nipples with his teeth and tongue while keeping his finger in her, his thumb moving over her clitoris.

She tightened, gripping him, her body getting hotter, wetter. He couldn't wait to taste her, but for now, this would do. He withdrew his finger, and worked two back in. Tight. So damn tight.

Bending one leg, Priss clenched, cried out, and then she was coming, her hips moving against his hand, heat pouring off her body. Trace took her mouth, swallowing down her moans and relishing every sound, every move.

Even after she quieted, he kept his hand between her legs, idly now, but unwilling to leave her.

"Oh, God," she said again, lazily this time.

Trace knew she needed a little time, but he couldn't accommodate her. Not yet. Not tonight.

He withdrew his hand and, watching her beautiful face, lifted his fingers to his mouth.

Through shallow breath, she whispered, "Trace?"

He kissed her parted lips, light and easy. Then her chin. He opened his mouth on her throat. Her breasts.

He wanted to consume her.

Settling her hand in his hair, she said, "I think I need a minute."

"Sorry." Thunder roared in his ears; waiting even a second more was as impossible as not wanting her. He teased her navel with his tongue, put a soft love bite on her taut little belly, and dipped down lower.

"Trace."

Nuzzling into her, he inhaled her spicy fragrance. Overwhelmed by her and what she made him feel, he pushed her thighs wider, parted her with his thumbs, and stroked his tongue into her.

Her recent climax had left her wet, and he loved it, but it wasn't enough. He stroked in again, holding her still when her hips lifted off the bed and she moaned.

He wasn't an inexperienced kid. He sure as hell wasn't a virgin. He'd had his fair share of sexual experiences, ranging from awkward to kinky and everywhere in between.

But this all felt so new, because everything with Priss was different.

When he licked up and over her clitoris, she cried out, her thighs closing on his ears, her fingers tight in his hair. Such honest reactions, and so hot.

He drew her in, sucking gently, working her with his

tongue, and within minutes she was coming again. Long, ragged groans told him how much she enjoyed this. He pressed his hips tight to the mattress and concentrated on not losing control. It wasn't easy, not with her so wild. It went on and on, until she gave a soft sob.

"Trace, no more." She inhaled shakily. "I can't."

Turning his face, Trace kissed the soft flesh of her inner thigh, lightly bit her again.

She moaned. "Will you please get naked?"

Yeah, he would. Pushing up and off the bed, Trace stripped off his pants and his boxers and left them there on the floor. Feeling Priss watch him with dazed eyes and curiosity, he grabbed for his wallet, and found a rubber. "Only one, damn it."

"I have more."

He looked at her in amazement, then shook his head and rolled on the condom. "I won't ask."

She gave his words back to him. "I figured we'd get together sooner or later, and I don't take chances."

Going along, Trace stole her sentiment, saying, "Responsible women are so sexy." It amazed him that either of them could still think enough to banter. When he turned back to the bed, she opened her arms to him, and he was gone. "Very sexy."

He didn't think it was the effects of the drug anymore. Now it was all Priss, everything about her, that made him uncontrollable with need.

As he moved over her, she naturally parted her legs for him. They fit together perfectly, her tender thighs cradling his hips, her breasts cushioning his chest, her mouth there for him.

"Like this, right?" Priss laced her arms around his neck, locked her ankles at the small of his back.

"Yeah." Closing his eyes, Trace tried to go slow, to ease into her. But she was so wet, so hot, and she lifted against him, urging him on. "Yeah," he said again, and pressed partially into her.

She caught her breath and tensed. He looked at her, but her eyes glittered with desire, not pain. Cupping a hand under her bottom, he lifted her more. Against her mouth, he said, "Tell me if I hurt you."

She swallowed, nodded. "It'll hurt if you stop."

"I won't." Hell, he couldn't. With every inch he sank into her, he lost more control. Her muscles were flinching, clenching, milking him and making him nuts.

"I won't break, Trace. I promise."

He groaned, and thrust into her. Squeezed by silky tightness, he withdrew and thrust in again. And again.

Holding on to him, Priss made small sounds of pleasure and surprise, then deeper sounds of excitement.

"You're…bigger than I expected."

"God, Priss…" He almost laughed. "You don't know enough about men to judge my size."

"I've seen plenty of movies, remember?"

Trace put his face in her neck. "Can we talk about that later?"

She tightened around him. "Yes." And then a few seconds later, *"Yes."*

A third time? He lifted up to look at her and saw the flush of her face, how her teeth sank into her bottom lip, the vagueness in her green eyes. Amazing.

"Let go," Trace ordered softly.

As if the words freed her, Priss softened on a moan. Her heels pressed into the small of his back, her thighs hugged him, her body arched—and she took him with her. The release was mind-blowing, draining him of need, and stripping him of tension. Somewhere in the back of his mind he knew Priss wasn't done yet, so he managed to stay with her until her legs fell away from him and she went utterly limp beneath him.

They struggled for breath together, their bodies damp, scents combined.

A gentleman would have moved off her; Trace couldn't. He didn't have the strength and, besides, he liked having her like this. It might have only been days, but it felt like he'd waited a lifetime to get her under him.

She proved she felt the same when she roused herself enough to kiss his sweaty shoulder, then flopped back, arms and legs sprawled out like a starfish. She looked suspiciously close to sleep.

Tenderness left Trace smiling, when he hadn't thought he had the energy for that. Not kissing her proved impossible, so he tipped up her face and brushed his mouth over hers.

Her eyes didn't open, but she said, "If you're thinking of doing anything more, I swear, I need a nap first."

The reminder of her exhaustion brought home all the trouble waiting for them. Murray would hit the roof when he discovered Helene's perfidy—and it was anyone's guess who would be the recipient of his rage. How that'd affect Priss…he just didn't know.

But he wouldn't take any chances on anything happening to her. From here on, she was out of the picture. Trace didn't care what conclusion Murray came to, but Priss wouldn't see him again.

With Priss out of the way, he could handle Murray. He could handle Helene, too.

Hell, he could handle just about anything…except losing her.

PRISS WOKE SLOWLY. Unfamiliar aches reminded her of where she was, what she'd done and whose hairy leg had her pinned in place.

Trace.

She smiled without opening her eyes. Through the

long night, Trace had awakened her twice more. He'd taken her over the side of the bed, his hands holding her breasts, his mouth on her shoulder while he went so deep that she'd felt wild.

Later he'd lain on his back, her riding him, and he'd watched her intently while she came. It was both unsettling and intimate and very exciting. Seconds after she collapsed over him, he'd held her tight and gained his own release.

She was now sore in places she'd never noticed or thought about. She was also so content that it was hard to remember she had a plan, a duty and revenge to fulfill.

The sooner she wrapped up her business with Murray, the sooner she could concentrate on Trace.

Wondering about that, what the future might hold, she turned her head and found Trace watching her.

He looked so serious that it startled her. "You're not sleeping?"

"No." When his fingers moved, she realized that he had his large hand cupped over her breast. His gaze went to her mouth. "How do you feel?"

Oh, she knew that look only too well now. Much as she'd like to jump his bones—again—reality took over. "Sore. In need of coffee." She winced, hating to disappoint him. "And I have to pee."

The heat dimmed in his amazing hazel eyes, replaced with humor. "I should have realized." After he kissed her shoulder, he said, "Go on. I'll get the coffee ready."

"Thank you." But she hesitated. She was naked. He was naked. And now, with morning sunlight slanting through a break in the curtains, well…it was different.

One brow lifted and he rose up to an elbow. "Feeling shy?"

"Maybe a little."

His grin warned her seconds before he whipped away

the covers. She smacked at him, but that only got her kissed again. "Come on." He left the bed and pulled her up with him. "Do what you have to do, then come back to bed. We'll drink our coffee there."

"I think I need a shower." The excesses of the night had left her a little sweaty.

Trace hesitated, then nodded. "Okay."

She didn't understand his quick agreement until she was in the shower, hot water easing the aches of her body. The curtain pulled back and Trace, still naked, handed her a cup of coffee.

She'd touched his body everywhere, tasted him all over and yet, seeing him again, even without the kick of caffeine, left her taut with renewed interest.

She reached for the coffee cup, got about half of it gulped down, then stepped back. "Care to join me?"

Already stepping in, he said, "I was going to insist." He took the cup from her and set it outside the tub, closed the curtain, and reached for the soap.

"What are you going to do?"

"Bathe you." He turned her so her back was to his chest, the water sluicing over her breasts. "You hadn't danced, hadn't made love. I'm guessing no one has ever pampered you, either."

The feel of his soap-slick hands sliding down her body made her eyes heavy and her breath shallow. "No."

"Good." His erection nudged her backside as he whispered, "Then I can be first at this, too."

OVER AN HOUR LATER, after they'd run out of energy, Priss curled up against Trace in the bed. She loved how familiar it already felt to be with him like this, her head on his shoulder, his hand curved over her hip.

Staying like this for…oh, *forever*…would be heavenly. But they both knew reality would soon interfere.

Priss hated to ruin the moment, but it wasn't in her nature to stew in silence. And after the closeness they'd shared in the last twenty-four hours…well, she felt she deserved a few answers.

A hand on his chest, her leg over his, she tipped her face up to see Trace. "What are you really doing with Murray?"

Though his gaze slanted down at her, he stayed stubbornly silent. After all the tenderness, the intimacy, his lack of trust was almost palpable. Considering she could still taste him, and her heart still pounded with excitement, that should have been insulting.

But for whatever reason, it wasn't. Trace was who he needed to be in order to keep others safe, to rescue them from horrendous situations. She got it, more now than ever.

"You need me to go first, huh?" Her hand stroking his chest hair, Priss said, "I can understand that."

When dealing with Murray and his ilk, trust was an elusive thing.

She drew a breath, and burrowed closer to Trace's heat. The confession she needed to make left her throat feeling raw and her chest tight. But it had to be said.

She sensed Trace's stillness, maybe even a little dread. He wanted to know her secrets, but he intuitively knew that the truths would be ugly.

"Murray not only raped my mom, he passed her around to his friends and let them all rape her, too. That lasted for about two weeks before she found an opportunity to get away."

Tension suddenly gripped Trace. His arm around her back tightened. The seconds ticked by as the implications of what she'd said sank in. "You don't know if he's your father or not, do you?"

Priss shook her head. Years ago, she'd been ashamed

for what her mother had suffered, and how it had left her with no knowledge of her father. Later, she'd been wounded that anyone could care so little, be so cruel. And finally, when her mother began fading away from her stroke, she'd gotten angry.

The anger had saved her from despair, leaving her with a single purpose to focus her life.

Until she'd met Trace. She still wanted to kill Murray, but she also wanted to somehow protect the tentative relationship with Trace.

She doubted it was possible to do both.

"My mom never knew." She tucked her face into his throat. "She didn't want to know. For most of my life, she was scared to death of any man who tried to get close. When she knew she was dying, it took all her effort to tell me that not all men were monsters. She said she wanted me to be careful, to always be on guard, but she didn't want me to live with her hang-ups."

Quietly, Trace asked, "When did she tell you about Murray?"

"When I was fourteen. I was selfish and bitching about wanting to go to a public school, to date and have friends."

"That doesn't sound selfish to me at all. It sounds really normal."

"For a normal kid, maybe it would have been. But that's not me. Because of what Murray did to my mom, we could never be normal like that."

Trace turned on his side toward her, and Priss ended up on her back. He smoothed her hair from her face, traced one of her eyebrows with his thumb. "You aren't normal, Priscilla Patterson. You're unique." He kissed her, very soft and sweet. "Extraordinary." Another kiss, this one lingering. "And exceptionally hot."

Priss smiled. "The only other person to tell me that is Gary Deaton, and he just wanted in my pants."

"I've already gotten in your pants, so you can believe me when I say it."

"Maybe."

A little sad, Trace braced himself over her. "So let me understand this. When you were an impressionable fourteen-year-old child, your mother told you that she'd been held captive by a madman and passed around sexually with his friends?"

It sounded horrible, even to her. "She had to tell me then, to make me understand why I couldn't sneak off to parties or football games. And she had to know if any man looked at me too long, if anyone ever took my picture. She needed me to understand the risk, to know what could happen if anyone had ever found out about me, that I could be Murray's daughter I mean."

Though he didn't look convinced, Trace kissed the top of her head. "I'll kill him for you."

He sounded so sincere, and so accepting of her dysfunctional childhood, that a smile bloomed in Priss's heart. "Thank you." She drew him down to her for a longer kiss, one he gladly accepted. "That's sweet of you, but no."

His eyes narrowed. "Sweet? I offer to kill a man and you think it's sweet?"

"You wanted to kill him anyway. And so do I." The hair on his chest fascinated her, so she concentrated on that. "You've never come right out and said so, but I've known for a while that you're a good guy, Trace."

He gave her a cautious survey. "I'm not sure that accurately describes me."

"Of course it does. From the very beginning, you were making moves to protect me. When you kept my license, it was so that Murray couldn't run a check on me, and that was before you had any idea who I was or what I wanted. Everything you've done since then has been a balancing act of fulfilling what Murray expects of you, while at the same time trying to keep me from getting too involved."

"As of this minute, you're not involved, not in any way."

If only that were true. For some, it'd be so easy to step back and let Trace do his thing. Especially since he did it so well. He would kill Murray, she knew that. But she couldn't delegate the responsibility. She'd never be able to live with herself. "Sorry, Trace, but I'm involved up to my eyeballs. There's no changing that."

He sat up suddenly. "Wrong. It's changed."

Worry niggled up her spine. "What do you mean?"

"I mean that you're out of it." He took his watch off the nightstand and strapped it around his wrist. "I'll tell Murray that you ran off, that I don't know where you went. He won't be able to find you, and after sending Helene after you, it's a believable lie."

"No." She wouldn't let him be this autocratic. She wouldn't allow him to decide her fate—her *life*—for her.

He strode to the chair and picked up his slacks. "Jackson will take you to stay with Dare until I've wrapped up things here."

Meaning after he'd killed Murray and all his cohorts. Panic squeezed around her. She didn't want to be separated from him, and she didn't want him to rob her of the vengeance she rightfully deserved. "No."

He pulled on his T-shirt, now wrinkled. "You don't get a say in this, honey. Sorry."

The tightness in her chest made breathing difficult. Naked, irate, she left the bed to confront him. "You are not my keeper. You don't get to make those decisions."

"They've been made." He didn't look away from her. Something flickered in his eyes, something both dangerous and defenseless. His voice went hoarse. "I don't want you to get hurt, Priss."

She gulped back emotion. "It hurts me that you want to exclude me from this."

The vulnerability left, replaced by a hard glitter. "You'll get over it."

Desperate to reach him, Priss said, "I feel the same way about you, Trace." When he paused, she said, "About you getting hurt, I mean."

He stepped around her to get his shoes. "You should realize by now that I can handle myself."

"Because this is what you do?" Priss stormed after him, grabbing his arm and demanding his attention. "And that's *what* exactly? Tell me what you do, Trace. Tell me why I should trust you to handle things with Murray."

He went stony again, not answering, not even blinking.

Oh, God, this time his silence demolished her. "No, damn you." She shook her head hard. "You can't dictate things without telling me a single truth." He wanted to take over her life without giving anything in return.

He caught her arms and bodily moved her to sit on the edge of the bed. Going to one knee in front of her, he said, "You want truths? Fine. I was in an old factory with Murray."

As far as disclosures went, that was vague. "Why?"

"To beat the shit out of some scumbag buyer who dared to dicker price with him."

"Oh." Her heart pounded double time, part in relief that he was finally confiding in her, but also in dread for what she'd hear. There was something about Trace's mood, something darker and edgier than usual. She knew that whatever he told her, it wasn't going to be easy to take. "A guy who would buy...women?"

"Yes."

"And did you beat him?"

"Yes."

"Good." Anyone involved with Murray deserved that, and more. "Go on."

"After Murray sells the women..." Trace squeezed her hands. "The buyer stores them there at the factory. It's used in part as a place for transactions, and to keep the victims locked up until he can get them sold individually."

If she hadn't been sitting down, her knees would have given out on her. Her vision closed in. "You left women there?"

"No." His frustration crackled in the air around them. "No, I wouldn't..." He let that go. "The thing is, Murray mentioned that he'd kept women there long ago."

No air could enter past the restriction in her throat. "Long ago."

"Back when he was just starting down this road of human trafficking."

Back when her mother was a young, innocent girl. Her gaze focused inward as she remembered her mother's terror, a terror so strong that it became a phobia. For as long as Priss could remember, her mother lived in constant fear of being taken prisoner.

"I had Dare check it out, Priss, to see how long that factory had been shut down—"

"I remember you talking with him."

Trace stood and paced away. "You're smart, Priss. You know where this is going."

She nodded, but since Trace had his back to her, he didn't see. "Yes. You're saying it's possible that—that my mother was kept there. That place could be where he let his friends have her. It could be where he forced her…to share herself."

"Did she ever tell you?" He kept his distance, but did turn to face her again. "Did she give you details?" Before she could answer, Trace said, "Understand, Priss, I'm hoping she didn't. I'm hoping like hell that she let you keep some of your innocence, some of your childhood. Those details…they aren't something that a girl needed to hear."

"I know." When she shivered, Priss belatedly recalled her nakedness. She pulled the sheet around her.

"Priss?"

She looked down at her hands. No, her mother hadn't spared her. She'd considered it all too important. She'd considered it for Priss's own good. "I—I remember her telling me once that she was kept locked in a damp, windowless room with…brick walls."

Hands on his hips, Trace dropped his head forward. "Shit."

She stared toward him. "You think that's the place?" If so, she would raze it. She'd take a wrecking ball to it. Not a single brick would be left standing.…

"Priss, listen to me. You will not do a damn thing. Do you understand?"

Had he read her mind? He couldn't be serious! "Then why even tell me?"

"Murray has a deal going down there. He'll deliver the women to that location and they *will* be locked inside." He went back to dressing, strapping on his vest, his gun and knife and baton. "I can't concentrate on freeing them if there's a single possibility that you could get hurt."

Baloney. She had no doubt that Trace could do many things, multitasking one of them. "When?"

His expression darkened like a thundercloud. "It doesn't matter, damn it!"

Her chin went up. "To me, it does."

"Priss, I want…" He ran a hand through his hair, and then rubbed the back of his neck before appealing to her. "I *need* to know that you'll be out of danger."

Unrelenting, she pushed up off the bed. "What do you do?"

He lifted his hands. "I get the bad guys."

Such a simple statement for such an amazing feat. Thinking of Helene, Priss asked, "And the bad women?"

"It's happened."

Had he gone undercover to get a woman? How far would he go to accomplish that? "Have you…you know, ever gotten involved…sexually—"

His tone, his expression softened. "I'm thirty years old, Priss. I've had relationships. You know that."

"That's not what I meant." No one would ever mistake Trace for a monk. What she really wanted to know was if she was somehow special, but she didn't know how to ask.

He watched her a moment, and as usual, he deciphered her meaning. "As a rule, I stay emotionally detached from anyone connected to a case. Emotion can dick up perspective every time. It robs a man of the edge needed to do what has to be done, when it has to be done."

Like pulling the trigger. She nodded, her hopes dashed. "I see."

"Do you?" He smoothed her wildly tangled hair. "I tried, Priss, I really did. But I couldn't stay detached from you."

"You couldn't?"

He shook his head. "That's the problem."

So he saw her as a problem. Not that she'd expected much else, given his undercover position, and how her appearance had caused such a stir with Murray. "I couldn't stay detached, either."

He cracked a smile. "I noticed. And I'm glad." His put his palm to her jaw, curved his long fingers around her head, into her hair. "Now, will you please work with me instead of against me?"

"Yes." She would definitely work with him, but probably not in the way he hoped. Priss slipped her arms around him, and he felt so big and strong and safe that she could barely get the next words out. "You can go, Trace. I promise I won't get in your way."

Tangling a hand in her hair, he gently pulled her head back and put his mouth to hers in a kiss of relief. "Jackson should be here soon." He kissed her temple, and she felt his smile before he said, "If you could get dressed, that'd be great. I'd just as soon he not see you naked again."

Priss slugged him in the gut for that, and even though he grunted, he laughed.

"It's not funny." Her face flamed anew as she remembered how Jackson had seen her.

"Believe me, I know." Growing somber, Trace opened the sheet and looked at her body. "I'd have been a whole hell of a lot happier if no other man had seen you like this."

Her heart started tripping in double time. "Why?"

"Because you're mine." He stepped back from her. "And I'm starting to realize that I'm a territorial bastard."

On that note he walked out the door. Leaving her for Jackson, going to deal with Murray himself...

Trusting her to do as he asked.

Poor Trace. She loved him, she really did. But she wasn't a person to consign responsibility, to sit idle while others were at risk, or to take orders from anyone.

Even from a man who now meant the world to her.

CHAPTER EIGHTEEN

AFTER ARRANGING TO meet up with Murray at the offices, Trace called Dare.

He answered with, "What's up?"

"I'm cutting things short. Murray has to go. The sooner the better."

"Okay." Dare fell quiet a second. "Why the change in plans?"

"I know where the women will be taken. The deal is happening any day now. There's no reason to wait. I can round up the major players in one net, and then when they talk, we can get the rest."

"*If* they talk."

"They will." He'd see to it.

"And the sudden turnaround has nothing to do with Priss?"

Trace squeezed the steering wheel. "Actually, it has a lot do with her."

"I figured."

He owed Dare the truth. "I slept with her."

"So, you got carried away." Dare sounded unconcerned. "It happens."

"Not just once, Dare. All night long." And it had been amazing, so amazing that he knew he couldn't give it up. He couldn't give *her* up. "I know damn good and well I'm going to sleep with her again."

"It's like that, huh?" As usual, Dare stayed calm in

every situation. "So I take it that we need to remove her from the picture?"

Out of harm's way. "Absolutely."

Without hesitation, Dare said, "If you can convince her, she can stay here."

"Thank you." He'd known that Dare would offer, but having it confirmed put him at ease. "I already talked to Priss. Jackson can drive her down today. I want her out of the area completely."

"Today?" Dare hesitated. "You sure you know what you're doing, Trace? How are you going to explain her sudden disappearance to Murray? He's always suspicious, so he's not going to be real accepting that a daughter presented herself one day only to take off the next."

That was the first thing Trace had figured out. "He'll believe she bolted after Helene went after her."

"Hmm." Dare considered the theory. "Yeah, that might be a good enough reason. God knows Hell is enough to scare most normal people into bolting."

"It'll have to do, because I'm not letting her within a hundred miles of Murray. Never again."

"I take it Priss agreed with this decision?"

Not really, but she wasn't irresponsible, so he had to believe that she'd play along. "She'll be all right. I'll see to it."

Dare didn't push the issue. "Chris can get the guest room ready. If you need anything else, let me know."

Half an hour later, Trace got to the offices. He tried to ignore the prickling of unease that seeped into his every pore, but his instincts had never let him down. Something wasn't right; he felt it even in the air he breathed into his lungs.

Was Murray onto him? Was he walking into a trap?

A guard at the parking garage door greeted him. "The boss man is waiting for you."

Trace gave him an icy stare. "Since when do I need you to tell me that?"

The guy, a new recruit lacking smarts, quailed. "I—I dunno. Just saying."

"You think I don't know what Murray is doing at all times?"

"I guess you do."

Deciding the comment had been offhand, and not a warning, Trace wrote it off. "Next time, try keeping your mouth shut."

"Yes, sir."

Idiot. And here he was, taking his bad temper out on someone who, for all intents and purposes, was defenseless against him. Disgusted, Trace took the elevator to Murray's floor. Not knowing how Murray might react to Hell's perfidy, he was anxious to get the confrontation over with.

For once it was nice not to get sideswiped by Helene. Of course, she was probably still recovering, not herself one hundred percent yet. He assumed she'd made it home okay. Like a cat, Helene Schumer always landed on her feet.

Alice was sitting at her desk when Trace walked in. Odd how she was always there, night and day, workweek and weekends. If Murray showed up at the offices, Alice was there, too.

She kept her head down, typing away on the computer.

Frowning, Trace approached her. "Alice."

She glanced up and away, but smiled. "Mr. Coburn is waiting for you."

"Thanks." Trace paused beside her desk. "You're okay?"

Alarm flashed in her big brown eyes before she averted her gaze. Again. "Yes, of course."

She looked tired. "When's your day off?"

Mistaking his interest, she stared at her monitor and her hands started to shake. "Mr. Miller…"

"Trace."

She coughed, nodded. "Trace." Her mouth opened twice before she said, "Mr. Coburn doesn't allow any… personal relationships among employees."

That wasn't precisely true, but he understood her warning. "I wasn't hitting on you, Alice."

Her face went up in flames. "Oh, I know that. I meant… Well, I can't…"

Something cynical and angry unfurled. As gently as possible, Trace asked, "You can't what?"

Curling her hands into fists, Alice breathed heavily—then smiled up at him, her eyes wounded but determined. "Forgive me. I don't know what I'm saying. You're right. I mistook your interest. I'm sorry."

Trace straightened. He would recognize those signs of fear and intimidation anywhere. How the hell had he missed it with Alice? Murray hired lots of people straight up, people he kept disconnected from the seedier side of his true profession.

Apparently Alice wasn't one of them.

"I'm the one who's sorry, Alice." He nodded at her and headed for Murray's office. *So many reasons to kill Murray.* And soon.

Trace rapped twice on the door and entered.

Murray sat behind his desk facing the window and speaking on the phone. He glanced back as Trace entered, waved him in, and then returned to his call. "No, damn it." He paused before snarling, "Because the product is arriving early."

Just inside the door, Trace waited with his head down so that Murray wouldn't realize how intently he listened. Maybe this would all go quicker than even he had hoped.

"Enough." Murray jerked his chair around to face his desk. "This isn't up for debate. Get your money together and be there." He ended with slamming the phone down on the desktop.

Lifting a brow at the show of temper, Trace asked, "Should I come back?"

"No." Murray scrubbed his hands over his face in frustration. After a second, he picked the phone back up and, with more care, placed it in the cradle. "Come on in. I need a drink. You want one?"

As usual, Trace refused. "I just finished off a pot of coffee."

"Late morning?"

"Very."

"Maybe it was a full moon last night or something." He sloshed a generous portion of whiskey into a tumbler. "Helene was also running late today."

Was? "So she's here now?"

Murray downed the drink and poured another before reseating himself behind the desk. "She called ahead to say she had something important to share with me." He studied Trace. "You know anything about that?"

Trace took a nonthreatening stance to the side of Murray's desk. "I have doubts that Helene would share the whole truth, but that's actually what I wanted to talk to you about."

"Helene?"

"In part."

"Huh." Murray folded his hands over his cumbersome gut. "You've got me on pins and needles."

"Last night, she overstepped in a big way."

Murray waved that off. "I gave her permission to play with Priscilla."

Trace locked his back teeth. "I know, I was here." And he'd make the son-of-a-bitch pay for that. "But I don't mean with your daughter." He maintained eye contact with Murray. "She overstepped with me."

"You?" He huffed. "How so?"

"Helene was at my hotel when I returned last night after our business."

A frown pulled down Murray's thick brows. "But what about Priscilla?"

"I have no idea. I tried to find her last night and then again this morning. No luck."

He sat forward, his forearms on the desk. "You're saying that Priscilla is missing?"

"Seems so."

He searched Trace's face. "And you think Helene did something with her?"

"That, or she scared her off."

"I suppose that's possible. Helene can be very...exuberant at times." Rubbing his goatee, Murray thought about it. His gaze slashed up to Trace in suspicion. "What did you say to Helene when you found her there?"

"I told her to get lost."

Chiding, Murray said, "Trace. Tsk, tsk. That was unkind of you."

"You already knew my plans, and they didn't include secondhand bait from you."

"Oh-ho! If Helene heard you call her that, she'd castrate you."

No doubt she'd try. "I wanted a quick shower, a couple of drinks and a woman."

"Other than my Helene."

Trace shrugged. "As you just said, she's yours, and I don't share."

"A man after my own heart." He slapped his hands down onto the desk. "So. After you rejected her, what happened?"

Remembering brought new tension to invade Trace's muscles. "The bitch drugged me."

Murray lost his relaxed posture. "Come again?"

"She stabbed me in the ass with a hypodermic. Whatever it was, it left me dopey long enough for her to…"

Sitting forward in anticipation, scowling darkly, Murray demanded, "Don't keep me in suspense, damn it! For her to do what?"

"She tied me up. She was going to have her jollies regardless of what I had to say about it."

Murray simmered…and then burst out laughing. "By God, Trace, you sound like one of those little twit virgins I've brought to auction!" He slapped his hands onto the desk again. "Worried about your virtue, are you?"

There was no comparing him, a capable, hard-living grown man to a helpless, frightened and fragile girl. But yeah, it had given him a small—very small—taste of how those females probably felt being so helpless.

The difference was that he knew he'd get loose, and he knew he'd make them all pay. The women whose lives Murray had ruined never had that satisfaction.

Expression and mood dark, Trace said, "You like control, Murray. I like control. Anything else is out of the question."

"True, true."

It wasn't exactly accurate, but close enough. Trace said silkily, "If she wasn't yours, I would have killed Helene for what she tried to do."

Murray continued in a humorous vein. "Ah, so I take it you got free before she could…compromise you?"

"I was too pissed to deal with her, so I gave her a dose of her own medicine. Literally."

"No shit?" His brows rose high. "You doped her?"

Trace gave a hard nod. "And then I left. When I came back later that night she was gone."

"And yet she didn't mention any of this." Letting out a thoughtful breath, Murray stewed. "I got the feeling that whatever she wants to discuss with me, it has nothing to do with you."

"I told her that you wouldn't like it. And I told her that I'd inform you." Trace shrugged. "I don't think she believed me."

"I have to say, I'm surprised you didn't try to cover it up." He tilted his head, studying Trace. "You weren't concerned that I might put you at fault?"

"No, but it doesn't matter anyway. I wouldn't keep something important from you."

"You consider this important?"

Trace didn't like being played with. "You said yourself that Helene is unstable. You can best judge how unstable with reports of what she does."

"Right you are."

"I'm surprised you didn't already know." It never hurt to stroke Murray's colossal ego—or to show his own. "You've had so many tails on me lately, I don't know if I should be insulted at your lack of trust, or complimented that you're concerned enough to keep the dogs out on me."

"Take my advice. Be complimented." He pushed the intercom. "Alice, tell Helene to get in here pronto."

So Murray would waste no time in dealing with her. "Did you want me to stay?" Trace hoped so. As distasteful as he found the dynamics of Helene and Murray's relationship, he wanted to stay apprised of any status changes.

"Knowing Helene, I might need your protection." Murray smiled as he said it.

Given Murray's fluctuating mood, Trace didn't know if the lunatic would kill Helene, or applaud her audacity.

Helene barged in minutes later with a paper in hand.

Usually picture-perfect from her hair to her shoes, she looked less pulled together today. Besides her lank hair and her eyes dark with exhaustion, her sleeveless, pullover blouse had a few wrinkles, her split skirt was askew, and her shoes didn't quite match the ensemble. She looked... more average than not, a regular woman instead of a live fetish with evil intent.

When she found Trace standing there by the windows, she paused. Her worried gaze went to Murray—and she knew she'd just stepped in it.

Helene wasn't dumb, just insane.

"Yes, Helene," Murray told her with a heavy dose of apathy. "You're in trouble."

Trying to brazen her way through, she waved a paper. "I have something important to share with you."

"Really?" He turned to Trace. "And she looks so anxious to share. I suppose we can wait for our little disciplinary hearing, can't we?"

Hiding his frustration, Trace said, "Your decision, as always."

Murray left his chair and circled around to the front of his desk. He leaned back on it, arms crossed over his thick chest. "All right, Helene. Let's hear it. And it better be good."

Triumphant, she held out the paper. "The paternity results are in. That little fraud is *not* your daughter."

Trace was so stunned that he didn't know how to react. Murray seemed even more thrown, proving that he had believed Priss to be of his blood.

Neither of them reached for the paper.

"It's true," Helene declared. "I swear."

Softly, Murray said, "I'll be damned. I bought her act completely."

"But it *was* an act." Slapping the paper down on the desk beside Murray, Helene presented the epitome of false sympathy. "She was trying to use you, Murray." She stroked his goatee, the back of his head. "She wanted to take advantage of you, to take your money and your possessions. The evidence doesn't lie. She's not related to you in any way."

Frowning in distraction, Murray set her away from him and looked at Trace. "What do you think?"

He thought Priss had dug a very deep hole for herself, and now, for him, too. "Maybe you ought to give Priscilla a chance to explain."

Helene bristled. "Why are you deferring to him? I have the proof! Who cares what he thinks?"

"I do, obviously." He swept her away from him and gave his attention to Trace. "What's the point in that?"

"It could be a true misunderstanding instead of a deliberate ruse." He leveled a look on Hell. "And I'd double-check the results myself before taking her word for it."

"Bastard!" Hell launched at him, but Trace easily caught her arm and pinned it painfully behind her back.

Near her ear, uncaring of Murray's audience, he whispered, "I'm not drugged now, Helene, so don't even think about it." While she struggled futilely, gasping in pain, Trace conferred with Murray. "Think about it. Helene has proven herself untrustworthy. Instead of going to Priscilla as you gave her permission to do, she came to me. Priscilla is now missing, and suddenly Helene has these results?"

Murray rubbed his chin, pulled at his goatee thoughtfully. "It does seem rather convenient, doesn't it?"

Helene gasped again and went still. "No!"

Was it possible that Murray actually wanted Priss to be his daughter? More likely, he was just taken off guard at having his plans—whatever those plans might be—thwarted by a possible sham.

Was Priss capable of that much duplicity?

Helene struggled anew. "He's lying!"

Uncaring if he hurt her, Trace tightened his hold. "Wouldn't you rather know for sure?"

Eyes narrowed, Murray moved closed to them. "You know, I believe you're right, Trace."

There was so much finality in Murray's voice, Trace could guess what would probably happen to Helene now. He released her and stepped back.

Babbling, pleading, she threw herself against Murray. "You can't believe him, Murray. You can't!" She kissed his face, his fat neck. "Baby, you know I wouldn't lie to you."

Gently, Murray cupped her face. "Oh, I think you're most capable of anything, my dear. Most capable. I believe, as Trace suggested, I will have the results checked myself. But not to worry, in the meantime you'll be kept... safe."

She whimpered in the first sign of real fear Trace had ever seen from her. Eyes wide, pulse tripping, she whispered, "Murray..."

He smiled at Trace. "Call in security." He pushed Helene into a chair.

"All right." Trace gave a quick, pitying glance at Helene, but he knew better than to interfere. He stepped outside the door. "Alice?"

Startled, she jumped up from her desk and jerked around to face him.

Trace frowned. Her face was pale, her expression one of worry. She'd always been inhibited, but he'd never seen her so stressed. He felt very protective toward her. "Get security up here, will you?"

"Security...other than you?"

"Building security," he clarified. He tried a smile that

had no effect on her, so he gave up and prompted her to action, saying, "Thank you."

"Oh." She rushed to take care of the order. "Yes, of course. I'll see to that right away."

As she reseated herself behind her desk, Trace closed the door. "On the way."

"Excellent."

In one of the padded guest chairs, Helene sat in stony silence, her gaze lost, staring at nothing in particular. Trace couldn't help but wonder what had happened with her last night after Jackson dumped her.

"We need to find her," Murray mused.

"Her?"

"Priscilla." He scowled at Trace. "Keep up."

In a seeming reprieve from Murray's censure, Trace's cell phone rang. Jackson would only use the private cell, and he wouldn't call; he'd leave a code. While Murray waited expectantly, Trace had no choice but to pull out the phone to turn it off. "Sorry."

Murray gestured magnanimously. "Go ahead."

In his bones, Trace knew that answering the call wouldn't be a good idea. "Whatever it is, it'll wait."

"Nonsense. It could be Priscilla." Murray gestured. "Answer it already."

With no other choice, he conceded. "All right." Not sure what new game Murray played, Trace put the phone to his ear. "Trace Miller."

"Hey, Trace."

Priscilla. Good God, what was she thinking? He struggled to keep his expression inscrutable. "What is it?"

"Bad timing? Sorry about that. Nothing is tragically wrong, so don't worry. I just wanted you to know that I'm here."

Aware of Murray's unrelenting attention, Trace asked, "Here…where?"

"Right outside. At a pay phone."

Un-freaking believable. Priss sounded contrary and lighthearted and he wanted to throttle her. Jaw clenched, he asked, "How?"

"Cabbie. I skipped out before Jackson showed up, so if he calls in a panic, no worries."

Trace glanced at Murray. "I'm in an important meeting."

"Oh, with Murray? Awkward! I just wanted you to know that I'm coming in."

No way in hell. He held the phone tighter. "Negative."

"Positive," she replied without concern for the direct order he'd just given her. "Oops. Especially since the jig is up."

Why had he ever thought her reasonable? "Tell me where you are. I'll come and get you."

Murray's brows lifted.

"Too late for that. Some apes are headed my way. I don't think I can outrun them, so I'm guessing I'm being brought in. Real quick. Did you say anything to Murray yet? About Helene I mean."

"Yes."

"Oh. Well, I can only hope our stories match up— Shoot. Gotta go, Trace. See you soon." Almost as an afterthought, she added, "Smooches." The phone died.

Smooches? Was she out of her mind? Had being around Murray and Helene addled her wits?

With numbness creeping over him, Trace closed the phone and dropped it into his pocket.

"Who was that?"

No point in lying about it. "Priscilla."

Helene said, "Priscilla?" almost at the same time Murray said, "No shit? I thought she was long gone."

"Apparently not." He took up a stance by the door. "I

offered to go get her, but she said she was close by and that apes were coming after her. Your apes, I hope."

Murray examined a nail. "Most likely. I told the men that if she approached the building, or anywhere near the building, I wanted her brought to me."

"She *lied* to you," Helene insisted again.

Ignoring her, Trace said, "Then I assume she's on her way in."

"Splendid." He dropped his hands and again sat behind his desk. "I can't wait to…greet her." And then to Helene, "Not a word out of you. Do you understand?"

She hesitated, but then nodded.

A few minutes later, Alice beeped the office. "Mr. Coburn, some of your guards have brought Priscilla Patterson to see you."

Murray rolled his eyes. "Don't be a dolt, Alice. Send them in."

"Yes, sir."

It was the first time Trace had heard Murray speak to Alice with anything other than professional curtness. But he didn't have time to dwell on that, not when the same men he'd confronted in Priss's apartment parking lot entered the room, dragging Priss along as she carped and complained.

A man at either side of her gripped her arms, and another trailed behind. Through remaining bruises and some medical tape, they grinned when they saw Trace.

Priss tried to hide her grimace, but they were hurting her, and Trace wouldn't tolerate it. Staring at the men but speaking to Murray, he said, "Did you tell them to manhandle her?"

Amused, Murray said, "Actually…no." And then, in warning, "But this is my office Trace, so don't break anything."

"Only bones." Straight and hard, his fist shot out and

connected with the nose of the man closest to him with cartilage-crunching impact.

Stunned, the fool quickly released Priss and lurched back with a gurgling, *"Arrrr..."*

"Do *not* get blood on my carpet," Murray ordered one and all as he sat back to enjoy the show.

Busy cupping his hands around his spewing nose and trying not to pass out, the man couldn't fight. He left the room and stumbled to Alice for tissues.

Priss darted out of the fray and away from the remaining two men. Out of the corner of his eye, Trace saw her shift closer to Murray.

She said, somewhat approvingly, "Trace is very efficient at this."

"Indeed."

Because he felt uneasy with her so close to Murray, Trace finished off the second man in rapid order. A short kick to an already bandaged knee took one guy completely out of the fight and had the added benefit of being blood-free. All he could do was roll on the carpet, whining.

A punch to the solar plexus, and then the ribs, put the third man down, too. He wheezed for air, close to puking but holding it back in fear of soiling Murray's carpet.

"Excellent work, Trace." As he again left his desk, Murray waved Trace back, and then addressed his henchmen. "You continue to disappoint me. Now get out."

Shifting nervously, Alice held the door wide. After the men had cleared it, she asked Murray in a tiny voice, "Do you need anything else?"

Murray asked Priss, "Coffee? Soda?"

She shook her head. "No. I'm fine. I don't want to impose further."

Helene roused herself enough to scoff, but otherwise remained remote and quiet as ordered.

Trace took the doorknob. "That's all, Alice. Thank you."

She scanned the room, nodded and left. Trace closed the door.

Braced for anything, Trace aligned himself closer to Priss. If need be, he'd gut Murray and deal with the consequences as they came.

Murray smiled at Priss with the same attention he gave his financial reports. "Don't hover over her, Trace. She'll be fine." He lifted a brow. "Isn't that right, Priscilla?"

She made a noncommittal noise. "I'm not going to get weepy over a little physical violence, especially since they had it coming."

"Priscilla," Trace warned. He wanted to muzzle her. He wanted to whisk her away and forget the rest of the world.

He wanted to…maybe, keep her.

Entertained, Murray smiled at her. "Don't worry, Trace. She'll be good. Won't you?"

More than a little mulish, Priss crossed her arms. "If, by good, you mean I won't file charges against those goons…I don't know yet."

Murray barked a laugh. "Excellent."

Trace had to wonder when Murray's good humor would evaporate. "By necessity, Murray has to be very cautious." He stared at her, hoping to convey the message. "Don't press him."

Leering, Murray said, "She can press me a little. I don't mind." Then his gaze roamed over her jeans and loose, casual T-shirt. "What in God's name are you wearing?"

Priss smoothed her shirt and shifted her feet. "You don't like my clothes?"

"No, I don't." Propping a hip on his desk and lacing his hands together, Murray shook his head. "I had clothes specifically purchased for you so that I wouldn't have to see these…substandard rags."

Her face fell comically.

The little faker. Trace didn't buy any of it. *What the hell was she up to?*

"I'm so, so sorry. Really. I wanted to wear them." The picture of despondency, Priss bit her bottom lip, then lurched closer to him with theatric fanfare. "Oh, Murray, I hate to tell you this, but someone broke into my apartment last night and *destroyed* everything."

Trace stared at her in fascination. God, she was a fabulous liar.

"Destroyed?" Murray looked taken aback.

"Yes. I had gone out—"

Pouncing on that, Murray asked, "Where?"

Without missing a beat, she said, "To a Laundromat. I needed to wash my pj's and jeans and stuff." Injecting the perfect amount of drama, she groaned. "And good thing, since everything else is gone!"

"Gone *where?*"

"That's what I'm trying to tell you. While I was away, someone broke in!"

Murray looked from Trace, to Helene, and back to Priss. "You're sure?"

Rapid nodding sent Priss's beautiful hair spilling over her shoulders, distracting Murray. "I got home and all of my wonderful new clothes were ripped up, ruined beyond repair." She jiggled as if distressed beyond measure. "Oh, Murray, I didn't know what to do!"

Murray eyed her. "So what *did* you do?"

"I tried calling Trace." She cast him a worried, apologetic glance. "But he didn't answer."

Brows up, Murray turned to him. "Trace?"

He shrugged, trying to keep up with Priss. "Must've been after Helene showed up. I didn't get any calls that I know of, but during our…altercation, she took my phone and turned it off."

Helene started to say something, but Murray gave her a narrow-eyed stare that quieted her immediately.

Priss looked at them all with near-genuine confusion and concern. "I don't have a number for you, Murray. So…I got out of there. I was afraid to stay. I am so sorry."

"Hmm. So where did you stay?"

"I hung out in an all-night diner. That was kind of creepy, too, but at least I felt safe." She rushed on. "I loved the clothes. Really loved them. And I know they cost a lot. I guess—I guess I could work to repay you. Unfortunately I don't have enough money saved, or I'd just hand it over to you right now."

Murray finally collected himself. "Nonsense. The clothes can be replaced. It's your safety I'm concerned about now." He looked at Trace. "Any ideas who could have done this?"

What a joke. It hadn't happened, and Trace almost hated to further incriminate Helene; she was in enough trouble already. But since Priss had started this game, he had no choice but to play along.

When he gave Helene a pointed stare, Murray followed his gaze and sighed.

"Yes, I suppose that makes sense."

Helene's expression pinched, but she held her peace.

As if she needed comfort, Priss looked fearfully at Helene—and slipped closer to Murray. In a whisper, she asked, "What's wrong with her?"

Trace had to fight the urge to demolish Murray when he draped his ham bone of an arm around Priss. "She realizes that her actions have abrogated our association beyond repair."

Filled with false innocence, Priss stammered, "I...I don't know what that means."

"It means she's no longer under my protection, and that, young lady, is a very bad place to be." Almost fondly, Murray hugged Priss into his side. "You might want to remember that."

Forestalling any reply on Priss's part, Alice stuck her head in. "Security is here."

"Perfect timing."

Priss gasped. "The men who grabbed me?" She half crawled behind Murray, using him like a shield.

"No." Murray looked aggrieved by her seeming fear, and then lenient. "Building security, not my guards." He patted her cheek. "And they're here for Helene, not you."

Panicked, Helene tried to bolt. Trace had already moved to block the door when Murray caught her by the hair, viciously twisting to subdue her. Gasping in honest dismay, Priss backpedaled out of the way. And Trace stood there helpless, hating that Priss witnessed the brutality.

She'd already seen too much in her young life. He wanted to shield her—but right now, he couldn't do anything at all.

"Get the door," Murray told him. And then to Priss, "Don't you go anywhere, young lady. I'll be right back."

Wide-eyed, Priss nodded.

Trace stood aside as Murray dragged Helene out into the foyer. She was a tough one, but even she had her limits, and Trace found he wasn't immune in reacting to her pain and fear.

Through the open door they could see Murray talking quietly to the men, but couldn't hear what he said. Alice, on the other hand, was close enough to go alternately pale, then flushed.

For a moment, Trace thought she might faint. He wanted to protect her, too, but he had Priss to contend with. And then Alice stiffened her spine and he knew she'd be okay.

For now.

The guards, for their part, didn't seem to relish whatever duty had befallen them. When Murray shoved Helene toward them, they caught her awkwardly and she broke into sobs.

"Jesus," Priss whispered.

Teeth clenched and temper burning, Trace said, "Not. A. Word."

She glanced at him, and patted his arm. "Okay."

Now she was agreeable? With no other choice left to him, Trace slipped his hand into his pocket and sent a code to Jackson before saying to Priss, "If only you'd shown that much sense before now."

She kept her gaze on Murray through the doorway. "I'm sorry, but you can't cut me out of this."

God help them. Falling back into the role assigned him, Trace turned and grabbed her arm. He pressed her into the seat Helene had just vacated, saying low, "You need to trust me now."

"I do." Priss swallowed hard, her eyes bright, determined. "Now it's your turn to show a little trust in return."

CHAPTER NINETEEN

Despicable as Helene might be, it wasn't easy to see her dragged away. And with Trace so furious, it was even harder to maintain her pretense, especially when Murray strode back in as if he hadn't just physically and emotionally abused his lover. Horror would be the appropriate reaction, so Priss gave in to it.

Hand to her mouth, she stared from Trace to Murray. "What in the world did she do?"

"She destroyed your new clothes."

"Oh, but…" Surely Murray wouldn't pretend that was her only offense? "If that's so…why? Why would she do such a thing?"

"Jealousy, no doubt." Murray finished off a drink, and went to the liquor cabinet to pour another.

"Oh." What the hell could she say now? "I seriously doubt that."

Laughing, Murray sent a toast to Trace.

"Well, really, whatever the reason, I don't want to see her hurt.…"

"Don't worry about it, my dear. The authorities will deal with her."

Yeah, right. "You called the police?"

"Of course." He smirked at her. "What did you think I would do?"

Torture her? Kill her? Sell her to the highest bidder, or maybe pass her around to his associates for grins and giggles?

Saying none of that aloud, Priss shook her head. "I don't know. You've said yourself that you're a powerful man, and so many strange things have happened since I came here. I don't know what to think anymore."

"It's understandable." He knocked back the drink and poured another.

Was he getting toasted? That'd be convenient.

Almost to himself, Murray said, "You have actually seen far too much."

Wow, not a subtle threat at all. Priss eased out of the chair. "Maybe I should come back another time."

"No." The way he bared his teeth in the semblance of a smile certainly wasn't meant to reassure her. Stepping around her, he said to Trace, "The deal is happening today. I need you along."

The deal. Priss hoped and prayed he meant what she thought he meant, because she badly wanted this all to end.

Trace looked far from relieved. "What about her?" He nodded toward Priss.

"With villains pursuing her left and right, we can't very well leave her unprotected, now, can we?"

Face set and cold, Trace said nothing.

Murray clapped him on the shoulder. "I believe we'll take her along."

Afraid of what she'd see, Priss didn't look at Trace. She knew he'd be in a killing mood, but trusted him—yeah, she did trust him—to keep his temper under wraps so they could finish this properly, preferably with Murray finished once and for all.

In a pretence of excitement, she clapped her hands together. "To a business meeting? You mean it?"

Deadpan, he looked at Trace, then back to Priss. "I always say what I mean."

"Oh, Murray, I'd *love* to see what you do and how you

do it. But…" She looked down at herself. "I'm hardly dressed properly."

"I'll have Twyla send over something. She should have your size on record."

Priss gasped in credible awe. "You can do that?"

For an answer, he hit the button to summon Alice. When the poor woman entered, feet dragging, Murray said, "Priscilla will be joining me on my business meeting today."

Alice shot a pitying glance her way.

"Get Twyla to send over something nice for her to wear. Tell her I need it within the hour."

"Yes, sir." Alice waited to be dismissed.

Studying her, Murray tapped his thick sausage fingers on the desktop. "You know, Alice, it'd be nice if you dressed a little more appropriately, too. You don't have to look so dreary all the time."

She looked like she'd just been struck. Even more meekly, she said, "Yes, sir."

"We'll leave at two." His expression boded ill for all. "Clear my calendar for the rest of the day after that." When she still hesitated, he said, "That's all."

After she'd left the room, Trace frowned. "Alice is going along, too?"

"Always. She keeps the books."

Whoa. That was something Priss hadn't considered. Surely Alice wasn't a willing participant. Not that she was a good judge of such things, but still—Helene, she could see. Murray, obviously. But not Alice.

When Priss looked at Trace, he wore no expression at all. But she already knew him well enough to pick up on his escalating tension.

"I have some things to attend to." Murray moved around them, speaking to Trace as if she didn't exist. "Take her to the conference room. Alice will bring the clothes as soon as they arrive. Supervise her when she changes. I don't want any surprises."

"I'll get her something to drink in the meantime."

"Yeah." He glanced at Priss without much interest. "Make her comfortable." He went out the door with an intent scowl of preoccupation.

As he passed Alice's desk, she jumped up to follow… almost like a pet, eager to please—or fearful of disappointing.

When the coast was clear, Priss said, "Wow, that was—"

Trace caught her wrist, shushing her. She looked at him and he shook his head.

Bugged? she mouthed.

He shrugged, letting her know he wasn't certain. But he glanced at the intercom system Murray used, and she realized it could easily go both ways.

"Come on." Still holding her wrist, he led her from the room, down a hall and into another, even larger room framed by floor-to-ceiling windows on two walls.

Already feeling exposed, Priss wrapped her arms around herself. "I'm expected to change in here?"

Trace looked harsh, furious and determined. "You're expected to do whatever Murray tells you to."

"Yeah, I know. But…" She bit her lip, and nodded. "You said something about a drink?"

His left eye twitched before he turned away and went to a built-in bar. From under the bar he produced a Coke. He tossed ice in a glass and poured. "Have you eaten?"

"Not much."

That seemed to anger him more. "I can't leave you to get real food, so your choices are peanuts, pretzels or cheese crackers."

He treated her like a stranger, and even though she knew it was a precaution in case Murray listened in, it still hurt. She wanted to tell him that she'd be okay, that she did have a plan, but talking about it would be too risky.

Pulling out a padded chair at the long conference table, she seated herself. "Cheese crackers, thank you." She lifted free the long chain around her neck and toyed with it.

Trace didn't appear to notice.

He hadn't gone through her purse this time, either. He might do that yet, but would he recognize the heart-shaped key chain? Once she removed the cover off the heart, it was a sharp-edged weapon. And what about her pink cell phone? It looked innocent enough, but it was actually a 950,000-volt stun gun in disguise. Trace would probably know she didn't really have a cell phone, but would he recognize it for the protection it offered her?

One way or another she would choke Murray's fat neck with the necklace, or cut it with the key chain, or she'd fry him with the stun gun.

But she *would* do him harm—the same way he'd harmed her mother, and by association, her.

Trace set down the soda and a bowl of crackers in front of her. He stared down at her for a moment, but when she began to eat he strode to the window to look out. Priss noticed that he had one hand in his pocket.

Sending a code to Jackson?

She hoped so. They could probably use all the help they could get.

Being a nervous eater, Priss had just finished off the crackers when Alice came in carrying a bag of clothes. Trace met her halfway across the room, but Priss stepped around him.

"Alice?"

She paused, her demeanor reserved, worried.

Priss reached out to take her hand. "Thank you."

Expression pained, Alice swallowed and nodded.

"You're welcome." She made a hasty retreat from the room, closing the door quietly behind her.

It bothered Priss, how downtrodden Alice was. "She's more skittish than usual."

"She must have more sense than you."

Priss glared at Trace, but he didn't give up his belligerent attitude. Fine. Let him stew.

"Where can I change?"

He lifted a hand to indicate the entirety of the large, open room. "Anywhere you want, but I'll be watching you."

It was her turn to scowl. Sure, he'd seen her naked. But this was…different. "That's ridiculous."

"You heard what Murray said." His hazel eyes all but glowed with an eerie, angry light.

When she tried facing off with him, hoping he'd back down, he shook his head. "You're only making it harder on yourself."

Priss flattened her mouth. "I don't like you very much right now."

"You say that like I should give a damn."

Ohhh. Jerk! Okay, so she knew he had to play his role, but did he have to look so sincere and sound so convincing doing it?

She upended the bag of clothing on the table. A dress, minuscule panties and torturous heels. Great. Just freaking great. Changing was something she hadn't counted on.

Holding up the black tank dress to examine it, Priss saw that it was a size too small—meaning it'd be really tight. And it had lace insets all along the sides—meaning much of her skin would be visible. And it was short—so she wasn't going to be able to move without flashing the panties.

"Nice," Trace told her, deliberately provoking.

Priss ignored him as she looked at the panties next. She wanted to groan. Flesh colored, barely there and bound to be uncomfortable.

"None of this is appropriate for a meeting with my father."

"Quit stalling." He touched her arm. "I want you done before Murray shows up."

Oh, hell. What if she was in midchange when he walked in? If he were listening to them now, would he show up at the worst time on purpose?

Possibly.

Hastily, her back to Trace, Priss skimmed off her shirt and bra and, as stealthily as she could, pulled the dress on. She glanced at Trace, and saw him smiling at her ingenuity.

"Take the jeans off, too."

"I am." She wiggled and squirmed without showing too much by tugging the dress down as she pulled off her jeans and underwear.

He reached around her, the panties hanging off his pinkie. "Here you go, Priscilla."

Snatching them away from him, Priss started to bend down to step in, but she could feel Trace right behind her. *So* close. If she bent, she would surely bump into him.

Uncertain of his purpose, she said, "You're crowding me."

"Thought you'd be used to that by now."

Was that for Murray's benefit, or not? She just didn't know. "You're a bully."

"Just doing a job."

Definitely Murray's benefit. Sighing, Priss lifted one foot—and felt his hands settle on her hips with the pretense of steadying her. He was so warm, his hands sure, his comfort undeniable regardless of the games they were forced to play.

Staving off the emotion became more difficult. "Trace…"

The door flew open and Murray strode in, saying, "All ready?"

God bless Trace, he turned, and Priss was able to use his big body as a shield to hastily yank on the underwear. As she straightened, Trace stepped aside, and their moves couldn't have been more choreographed if they'd practiced them together.

Seeing her properly clothed, Murray couldn't hide his annoyance. "Where are the shoes?"

"Right here." Priss sat—her back to the men—and slipped on the narrow, pointy-toed stilettos. The absurd ensemble was in no way presentable for any afternoon event, other than perhaps stripping or…getting sold.

Voice strained, Murray said, "Let's have a look at you."

Tugging at the low neckline of the dress, Priss stood again. With no help for it, feeling very self-conscious, she presented herself to the men. "The dress is too tight."

"Nonsense." Murray licked loose lips, his narrowed gaze lingering on her breasts, and then her legs. "You look quite nice."

Her smile hurt. "Thank you." She busied herself by folding her own clothes and stacking them together.

Alice spoke from the doorway. "Everything is ready."

"Good, good." Murray reached for Priss's hand. "Let's go, then, shall we?"

She didn't want to touch him, but she didn't want to blow the opportunity, either. Leaving her sensible clothes behind, she nodded. "All right."

His fat, clammy fingers griped hers too tightly, and his thumb kept brushing over her skin in a suggestive way.

Priss's stomach roiled, and it took all her concentration not to react to his vile attention.

On the ride down the elevator, Trace stood with his hands clasped at his back, Alice stared at her feet, and Murray toyed with her until she wanted to scream and slap him away.

Perv.

Disgusting, abusive, evil. The world wouldn't miss him when he was gone.

Once in the parking garage, Murray finally released her, but his torment didn't end. At his insistence, Trace drove and Alice rode shotgun. She and Murray took up the backseat.

Twice he let his thigh touch hers, and when she moved away, he put his hand on her knee. Priss made a point of being so jumpy—just as any woman would be—that he finally gave that up. But nothing she did could dissuade him from sliding his sleazy gaze over her cleavage. She felt violated, and that made her imagine how her mother had felt dealing with so much more, with more than any woman should ever have to bear.

Anxious for her shot to hurt him, Priss kept her purse to the other side of her, away from Murray and his prying eyes. If need be, she could retrieve her weapons quickly, but she didn't want to do that until they'd freed Murray's latest victims.

And Alice. Somehow, difficult as the prospect might be, she wanted to help her, too.

Murray started a conversation on his power and connections that sounded more like a veiled threat than anything else. Priss pretended to listen, but instead she kept stealing glances at Trace. Because he looked alert and tense, but not really worried, Priss decided that she wouldn't worry, either.

He constantly scanned the area. Murray probably

thought the diligence was part of Trace's normal vigilance, but Priss wondered if he watched for something specific.

Like maybe Jackson. Or the police.

"Planning to shoot someone?" Trace suddenly asked.

Priss didn't understand until she realized that Murray had pulled a gun and had it resting across his knee—aimed at her.

Her breath strangled in her throat.

With his usual smarmy smile, Murray shrugged. "Only if necessary."

TRACE LET HIS INSTINCTS kick in. He kept things cool, detached, as he finished the ride to the factory.

Fulfilling her role, Priss gaped at the gun. "Oh, my. Is this trip dangerous?"

As if he bought her acting, Murray laughed. "Yes, child." And then, with ominous overtones: "More dangerous for some than others."

"Then I'm very glad you're prepared."

"Is that right?" Murray grinned. "What about you, Trace? Are you glad?"

Maybe Murray was onto him, or maybe he just wanted to be rid of Priss. Either way, Trace wouldn't make it easy for him. "It's unnecessary, because I can handle things, but I understand your caution."

Proving he didn't see Priss as a threat, Murray looked out the side window. "Yes. I thought you might."

Trace considered things, and decided that Murray wouldn't shoot Priss in his own car. Too many complications waited down that road: DNA evidence, false registration on the vehicle, even the clean up.

No, if Murray truly felt susceptible and chose to shoot anyone, he'd shoot Trace first. And knowing that, accepting that—at least for right now—Priss was safe enough, made it possible for him to keep up appearances.

Beside him, Alice closed her eyes and fisted her hands. She looked ready to come unhinged at any moment. Murray had bullied her one time too many, leaving her fragile and emotionally drained. Trace wanted to reassure her, but he couldn't. Not yet.

He glanced back at Priss and, though she smiled, he saw a taut expression on her face.

No fear or panic for her. When most would be falling apart, Priss reacted as he did—with cold anger.

Damn it, he did not want to admire that about her. He was trained, and she was not.

But in this situation, fear and panic could do her in. Rage, on the other hand, just might see her through this as long as she could keep her wits. His money was on Priss. With any luck, she'd follow his lead and they'd come out of this unscathed.

"We should be there in a few minutes." Trace glanced around the area again. Jackson had confirmed the code and would be within range, but he wasn't visible. A good thing, that.

Ohio lacked a human-trafficking task force but, to put a dent in the crime, county police were working with the federal law-enforcement agency, state and local police, and several social organizations. Through higher political contacts, Trace had an in with the county executive. That meant, with Jackson's coordination of everything, the right people should show up at the right time to shut down Murray's operation, ferret out all the involved parties, and keep Jackson and Trace clear of it.

There was no one on the street and very little traffic when they reached the factory a few minutes later. This time, several cars were parked in the secured lot and, off to the side by the loading docks, an old semi idled.

Trace knew what that semi meant, and judging by Alice's face, so did she. Priss hadn't yet noticed, and Trace prayed that she wouldn't.

"You get out first, Trace. Take Alice with you. Priscilla and I will follow."

While watching for a trap, Trace opened his seat belt. He touched Alice's arm to get her moving. "Ready?"

Tears swam in her eyes but she nodded and left the car.

Near the hood, Trace moved in front of her just in case anyone decided to take a shot. They waited for Murray and Priss to join them.

Though he wasn't overt about it, Murray kept the gun on Priss as they exited through her door. Priss held something in her hand. It looked like a pink cell phone, but Trace knew better. Damn it, if she tried anything at all, it would precipitously set the chaos into motion.

While Murray held her close and said something low into her ear, Trace caught her eye and ever so slightly shook his head to warn her off.

She winked at him in return.

Having witnessed the exchange, Alice muttered, "Oh, God."

"Quiet." Trace moved forward, anxious to divert Murray away from Priss. "Why don't I go in first, just in case it's a trap?"

Alice grabbed his arm in silent protest.

Snickering, Murray said, "I don't think so. You'll stay where I can see you." He slanted his gaze to Priss. "For everyone's safety."

Priss finally noticed the big idling truck, and her green eyes lit with fire. For a second there, she stared and looked ready to self-combust. But she shook off the emotion. "If it's truly dangerous, then I think you're right. I'd rather Trace say close. He is your bodyguard, right?"

Murray smiled at her. "Exactly." He gestured with the gun toward the door near the semi.

As Trace led the way, he marveled that Murray—who was usually so astute—could believe Priss was that vacuous.

"Still no need for your gun?" Murray asked him.

"Not yet, no." He glanced back at Murray with a partial truth. "I'm fast. If I need to take a shot, it'll be accurate."

"So goddamned confident." He chuckled and prodded Priss ahead of him. "Have you ever known anyone that cocky?"

Priss giggled. "I'm guessing you're every bit as sure of yourself."

"True. With good reason."

Trace was barely in the door when Dugo, shoulder wrapped and forehead badly bruised, stepped into view. He saw no one else.

Alice and Priss crowded in behind him, but Trace didn't budge. Not yet.

"How's the shoulder, Dugo? I hope you got that looked at."

Dugo pointed a meaty finger at him. "You shut up."

Trace looked beyond him as Mr. Belford presented himself. He was barely upright, still in obvious pain. Shaking his head, Trace said, "Jesus, man, you look like you should be home in bed."

"I was," Belford complained. "But plans got changed."

Ah, the phone call he'd overheard. Trace nodded. "And you wisely chose to man up and drag your sorry ass here?"

Disgruntled with the insults, but unwilling to push it, Belford gave the slightest of shrugs. "Something like that, yes."

Murray forced his way in, shoving Priss and Alice aside. "The truck came in early. No choice."

Limping, Belford moved to lean on a wall. His face was so badly battered that he was almost unrecognizable.

Priss, always on game, asked, "Whatever happened to you? Were you in a car wreck?"

Alice groaned. She hovered close by Trace's back, no doubt sensing he could, and would, protect her from Murray. Or at the very least, she found him to be less of a threat.

Murray laughed. He looked at Priss, and laughed some more, almost bending double with hilarity.

Frowning, Priss put her hands on her hips. "What is so funny?"

Still amused, Murray wiped his eyes. "I'd say you're priceless, but that wouldn't be entirely accurate, would it?" His gaze skipped over to Belford's. "What do you think?"

That bastard straightened with new awareness, his swollen eyes directed on Priss. In the killer dress and fetish heels, her long reddish hair hanging loose, she looked like a walking wet dream.

Trace had no doubt that Belford would be interested.

Bent like an old man, Belford pushed away from the wall and moved closer to size her up with his leering gaze. "A bonus?"

"Ah, no. Never that." Murray gripped Priss's bare arm. "But I'm sure we can work out something."

Priss reacted as any young lady would when sensing imminent peril. Eyes wide and body stiffening, she leaned away from Murray as far as she could. Her voice sounded appropriately high when she asked, "What are you talking about? What do you mean?"

Murray jerked her closer again, almost tumbling her

off her shoes. "I've decided, Priscilla, that you should see the…extent of my business."

"I don't understand. What does that have to do with him?" She pointed at Belford.

Trace watched her—and even though it amazed him, he knew that she wasn't truly afraid. Again, that damned admiration hit him.

Unbelievable.

As Murray led her toward the loading dock and the back of the semi, Belford followed, all but drooling on himself as he eyed Priss's ass in the snug dress.

The idiot couldn't know how he tempted fate.

"Get a move on," Dugo said.

Unnerving him with a slow smile, Trace said, "You first."

He could tell that Dugo didn't want to, but he also knew that Trace wouldn't give him any choice. Until the bosses said otherwise, Dugo wouldn't risk a conflict.

He locked his jaw and fell into line.

Trace took up the rear. Was Jackson in place? Damn, he hoped so.

At the back of the locked semi trailer, Murray paused. "Priscilla, dear, I've given this some thought, and before we further our relationship, I've decided that it'd be wise for me to do a DNA test myself to ensure that you're truly my daughter."

Hearing that, Belford stopped short in disbelief. Dugo almost plowed into him.

"Daughter?" they asked in unison. Their gazes went from Priss to Murray and back again.

Priss nodded fearfully. "I understand. Of course, I'd be happy to do whatever you need me to."

"Lovely Priscilla." Murray cupped her cheek, smoothed back her hair. "I certainly don't need your cooperation, but I thank you all the same. The thing is, until I have confirmation, I'll need you...contained."

She quailed. "Contained?"

"Kept safe," he clarified, when she knew her safety was the last thing on his mind.

"Oh, but..." She looked around at all the male faces, including Trace. "But...I don't understand."

"I can't have you gossiping about me. I can't risk you talking to the wrong people."

"I wouldn't!"

"My patience is running thin. You'll do as I say." Murray fisted his hand in her hair and turned them both. He called out to the driver of the semi, saying, "Come open the trailer."

Nothing happened.

Louder, Murray ordered, "Open the damn trailer."

Knowing what he'd see, Trace went to the edge of the loading dock and peered out. He whistled, and ducked his head back in. "I don't think the driver can do that."

"Why not?" Murray pulled Priss forward by her hair. She flinched, but didn't lose her cool.

"Given the unnatural bend in his neck, my guess is that he's dead."

Murray expanded with fury. Teeth clenched, he waved his gun at Dugo. "What the fuck did *you* do?"

"Not us!" Belford went red-faced with anger. "We got here just before you."

Dugo did a fast turn, searching the interior around them. When he saw no other threats, he directed his rage at Murray. "It's your man who's dead. What did you do?"

Murray's eye twitched. In a voice more fearsome for the quietness of it, he ordered Dugo, "Open it."

Gaze alert, Dugo inched over to the trailer. Using his

uninjured arm, he worked up the heavy latch and swung the first door open. With haste, he retreated again.

Inside the dark trailer, bodies stirred.

While Priss stood there shaking with barely contained rage, and Alice looking stoic, fifteen women hesitantly peered out. Wincing at the light, emaciated, dirty, bruised and disoriented, they climbed from the trailer. Two younger women, maybe even underage, clung to others who tried to shield them protectively.

Red-hot fury expanded in Trace's heart. God, that any of them should have suffered this...

Suddenly, out of the corner of his eye he saw Dugo pull his gun. Trace had it under control; he was ready and would have shot down Dugo before he could get his finger in the trigger.

But for the first time, Priss panicked.

She yelled, "No!" and at the same time, jerked her elbow back hard into Murray's big gut.

What the hell? Already on the move, Trace wondered if Priss thought she could block bullets.

She did manage to free herself from Murray, but also gained Dugo's attention.

"Stupid bitch!" Murray railed as he ducked behind empty shelving and debris and, jumping the gun to protect his own ass at all costs, started firing.

Trace thought only of protecting Priss. He tackled her to the floor, rolled to put her up against the wall and hopefully out of range. Even with her resisting, he kept her shielded with his body as he fired off two shots, one at Murray to keep that bastard cowering, and then one at Dugo.

He winged him, but didn't get in a killing shot.

Before Dugo could aim again, a bullet hit him square in the chest. The force of the shot sent him reeling back into the brick wall. He looked down at the blood on his chest, then at Trace. He sputtered and dropped.

The just-freed women screamed and hunkered down by the back of the semi.

For an injured man, Belford still moved fast. He grabbed one of the women and used her as a shield. She screamed—until his gun levered under her chin. "Shut up."

"Bad plan," Trace told him. "Let her go."

Instead, Belford roared toward Murray, "What the fuck is this?"

Hidden from sight, Murray said, "Obviously, I've been betrayed, you ass." And then to Belford, he said, "Kill them! Both of them."

In his surprise, Belford shifted just enough.

Trace shot him in the knee, and then the shoulder. With a roar of pain, he passed out and dropped the gun. It skittered across the floor.

Sobbing, close to hysteria, the woman scrambled toward the others.

Murray, the lunatic, laughed loudly, even as his retreating footsteps echoed around the cavernous room.

Damn it. Trace sat up, but kept Priss behind him while he assessed the room.

Against his back, she asked, "That was Jackson who shot Dugo?"

"Yeah."

"You didn't kill him?" she asked of Belford.

"No." The beating had nearly done him in, but two immobilizing shots had really put Belford down. "Dead, he's useless. Alive, he can help flush out the rest of the rats."

Not overly upset with the bloodshed, Priss said, "Oh."

"Stay put." He caught her chin, his hold firm. "I mean it."

"I won't budge an inch."

He searched her face, and decided she meant it. But just in case, he added, "If you move, you won't like the consequences."

She dismissed the threat without concern. "Go. I'm fine."

Yeah, but only because Jackson was one hell of a sniper, and he'd had a clear shot through a window. Trace's head still reeled over how easily Priss could have been hurt. Hadn't he told her a hundred times that he was more than capable of handling things?

And still she'd thrown herself in the way of danger.

Pushing that thought aside, Trace went about securing the scene in efficient haste. He handcuffed Belford's unconscious body to the truck hitch and collected anything that could be used as a weapon.

All around him, abused women cowered. They stayed out of his way while watching him warily. If he'd had time to explain things to them, he would have.

Less than half a minute passed before he came back to Priss to press Belford's gun into her hand. "You know how to use that?"

"Yep." Distracted, she looked around at the women, and her heart showed in her eyes. Holding the gun loosely in one hand and, offering a tremulous smile, she said to the women, "It'll be all right now. We're here to help."

God bless her. Trace knew he should be on his way but he couldn't pull his gaze from her. Her beautiful hair hung tangled around her face. As she steadied herself in the torturous high-heeled shoes, a red swelling showed on her cheekbone, probably from where he'd taken her to the floor. Thanks to the dirty factory, she had a dead bug in her hair and cobwebs clinging to her dress.

Yet she was ready to take control.

"Trace," she whispered out of the side of her mouth. "Get a move on, will you?"

"Right." After quick consideration, he told her, "Take them out that way. Don't let them scatter, okay?" Trace indicated a door. "Jackson is out there so it'll be safe enough."

"Got it." Glad for the instruction, Priss started to follow through, but she turned back with a frown. "Where did Alice go?"

Damn. Somehow, he'd lost track of her. Trace glanced over at Dugo's body, and realized that when he'd collected weapons, Dugo's had been missing.

"You're a damned distraction, you know that?" He had to move—*now*. "Listen to me, Priss. Get them out of here, away from the building, and don't trust anyone except Jackson. You understand me?"

"Yes."

"Shoot if you have to." He grabbed her by the back of the neck and gave her a quick, hard kiss. "I'll be back as soon as I can."

"Be careful, Trace. Please."

He would have told her that he was always careful, but he wasn't willing to lose Murray. Gun in hand, he went in pursuit.

For once, he had to put Priss completely from his mind.

CHAPTER TWENTY

PRISS'S HEART HAMMERED in dread at how things had unfolded. Despite her palpating fears, she forced herself to patience as she got each and every woman out into the sunny yard. "Please trust me," she called out to them. "I need you all to stay together, and I need you to move a safe distance away from this building."

Under the circumstances there could be stray gunfire, and Priss didn't want any of the women to inadvertently get in the way. She didn't see Jackson anywhere, but she had no doubt at all that he'd keep them all safe from any direct threats.

Only problem was, if Jackson kept watch over them, he couldn't help to keep Trace safe.

And Trace needed him more than they did.

He was alone with a madman, trying to maneuver through a web of dark and winding corridors in a collapsing factory. Murray could conceal himself around any corner and then attack when Trace came into view.

No, no, no.

Few men could boast of Trace's skills; she had to keep reminding herself of that.

But could he be as ruthless and cold as Murray?

Her eyes burned, but she couldn't give in to her worry. Trace had entrusted her with a job, and she would do it the best she could.

Right now, the women were rightfully panicked and so emotionally damaged that it ripped Priss's heart to shreds. They were a variety of ages with differing reactions, some appearing braver than others, some angry, a few crying. But none of them really knew what to think about their rescue.

With everyone safe outside, Priss put a hand to her eyes and surveyed the area. In the distance, she could hear police sirens. Thank God.

One woman stepped up. She stared at the gun Priss held. "We're being let go?"

"Oh." Those tears burned hotter, forcing her to blink quickly. On impulse, Priss reached out a hand to touch her arm—making sure to keep the gun behind her back. The woman was stiff, not very receptive, but she didn't run away. "Yes, you are. I'm sorry we were unable to explain—with everything going on and the gunshots....."

The woman nodded tiredly. "The men who were shot— they were the ones responsible for...taking us?"

"I believe they were buyers."

"One got away."

Priss measured her reply. "That's Murray Coburn, the one most responsible. But someone went after him." Her stomach cramped anew thinking about what could happen. "Don't worry. We won't let him escape. You truly are safe now. I promise."

"Thank you." With a shaking hand the woman pushed dirty brown hair out of her face and looked around. "What now?"

"That building across the street. It looks abandoned." Everything in the area was deserted, which is why it made such a great location for trafficking. "You could stay over there until the authorities arrive." And then she'd be free to go after Trace.

"I'll get everyone together."

Before the woman walked away, Priss had to reassure her. "Just so you know, someone will be watching over you. One of the good guys, I swear. He won't let anyone else hurt you."

"The sharpshooter."

"Yes." Jackson had been rather effective with his aim. "He'll stay close until after the police arrive and take control of everything."

Trace had never fully explained, but Priss assumed that he and Jackson would want to stay anonymous. Being drawn into a trial would only expose them. How effective could they be as undercover heroes if everyone knew about them?

Likely, Trace planned to pull back before the cops got on the scene. Though she wouldn't take anything for granted, Priss hoped he took her with him. She didn't relish explaining her role in all this, or dredging up stories of her mother, *or* explaining why she had hidden weapons with her.

And really, there'd be dead bodies left behind—but only those men who deserved to die.

As proof, someone started softly sobbing. Another woman crooned to her. Hurt, bound by their experience, they pulled together.

Never in her life had Priss witnessed so much misery. Her mother's pain had been great, but tempered by time.

This pain, so fresh and raw, was nearly unbearable. "They'll all pay," Priss whispered, almost choking on emotion. And those damn tears leaked out to burn down her cheeks. "I swear they will."

The women didn't seem to hear. With a stilted walk, one woman went to another and gathered her close. She started them all across the street to meager safety.

Angrily, Priss scrubbed at her face, wiping away the tears. Later, she'd no doubt bawl her eyes out. But right now, she had to be backup for Trace, and she had to find poor Alice.

Retracing her steps through the factory proved difficult in the mega-high heels and too-tight dress. She headed in the direction that Murray and Trace had gone, but ran into steps, heaps of crumbling bricks and broken machinery.

The dark hallways seemed to go on forever. At first, she didn't worry about making noise. But when she heard something, a faint sound, she quieted.

With both hands she held the gun at the ready. Prickling sweat gathered at her nape, and her lungs labored on hot, dusty air. Like the steady rhythm of a base drum, her heartbeat sounded in her ears.

She'd never shot anyone before, but she'd be happy to make Murray her first.

Hearing another sound, an indistinguishable dull thud, Priss crept farther along the hallway. It opened into a yawning room cluttered with busted shelving and empty boxes. Very little light penetrated the blackened windows, leaving everything eerily dim and shadowed. Eyes wide, Priss stopped just inside the door and listened again.

The next sound she heard was definitely a grunt.

She moved through the shadows to the farthest side of the room and found Trace and Murray battling. Murray was thicker in every way. He was also bleeding out of his nose, from the corner of his mouth and from a cut on his forehead.

Murray's gun had been knocked to the floor, and as he made a move toward it, Trace's foot hit him in the face, sending him reeling back. He floundered into a mountain of empty, splintered wooden flats. They crashed down around him, causing a deafening racket.

His own gun drawn, Trace started toward him. He would kill Murray now.

Bile burned up the back of Priss's throat. Her hands went cold but damp as she lifted the gun and stepped forward. "Move away from him, Trace."

Trace froze, cursed softly—and stayed put. "Get out of here, Priss."

"I can't."

Without looking at her, he said, "I won't let you do this."

Priss understood his predicament. He didn't dare take his attention from Murray, but she was now on the scene, ruining his plans.

Too bad. They were her plans long before he'd ever learned of Murray.

"Move." She swallowed hard, doing her best to fight back churning nausea. "I mean it, Trace. I might not be the best shot and I don't want to accidentally hurt you."

He widened his stance. Tone cold and commanding, he said, "Put down the gun and walk away."

"Sorry...no." Her knees started to shake. A peculiar weakness overtook her, making her shake all over.

Sprawled on the floor, Murray studied her, and laughed. "Oh, God, this is rich."

"Shut up." She took another step forward...and stumbled.

He dared to smile at her. "Why, Priscilla?"

She shook her head and Trace, damn him, still hadn't moved. Her palms felt slick with sweat. An unnerving chill crawled up her spine. The gun was starting to feel far too heavy.

She needed to end this!

But she couldn't shoot Murray with Trace standing there. Never would she risk him. "Trace," she pleaded.

"Enlighten me," Murray insisted. He half sat up, leaning on one arm. "I mean, I know why I wanted rid of Trace. He knows too much about me for me to let him go, but a man like him would never be content as my lackey. Eventually he would have challenged me."

"No." Trace shifted slightly. "You have nothing I want, Murray. From the day I met you, my only intent has been to destroy you."

"No shit?" He wiped blood from his mouth. "I always did say you were good. But why come after me?"

"My sister was taken by traffickers."

Priss knew it was true, and still it stunned her. Why was he sharing this now? Why couldn't he just get out of her way?

"Huh?" With the back of his hand, Murray wiped blood from his left eye. "I had something to do with that?"

"No. Those involved with her kidnapping are all dead."

How could Trace sound so calm, so detached?

"Then why the hell are we here?" Murray asked.

Priss shouted, "Because you're a monster!"

Unconcerned with her loss of control, Murray snorted, "Can you be more specific?"

She meant to shout again, but the words squeezed out around a lump in her throat, barely above a whisper. "You—you killed my mother."

His disdain couldn't be more obvious. "I killed a lot of people," he snapped. "For clarity, I need you to be more specific still."

As Priss gasped in pain and started to squeeze the trigger, Trace stepped in front of Murray, blocking her.

She cried out in frustration. "Trace!"

"I'm not letting you shoot him, honey."

"Honey? Does that mean you two are in cahoots?" Murray leaned to look around Trace. "Priscilla, have you been fucking my number-one bodyguard?"

Trace's boot connected with Murray's chin again.

His head snapped back and he slumped on the floor,

fuming and cursing and spitting blood. "Son-of-a-bitch."
He said, almost with admiration, "You are so fucking fast.
I didn't see that coming."

"I'd suggest you keep your mouth shut."

"Or what? You'll kill me?" He scoffed at them both.
"She plans to do that anyway."

Priss didn't want to cry; she didn't want to give Murray
the satisfaction of seeing how he'd affected her. But the
hurt was deep inside her, ripping her in two. He'd done
so much damage, destroyed so many lives, and yet he
remained cavalier about it all.

The gun grew more cumbersome, her arms weaker,
her heart as heavy as lead.

"I think you broke my jaw." Murray struggled to sit upright again. "So, Priscilla, your mother was my first?"

Priss shook her head. "I don't know and I don't care.
You need to be dead."

"We'll see. Until then, at least tell me if I'm your
father."

She managed a shrug. "Don't know, and don't care."

"So Helene was right? Instead of waiting, I should
have killed her before we left the office." The shock of
that was still sinking in on Priss when he continued. "I
guess it's hard to pinpoint a sperm donor with so many
participating."

Priss bit her bottom lip to still the telltale reaction to
his callous news; Helene hadn't been much better than
Murray, and she got what she deserved.

So why did hearing it cause her so much distress?

Ready to be done with it all, Priss lifted the gun, but as
she moved, Trace did, too—and Murray escaped further
repercussions for his foul mouth.

Priss didn't know how much more she could take.
"Trace, *please* get out of the way."

"Not going to happen." Never looking back at her, he hesitated, and said, "It's not for you to do this, honey."

"It's not for you, either!"

"No." Alice stepped out of the shadows. "Killing him will be my privilege." Unlike Priss, she didn't waver. She didn't look weak or emotional. She held the gun out straight, her finger on the trigger, her normally plain face now hard with iron will.

"This is bullshit!" Murray railed.

Trace cursed—and started backing toward Priss. "Alice, you don't want to do this."

"I'm not her, Trace. You can't talk your way around me. I've been waiting for this opportunity for a long time. I've been waiting for someone like you, someone who wasn't totally corrupt. This is the first chance I've had, and no one is going to stop me."

Mesmerized, Priss watched as Alice smiled, a genuine smile of anticipation.

Trace backed up until Priss had to go on tiptoe to see over his shoulder. "Hear those sirens, Alice? The police are on their way. It's over for Murray. Why don't you give me the gun, and then we can all get out of here?"

"No."

"Fucking police, Trace?" Murray mocked. "Really?"

He probably realized that they wouldn't be able to hold him. Not with his connections, not with his far-reaching influence. Somehow he'd worm out of the charges; there would be a technicality, others would take the blame for him, or someone would get paid off by scumbag lawyers.

Priss held the gun tighter. She wouldn't let that happen. This ended with Murray today—here, right now.

"You won't be seeing the police, Murray." Trace crowded her back, away from Murray and Alice. "You'll be dead before they get here."

"You'll let me shoot him?" Priss asked.

"No." His shoulders went rigid. "I'll take care of it."

Murray's gaze darted around the room, from Priss to Trace and finally, maybe because she was so silent now, he settled on Alice. "How about we agree that no one should kill me?"

Several things happened at once.

Trace turned fast and snatched the gun out of Priss's hand.

Before she could protest that, Murray vaulted to his feet.

And Alice, without hesitation, shot him in the middle of his chest. Once, twice, a third time. Each strike sent him back a step.

With the blast still echoing around the cold, dark room, Murray went utterly still. Eyes unseeing and mouth gaping, he wavered on his feet, and then buckled backward in an awkward heap.

Dead.

While crimson blood blossomed over Murray's expensive dress shirt and spread out in a puddle beneath his corpulent body, the smile faded from Alice's face.

Priss stared in shock at the carnage. It was over, and she'd had nothing at all to do with it.

That would have been devastating beyond measure, except that Alice slipped down to her knees and her sudden, wrenching sobs would shred the coldest heart.

Trace's hand on Priss's arm tensed with emotion. "Alice…"

"No. No, no, *no!*" Alice pounded her fist on her thigh. "It doesn't—doesn't matter. Not anymore." And with that, she started to turn the gun on herself. Priss gasped, and Trace started toward her, but he wouldn't be in time.

Priss caught his hand, at the same time, saying, "Thank you, Alice. Everything will be okay now."

Alice kept the gun to her temple. She gulped hard, hiccuped on her tears. "What are you talking about? Nothing will ever be okay again."

"It will." Priss did her best to sound confident. "Trace will help you. Whatever happened—"

"He stole me." Alice looked at her with empty eyes. "He took me from my home, from my family...." She choked on the words, her eyes liquid with tears that spilled over and left trails down her cheeks. "He told me if I tried to leave he'd steal my little sister, too, and then he'd rape me. He said he didn't want to. Even when he made me be naked around him, he said that I repulsed him, but that he'd rape me anyway if I gave him trouble."

Bastard! Priss didn't look at Murray's body. His death had been too easy, but he was dead, and that's what mattered most. "He was a monster, Alice, but not anymore. Thanks to you, he'll never hurt anyone ever again." Priss inched toward her. Trace didn't want to let her go. He was worried, and she understood, but she *had* to do this. "Your family must be frantic. I know they would love to see you again."

"It's been over a year. A year of them not knowing. A year of me locked away, forced to do his business. Forced to silence, living in fear and—" she swallowed audibly "—nothing is the same anymore. I'm not the same."

"That's okay, Alice." Priss kept moving toward her, step by step. "You still love them, and they still love you. They'll be so relieved to have you back."

Alice squeezed her eyes shut. "Not after what I've done, what I've let happen to all those poor women...."

"What you were forced to do."

She nodded slowly. "I never had another chance, not once. I couldn't stop things. If it had only been my life..."

What? She would have willingly died? Maybe.

"But rape? Being sold?" Alice shivered. "What he threatened, what he did to others, would be worse than death."

Trace reached her in two long strides to gently, and cautiously, wrested the gun from Alice's hand.

She didn't fight him.

He turned to Priss. "We need to get out of here."

Nodding, Priss knelt down beside Alice, their shoulders bumping. "He raped my mother, and then shared her with his friends. She escaped him, but she never really recovered. I used to think he'd ruined my life, too."

Face downcast, Alice swallowed hard and nodded in understanding.

"But he didn't." She took Alice's hand. "He can't hurt me, and he can't hurt you, unless we let him. He made you a victim, Alice, but you didn't stay a victim. And thanks to you, no other woman will have to fear him."

Voice faint with fear, Alice whispered, "I don't know what to do."

Trace said, "You come with me. Now."

His control, his certainty, seemed to revive Alice. She drew in a deep, steadying breath. "I've always trusted you, Trace. I knew you were different."

Though emotion weighed heavy on Priss, she smiled. "Me, too." She stood by Trace's side, put a hand on his shoulder. "Murray was the only one dumb enough to believe that Trace was like him."

Trace reached out his hand to Alice.

After a deep breath, she dried her face, gave one last look at Murray's unseeing corpse and accepted his help.

WELL AWAY FROM THE SCENE, Trace put Alice in a cab. He leaned in the back door, speaking close to her ear. "You're going straight to the address I gave you, Alice, understand? I have someone there waiting for you. If you need anything, you have a number to call."

She nodded.

That didn't quite satisfy him. He needed to know that she'd be okay. "Tell me you understand."

"I understand."

But she still looked too numb, and it bothered Trace. "Alice?"

Eyes big and sad, but no longer stark with fear, she looked up at him. Trace touched her cheek and smiled. "I always knew you were different, too."

That admission seemed to break the fog, and she threw her arms around him, squeezing tight as if she didn't want to let go. Trace awkwardly patted her back until she regained control.

He lifted her chin. "I'm sorry, hon, but Priss and I have to go."

"I know." She wiped her cheeks, and summoned a shaky smile. "Thank you. For everything."

He hated to let her go like this. "You'll get hold of your family?"

"First thing, I promise."

He had nothing more to say, so Trace closed the door and stepped back.

Before the cab could pull away, Priss put her hand on the glass of the window. Alice drew a deep breath…and put her hand to the glass, too.

Both women looked on the verge of tears, and Trace wasn't sure he could bear it. He kept thinking about what Murray had intended for Priss, how she'd been in the middle of flying bullets.

He kept remembering her standing there, a gun in her small hand, ready to kill Murray.

She should never have been there, and no way in hell did she deserve to have Murray's death laid at her door.

At the moment, equal shares of rage, urgency and compassion vied to flatten his self-control. But damn it, he was a pro. He had things to do, and those things had an order to them. Getting sidetracked by his feelings wasn't on the agenda.

He took Priss's arm and pulled her back.

The cabbie drove away from the curb. Putting his hand to the small of her back, Trace prodded her toward the car. They had to ditch it, get another ride, and get the hell out of town.

Later he'd deal with the bombardment of emotion. Right now, he had to focus on details, and hopefully that would see him through.

CHAPTER TWENTY-ONE

As Trace drove away from the area, a fierce emotion settled over Priss. It was final and dark, and scarier than facing off with Murray in a deserted, musty factory.

Now that Murray was dead, what would she do?

She glanced at Trace. What would *they* do?

Even though he'd been careful with Alice, Priss could see that Trace was in a killing mood, silent and distant.

He probably resented her involvement, because he saw it as interference.

Given all that had transpired she understood his reaction. He'd had a long-term plan, and she'd thrown a kink in the works. Poor Trace. He was so methodical, so detailed in what he did, so quick to react in every situation, having someone like her around must have been a trial.

What to do? When Priss lifted a hand to push her hair from her face, she noticed that, with the adrenaline wearing off, she shook like a freezing, wet cat.

She also realized how badly her feet hurt in the stupid heels. Fighting back useless tears, she bent and removed the shoes. Trace glanced at her, at her naked feet, and then her legs. His look was narrow-eyed and mean.

Enough already.

Drawing up one leg, Priss turned to face him in the seat. The new position hiked the dumb dress up farther, but she didn't care. "What are we going to do now?"

Other than a slight shifting of muscles, he didn't move.

He stared straight ahead at the road. "*We're* not doing anything. I've got follow-up work to see to."

"What kind of follow-up work?"

"Twyla, Helene, the entire business office…" His hands tightened on the wheel. "And you're going to keep your nose out of it."

Exasperating man. "I hadn't thought about all of that. All I wanted was Murray."

His jaw clenched noticeably.

Priss rolled her eyes. "That's not what I meant anyway." Her mouth felt dry, so she licked her lips. "I meant us—as in you and me."

His forearms flexed and his knuckles turned white.

Not real encouraging. If he tensed any more, he'd end up breaking something.

"Because, like—" Priss cleared her throat. No point in dithering. "I really need to see Liger. I've missed him horribly. I know your friends are taking care of him, but it's not the same. And I need to get back to the shop, too. I need to check on things." She lifted her shoulders. "My life—my *real* life—is waiting for me."

Braking in the middle of the road, Trace turned to stare at her. His fair hair was mussed, his T-shirt dirty. He stared at her with hazel eyes so bright, they looked lit from behind. His jaw ticked.

And damn it, she just didn't care. She didn't want this to end. "I want to see you again."

He went comically blank. "What?"

Why did that surprise him? "You know." She gestured with her hand. "*See* you." She could really use some comfort right now, but he didn't look all that receptive to the idea. "Like…date? I've never dated, remember?"

Brows pulling down into another frown, heaving a little, his nostrils flared, Trace continued to stare at her.

His attitude was starting to annoy her. "Okay, look, I

know it's a stretch, you and me together in a relationship, but you don't have to act like—"

So fast that she yelped, Trace reached out and caught the back of her neck. As he leaned in, he hauled her across the seat so he could close his mouth over hers. Her lips parted in surprise and his tongue moved in, thorough and hot and definitely possessive.

Wow. It wasn't exactly comfort, but it'd work. On a soft, accepting moan, Priss slid her hands up his hard chest and around his neck. No one else could possibly feel so solid, so safe and sexy and…perfect. He pressed her back into the seat, his kiss consuming her.

A horn beeped.

Reluctantly, Trace drew back in infinitesimal degrees. He had one hand on the steering wheel, one on her neck. His gaze moved over her face, and then he shook his head. "You're going to make me nuts, Priscilla."

He reseated himself and drove forward again.

Nonplussed, Priss settled back in her seat. The way his moods blew hot and cold was addling her brain. "So…that kiss. Does it mean you want to keep seeing me, too?"

"It does."

He didn't seem all that happy about it. After a few minutes of silence, she said, "I still have to get Liger and go to the shop to check on things."

"When?"

She didn't really want to go anywhere without Trace, but with the danger over, she couldn't bear to be apart from Liger any longer. And really, the shop required her input. Her one and only employee, Gary, could only do so much on his own.

Downcast, Priss admitted, "The sooner, the better."

He nodded. "If I arrange it, will you agree to let Jackson take you to Dare's until I can wrap up things here? Then I'll go with you to the shop."

He wanted to accompany her? Priss wasn't sure what to make of that. "How long will it take you?"

"A couple of days." He glanced at her. "Everything's already in place, so it won't be long."

Her spirits lifted as she looked out her window at the passing scenery. "All right."

"You mean it this time? I'd like to trust you, Priss."

She'd like that, too. "I promise that I won't ever mislead you again."

"That's a start."

A start to what, exactly? Happiness? She wanted to be happy, but Murray had disrupted so many lives that she couldn't think about herself too much right now. "Do you really think that Alice will be all right?"

"Yes." Trace firmed his mouth and nodded. "I have to believe that, or I'd go crazy thinking about what my sister has been through."

Her heart skipped a beat. "Your sister?"

"Trust goes both ways, honey."

"What does that mean?"

Visibly bracing himself, Trace said, "My last name is Rivers, not Miller."

Her eyes widened. "Oh, my God, I was right about your name."

"You've been right about a whole lot of things."

She whispered the name, "Trace Rivers." Nice. "That sounds better."

Trace wasn't done. "My sister, Alani, was taken. Not by Murray, but others like him."

There was no mistaking the gravity of the subject for him, and Priss, although she'd already heard him say as much to Murray, recognized that he'd just taken a giant step toward trusting her. It was such a fragile thing, so incredible, that she wanted to throw herself against him.

"And you've been set on wiping out human traffickers since then?"

"Something like that."

Having it hit close to home had probably spurred Trace, but Priss knew he'd never turn a blind eye to injustice or cruelty. Keeping her tone gentle, she asked, "How long did they have her?"

"Only a few days. But they took her across the southern border into Tijuana." Trace flexed his hands on the steering wheel. "I couldn't go after her. She was kidnapped by people who knew me."

Guessing how devastating that'd be for Trace, Priss covered her mouth. "So if you'd gone, it might have put her at more risk?"

Restless, he pawed the steering wheel as if he wanted to break it in two. "It still burns my ass to think about it."

Because he was a take-charge man, but when the one person he cared about most had needed him, he'd been forced to sit back and entrust her rescue to others. "How did you get to her?"

"Dare went instead, and I…" He sucked in an angry breath. "I waited for news."

She put a hand on his thigh. "I'm sure Dare is… competent?"

That made Trace laugh, but it had more to do with irony than with humor. "Yeah, he's competent."

"Good."

Trace gave her a look, and then shook his head. "Dare killed all of the bastards, freed the women and came home not only with Alani, but with an additional surprise."

"What do you mean?"

A genuine smile tipped the corners of his mouth. "That's where he met Molly."

Priss's hand fell away and her mouth dropped open. "You mean…?"

"He found her in Tijuana when he went in after my sister. Molly had been taken, too, and he brought them both back across the border."

It made sense, now that she knew. She remembered how the men had shielded Molly, their concern, when Priss had mentioned Murray to her. "I thought there was something about Molly.…"

"She's a strong woman."

"And your sister?" She touched him again, his biceps, then his shoulder, and she wanted to go on touching him, everywhere. "She's strong, too?"

"God, I hope so. She seems to be dealing with it okay."

Priss didn't push, and then Trace pulled out his cell. "That reminds me, I need to call Jackson now that we're clear. I'll be just a second, okay?"

Nodding, Priss retreated back to her own side of the car. She let out a breath and stretched out her legs. A yawn took her by surprise. "Take however long you need. I don't mind."

TRACE MARVELED AT THE odd sort of serenity that settled over Priss. She held up better than any woman should have, but then, Priss was unlike any other woman he'd met.

Jackson answered on the second ring. "What's up?"

"Just checking in." Trace watched the road, but he also stole glances at Priss. Her relaxed posture and even breathing belied any stress at all. Amazing. "The authorities handled things?"

"Like pros. They might not have a proper task force, but they know what they're doing. All's well."

Trace had expected no less, but he wanted to hear Jackson's take on things. "How so?"

"Several female officers were on the scene. They brought an unmarked van instead of a paddy wagon, food, blankets, drinks… It was the best anyone could hope for."

It relieved Trace to know the department had shown some sensitivity. "And the offices?"

"They closed in right on cue. Rounded up everyone." In a hasty afterthought, Jackson asked, "Did you know Murray had Helene tied up, gagged and doped to the gills with one of her own psychotropic concoctions? I'm told she was totally out of it."

He'd known that Murray planned to kill Helene, but not the details. "She'll be okay?"

"If a life behind bars is your definition of okay." Jackson made a sound of impatience. "So. If that's all you wanted—"

Trace frowned. "Is there a problem?"

"Nope. No problem."

That curt answer did nothing to reassure Trace. "Then why are you rushing me?"

"Did you want something else?"

"No, damn it." Priss looked at him with raised brows, so Trace moderated his tone. "But unless you have somewhere to be—"

Jackson let out a disgusted breath, then admitted, "I've got your sister on the line."

Of all the… "Alani?"

"You have another sister I don't know about?"

Next time he saw Jackson, he just might have to clout him. "*Why* are you talking to Alani?"

"Remember, I told you that I wanted to hire her to redo my place."

He remembered and he hadn't liked it then, either. "You said it wasn't happening."

"I know, but I felt bad at how we left things."

"Things?"

"Yeah, *things*." Annoyance crept into Jackson's tone. "And for the record, Trace, this isn't any of your damn business."

Trace snarled, started to issue Jackson a very real warning, but at the last second he glanced at Priss, and changed his mind. More moderate now, he asked, "Are you making moves on my sister?"

"Possibly."

God help him. "And she's allowing it?"

"She's not running from me, if that's what you mean." A little more frustrated, Jackson added, "I can't believe you're chewing my ass after you let her get involved with that idiot financier guy."

He hadn't liked that much, either. "Decorating is her *job,* Jackson."

"Yeah, but you can believe *he* made moves on her." And then, with an edge of anger, he added, "Luckily for him, Alani turned him down flat."

Trace couldn't believe Jackson's nerve. "Just how do you know all this?"

A long hesitation, and then with belligerence: "I've been keeping tabs, all right?"

Unbelievable. "Does Alani know you're spying on her?"

"No, and don't be so dramatic."

"I am *not* dramatic." Trace heard Priss snicker and shot her a look, but she pretended to whistle.

"Look, I'm keeping an eye on her for her own good. We both know she was skittish for a while there, but still determined to be on her own."

It sounded to Trace like Jackson had an awful lot of

interest in his baby sister. "You're trying to make yourself sound noble," Trace accused. "Just admit that you want her."

"Damn straight. I'm not blind."

Unbelievable. Trace straightened. *"Jackson—"*

Jackson laughed at him. "Look, Trace, I get the whole big-brother routine, I really do. But you know I'm not an idiot. I'm well aware of what Alani went through and I wouldn't do anything to pressure her."

"You have her on hold? Right now?"

"Yup."

"She's *willingly* talking with you?"

"If she didn't want to, she'd hang up, right?"

Interesting. Far as Trace knew, Alani wouldn't look at any guy, but she was putting up with Jackson? Grudgingly, he said, "Fine. But Jackson, if she tells you to back off—"

"I'll back off. Now give it a rest, will you? I don't like to keep a lady waiting." He disconnected the call.

Not quite sure how he felt about all that, Trace dropped the cell phone on the seat between them. He stared straight ahead, his thoughts jumbled.

"So. Jackson and your sister, huh?"

He could hear Priss's smile even before he looked at her. How she could smile right now, he had no idea. He shrugged. "Maybe."

"I told you so, didn't I?"

Teasing, too? Trace reached for her hand, and found her fingers to be icy cold. The day was warm, so he knew she wasn't as indifferent as she tried to pretend. He decided to divert her. "What'd you do with your toys?"

"Toys?"

He nodded toward her purse. "That cell phone stun gun, the barbed key chain."

"Oh, those." She peeked at him. "I figured you wouldn't be fooled."

"You still have them?"

She put her head back against the seat. "Since I didn't get a chance to use them…yeah."

"I'll take them off your hands."

"Why?"

Because he didn't want her to keep reminders of the day.

And he didn't want her playing around with dangerous gag weapons.

If she needed protection, he'd damn well protect her. But it wasn't the time to lay all that on her.

"Better to have them destroyed than to run the risk of someone later finding them, and maybe tying you to the scene."

Her hand squeezed his, and she said faintly, "And the deaths."

Trace kissed her knuckles. "Exactly."

She nodded agreement. "So…Alani." She turned toward him again. "You two are close?"

"Very. We always were, but especially after my parents died. She's eight years younger than me, so I've been sort of a stand-in parent as well as a brother."

"Eight years younger, so that makes her…?"

"She recently turned twenty-three." Too damn young for Jackson. Unless…unless Jackson was the one she wanted.

"I know what you're thinking," Priss told him. "But she's not much younger than me. Definitely not a child."

"No." Losing both her parents had forced her to grow up quick. "She's been throwing herself into her work. After what happened, with the abduction I mean, I wanted her to take some time off, but she said that she needed to stay busy."

"That's what I'd do."

No. Priss would go after the one responsible. Trace had to give thanks that Alani had the good sense to leave the destruction of bad guys to him.

"She's an interior decorator or something, right?"

"Yes." Trace brushed his thumb over Priss's knuckles. Other than Dare, he hadn't talked with anyone about Alani. But talking to Priss felt right. "I backed her financially and helped her get set up, so she owns her own design business. She can set her own hours, but instead of taking it easy, she puts in fifty-hour weeks or more."

That amused Priss. "So even though you're rich, and even though you've probably done your best to spoil her, she still has a great work ethic."

Pride swelled inside him. "I tried to give her every advantage, yeah. But she's still grounded." Still very sweet and unspoiled.

Like Priss. She'd never had anyone to spoil her, but that would change now. Her mother's fear had handicapped her upbringing, depriving her of so much. Trace had the means to give her a taste of everything she'd missed, and then some.

He was due a little time off. Unless Dare or Jackson needed him, he'd be free to dedicate plenty of attention to Priss. That decision was as much for him as it was for her. Even in the middle of chaos, he wanted her. Maybe with enough alone time, he'd finally be able to blunt the sharp edge of need.

But probably not. And truthfully, he was starting to enjoy the way she made him feel.

AFTER DROPPING HER OFF to "visit with Molly and Dare" earlier that day, Trace had left her. He hadn't specified where he was going, or when he'd be back, but he'd already been gone for hours.

Dare was working in the yard, and Molly got a phone call from her agent, so Priss decided to swim in the lake. Chris and Matt were already down there, and the animals—including Liger—had joined them. With the sun so bright and the sky so blue, a swim just might cool her temper.

It wasn't that she needed Trace's constant attention, but she resented the secrecy surrounding his absence today.

For two months now, they'd spent the better part of each day together. Trace woke her with kisses, held her while she slept, and between those times he alternately made love to her and treated her to one adventure after another.

She was happy. Happier than she'd ever known possible, and with every minute, she loved him more.

Normally she'd be worried about the shop after being away so long. But she and Trace had been there twice to check on things, and surprisingly, Gary did a great job running it. Once the responsibility fell to him, he'd stepped up and proven to be even more attentive to details than Priss herself. During each visit, she'd found the shop well organized, the stock in order, all the computer work up-to-date and not even a speck of dust marring the appearance.

It was nice not having to think about the shop.

In fact, she didn't have to think about much of anything. Maybe that was part of the problem. She was so used to focusing on how she'd get to Murray, how she'd make him pay, and now…she felt in limbo.

Blast him. Where had Trace gone and why did he still not confide in her?

As Priss strode onto the sun-warmed dock, the dogs looked up at her, and Liger stirred. He tended to trail the dogs wherever they went, but he drew the line at actually getting in the water. He'd walk along the shore on the rock retaining wall, and the fish fascinated him. But most of all he'd taken to sunning himself. Now, with Priss smiling at him, he got up to wind in and around her bare legs.

"You've been even more pampered than me, haven't you?"

Liger brushed his teeth over her knee, gave her one of his sweet meows and then fell to his back again, stretching out and closing his eyes.

Matt popped up over the end of the dock. "He's really taken over running the place."

"I can see that." Liger got attention from everyone, sat where he wanted, slept when he felt like it, and enjoyed playing with Sargie and Tai. While she and Trace traveled, Chris insisted on keeping the cat. Liger didn't need constant supervision, but Chris had gotten close to him, and vice versa.

With Liger now resting, Priss pulled off her cover-up.

Matt whistled. "Nice suit."

She looked down at herself. The suit was pretty basic; beige with no adornment, not an itty-bitty bikini but not overly modest, either. It was almost the exact color as her skin, so it didn't clash with anything, but the material was thick enough to conceal all things vital. "It's the first one I've ever owned. It looks okay?"

Chris swam over to the dock, too. Crossing his forearms over the end, he surveyed her. "Trace hasn't seen it yet, has he?"

She shook her head, and tried not to sound sour when she said, "He's out and about somewhere." She flapped a hand. "Don't know where, and I don't know when he'll be back."

Matt dunked his head, then came up for air. His

bleached hair stood in wet, spiky disarray, but as always, he looked good. "I'm surprised anyone could separate you two." He swiped water from his face. "It's been what? A couple of months together now, right? All of it nonstop clinginess."

Dropping her towel and cover-up on a chair, Priss pretended annoyance. "Why are you here again?"

He preened theatrically. "Molly liked what I did with your hair so much that I do hers now, too. Dare even added a regular salon room in the basement for me. Makes it pretty easy to work and it saves Molly from having to suffer through the crowds and incompetence in town."

Priss was willing to bet that Dare enjoyed knowing Molly was safe. They all trusted Matt, as far as it went, and he did do fabulous work.

Chris still hung off the end of the dock looking all too serious. "So." He splashed Priss with a cupped hand. "What exactly are you doing down here?"

"I'm getting ready to swim with you guys."

"No, I meant with Trace." He glanced past her up the hill toward the house, then back again. "If that suit is supposed to push him over the edge, I'm guessing it'll work."

Priss doubted anyone or anything could push Trace anywhere that he didn't intend to go. "I needed a suit, so I bought one." She sat on the end of the dock next to Chris and let her feet dangle in the water. "And why do you always attribute ridiculous childish emotions to everything I do?"

He shook his head. "Just wondering why you haven't yet told Trace how you feel."

"How do you know I haven't?"

Matt laughed. "Your baleful expressions of discontent?"

Chris just stared at her, waiting.

Fine, why not be honest? "I don't know how he feels, that's why."

"That's so lame." Chris splashed her again, harder this time, so that the water hit her in the face. "Who says the guy has to spill his guts first?"

Her temper sparked. "I've spilled plenty of guts for him! I confided in him about my mother long before he'd tell me anything. Do you know how long it took him to even admit—"

Matt said, "La, la, la…" and wisely dunked his head under the water again.

"—that he was undercover?"

"You know why," Chris told her.

It annoyed Priss that she'd forgotten to be cautious. Obviously Matt was a welcome, trusted friend, but he wasn't in on the business, and she knew better than to mention anything about it. "In the beginning, sure."

"And now?"

"Now I don't need him to tell me." She looked out across the water. "I've figured it all out."

"So what's the problem?"

"He took off again today, all hush-hush, and *still* didn't trust me enough to say where he had to go."

Matt resurfaced. "Sorry." He gasped for air. "Can't hold my breath any longer."

"No problem," Priss told him. Maybe she'd catch Chris later and talk with him more, but for now, she'd show some discretion. "Conversation is over. I'm ready to swim."

Chris tilted his head to study her. "You're getting red."

"I am *not* embarrassed about any of this."

He rolled his eyes. "I meant from the sun. You need sunscreen if you're going to be down here. The water reflects everything, and you're fair-skinned."

"Oh." She looked at her shoulders with disinterest. Indeed, they were already turning pink.

Matt swam over to the ladder and climbed out. Just as Sargie and Tai might do, he shook off excess water, sprinkling Priss in the process. "I'll do it."

She eyed him. "It?"

"Put sunscreen on you." He dripped water beside her as he held out a hand. "Up."

After she took his hand, he hauled her to her feet. Picking up the big tube of sunscreen, Matt filled his palm. While he spread it over her shoulders and back, he said, "You know, all kidding aside, I like you, Priss. You're a good sort."

"Ditto." What brought that on?

"I don't like seeing you unhappy." Before she could object, he continued, "I know. You and Trace have been hitting it off. You've enjoyed every moment. You're *deliriously* happy."

She frowned at him. "I would never be that dramatic." But the description sounded about right to her.

He cupped her shoulders and smiled down at her. It was a very brotherly look, and Priss enjoyed it. She hadn't thought to stay friends with anyone, but now she knew that, even if things didn't work out between Trace and her, she'd keep in touch with these people. She liked them all a lot. She was especially taken with Matt.

Until he said, "It's time to fess up, hon. Tell Trace how much you care. You'll feel better when you do."

Climbing up the ladder, Chris said, "Better sooner than later." He nodded at the hillside behind them. "Because here comes Trace, and he doesn't look happy."

Both Priss and Matt turned, Priss with anticipation, Matt with tempered dread.

Dressed in jeans and a snowy-white T-shirt, Trace stalked down the hill.

Priss shielded her eyes to better see him. When he'd left, being so guarded about his mission, she'd half wondered if he'd return before dinner.

Trace wore reflective sunglasses, so she couldn't see his eyes, but his entire demeanor—heavy stride, rigid shoulders, tight jaw—bespoke annoyance.

As soon as he was close enough, Priss called out, "What's wrong?"

Without answering her, Trace continued onto the dock. He didn't stop until he stood right in front of...Matt.

Backing up to the edge of the dock, Matt said, "Uh... Hello?"

Trace didn't say a thing; he just pushed Matt into the water.

Arms and legs flailing out, Matt hit the surface with a cannonball effect.

Stunned, Priss shoved his shoulder. "What the hell, Trace! Why did you do that?"

Trace took off his sunglasses and looked at her, all of her, from her hair to her body and down to her bare toes. After working his jaw a second, he said, "If you need sunscreen, ask me."

Her mouth fell open. Of all the nerve! He left her at Dare's, took off without telling her a damn thing and then had the audacity to complain when a friend tried to keep her from getting sunburned. "Maybe I would have, if you'd been here!"

"I'm here now."

Emotions bubbled over. "So you are." With a slow smile, Priss put both hands on his chest. The shirt was damp with sweat, the cotton so soft that she could feel every muscle beneath. "And you look a little...heated."

Trace's beautiful eyes darkened, and he reached for her.

"A dip will cool you down." Priss shoved him as hard

as she could. Taken by surprise, fully dressed, Trace went floundering backward off the end of the dock.

Priss caught a glimpse of the priceless expression of disbelief on Trace's face before he went under the water.

Excited by the activity, the dogs leaped in after him. Liger roused himself enough to move out of the line of splashing.

Chris climbed up the ladder. "So that's the new game, huh?" He laughed as he scooped Priss up into his arms.

"Chris!" She made a grab for his shoulders. "Put me down!"

"Afraid not, doll." Just as Trace resurfaced, Chris jumped in with her. They landed between the swimming dogs.

Sputtering, her hair in her face and her skin chilled from the shock of the cold water, Priss cursed. Trace had already waded toward the shallower water off the side of the dock. His fair hair was flattened to his head and his T-shirt stuck to his body.

"Wait!" Priss shouted at him.

He was still waist-deep as he turned to glare at her.

Kicking and splashing, Priss doggy-paddled over to him, grabbed his shoulders and wrapped her legs around his waist. "Oh, no, you don't!"

Startled, Trace scooped her bottom in his hands and struggled for balance on the squishy mud bottom of the lake. "What the hell?" And then lower, "You look naked in this damn suit."

Matt and Chris found that hilarious.

Priss looked at Trace's handsome face, a face she loved, and she kissed him. Hard.

For only a second, he allowed the sensual assault. He even kissed her back. Then he levered away from her. "You ruined my clothes, damn it."

"Only because you were being a jealous jerk."

His expression dark, he glared toward Matt.

Chris started humming, but poor Matt said, "Yeah," and shrugged. "If you think about it, you'll agree that you sort of were—and we both know there's no reason."

Trace started to wade toward Matt, still with Priss wrapped around him, and she blurted, "I love you, Trace."

That effectively drew him to a halt. His hands contracted on her backside. "What?"

"I love you." Then she pointed at Chris, and to where Matt had disappeared. "They told me to fess up, so I am, and if you reject me, I swear I'll drown them both."

Very slowly, Trace's expression changed from the heat of anger to a different type of heat. "Say it again."

"Why?" She frowned at him with challenge. "Why don't you say something first?"

"All right." Sliding his hands up her back, over her shoulders, and into her wet hair, he kissed her. "You make me nuts, Priscilla." He turned his head and kissed her again, a little longer that time. "You make me hot as hell, too."

"I love you," Priss reminded him, hoping it might prompt him to a more telling declaration.

His next kiss lasted long enough to take the chill off the lake, and Priss got so wrapped up in the taste of him that she almost forgot what she wanted to hear.

Chris didn't. From the dock, he said, "If you're going to keep her waiting like this, someone needs to finish putting sunscreen on her."

Trace moved fast, grabbing for Chris's ankle, but Chris jumped back out of reach.

Priss, feeling very affected by that kiss, nuzzled Trace's neck and stroked his shoulders. He smelled delicious, felt even better. "Stop being a voyeur, Chris, and go away."

Having joined Chris on the dock, Matt asked, "Does that mean I can stay?"

Trace lurched forward again, and Matt jumped back so quick he fell on his butt. "I'm going, I'm going!"

To bring Trace's attention back to her, Priss bit him. Not a hard bite, but she left the impression of her sharp teeth on that sensitive spot where his neck met his shoulder.

Trace shuddered. "I love you, too."

She licked the bite mark. "I'm so glad."

He hefted her higher and waded over to the rock retaining wall built along the shoreline. He sat Priss down on a smooth slab of rock, looked at her in the bathing suit, and shook his head. "It should be illegal for a woman to look as good as you do."

"Really?" She peered down at herself again, but saw nothing all that spectacular. "I'm glad you like it."

"I love it. I love *you*." He dug in his pocket. "When I left today, it was for this."

Speechless, Priss watched as he opened a now-wet jeweler's box. Inside, securely nestled in velvet, was a beautiful diamond engagement ring. Her heart nearly stopped.

"I wanted it to be a surprise."

There were no words. Her eyes suddenly burned and her throat went tight.

Trace took her hand and slipped the ring on her finger. The fit was perfect, but then, anything Trace did, he did right.

"Priss?" Using the edge of his fist, he lifted her chin. "We've been to movies and plays, to small diners and fancy restaurants. I've taken you dancing and hiking, to the amusement park and the zoo."

Sounding like a choked frog, Priss said, "All the things I never got to do growing up."

"But there's so much more, honey." He moved wet

tendrils of hair away from her face and over her shoulder. "I was trying to give you time to enjoy it all."

"No!" Priss did not want him second-guessing his intent. "I don't need any more time. Really I don't."

Both still very attentive, Matt and Chris snickered. Trace just smiled at her.

Closing her hand into a fist, she held the ring tight. "All I need, all I want, is you."

"Glad to hear it, because I'm not an overly patient guy. Hell, I think I knew you were the one for me the day you showed up at Murray's office." He kissed the tip of her nose, her lips, her chin. "You were so damned outrageous, and so pushy, that you scared me half to death."

"You felt me up," Priss reminded him. "But that was a first for me, too."

"I remember it well." He treated her to a deeper kiss, and ended it with a groan. "Every day since then, I've wanted you more. Even when you worried me, or lied to me, or made me insane, I admired you for it."

Priss nodded. "Okay."

This time, Trace laughed out loud.

"Come on," Matt said. "Stop being so easy, Priss. Let him do it right."

Priss scowled at him, but Trace brought her face back around. "My job isn't going to change, honey—and no, Matt, you don't need to slink away."

Matt, who'd already been in the process of leaving, now waffled. "If you're sure?"

"Priss knows what I'm talking about." And with that, Trace ignored Matt. "Sometimes I'll need to be gone, and sometimes you're going to be afraid for me."

"Oh, Trace." She blinked fast, thankful that they were still mostly in a lake, and mostly wet from the dousing; it helped to hide the silly tears. "I'm going to do that whether we're together or not."

He put his forehead to hers. "I like my house, Priss. The location is secure, so I'd prefer not to move."

She laughed around a lump of emotion. Trace's home was within half an hour of Dare, on a similar scale but in a different style, and also backed up to a large lake. Priss had a feeling that the guys used the lake as a natural barrier to prying eyes.

"Liger will need a few things," she warned, thinking of his cat box. "And he can shed a lot in the summer."

Trace looked over at the big cat. Stretched out on his back, his legs flopped open, he rested next to Tai. Even with the dog dripping lake water, Liger looked content.

When he realized that he had Trace's attention, Liger lifted his head and said, "Merrrowwww...." in his sweet voice, making Trace laugh.

"You two are a package deal, and Liger's already my buddy. I'm every bit as pet friendly as Dare, so don't worry about that."

"Good. Because I like your house, too, at least, from what I got to see of it." They'd only been there a day. And most of that day had been in Trace's bedroom on his massive bed. The next morning, he'd flown her to New York City, and from there, to Las Vegas. "I've loved all the places we've been and all the fun we've had, but I wouldn't mind settling down a little, too."

Being in one place with Trace, having a routine with him—making a life with him—appealed to her in a big way.

"What about your shop?" And before he let her answer, he said, "I'm not keen on you being away from me, Priss, and no, it has nothing to do with the type of shop it is."

"Fibber." She still recalled Trace's unease as she'd shown him through the shop with Gary dogging their heels. He'd tried to hide it under compliments on her management skills, but she knew that Trace hated the thought of her working there.

"It has more to do with it being too far away, and not in the most secure location—"

"Gary can buy me out. He wants to do that anyway."

Trace stalled in midsentence. "You're okay with that?"

"With not owning a porn shop?" She shrugged. She was more than okay with it. "It doesn't hold any sentimental value, believe me. It was always a means to an end."

He stroked her cheek with his thumb. "It was your independence."

And a way for her to hide from Murray while plotting her revenge. Priss shook her head. "I still want independence, so I'll be getting a job." She was hoping to find some way to assist Trace in his work. Not by accompanying him, because she knew he wouldn't have that. But maybe she could do some computer-type screening stuff, looking up facts and histories. Now that she'd had a small taste of helping others, she wanted more.

She wanted to make a difference, the same way that Trace did. But she'd broach that topic later. "I'm not a person who does well with idle time."

"Seriously? I never would have guessed."

His teasing didn't bother her, especially when she looked at her ring again. Smaller diamonds surrounded the impressive princess-cut stone, making it glint brightly in the sunlight. "It is so perfect."

"If it's not, we can exchange it—"

She snatched the ring up close to her chest. "Never."

Trace gave a slow, sexy grin. "So, Priscilla Patterson, since you approve of my job, my home, my friends and my ring, will you try another new experience—and marry me?"

Joy bubbled up, but she didn't want to shout just yet. "When you go off to—" she glanced at Matt "—work, will you at least tell me what's going on?"

"Yes. As much as I can."

"Will you be honest about the danger involved?"

"I'll be honest with you about everything."

"Okay." She peeked at him, and winced in dread. "Did you want a big wedding?"

Trace frowned at the continued line of questioning. "I want whatever you want."

That almost made her cry, too. "Another first," she whispered, because before now, what she wanted hadn't really mattered. She kept smoothing her hands over his chest, as always drawn by his physique. "You should enter a wet T-shirt contest. You'd win."

Chris snorted, but Matt agreed.

Priss ignored him. "If you're sure it doesn't matter to you, I'm not keen on the idea of anything too fancy."

Trace pulled her off the rock ledge and into his arms. "Small works fine for me. Just family and friends?"

"All right." She looked over at Matt. "I'll invite him. Everyone else will have to come from your side."

"Me?" Matt choked. "I mean, I'd be honored, but—"

Trace's crooked smile put Matt at ease.

"Well, I'm flattered." Matt put a hand to his heart. "Thank you, Priscilla."

She grinned at him. "I'll need you there to do my hair anyway."

Chris pushed up from his seated position. As if he were the Pied Piper, the dogs and cat followed suit. "I think I'll go tell Dare to figure on something nice for dinner. That is, if you two want to celebrate with friends?"

Friends. Thanks to Trace, she had them now. "Will you invite Trace's sister so I can meet her?"

"She'd skin me if I didn't," Chris told her.

"And Jackson?" Priss asked.

"Why not?" Trace gave her a teasing smooch, and then said in a lower voice meant just for Priss, "I might as well see the two of them together so I can gauge the situation myself."

He was so wonderful that Priss felt giddy. "When I took self-defense training, when I spent so many nights thinking of how I'd confront Murray, what I'd accomplish, never—not once—did I figure on meeting someone like you."

"Someone you love."

"Yes."

He waited until Chris and Matt had gotten far enough way. "Do you really think you can redirect all that awesome energy now that Murray is gone?"

"To love you? To be this happy?" She leaned into him for a kiss. "Absolutely."

Eyes blazing, Trace lifted her up and headed deeper into the water. His jeans dragged and his shirt stuck to his body.

Confused, Priss asked, "What are you doing?"

He moved under the dock, behind the ladder. Voice deeper now, he said, "Making love in the water."

She gasped. "In *daylight?*"

"They like to tease, and God knows they can be annoying—especially Matt—but I promise you that no one will be watching." He pressed her up against the ladder. "And now that you've agreed to marry me, I need you."

Priss looked at the wooden boards over her head, allowing only thin strips of sunshine through. The air was warm, the water cold. She felt Trace's jean-covered legs against hers, his hands slipping into the back of her bathing suit bottoms.

And she saw the love in his eyes.

"Okay, then." After a lifetime of anticipating Murray's

death, she feared she'd lose herself to the need for vengeance. Instead, she'd gained so much more. "Another first for me, and thanks to you, they just keep getting better and better."

"For the rest of our lives."

Now, with Trace, that idea held promise and contentment. Her mother had never found peace, but Priss had. She only wished everyone could find the same happiness.

EPILOGUE

JACKSON STOOD QUIETLY as Alani came into the house. Unlike the other women, she didn't wear a swimsuit. Shame. He'd love to see her in one. Everyone had duly celebrated Trace's engagement, and Alani seemed taken with Priss—but then, who wouldn't be? Priss was funny, smart, cute and—luckily for Trace—stacked.

Unaware of Jackson, Alani stopped to look out the patio doors. She looked…wistful. Like maybe she wanted to take part, but couldn't.

In so many ways, despite being kidnapped by flesh peddlers, or maybe because of that, she was still an innocent. At just-barely twenty-three, she acted much older.

Like a virgin spinster.

Every night, in his dreams, they burned up the sheets.

Here, in reality, she avoided him. She avoided involvement.

But he'd get her over that. Somehow.

Suddenly Priss came in, wet hair sleek down her back, rivulets of water trailing between her breasts. She spotted Jackson right off and, after smiling at Alani, asked them both, "Why aren't you guys coming down to swim?"

Alani jerked around to stare at Jackson with big eyes.

His crooked smile told her that he had her in his sights. "I was just about to ask Alani that."

Priss laughed. "You're still dressed."

"I can undress fast enough." He looked at Alani. "What about you?"

Her lips parted. "No, I...didn't bring a suit."

"Pity. Maybe we could move up to the cove and skinny-dip in private?"

Pointing a finger at him, Priss said, "Behave, you reprobate!" And then to Alani, "Beware of that one."

Still watching him, Alani nodded.

Priss put her hands on her hips and considered the situation. "Molly might have a spare swimsuit. I'd offer to let you borrow one from me, but this is the only one I have."

"It looks great on you, too," Jackson told her.

"Ha. Trace doesn't like it."

"Because you look naked," Jackson told her.

Priss went three shades of red. Her eyes narrowed. "Ever mention that again, and I'll throw you in the lake and drown you."

He pretended to button his lips, but he couldn't stop grinning at her.

Not being a dummy, Priss looked at them both, shook her head, and said, "Well, I'm heading back down. I'll tell the others that you'll be joining us soon." With a careless wave, she ducked back out the door.

Jackson moved closer to Alani. She backed up.

So he stopped. "What's wrong?"

"Why did Priss blush?" Her brows came down. "What's going on between you two?"

"Nothing." He didn't appreciate her subtle accusation. "You think I'd disrespect your brother's claim?"

"His *claim?*"

"Now, don't go getting all riled. You know what I mean." Jackson tried to dig himself out of a quickly yawning hole. "He and Priss are together. I get that. I wouldn't do anything inappropriate with her. Not that she'd be willing anyway—"

"So you *did* try?"

"No!"

"Then why did she turn scarlet?"

He rubbed the back of his neck. "She's still embarrassed because I saw her—there was this situation…"

Alani crossed her arms.

To hell with it. Jackson moved closer and if she didn't like it, too bad. But this time she didn't retreat. She just stared at him with something akin to challenge. "Look, Priss still gets red-faced because I had to steal her out of the shower and hoist her out a narrow window."

Alani's mouth fell open.

"She was buck-ass, and you can believe me, it was awkward for both of us." He thought about it, and couldn't help but grin. "Probably more so for her, but it wasn't what I was expecting, either."

Alani continued to stare at him in surprise. "Unbelievable."

"Tell me about it." Trace still looked riled every time he spoke to Jackson. "It's probably going to take your brother a little while to get over it. I mean, I saw things that he probably hasn't even seen yet. I mean, with Priss. You know, because they haven't known each other that long. I'm sure eventually…"

Her loosened jaw snapped shut. "God, you are so crude!"

How the hell did she figure that? "I was trying to be honest with you!"

Pushing him out of her way, Alani said, "Well, from now on, don't bother."

Damn it. Jackson watched her slim backside as she disappeared out the door. Frustration galvanized him into action.

In only a few long strides he followed her out. Alani hadn't gone far yet, and he reached her easily. "Hold up."

She froze in her tracks, then slowly turned to face him.

Trace, always aware of every damn thing that happened concerning his sister, looked up from the dock. Far as Jackson was concerned, Trace's overbearing protectiveness wasn't helping Alani one iota.

"What is it?"

Damn, she was beautiful. A light breeze teased through her fair hair; her golden-brown eyes glittered in the sunshine, shaded only by long, curling eye lashes. She didn't have the same lush shape as Molly and Priss, but her willowy, delicate curves pushed all the right buttons with him.

"I'm heading out."

Her gaze searched his and, a little breathless, she asked, "Leaving?"

"Yeah." He stepped closer. Any second now Trace would intrude. "Thing is, Alani, I can't be around you without wanting you. Bad. *Really* bad."

"Oh."

"If that's crude, well, then, screw it, I'm crude. I know we'd have a great time in bed, but since you aren't ready for that yet, well…I promised Trace I wouldn't pressure you."

Her neck went stiff. "Dear God. You discussed this with my brother?"

"No!" He cut a hand through the air and his voice lowered. "When…*if*…I get you out of your panties, believe me, it'll be a private thing between us. No way in hell would I discuss that with anyone else."

Her face went as red as Priss's had.

"Trace and I talked about you maybe decorating my house, that's all."

"Oh." Face still hot, she said, "I—"

"Yeah, forget it. That's off. Like I said, I'd just hanker for you, and you aren't exactly reciprocating. So that's that."

She blinked fast.

"But if you ever change your mind, all you have to do is let me know." He reached out and touched her cheek. Her skin was soft and warm and he wanted to feel her all over.

All over *him*. Naked. Hungry. Wet…

Damn, he had it bad. "I can promise you, if you do come to me, you won't regret it."

She swallowed, licked her lips and damned if her eyes didn't heat. She wanted him, too. He had to believe that. But Trace was starting up the hill, and the others were looking on, and the last thing he wanted was to make Alani uncomfortable.

"Tell everyone I said goodbye. You make up any excuse you want." And with that, he left Alani standing there, watching after him as he walked away.

God willing, she'd contact him soon.

He wasn't sure he could stand it if she didn't.

* * * * *

So you think you can write?

Mills & Boon® and Harlequin® have joined forces in a global search for new authors.

It's our biggest contest yet—with the prize of being published by the world's leader in romance fiction.

In September join us for our unique Five Day Online Writing Conference **www.soyouthinkyoucanwrite.com**

Meet 50+ romance editors who want to buy your book and get ready to submit your manuscript!

So you think you can write? Show us!

A sneaky peek at next month...

INTRIGUE...

BREATHTAKING ROMANTIC SUSPENSE

My wish list for next month's titles...

In stores from 21st September 2012:

☐ Colby Law – Debra Webb

& At His Command – Karen Anders

☐ Spy Hard & The Spy Wore Spurs
 – Dana Marton

☐ Cavanaugh Rules – Marie Ferrarella

& It Started That Night – Virna DePaul

☐ Rancher Under Cover – Carla Cassidy

Available at WHSmith, Tesco, Asda, Eason, Amazon and Apple

Just can't wait?

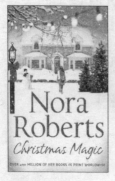  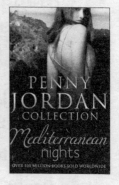

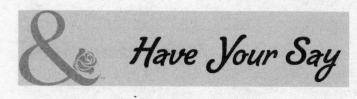

Have Your Say

You've just finished your book. So what did you think?

We'd love to hear your thoughts on our 'Have your say' online panel
www.millsandboon.co.uk/haveyoursay

- 🌹 Easy to use
- 🌹 Short questionnaire
- 🌹 Chance to win Mills & Boon® goodies

 Visit us Online

Tell us what you thought of this book now at
www.millsandboon.co.uk/haveyoursay

YOUR_SAY